Maplewood

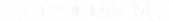

Maplewood

AMY Q. BARKER

Maplewood

Editing and layout by Kira Freed
Cover design by BespokeBookCovers

www.amyqbarker.com

ISBN: 978-1-7353581-3-0
Library of Congress Control Number: 2021925326

Printed in the United States of America

Also by Amy Q. Barker

Rue

Punk

Bibliointuitive

For the Maplewood Gang
Past, Present, and Future

❧ Chapter I ❧

Carmel, Indiana
May 2018

Murder. Senseless. Without reason. Torturous. Heartless. Soulless. Evil incarnate.

It had been two years. Mom begged me to come home and leave that hollow, haunted place where my heart used to live. To walk away from the anger and the agony. As if that were possible.

She called me and said, "Amanda, you're never going to believe this. Our old house is for sale."

"Hmpf," I grunted with little interest. "Really? How much?"

"That's not the point," she explained casually. "You're gonna buy it."

I scoffed. "Mom, please. Right, good one."

"I mean it. Why not? You've always loved that house. And the neighborhood is just the same as it always was." She paused and added softly, "I think it would be good for you. Something old…something new."

"If you say 'something borrowed, something blue,' I'm going to scream," I said with a laugh, keeping it light. She couldn't be serious. I hadn't seen my childhood home in years. Hadn't even thought about it. Even now, it was like a faded memory that pops back into view when you look at an old photograph—a bit of nostalgia that has long since been replaced with life's harsh realities.

The silence on the line was deafening. I finally said, "Mom, *no*. What good would that do? Running away. Plus, my job is here. And Shawn's family. I can't just pack up and leave."

"Sure you can," she replied flatly.

I didn't say anything, breathing hard, trying to think of more excuses, more reasons to deny that a change was needed, that my life was no longer

my own. Instead of answering her, I talked about the weather and my latest
work project as my mind churned on her suggestion.

Finally, as the conversation wound down, she added, "Just think about
what I said. I want you *home*. Close to me. Close to *your* friends and family.
It would be…a new beginning. A way forward."

We hung up and I stared out the window, wondering about the word
forward. Movement in a direction. Onward. Upward. Going *some*where. Intentionally. Not backward. Not stuck. Not sinking. Not drowning.

A way forward.

But how?

That was the question.

One night a week later, I sat down at the kitchen table and wrote this word
on a yellow lined notepad: *Maplewood.*

I let the notepad sit there for a few weeks, the word telescoping up like a
set of eyes trained on me from afar. There it was as I got ready for work in
the morning, as I ate very little for dinner sitting by myself in front of the
TV every night, as I let my incoming phone calls go to voicemail, as I stood
absently at the sink washing dishes, as I stared out the window at the crocuses
and daffodils popping up in the yard and wondered what right they had to
look so chipper and hopeful.

The notepad. That word.

Maplewood.

What did I even remember of it? It seemed like a lifetime ago, like a life
lived by someone else. Someone entirely different from the person I was today. Like a happy, cheerful, fun-loving person. Someone without a care in the
world. Who laughed. Who was silly and spunky and spontaneous. Who tried
new things. Who dreamed. Who cared. Who loved. Who was loved.

Maplewood.

Those rich, hot, green, humid summer nights when the world would come
alive. Children's laughter. Bicycle spokes clickety-clacking with interwoven
playing cards, skateboards, whippersnappers, cap guns, pogo sticks, Frisbees,
go-carts, running, shouting, playing, eating, drinking, boasting, ribbing, argu-
ing, racing, testing, riding, skipping, waiting. And rarely a breath of "I'm tired"
or "We should get home." But inevitably, after five or six hours of terrorizing
the neighborhood, some parent would holler out the front door, "Hey, kids!
It's late. Better call it a night," leading to the sad trudging home to respective
warm beds, with the promise of doing it all again tomorrow.

Then there were the cool early mornings sitting on the front porch swing reading a book and watching the tunnel of maple trees reflect their dappled shimmer of light across the sidewalk in a kaleidoscope of colors. The sound of robins and cardinals and finches, like a symphony composed by nature and transmitted in its own perfectly tuned acoustic amphitheater. Mr. Hawthorne coming out onto his front stoop in his bathrobe and slippers, coffee mug in hand, to retrieve the morning paper and savor an appreciative glance at his perfectly tailored lawn before slipping back inside. Mrs. Roberts sneaking a cigarette on her side porch and drinking a glass of Ovaltine. Donny Brewer rushing down the street being led by his Great Dane, Tandy, her nose taking in every curb, fire hydrant, and tree trunk.

And who could forget winter, when the snow would fall in feet instead of inches and we would spend hours constructing igloos and caves, inserting ourselves one at a time like mummies into the mouth of the construction, feeling as if we had accomplished a massive feat of engineering. When our toes and fingers were numb, we would stomp into someone's warm house to shake off our snow-encrusted gear and get cozy with cups of marshmallow-laden Swiss Miss hot chocolate. Then the next day there would be snowball fights, snow angels, ice-skating, skiing, sledding, and made-up games of intrigue, war, and spies hiding behind enemy lines of snow encampments and trenches.

Maplewood.

I began to think about it. Then I began to dream about it. Not in the ethereal sense, although yes, I sometimes found myself daydreaming about it in the middle of a conference call at work or during my lunch break or while waiting in line at the post office, but I also started to have sleeping dreams about it. The street, the surroundings, the town, the people, the parties, the memories. My house. My family. My friends. My life. My prior life. My life in another lifetime.

Then the numbers started to appear without warning in my field of vision at the most inopportune times, like while I was giving a presentation or when a server crashed and my boss was breathing down my neck to fix it. Or in the car. A *lot* of times in the car. I guess since my body was on autopilot, driving to and from work, to the grocery store, to the pharmacy, wherever, my brain was free to focus on the most pressing thing I was attempting to avoid. 128. One. Two. Eight.

128 Maplewood Avenue.

Mom didn't bring it up again. She knew how my fragile psyche worked—
it needed time to ruminate, to stew on the possibilities, the unknowns,
the fear, and, scarier than the fear, the hope. Several weeks later, I sat down
at the kitchen table again and wrote this on the notepad, below the word
Maplewood:

<u>*What would it take?*</u>
Sell a house.
Buy a house.
Quit my job.
Find a job.
Reverse those.
Pack.
Go to the cemetery.
Say goodbye.
Stay upright. Must remember: a way forward.
Rent a moving van.
Load up.
Drive six hundred miles.
Unpack.
Begin again.
Born again?

Two weeks later, after a short plane ride, I was walking through my childhood home with a very chatty real estate agent named Marsha. In between
polite nods to her inquiries and observations, I marveled at how small every
single aspect of this house was compared to the veritable colossal mansion
it seemed during my growing-up years. It was as if the entire interior of the
house had been shrunk down to a perfectly proportioned miniature doll-
house. Had my bedroom always been the size of a prison cell? It had just
enough room for a twin bed, small dresser, nightstand, and closet wedged
in under the attic stairs (hardly tall enough to hang anything besides a knee-
length dress, although, I thought with a chuckle, I suppose I never owned or
wore anything *below* a knee-length dress back then and probably not many
dresses at all, for that matter). But how had my creative world of imagination
been constructed and crushed in such a small space? It seemed impossible
now, but it was true—my every thought, feeling, attitude, and activity began

right here in this tiny dungeon of a bedroom. And yet, even now, years later, I remembered it fondly with a sort of squishy warmth coming to my rescue as I blinked back a few tears hearing Marsha observe, "This would be a perfect room for a little girl, don't you think? Or a boy, I suppose. You could remove the wallpaper or paint over it. So many options, just simple cosmetic touches, really. I'm sorry, I can't remember if I asked already—do you have kids?"

I tucked my head into the closet and cleared my throat to avoid the question, noticing that the door still stuck unless you lifted the glass doorknob up and turned it slightly. I smiled despite the flame in my throat. It felt right. That doorknob. And there, to bring me more into focus, etched in the wood of the back baseboard, were my initials, still plain to see: ASH, Amanda Stacy Holmes. I bit my lip and touched the letters with my fingertips, ducking down to get closer and so my head wouldn't hit the eaves. Marsha was taken aback, advising, "Oh sweetie, you don't need to check every square inch. I can promise you everything is constructed with the utmost sturdiness; you know these old-fashioned hardwoods, baseboards, moldings—they didn't mess around back then. They're solid as a rock; truth be told, you simply can't find this type of craftsmanship anymore. The newer developments can only *wish* for this level of quality, materials, construction, attention to detail. I tell you what…if only…anyway, here's the bathroom across the hall, fully remodeled…"

Thirty minutes later, I was back in my rental car with visions of the coat closet and attic and basement and kitchen counter and built-in bookshelves and (despite Marsha's request) every square inch of the house still swirling in my head like a funnel cloud. It was surreal, this feeling of me in that house, in my old bedroom. A blond curly-haired toddler being tucked into bed by Mom or Dad, a rambunctious kindergartner singing nursery rhymes and playing with Fisher-Price toys, a middle grader trying to find style with a battered pair of blue jeans and feathered hair, a teenager drawing hearts around the cutest boy's photo in the yearbook, a college student coming home to decompress and eat as many home-cooked meals as I could manage during winter break.

It was all right there at my fingertips—a flashback in time, set like a photograph in a frame. And yet, in my logical mind, I knew it was all just an illusion. It was gone like a popular TV show that had long since been canceled, the cast of characters moved on to their next gig, the plot a distant memory that no one thought or spoke about anymore, the set torn down and replaced with a replica that looked similar but was actually made of spun glass ready to be annihilated at the slightest touch.

Oh, but how hard my heart wanted to ignore my logical mind and jump right back into that photograph, that safe space!

Back in my house in Indiana, I wrote this word on the yellow notepad (underneath "Born Again?"):

Courage.

CHAPTER II

Siesta Key, Florida
May 2016

LUXURIATING ON A LOUNGE CHAIR on the Sunday before Memorial Day, I glanced up from my book to look out over the waves that stretched past the white crystalline sand. I felt the essence of nature's rapture encapsulated in the sparkling reflection of the sun's rays upon the water's rolling waves. Every hue of blue, green, and gray swirled in undulating laps against the surf. A snowy egret's yellow feet plodded slowly past a fisherman's bucket, at the ready to plunder the spoils while ten sanderlings scurried away from the incoming tide. Billowy white clouds painted a picture of ethereal wonder across the lapis-infused sky. The wheat-colored reed grasses fringing the condo complex behind me were waving in soft, rhythmic motion against the wind. The sun's white halo beamed down onto my body, and I drank it in like a sponge absorbing every ounce into my not-yet-sated skin.

As I listened to the light tinkling of children's laughter in the background, I thought to myself, this is heaven. If only I could capture this moment and hold it like an egg in my hand. Then when I returned to work in a few days, in the midst of stress and craziness, I could crack it open and be transported back to the sound of crashing waves, the taste of salty sea air, and the feeling of pure, unadulterated serenity radiating through me.

I sighed, leaned back, and closed my eyes.

My mind wandered. It would be wonderful to retire here someday. Siesta Key would be the perfect location—quiet, sleepy, easygoing. Not a party beach at all—more like a family destination. Such a good fit. We could walk every day, bike into the village, or take the Legacy Trail into Venice, brush up on our yoga moves at that class down the way, kayak on weekends, eat out every night, go boating with friends. So many options. Plus, all the live music around town, dinner overlooking the intercoastal, museums, shopping, ice cream, sunset cruises, and on and on. This beach was made for retirees. Heck, we had already made a habit of coming here at least once a year for ages, sometimes with the kids, sometimes alone. I liked alone better.

Anyway, it didn't matter because we weren't retiring anytime soon. Still too young and poor. Well, not really *that* young or *that* poor, but still…we had years to go, not to mention a mortgage, two car loans, child support, the Roth IRA accounts for the kids' college, expenses for school trips, soccer gear, braces, shoes, clothes, insurance, and about a million other things that should have kept me from even putting one tiny pinky toe in the waters of the retirement dream world that was definitely not yet a reality. But I did it anyway… for a pleasant hour or two…wallowing in that little slice of yearning heaven, if only, if only, if only…

Finally, snapping out of it awhile later, I opened my eyes and sat up, trying to focus on my book, but instead found myself observing four suntanned middle school children building a sandcastle a few feet away. They had segmented their work into an assembly line like busy honeybees. One child went back and forth to the water, filling buckets. Another compacted the sand into tightly formed castle walls and towers. Another dug a moat around the castle's platform using the water to hard-pack the sides of the trench. And the last used a carving tool to insert windows and doors into the tower's face. They were strangely quiet and intense in their work. I sat staring, somewhat mesmerized, when—*RING*.

The jarring sound startled and irritated me. I blinked and reached into my beach bag with a curse, pulled out my phone, and saw that it was my brother, Dustin. Why was he calling? He never called me. I picked up.

"Hey, Dustin," I said, trying to hide the impatience from my voice.

"Amanda! Where are you?!" A shout. I had him on speakerphone, and the sandcastle kids looked over curiously. I gave them a shrug and a small smile, and they went back to work.

"Um…Siesta Key, on the beach, lying on a lounge chair, relaxing with a book—why? What's going on?"

"Amanda! Is Shawn with you?" He was out of breath and still too loud. It was the strangest thing—I couldn't remember the last time I had heard Dustin raise his voice like this.

"No, why?" I asked as something in my mind suddenly clicked, causing my heart to beat faster in my chest. It was almost like being awakened from a deep sleep with a gunshot.

He said slowly, succinctly, "Go find a TV, *right now.*"

Without another thought, I grabbed the key out of my bag, leaving everything else on the beach, and ran, in what seemed like quicksand, to the condo, my phone shaking in my hand, trying not to raise my voice as I cried, "Dustin, what? What is it? Tell me *now.*"

"Listen, Amanda," said Dustin. Detecting my rising panic, he now used a calm voice. "I was just watching the race and—"

My phone started to vibrate. Mom calling. Then Shawn's daughter, Sissie, calling. Then Shawn's mom calling. Then my sister, Nikki, calling. Call after call. I couldn't hear Dustin, couldn't process what was happening, couldn't understand. As if to make sense of this, I said out loud, "I don't understand." Then, a second later, now fumbling with my key in the door of the condo, I said into the phone, "Hang on, hang on, I'm back. Let me get the TV on."

I grabbed the remote, and just as the TV came into focus, my stomach sank as I had this random dreaded thought: why was everyone else calling, but not Shawn?

Losing it, I yelled into the phone, "Dustin, *I have to go!*"

I tried Shawn's cell phone at the same time that I scanned the channels to…*what?* Was it ABC, CBS, NBC?! Good God, I couldn't think straight. My mind was racing, disjointed, my fingers like putty, I clicked through, trying to remember the local Florida TV stations, my breath coming in jagged gulps.

Then, there it was, right as Shawn's phone went to voicemail—I saw it and stared in horrified comprehension mixed with disbelief and shock. A news commentator was standing on the street just outside the track, shouting over the sounds of helicopters, police and fire sirens, people screaming, car alarms. A dark, suffocating plume of smoke billowed into the air behind him. Debris scattered in every direction, pieces of broken and bent metal and glass, chunks of concrete, wisps of paper and plastic drifting in every direction.

"…it looks like the blast occurred behind the tower, near the west entrance…we're still assessing the scene. The police are clearing the area. Ambulances are starting to arrive. Emergency evacuation proceedings have begun, although all we can see from this vantage point is…well…there's no other way to say it…mass chaos. For those of you just joining, I repeat, there has been an explosion at the Indianapolis 500. We're not sure of the details yet. Hang on, oh, okay, yes, we have confirmation that the race-car drivers have stopped their cars and are being assisted to safety, along with their pit crews. Thousands of spectators are on the move, being directed to the exits as quickly as possible. Folks, as you can see, we are in the midst of a disaster, under attack here. Okay, um, I repeat, we are coming to you live from the Speedway. The Indianapolis 500 has been bombed, I repeat, there has been an explosion at the track..."

I got down on my knees and nearly pressed my face to the TV, my hands reaching up to the screen, focusing on the throngs of people walking, running, scattering in all directions like lost children. *Where was he?* Where? He must be in this crowd, this seething, swarming pack of panicked people. *Where?* I scanned every face, every body, every piece of clothing, every glimpse of anything that might remotely be male, tall, mid-forties with dark hair and dark eyes, a teenage boy at his side. Of course, they would be together—Shawn would never leave Cole. Was that them, running away toward the side street? No, that boy was a redhead. What about that guy holding someone in his arms, was that them? No, that man was with a toddler. Was that Shawn with a bloody napkin pressed to his forehead? No. What about that guy being lifted by two ambulance workers onto a stretcher, his hand dangling off the side? No, I didn't think so...I couldn't tell. I stood up, blinked back frustrated tears, and screamed into the empty condo, "Shawn!"

I kept dialing Shawn's and Cole's phones over and over again. No answer. At the same time, I kept receiving calls from my friends and family that I let roll over to voicemail.

I started to rationalize in my mind: Could they even hear their phones in that chaos? Maybe they were on the other side of the track, rushing to evacuate. Of course, it would be the last thing they would think about right now, picking up the phone. Their focus would be on getting to safety. Plus, knowing Shawn, he would be helping. He was always so level-headed in an emergency. Unlike me, who would run away from anything remotely gory or traumatic. If Shawn saw an emergency, he would dive right in and make himself useful. It was one of the many things I admired and loved about him. Once, at a neighborhood barbecue, our friend Tim let the propane run too long before hitting the ignition on the grill and burned his face. When it happened, I looked away in horror, whereas Shawn jumped up from the picnic table and ran (not walked) toward Tim. Grabbing a cooler full of pop and melted ice water, he flung the pop onto the ground, took Tim, set him down on the ground, and promptly placed his entire head into the water. How did he know instinctively what to do? Without a split second's thought.

So, I thought, that's where he is right now—he's helping. Probably ran right to the explosion site, trying to gather someone in his arms, cover a wound, calm everyone down, direct them away. If that were the case, then of course he wouldn't be answering his phone. Cole's probably right there with him, taking his dad's lead.

Okay, okay, okay. That makes sense. That could be the case. I shouldn't be jumping to conclusions. I should assume he's fine and Cole's fine. Going on this premise, I took a deep breath and answered an incoming call on my phone.

"Mom?" I asked. "Is that you? Oh my goodness, Mom."

She replied quickly, "Yes! Amanda! Oh, thank God you answered. Are you watching this? Have you talked to Shawn? Is he okay?"

"No, I mean, I don't know! He won't pick up. What—what do I do? Should I just wait? Should I try to call his parents? What do I do? Cole isn't answering either. What on earth has happened? A terrorist attack? In Indy? It doesn't seem possible...." My voice trailed off with a gasp.

"Amanda..." She sounded firm, but with a tremor in her voice. "You listen. You don't know *anything* yet. Let's just assume they're fine. Stay calm and be patient."

"Okay, but how? Good God, *how*?!" Talking about it and thinking about the implications as I saw yet another body being placed onto a stretcher, the news commentator droning on and on, I started to hyperventilate. After a minute, I panted, "Mom. I'm—scared!"

"I know, sweetie..."

Shawn's mom was calling me.

"Mom, I have to go. Karen's calling me. Maybe she's heard from them..."

"Okay, call me back right aw—"

I hung up and quickly pressed the accept button. "Karen! Have you heard anything?"

"No." Her voice was an octave higher than normal but relatively steady. "You?"

"Me either," I replied, closing my eyes as my shoulders slumped. "Has anyone? Why aren't they calling us? Do you think it's just that the phone lines are down? Or they're lost in the chaos or helping or dazed? I—I can't believe what's going on there..." I struggled to think and talk at the same time, still absorbing the scene on the TV. Finally, I said, "What do we do?"

"Well, Ed's just called 911 and talked to the dispatcher. I guess she sounded frazzled and said they were getting a ton of calls but didn't have any information yet and for everyone to stay put. She said we could keep trying to reach out to loved ones, stay glued to the news, and check back later when they had more information."

"That doesn't seem helpful right now," I said with despair. "What about the hospitals? Are they bringing casualties to the hospitals? Maybe we can call around? I'm thinking Methodist or Community North…"

"Ed's already called, but they told him they're not releasing names or any other information right now. At this point, they said they're not even able to keep up with the triage. Channel thirteen said they're sending the injured to the local hospitals, and not just the ones downtown. Listen, if we don't hear anything in the next hour, Ed said he and Tom are going to start driving to the hospitals. They might be able to find out more in person. Plus, Tom's on the phone right now, chasing down some connections through his old station. By the way, when is your flight back to Indy?"

"Tomorrow afternoon," I replied, thinking for the first time that there must be a way to get back sooner. I would need to call the airlines. I wondered absently if they had some type of emergency seats reserved for people like me.

"Karen, what do I do? I can't just sit here and wait—" I sobbed into the phone, sinking onto the couch.

"Sweetie, listen to me. Let's not get ahead of ourselves right now, okay? Ed and Tom will follow up."

"Uh-huh," I stuttered into the phone in between sobs. The only comfort pushing through the panic and pain was the fact that Tom, Shawn's brother-in-law, was a retired cop, and if anyone could get reliable information, and quick, he could.

Karen continued, "Amanda, why don't you get on your computer and see if you can get an earlier flight? Maybe tonight instead of tomorrow. And wait for our call. Okay?"

I sniffed and replied with a tiny "Okay, bye."

Glancing warily at my phone, which was still buzzing and ringing incessantly from what seemed like every person on my contact list (everyone except Shawn and Cole!), I threw it down on the couch in frustration, cupping my face in my hands and sobbing uncontrollably.

My mind, like the ocean waves I had just been listening to not fifteen minutes ago (and a lifetime ago), opened up onto a sea of memories from this past week. An amazing, unforgettable week with Shawn. Walking on the beach, swimming in the ocean, relaxing in the sun, eating at our favorite restaurants, playing trivia at the local bar, trying out a new hoppy IPA, making love, holding hands, kissing, talking, sharing, connecting.

Then my mind flashed to yesterday. On the drive to the airport.

"Honey, aren't you going to miss me?"

He turned to me without a word, his eyes fixed on mine, with a small smile. He took my hand and kissed it. Then a moment later, "Of course. Aren't *you* going to miss *me*? You'll be all alone."

I tried to make light of it, shrugging and grinning. "There's always Paul the pool boy."

He replied with a chuckle, "Ah yes, Paul the pool boy. I hear he services all the lonely ladies—oh, I mean, all the pools around here."

I smiled, leaning my head against the car seat, still staring at him, my handsome husband. Suddenly serious, I added, "Do you really have to go?"

He exhaled, his eyes softening. "We had a great week."

"Yes," I agreed with a whisper.

We were quiet for a while. Pulling into the airport terminal, he added, "Cole is really excited. I can't let him down. Plus, it's the one hundredth running. That only comes once in a century."

"True," I said with a nod, then, "I'll miss you."

"Me too, babe."

We got out of the car, and he grabbed his suitcase from the trunk, handed me the keys, and said, "Don't do anything I wouldn't do."

I put my arms around his waist, staring up at his face, and said with a laugh, "Well, that doesn't narrow it down very much, does it?"

"Nope. Have fun. I'll call you tonight. Be safe."

I nodded, we kissed briefly, and he was off. I stood staring after him until he turned around and waved from inside the double doors. I waved back with a smile. Then I got into the car and drove away, thinking, wow, two whole days of freedom! What will I do with myself?

In a flash, my mind snapped back to the present, and I shuddered. Had I really thought that? *Freedom?* As if it was a chore to be with him. As if I deserved time to myself and would enjoy that more than passing my hours by his side. Was that really what I felt? Now, under these horrific and insane circumstances, I would give all the money in the world to see Shawn for thirty more seconds. How could I have thought that I wanted to be "free" of him for two days? God, I was awful.

My next thought was this: I had a bad feeling. *Such* a bad feeling. A sinking feeling, as if someone had pulled the rug out from under me. It reminded me of a time at work a few years ago when I accidentally sent a sensitive email to the wrong person. I felt an abject terror two seconds later when I realized my mistake. All the blood drained from my face, and my fingers started to tingle. I think if someone had waved their hand in front of me, I wouldn't have seen it. This was the same feeling, but a million times worse. With the email, I was able to recall it and, for safe measure, let the recipient know about the error. With this…what was to be done? Nothing! Absolutely *nothing*. Wallow in the feeling. No turning back time. No way to pay any price to have Shawn sitting here with me instead of lost in that whirlwind of horror. No way to unsee the truth of what I was seeing on TV.

There was also the *knowing* that was seeping slowly like toxic mercury into my veins. The knowing that no matter what Ed and Tom did, no matter how many times I called Shawn's phone, no matter how much I wished and hoped and prayed, the outcome was already right there, right in my consciousness, right in my pores, searing like a branding iron into my heart.

He was gone. I felt it. I *knew* it.

❧ Chapter III ❧

Heathport, New York
July 2018

Enough, Amanda.

It was *enough*.

My drug, my addiction.

As I stood in the kitchen looking around the quiet house, I felt alone, so alone.

Before I could even begin to approach the idea of unpacking, I wanted a hit.

In my mind, I struggled against it, but then I thought, just one hit won't hurt.

Take the edge off.

I picked up my phone and went into voicemail.

Ahhh. There it was. So smooth and warm and comforting.

"Hi, it's me. Where are you? Give me a call…or I'll try you later, bye."

Shawn's voice, alive again.

Yes, an illusion. The message, left in haste on the morning of his death, was an aberration, a blip, a slice in time.

But it filled the emptiness that had invaded my soul.

If only for a moment.

It was my pathetic little addiction. To hear his voice again, to soak it in, as if he were still alive, as if he could walk back through the door at any moment.

Being my only drug of choice, I sometimes listened to it a hundred times a day, sometimes only five, but it always gave me that same rush of fleeting joy, calmness, and a state of suspended animation.

No, it wasn't alcohol or drugs, but it was my own personal brand of masochism, and I clung to it like a baby to a bottle.

Our phone calls since the very beginning had always been like this, short and sweet, never an extra "I love you" or a drawn-out conversation or explanation.

Just the essence.

Like *our* essence. A symbol. Our way of showing all the things that didn't need to be said. The unspoken manner of our love, revealing, in place of words, the connection we had from the first and that was always there. We didn't have to state the obvious. Words would have taken away from that.

But that was gone now.

And I was here. Alone.

I placed the phone down on the counter.

I still felt the hit coursing through my veins, bringing me back to that safe space.

I decided to take a walk around the house. Of course, I had been through it with Marsha a couple of months ago, but back then I had been lost in a world of nostalgia and conjecture. I hadn't really looked at things, taken them in, noticed the details in the context of what they could mean to me, if I let them, if I opened my heart a pinch from where it had lain dormant, stagnant, dead for over two years. Mom and Dustin had managed the home inspection in my absence and the few required fixes. The house keys that had been handed to me at the closing were sitting by my phone like a passageway into my past, into my present, and maybe, I wondered, hoped, and speculated, into my future.

This was my first time alone in the house in well over twenty years. A wash of memories hit me as I walked down the corridor toward the front hallway, touching the wooden slats of the coat closet doors with a sweep of my right hand. The original pine floors were golden brown, and the tapping of my shoes on them echoed up into the open space that was the second-story stairwell. As I came around the corner into the living room, I stared at the blank walls and barren windows, remembering the year that Mom hung Vermont Country Store curtains and Dad said he felt like he was living with Martha Washington. There was the space where the tall brown bookcases used to flank the entryway into the dining room. And the big formal couch and two high-backed wing chairs that were like a blueprint of invitation for guests as they came through the front door into the foyer and turned into the welcoming space.

Everything in my mind was exactly as it had been, except of course, it wasn't. The sounds were all wrong, the emptiness palpable, the illusion a memory, a faded, dissipating vapor. I sighed. Nothing stays the same. Even packages tied up with string in our minds are eventually ripped open and left on the floor in a mutilated heap.

The movers had put the downstairs furniture in the dining room and the boxes in the kitchen. There was barely space to move in those two rooms, so I knew I had my work cut out for me. I wasn't even sure where to begin. Very daunting, and I hadn't even gone upstairs yet. The first thing, though, was to get my bed set up so I had a place to sleep tonight. Walking by the tiny office on the way up the stairs, I smiled seeing the old oak desk—the one piece of furniture that had never been moved from the house (and maybe had even been built in as part of the original construction in 1910). No one really knew for sure, but it was too large to have ever fit through a doorway, and it was of the same era, so it made sense. I'd spent hundreds of hours doing homework and reading and crafts at that desk. It was almost like an old, cherished antique family heirloom that had been passed down from previous generations.

On the landing, the halfway mark at the turn of the stairs, I chuckled when I noticed the broken pane of glass in the window backdrop where Dustin, at the age of thirteen, in a fit of rage (for borrowing his guitar without asking), threw his shoe at me. When I ducked, it sailed straight through the irreplaceable leaded glass pane. I remembered both of us gasping and screaming blame at each other as Dad promptly ordered us to our rooms with a week's grounding.

Stepping from the top stair into my old bedroom, I had flashes of memories scrolling through my mind: Sitting on the floor crossed-legged with Michelle and Kelly playing Go Fish, Old Maid, Candyland, and Life. Sucking candy sugar out of paper straws and drinking Dixie cups of Kool-Aid while reading *Teen Beat* and *Highlights*. Writing notes back and forth to each other, usually about boys, folding each one into an intricate origami shape before handing them over. Listening to the Bangles, the Cure, Depeche Mode, Tears for Fears, Bon Jovi, Duran Duran, and U2 on my boom box cassette player.

I walked over to the room that used to be my parents' and that seemed completely unfit to be mine now, but it was the biggest and had a walk-in closet, so there it was—my new digs. The mattress and box spring were shoved up against the back wall, and the frame was in pieces on the floor, a Ziploc baggie filled with loose parts taped to the headboard. Ugh. It dawned on me that I had to assemble it. I sat down on the floor and cried.

I knew it was pathetic. *I* was pathetic. I had always considered myself a practical, reliable, self-sufficient kind of person, and yet when Shawn and I got married, without discussing it or even thinking about it, we both fell into the usual traditional marital roles (me cooking, cleaning, taking care of the house; him mowing the yard, working on the cars, assembling and fixing things). In the past two years since he died, I had learned a few rudimentary skills like how to replace the parts in the back of the toilet tank and how to swap out the propane tank on the grill, but otherwise I left things broken or, if the situation was dire, phoned a friend or hired a handyman. Of course, to sell the Indiana house, I had to put a bit of money into the repairs I had neglected, but thankfully it sold quickly and was now someone else's burden.

Which was good because now I had my own problems. Like trying to find a screwdriver. I had shipped Shawn's toolbox with the movers, but who knew where it was? Out in the garage with the mower and shovels? I put my face in my hands. At this moment in time, for whatever reason, the insignificant, completely innocuous challenge of putting my bed together threw me into a fit of despair. Everything seemed too much. Why did I always have to be reminded that I was alone and that everything was left to *me* to figure out? And why did it always come out of the blue like this? Was God trying to test the strength and veracity of my heart, my muster, my grit? Because I was ready for a white flag. I was ready to cry uncle.

But instead, I simply cried.

Then the doorbell rang. I lifted my head in surprise. Wow, I hadn't heard that sound in a while—the same old doorbell I remembered from my childhood—ding-dong-ding. I wiped my eyes and stood up. I glanced at my watch: three forty-six. I wondered who that could be. I'd only been in the house for less than an hour. But after a second, I thought, of course, Mrs. O'Connor. The welcome wagon. She was seventy-five if she was a day, she'd lived in the farmhouse across the street for fifty-plus years, and her hobby was to know everyone's business. She was basically the mayor of Maplewood Avenue. So, it made sense that she was the first one to check in on me.

As I descended the stairs, I wondered if she would corner me with the same look of pity I had grown to deplore in everyone from Indiana. It was one of the many reasons I had moved away—to get away from *that* look.

"Yoo-hoo! Amanda?" she called out, opening the front door as I came down into the foyer.

"Yes, Mrs. O'Connor. Hi!" I said, giving her a hug. Thankfully, her face was clear, open, and welcoming. Her blue eyes were like the color of a sunny summer day. She was just as spry and solid as I remembered.

I breathed out and laughed. "It's so great to be home," I said with a look of unmasked relief. Not a stitch of pity on her face. Just seeing her was like going from night to day. "Thanks for letting the movers in yesterday. It looks like everything arrived in good order."

"Oh, sure thing. They were sweet young boys, a bit quick with the shuffling in and out. I was worried they might drop something, but no, I made sure that everything was just as you had instructed. I could see they ran a very tight ship."

I nodded. "Well, good."

Then she stepped back and said, "So, let me look at you. Miss Amanda Stacy Holmes, as I live and breathe!" I laughed again at her funny, old-fashioned expression and her use of my full, middle, and maiden name. I hadn't heard that in a while. "We've all been looking forward to your return! Like old home week. I know it's been twenty years or more, but the old haunt hasn't changed a bit. The Abernathys and Brewers and Hawthornes are still here, not to mention the Sullivans and Derrys and Roberts."

"Yes, I heard that. Michelle filled me in. Hard to believe Donny Brewer could ever turn out to be a responsible husband and father and buy his childhood home just like I did," I said with a laugh.

"Certainly was a shock to me!" she agreed with a wink and a grin. "You kids all do eventually grow up, though—even Donny. So, do you need any help around here?" she asked as she peered around at the unpacked furniture and boxes. "Not that I can lift anything nowadays. My sciatica's been acting up lately. But maybe I could help you sort through dishes or something…"

"Actually…," I began, thinking how ridiculous I had been not five minutes ago, "do you happen to have a screwdriver I could borrow?"

"Phillips head or flat?" she replied, not missing a beat. God, she was sharp as a tack.

"Um, I think flat, one of those big ones…for the bed frame."

"Oh, right, well, let me bring you both to be on the safe side. I'll just pop over to my house and come right back."

As I watched her retreating form walking across the street, my phone rang from the kitchen.

"Michelle, hey!" I answered.

"EEESHHHHHHWOOOOHOOOO!" was the response, as I held the phone away.

"Good Lord, Michelle!" I laughed.

"Are you home?"

"Yes."

"We're on our way." I could hear Kelly in the background, softer, saying, "Hi, Amanda."

"Hi. Okay, thank goodness. I have no idea where to begin. It looks like Armageddon in here. Mrs. O'Connor just stopped by. I sent her to retrieve a screwdriver because there's this bag of nuts and bolts and screws taped to my headboard…it's very intimidating."

"Whoa, sounds complicated, but no worries—we're on our way."

I exhaled with a laugh as I shook my head. Then I found a tear rolling down my face. I wasn't alone. I didn't have to figure everything out on my own. My silly, zany, wacky, loving, amazing two best friends were within a short drive of me now. I was *home*. In that moment, it all began to sink in, and I was simultaneously shocked and happy and grateful.

I said, my voice revealing a saturation of emotion that was completely unwarranted for this specific conversation, "There are just so many parts, and I wasn't sure where to begin…"

Michelle scoffed, "Parts, schmarts. Never fear. Michelle and Kelly to the rescue. We'll have it put together in no time flat."

Then Kelly corrected her in the background. "She means that Andy and Peter will figure it out."

Michelle paused, then admitted, "Well, yeah, we kind of convinced the hubbies to come over and do the heavy lifting. The point is, though, that *we* could have put Amanda's bed together, but I mean, they'll do it much faster—why not leave it to them?"

"Right. Exactly," I agreed.

"Okay, sweet cheeks, be there in five," Michelle screamed into the phone before hanging up.

I grinned and set the phone back down. Crisis averted. And the advent of my new normal.

❧ Chapter IV ❧

Carmel, Indiana
December 2016

Seven months later and they still hadn't solved the explosion at the track. If I could have crawled into a hole in the ground and stayed there, I would have.

The interviews, investigations, press releases, round-the-clock coverage of every single detail of that day and the analysis of thousands of videos, photos, and webcams, and yet they didn't know who did it. How was that possible in this day and age?

And under these circumstances, there was no avoiding it. I already knew there would never be a day when I didn't think about Shawn and Cole, but would there ever be a day when I wasn't inundated with reminders of the tragedy from sunup to sundown?

Plus, did I really need to know whether it was a crazed loner, skinhead, neo-Nazi, mentally ill person, ISIS, the Islamic State, al-Qaida, or whatever flavor-of-the-month terrorist caused this week's news story? It didn't bring back Shawn or Cole or any of the other victims. It didn't change anything. For me, it was better to imagine a Grim Reaper in a black cloak, with dark, empty holes for eyes, walking into the track that day with a scythe to decimate the future.

Of course, the FBI had seen the surveillance videos and had observed the primary suspect, the potential patsy: A man in his late twenties or early thirties, average height, with long, dark, curly hair and a beard, wearing shorts, a T-shirt, and a race-car driver baseball cap pulled down low over his face. Looking exactly like every other person who was there that day. His "disguise" was ingenious. Invisible in plain sight. He had kept his head down, gone through security with a normal-looking cooler of beer, and then simply placed the bomb (the cooler) under the stands in the place where it would inflict the most damage. After that, he walked out of the track, down the street, out of the range of cameras, and out of any consequences for his actions. The bomb detonated fifteen minutes later.

And seven months later, I wished for the day when he would walk out of the range of my conscience and hatred.

A few weeks after the bombing, I went to a grief counselor. He suggested within the first five minutes that I start on a course of antidepressants and sleeping pills. This seemed counterintuitive to me. How would masking the pain help me? Or running away from it? Wasn't that just a temporary solution? What would happen the moment I went off the pills? The pain and agony would be festering and waiting to pounce like a tiger crouching in the tall grass. How would that *fix* anything?

Not that I thought I was fixable. This situation, this loss, this torture, this *grief*, seemed to stretch out in front of me like a vast sea of darkness. What was the point of trying to fix something that would never end? It was cataclysmic, apocalyptic, unendurable.

And yet I endured, or at least existed, one day after the other after the other.

Sometimes, in the middle of the night, when I would wander around the house, lost in a state of perpetual insomnia, I would find myself laughing about it. Yes, *laughing*. Here's where the joke came in. The joke that was on me. I had sown my wild oats for years in college, having fun while I held out for Mr. Right. I promised myself nothing serious until I knew he was *the one*. I had been discerning, wanting to find someone who matched and respected me on my level, and in the meantime I had focused on my studies, on finding the best job when I graduated, and on finding myself. And despite the fact that Shawn was probably the least likely candidate to fulfill my early girlhood dreams of a perfect man, he'd been it, the one I'd been looking for, and we'd created our circle of happiness and stayed blissfully cocooned inside that reality.

And now, as I thought about how I had tried so hard to do everything right, based on the world's formula for seeking and obtaining the best love match, I was thirty-six years old and alone. And when I thought these thoughts, that's when a little voice popped into my head, channeling Charlie Brown, and said, "Good grief!" which made me laugh. Yes, it was a *good* grief, Charlie Brown—a grief that wasn't going away and that lived inside me, and was warranted, necessary, and *right*. In fact, I think I was falling in love with the grief. All that time it took to find and fall in love with Shawn, and yet, this new love came to me so suddenly, effortlessly, naturally. The grief seemed like the perfect love. It seeped into my pores and filled me up, like a warm bath, and lived with me as my best friend. It was such a *good* grief. It didn't ask for anything in return—it simply let me live with it, hand-and-hand, day after day, night after night.

It was around this time, when I had started to have full-on conversations and laughing spells with myself in the middle of the night, that something happened. It was a typical Tuesday at work, and a woman stopped by my desk. She worked in the next department, and we hadn't spoken in a while, but she came and sat down beside me. I was somewhat taken aback because the first words out of her mouth were "Amanda, I can't—anymore—I can't."

"What?" I asked, confused and a little scared.

She explained, with a wave of her hand at my face, "That. You. This."

I frowned, even more perplexed. She told me a story about her son, who had died seven years ago from cancer, and said she could spot the "fog of grief" from a mile away. She patted my arm and told me about the only thing that helped her: Beverly. Some shrink, I supposed. "You need to talk to her. Right away. I promise, you won't regret it. Here's her card, sweetie. Don't wait. Set up an appointment today." I thanked her with a narrow smile and promptly shoved the card in my drawer under a stale pack of gum, twenty thumbtacks, and an old dollar bill.

Days went by, and every time I opened that drawer, I saw the card peeking out, beckoning me, reasoning with me, persuading me. Eventually, I felt myself listening to its pull. I had the distinct impression that it knew I needed help and wouldn't let me ignore it, wouldn't let me stare out at the sea of endless darkness anymore. It wouldn't let me call it my *good grief* anymore. After a while, my fear and loathing of that card turned to curiosity, but still, I couldn't seem to pick it up. Finally, feeling as if the card had grown to be the size of a colossal inflatable lifeboat, I reached for it one day and called the number.

A week later, I was in a waiting room, wishing the floor would swallow me. She called out my name from her office, and I dutifully stood up (trying not to let my legs buckle underneath me), approached her, and held out my hand as she introduced herself, "Hi, I'm Dr. Flagg, but please call me Beverly."

"Hi, I'm Amanda Morgan." My smile was tight-lipped as I shook her hand and put on my best brave face. The face I'd learned to plant there, not for my sake, but for everyone else's. Act fine, act strong, act with-it, act like you're up for an Academy Award. It's much easier than the opposite, which always solicits the inevitable response of pity, fear, confusion, panic. So, brave face. Throughout the day, I would actually think the words *brave face* to myself, as if that were my name. You can *do* this, brave face. You can make it through this session, brave face.

"Please take a seat," she said as she pointed to a large brown leather chair. She sat in a matching chair beside an antique writing table. Her office was a warm mustard color. She had it decorated in a peaceful, homey kind of way: a navy couch in the corner with brick-red pillows and painted wooden boards on the walls with cheerful expressions like "Be Still and Know" and "Let Your Faith Be Bigger Than Your Fears."

"How can I help you today?" Beverly asked with an open smile.

Good Lord, how to begin? Just the facts, brave face, just the facts. "Well, I've been feeling…kind of down lately, and I've been having—having some—some trouble eating and sleeping." I found myself nervous and fumbled over my words, staring down at my hands as I sat wringing them in my lap.

I could feel her examining my face and body language. She said, "Okay, well, I'd like to help with that. Tell me more."

I took a deep breath and looked up at her. "Well, it's Christmas next week, and I've never dreaded a holiday so much in my life."

Her eyebrows arched, but she didn't say anything. I noticed her eyes were kind and warm, a friendly shade of deep brown, a shade lighter than her pupils, similar to the color of the chairs we were sitting in. For some reason, they reminded me of a dog's eyes, the kind of dog that jumps in your lap with unconditional love when you're at your lowest. For some reason, this thought gave me strength.

After a moment, when I didn't say anything else, she said with an encouraging upturn to her mouth, "Holidays can be a difficult time of year for many. The rush of shopping, family, meals, travel, alcohol, parties…quite overwhelming."

"Yes," I agreed easily.

Another silence.

"Is there one thing in particular that you're dreading? Or just everything in general?"

I stared at her for a moment. Then I said, "I guess I'll just come right out with it." After biting my lip, I opened my mouth and raced to get the words out. "My husband and stepson were killed in the explosion at the track, and I guess I'm having some difficulties trying to deal with that, and with the thought of a Christmas without them."

Her eyes widened, a slight crack in her perfectly composed exterior. Recovering quickly, she nodded, a slow crease of concern puckering her eyebrows. She said, "Oh. I'm very sorry."

I nodded back, my head down, trying to keep the tremor out of my voice as I continued, "I went back to work after a couple of weeks, but I don't know, maybe that was too soon…? I find myself living in a sort of dream state. Some days, I don't remember having been in the office at all. Other days, I stay at the office late, wishing I didn't have to go home. And then everyone has been so nice, dropping off food, calling and texting, offering to clean my house or decorate my tree. Even now, all these months later. And with Christmas coming, it's gotten worse—the casseroles, the cookies, the cards. It's really very sweet, but all of this…attention somehow makes me feel worse."

I glanced up guiltily. Her countenance listening, studying, quiet. I went on, "The sympathy from every angle makes me walk on eggshells, not knowing when someone, out of the goodness of his or her heart, will unintentionally drag me back down into the horror again. It's right there, fresh and throbbing in my heart, waiting to be wrenched back up, and I can't seem to get away from it. And to make matters worse, I somehow feel obligated to ease *their* discomfort. They don't know what to say or how to act, and I don't either, so we do this dance where they say how sorry they are and what a tragedy it is and ask how I'm doing, and I lie and say, 'Better—a little better every day.' It feels like an endless loop of platitudes and a pendulum of pain, and I'm left in the dust afterward, wondering when or how it will end, and then I feel bad because I wonder if it ever should." I paused, then added, "On top of that, at night, when I actually probably could use a little company, I'm home alone trying not to think about everything—my desolation, my shattered life, my mortgage, my husband—especially my husband, whose smell still lingers on his clothes in the closet and under the sink where he kept his cologne. What do I do about that?"

My brave face fell, and the tears began to fall. Beverly handed me a tissue box. I plucked several out and cried into them.

Eventually I sputtered, "I just feel like I'm an empty balloon floating above myself…held to the earth by a very fine piece of thread. Sometimes, the thread is short and I'm able to walk among people on solid ground and be myself, but lately—most of the time—I'm hovering up high, big and empty, looking down and wondering who that person is. I don't feel attached or tethered somehow to my life or to this earth anymore, and I don't know what to do about that."

She let me sob for several minutes. Then, when I finally looked up, blowing my nose, she said thoughtfully, "Yes, I see. You know, I see. You, I mean. I see what's happening. Grief is not an easy thing, and it comes in waves and in many forms. For you, I believe you have let yourself drift, or split, into two; in the forefront, you're portraying someone who has a handle on things— your routine, your work, your logistics—and in the secret background, you're hiding your grief from everyone, and even from yourself. I would like to try to get these two layers of your being put back together again, and maybe then we can work on an integrated solid footing here in the real world."

I nodded and muttered in agreement, "Um…okay."

She paused, her mouth a thin, hard line, waiting for my full attention, which I readily gave as she said, "I can help you. But it may take some time and work. Although I can't bring your loved ones back, I can certainly provide tools and counseling to get you moving in the right direction. My goal is not to recreate what you had in the past. I'm afraid *that* life for you, sadly, is gone, and I'm not in the business of selling miracles, but what I *can* do is help you create a new space—one where the potential exists to achieve a new kind of hope and happiness. You have to be willing to come along on the journey with me, though. It won't be easy. It may require some work on your part. Are you willing?"

I faltered, feeling the weight of her words in my chest. Didn't she see I was broken, unable to provide an ounce of anything, let alone whatever she meant by "work"? But then I swallowed, thinking, what was the alternative?

Her stern face regarded me, waiting. I pursed my lips and finally said warily, "Alright."

With that, her eyes turned on a dime to warm and caring, the hardness completely disappearing, like a wash of sunshine that blanched a dark shadow. She gave me an encouraging smile. "Good. For starters, I think it would be helpful for you to come at least once a week for a while. And I presume you're already on some medications?" I shook my head. "No, hmm, okay, that's fine. We won't need them. We're going to try a different approach."

I blinked several times in succession. I found my face forming something unnatural and unfamiliar—a faint smile. Could it be? Would it be?

Was it possible? Did I actually feel something close to…what was it? Hope? Yes, *hope*.

She began again, "I know you're worried about Christmas, but first tell me a little bit about yourself. And about your husband and stepson. And anything else you're willing to share. I'd like to get to know you better." She paused and then added, "And if you don't mind, I'm going to take some notes."

"Sure." I took a deep breath, more in control of my voice now. "Shawn is—was—sorry—well, he was a great guy. That's usually how people described him. A great guy. You know, the type who would give the shirt off his back to a complete stranger. Grew up on a farm, smart, funny, kind, mechanical—he could fix anything—good at sports and work. And Cole, he was a lot like him. Into sports, had a lot of friends, active in the church youth group. I don't know…that's what's so heartbreaking," I paused, the burning beginning in my throat again, "they were two peas in a pod, and now they're both gone. And it's just me and Sissie left to pick up the pieces. How are we supposed to do that without them? Without him? Shawn was always the one who managed everything, not to mention the glue that kept us all together."

"Who's Sissie?"

"My stepdaughter."

She nodded. "No kids of your own?"

"No," I answered softly, shaking my head.

As I thought about how to frame this part of my life, I felt Beverly examining me, seeing that I was reluctant to expand; it was my sore spot. But I thought to myself, better rip the bandage off quickly. I added, "Shawn and I were married for almost eleven years when he died. It was a few weeks shy of our anniversary. I was young when we married—just twenty-five—but he was thirty-five, and he'd already had his children and figured they would be enough for me too."

"And were they?"

"Well…yes…and no. I mean, as much as I loved helping raise Cole and Sissie, I'm not their mother. And sometimes it's just hard to compare. As my friends and coworkers have become pregnant and started having kids, I find myself being jealous. They complain about having pregnancy cravings and gaining weight, and then when the babies come about how awful labor is, but all I can think is how much *I* want that. I want to experience that. But Shawn didn't understand, couldn't see it from my perspective. He just kept pointing out that we already had our hands full with Cole and Sissie, which of course was true, but that didn't mean I stopped yearning for my own maternal experience."

Beverly looked at me with her kind, all-knowing eyes and said, "What you wanted was perfectly natural, especially for a twenty-five-year-old. As much as you loved Shawn, he should have considered your feelings too…"

I nodded. She had hit the nail on the head. Why couldn't Shawn have given me a child of my own? Before we were married, he'd told me it was certainly a possibility, but afterward, he changed his mind. I tried to push it, but he always put the discussion on the back burner, saying now wasn't the time. And here I was, essentially alone without even a piece of Shawn of my own, without even a hope of having a child at all.

When I paused, Beverly asked, "Did you ever consider having a child anyway?"

I knitted my brow, confused. "You mean, without Shawn?"

"Yes. Or with Shawn," she said matter-of-factly.

I looked up and blushed. "Yes, I did consider both options. The thought of divorce crossed my mind, but that seemed so ugly to me. It would have been especially hard on Cole and Sissie to go through that again. Not to mention, I didn't think I'd be able to find someone else as well suited for me in every *other* way as Shawn. And because I could see that Shawn was such a great father, I really wanted a child with him, if it was possible." I stopped and looked down at my hands. "And at one point in our marriage, I…well, I removed all preventative measures. I didn't tell him. Of course, this was wrong of me, but I figured he'd have to become okay with it and that it would all work out in the end."

Beverly nodded and said, "You wanted a baby, but he wasn't willing to compromise. I get it."

I smiled grimly. I still felt bad about it. It was the only deception, the only thing in our marriage that wasn't aboveboard and honest.

"So, what happened?" she asked.

"Nothing. Nothing at all. I never got pregnant. I guess it served me right."

"Oh," she said. "Well, I don't know about that…"

I regarded her and effectively ended the conversation with, "After all, what does it matter now? I should probably be happy it didn't work out because I'd be left raising a child on my own, and maybe it's a blessing that it never happened." It was strange for me to think about the fact that a few years ago, having a baby was a sort of obsession with me, and now it just seemed so insignificant. What did it matter? Shawn was gone. No baby or anything else could fix that, could fill that void, and I wished I could take back every argument we ever had about it.

"What about Sissie? How is your relationship with her?"

I sighed. It was complicated. I figured I'd start with the positives. "Actually, Sissie and I are getting along pretty well lately—much better than we ever did when Shawn was alive. We both loved Shawn so much. Sometimes we talk about him like he's still around. I think it's helped keep his memory alive. We're both sad, but we're more *together* now." I paused, thinking about the irony of the past seven months, that Sissie and I were finally, after all of these years, connecting on a sort of mother-daughter-friend level, and yet Shawn wasn't around to witness it. He would have loved it.

"So, does she live with you then?"

"Well, sometimes she stays with me, but mostly she lives with Shawn's parents."

"Not with her mother?"

"No, there have been some issues over the years…it's a long story. But now that school's back in session, it's better for her to live with Shawn's parents because she can get back into a routine with the bus and homework and everything. Plus, with my insomnia and crying at night, I think I was keeping her up…she's never said a word, but I know it was starting to affect her."

I paused as I noticed that Beverly had stopped writing and was looking up at the clock. She said with an apologetic smile, "We're at the end of the hour. With regard to the holiday, I know this season will be difficult without Shawn and Cole, but perhaps think through other times in your life when you had to dig deep and draw on your inner resources to get through a tough time. You may already have the strength within yourself and the necessarily tools to persevere. And another thought: although Shawn and Cole can't be with you, you might find a way to include them anyway. Say a prayer for them before the meal or buy them a gift or fill their stocking. Whatever your normal tradition would be, see if there's a way to make them a part of it. They may not be here in body, but they will be in spirit."

I didn't respond, but as we both stood up, I nodded, grateful because I had to admit I felt better than I'd felt walking into her office an hour ago, less stalled, less likely to allow my thoughts to run in the same downward spiral as before. Now I had some concrete thinking and processing to do, and I appreciated and yearned for that.

✣ Chapter V ✣

Heathport, New York
September 2018

I woke up and looked out the window at the backyard. The sugar maple leaves were just starting to turn, and they shimmered in the morning light with hints of yellow, red, and orange fringing the tips. It seemed as if fall was nearly upon us, still warm and clear with just a hint of crisp autumn air and cut grass.

I sighed. Months had gone by, and I was sleeping like a rock now. Even after that first night in July, in my newly assembled bed miraculously screwed together in fifteen minutes flat by Michelle's husband, Andy, and his nifty cordless screwdriver (didn't need Mrs. O'Connor's manual kind after all), it had become easier, more natural to fall asleep and stay asleep. After the bed was done, Andy and Peter (Kelly's husband) went downstairs and moved the heavy furniture into place while Michelle and Kelly stayed upstairs with me to put the rest of the bedroom together, including hanging pictures and stowing all my clothes in the closet. Somewhere along the way, we ordered take-out Chinese, and the five of us sat out on the back deck with beers, eggrolls, and fried rice, taking in the night sky, shared memories, and laughter like a new constellation of friendship forming right there in the middle of Maplewood Avenue.

Now, as I stared out the window, I couldn't keep a tear from escaping down my cheek. I was home again. Really *home*. In my old house on my old street with my old friends. And yet everything felt new. Something new couched in something old, something familiar, fantastic, and right. What did I ever do to deserve this? It seemed like not enough. It almost didn't feel real. Or earned. But I couldn't deny that it felt like fate or a dream that actually came true for once.

The paper birch trees in the backyard reminded me of the Fox and Geese game we used to play for hours, a sort of tag that involved arranging the leaves into an intricate maze of trails, zigzags, and switchbacks, complete with a penalty box and time-out area. We ran for hours and left the trails in place for days until my parents inevitably broke up the fun with the announcement that it was leaf pickup day, at which point we would spend the next eight hours raking our maze to the curb. That's when we knew the season was coming to an end.

But today, as I noticed the bright sunshine breaking through the clouds in streaks of gold on my bed, I raised my arms above my head in a big stretch and said out loud, "Not today! It's your birthday, Amanda Morgan! And you are waking up on Maplewood Avenue! Thirty-eight years old and starting over. How about that?!"

As I slid my robe over my nightgown and walked down the stairs to get breakfast ready, I had a funny thought cross my mind: I'm kind of like the autumn trees, aren't I? First decaying, then falling down, then dying off for a season (or two, in my case), only to reappear again in the spring. Is that what I'm meant to do now? Grow new roots, send out new tendrils, spread my seeds across the ground in the hope that one will take root? Maybe this fall would actually be my spring—my renewal, my regrowth, my reentry into life.

I was taking the breakfast things out of the fridge when my mom called and insisted on singing me happy birthday. It was sweet. I told her I'd pick her up tomorrow at ten thirty for brunch at my sister's. In the meantime, though, I had to power through today. Michelle and Kelly were coming over for a "surprise." They wouldn't tell me what, and I had a stomach full of butterflies. I offered to make breakfast and they hadn't refused, so I began by browning sausage in an iron skillet for the beginnings of biscuits and gravy, one of my Indiana specialties. I added a bit of vegetable oil and some shredded potatoes into another skillet and turned the burner on medium. In between responding to birthday texts, cutting strawberries, and sticking the biscuits in the oven, I heard the doorbell ring, followed directly by a singsong "Hey-hey-hey-hey, birthday girl, we're here!"

I put the phone down just as Michelle and Kelly came rushing through the door laden with flowers and balloons. In the middle of a chest-crushing hug that I felt in my bones, Michelle screamed, "Holy moly, it smells good in here! When do we eat?"

"Soon," I said with a laugh, taking a vase out of the cupboard and filling it with water to hand to Kelly as she pulled the scissors out of the drawer and cut the ends off a beautiful set of long stem yellow roses, arranging them strategically in a neat bouquet.

I smiled, drinking in the smell of one rose while laughing at the balloons that said, "It's a girl!" and said, "Aw guys, you shouldn't have...so sweet."

I turned back to the skillets, drained the sausage grease into an empty coffee can, then seasoned the browned sausage with salt and pepper, coated it with a heaping pile of flour, and finally gave both the sausage and the potatoes a good stir. The whole time, I was trying to hide the tears that had welled up in my eyes. God, the slightest kindnesses set me off lately. I wondered when or if that would ever get better.

I cleared my throat and sniffed, turning to Kelly and saying with a nod, "Nice balloons."

Kelly started to say, "Oh, I know, I told Michelle that was stu—"

Michelle jumped in, "I thought this one was more fitting. Having a *birth* day, not just your birthday."

My teary eyes grew big as I stared at her. "What does that mean?"

"Oh, I don't know. I thought about you moving home and being part of the Maplewood gang again—it seems almost like a rebirth of sorts. And well, you're a girl," she said with a laugh.

"Yes, that much is true," I conceded with a grin. It was almost as if she had read my mind about those autumn leaves and how this fall was my spring. I turned away as I poured the milk into the powdery sausage mixture, stirred, and asked, "So, are either of you going to tell me what my surprise is? What exactly are we doing today?"

Neither of them said a word, so I looked to Kelly, the voice of reason, and asked, "Nothing illegal, right?"

She shrugged. "One would hope."

"Great," I laughed. "Very reassuring. Can you two set the table? This is just about ready."

As they shuffled around the cupboards, kitchen, and dining room, I continued to stir and also began to wonder how I had lucked out—my family had moved kitty-corner across the street from a family of eight girls when I was six years old. Michelle and Kelly were the two youngest, Michelle one year older than me and Kelly one year younger. I was happily squashed right in the middle and spent nearly every waking hour from that point forward in their presence. It was a wonder their parents didn't kick me out, I pilfered so many snacks, candy, cereal, and treats from their house, not to mention enough hand-me-down clothes to last a lifetime. My sister, Nikki, was three years older than me and my brother, Dustin, three years younger, so I spent many of my early years feeling like an only child until I met the Abernathy sisters, who became like sisters to me. In fact, all these years later, we still referred to each as "seesters." And we even had a running joke that we were each other's "semesters" because this is how autocorrect translates "seesters." When we were being lazy or funny, we left it as "semester." "Miss you, semester." "How are my semesters doing?" "When can the semesters meet up?" "Love you like semesters."

As Michelle grabbed the bowl of strawberries off the counter, I noticed how little she had changed in the past thirty-plus years. She was still tall and willowy, and always boisterous, funny, gregarious, and bold. With her broad shoulders and thick chestnut hair, she always turned heads when she walked in a room. In contrast, Kelly was shorter and heavier, with bobbed curly auburn hair and a shy smile. She was more of a listener than a talker, but on occasion when she got lost in the shadow of Michelle, she would hold up a hand and say, "Excuse me. I'm talking now." That always ruffled Michelle's feathers and forced me to hide a grin. Having grown up in such a big family, they had each perfected their own strategy for how to be heard.

Before we moved to Maplewood, my parents thought our family of three children was large, but we realized quickly that a family with three children was on the small side in this town that was mostly filled with Catholics and Protestants of Irish, Italian, and German descent. It made for some raucous, rowdy neighborhood parties, with a veritable bursting at the seams of kids of all ages.

Both Michelle and Kelly lived in Pittsford now, about a half hour away, so when they came to see me, they would often also stop and see their parents, who still lived kitty-corner across the street. Kelly didn't have any children, but Michelle would use these opportunities to drop her two boys off at Grandma and Grandpa's so "Mommy could have a time-out," as she called it, which was the situation today. At one point about a month ago, Mrs. Abernathy had come by and thanked me (with the *most* delicious chocolate chip banana bread) for being "the reason I get to see my daughters and grandchildren more often now."

Michelle and Kelly still thought of my stint in Indiana as a brief bout of insanity. Why would I move away from New York and settle in "flyover country"? And they made fun of my "accent," which I thought was ridiculous since Indiana couldn't be more midwestern, meaning essentially no accent at all. I often reminded them that just because I didn't say *cat* and *hat* with the hard "a" and I didn't call my soda "pop" anymore, it didn't mean I had lost my New York roots. And truth be told, I still called soda "pop" most of the time. Old habits die hard.

The table set, the food done, we each grabbed a cup of coffee and tucked into our meal at the dining room table. For a few long minutes, we sat silently and happily eating. Then, as Kelly bit into a strawberry, she asked Michelle, "Have you seen Mom's tomatoes?"

"Yes! Oh my God, so good. It's September, and those plants are still weighted down with fruit. She keeps giving me bags and bags. I swear I ate like fifty cherry tomatoes last week."

I said, "She's given me a whole bunch too." I pointed to the brown sack on the kitchen counter. "I already used the big ones to make a caprese salad last night. It was delish!"

"By the way, Amanda, *this* is really good," Kelly said, pointing with her fork at the biscuits and gravy. Michelle nodded and agreed.

"Thanks, glad you like." I smiled.

"So…how are you feeling about this birthday?" Kelly asked tentatively.

"Well, outside of not knowing what kind of shenanigans you two have in store for me," I answered with a laugh, "I'm mostly feeling pretty good." I sighed and thought for a minute. "Compared to last year and the year before that, it feels like a one-eighty, so I guess that's good. I was in such a bad place back then. I couldn't see a way out, you know?" Kelly reached over and squeezed my hand. They had both been in the trenches with me over the past two years, coming to Indiana (sometimes for a weekend, sometimes for a week), holding me when I couldn't stop crying, forcing me to get out of bed, shower, and feed myself, helping me with the arrangements and household matters. I squeezed back with a smile, gulping down a tear, and said, "I know I've told you both a thousand times, but thank you for everything."

Michelle said softly with a grin, "Well, you owe us big time, that's for sure." Then, more seriously, "I'm just glad you found Beverly when you did. I noticed a marked difference in you after that. She was a godsend."

"For sure," I agreed.

Kelly nodded.

Then Michelle quickly changed the tone with "Well, *this* birthday, we're going to whoop it up and have some fun! We have the whole day planned out, and you're gonna love it!"

"Woot! Woot!" I exclaimed. "I'm putty in your hands, Lord help me."

Kelly looked around the room and said, "By the way, how funny is it that we're starting your birthday right here in this dining room? Remember how your mom used to have your birthday parties in here, and there was that jungle of houseplants in the bay window and an old clock on the mantel over there? I'm feeling such a sense of déjà vu right now."

I exhaled and shook my head. "You have no idea...I've been feeling that for months since I moved in. It comes in spurts. The other day, I remembered the year when I hid a bag of Halloween candy under the kitchen sink and then promptly forgot where I hid it until Dad came upon it six months later when the garbage disposal went on the fritz."

Michelle laughed. "I remember that! We had such a good cache that year too, and you were so mad you couldn't find yours."

"Total childhood trauma," I teased.

We giggled over more childhood stories until our plates were empty and our stomachs full.

As I rinsed and stacked the dishes in the dishwasher, Kelly asked me, "So, are you lonesome here all by yourself? How is it at night?"

"I'm fine. Well, I'm maybe not totally 'fine,' but pretty good. I sleep a lot better here than I ever did in Indy. It was so hard sleeping in *our* house because everything reminded me of Shawn, and every noise seemed like it might be him." I gave an embarrassed shrug. "Hard to shake something like that. Here, I don't have to worry about that. I still think about him all the time, and I know he's still...watching over me, but it's just...different here."

Kelly nodded. "Well, you *look* better." She blushed a little and added, "Not that you ever looked...horrible or anything. It's just that now you look healthier, less strained. For a while there, you were scaring us—losing all that weight and the lack of sleep."

"Well, to be honest, losing a few pounds wasn't such a bad thing, although not a diet plan I'd wish on my worst enemy, but yeah, I get what you mean— for a while there, I was scaring *myself*. I'm glad to be back in a good routine. That helps a lot."

"Speaking of that, how's the new job?"

"Great so far. It feels like starting my career all over again, which seems crazy at my age, but yeah, I mean, it's pretty good. Maybe not my most desired dream job, but I like it. Everyone's really nice over there."

I took a few minutes to talk about my new job as a project manager at a small start-up software company on Ridge Road. It was a step down from my prior role in Indy as an IT director at an insurance company, but this new job was a good first step in establishing myself and building a network in New York. I figured I'd ride it out for a while, then look for something else in a year or two. I asked Kelly about her job (as a music teacher) and Michelle about her kids' activities, and before long we were done with the dishes, and Michelle looked at her watch and said, "We need to get a move on. Go ahead and get ready. You have exactly, let's see…ten minutes."

"Okay, but you still haven't told me what we're doing," I said incredulously. "I don't even know what to wear or what to bring."

Michelle said, "You don't have to bring a thing, and just wear something comfortable and pack a bag with a few extras and a swimsuit, and we'll manage the rest."

I ran upstairs to get ready, my stomach in knots. What did they have in store for me? I knew it would be fun no matter what, but I still wracked my brain trying to think of what might require "extras" *and* a swimsuit. God, I hoped it wasn't a surprise pool or beach party. Did we know anyone who had a pool or lived on the beach? I didn't think I could handle that. My new, thinner body was not in prime viewing order yet, nor was my fragile psyche. Being the center of attention was not my cup of tea, to say the least. It was still so hard to be seen by others because every narrow spotlight focused on me summoned their questions and, worse, their inevitable pity. I had moved six hundred miles to get away from that and from the constant in-my-face memories, and I certainly didn't want to go back down that road, especially today. But surely Michelle and Kelly knew that, right?

I scoured my closet and drawers. I finally settled on a pair of cutoff jean shorts, a close-fitting navy T-shirt, and beige strappy sandals. I tied my wavy blond hair up into a high ponytail and carefully applied some makeup, thinking I looked quite good, maybe even *cute*. Or rather pretty anyway. I smiled.

When I came downstairs, they were sitting out on the front porch swing, laughing, and I blew out a sigh of relief. They would never put me in a situation where I wasn't comfortable. These were my two best friends, who had taken an entire day out of their lives to make my birthday special. No matter what they had in mind, I'm sure I could face it, and damnit, I would! After all, it was a beautiful morning—bright and sunny, as if fall had decided to hold off for another week, and the birds were singing, so I was going to buck up and go with the flow.

Closing and locking the door behind me, I proclaimed, "Okay, let's hit this!" and secured my bag over my shoulder as they both stared at me in shocked, happy surprise.

"Well, alrighty then," Michelle replied in her best Jim Carrey voice.

"Who's driving?" I asked.

Michelle said with a big grin, "We're taking Kelly's Lexus!"

"Woot! Woot! Shotgun!" I cried triumphantly and started running down the porch steps. Michelle almost always called it first, and she came tearing after me echoing, "Shotgun! Shotgun!" but she was too late. I snagged the front seat with a swift butt bump to her side and a dive into the soft leather.

Kelly ambled down after us, laughing. As she backed out of the driveway, we all waved at Mrs. O'Connor, sitting on a stool weeding her flower bed, and at Mrs. Roberts, out on her side porch with her Ovaltine and cigarette.

Kelly observed, "Some things never change, do they?"

"Not around here," Michelle answered. She took a minute to roll down her window and holler at her boys, who were riding scooters down the middle of the street. "Get out of the road, you goobers! You're gonna get yourselves killed!" I turned to look at her in the back seat as she shook her head and smiled.

I said with a grin, "No they don't."

❧ Chapter VI ❧

Carmel, Indiana
February 2017

As I was getting ready for work, I noticed it was snowing outside. I was glad I had scheduled a morning appointment with Beverly because at least I wouldn't have to commute downtown until after rush hour. I'm sure the roads would still be clogged at ten, but not as bad as seven or eight. I logged into my computer before leaving for my appointment, answered my emails, and prepared for a meeting I had at one. After that, I drank a cup of coffee while watching the snow drift down like wisps of white cotton from the sky. It was pretty. Snow always made me think of my childhood home back in New York. Maplewood. All those years growing up in a small town on the banks of the Erie Canal, covered by a layer of snow for much of the winter months. An idyllic setting for warm memories (ironically) like coming inside after a day of sledding or skiing to be told to strip down to skivvies and hang wet snow-encrusted clothes on the line by the furnace, then to be diverted with mugs of hot chocolate and marshmallows while being wrapped in blankets in the rec room, where a holiday movie was slipped into the VCR.

What was great about those times and our town was that everyone knew everyone. The kids all played together outside, no matter what the weather. And there was something special about the snow that got everyone excited. It made the salty roads, dirty cars, and mushy ground become new again—crisp, white, pure, fresh. When we saw snow, we knew we were ready to take on the day. Even if it was a school day, there was an unwritten rule that the moment we arrived home after the bus dropped us off, we would meet out in the middle of the street to figure out what activity we were going to tackle. Build an igloo? Sled down the Hawthornes' hill? Snowball fight in the Brewers' yard? Ice skating on the Derrys' pond? Snow sculptures at the Abernathys'? Hockey on Roberts' iced-over basketball court?

There were endless possibilities, and there was not even the slightest thought about the inconvenience of snow, as I was imagining today here in Indy with the commute. Of course, back then our parents probably had different thoughts about driving in it, but we only saw it as a barrel of fun to be taken advantage of in every possible way while it was available and there for the taking.

Cradling my mug of coffee in my hand and watching the flakes drift down, I sighed. If only my life were that simple again. If only I could take back time and hold it in my hand as tightly and snugly as a smooth, flat stone. Then I could go back to that simple time and stay there. And not think or deal with this time I was living in now, where everything seemed so complicated, dark, and unendurable. If only I could blanket my life with this white layer of snow and cover the darkness with light.

Granted, I thought, things were better than they had been, weren't they? Just a smidge. It was hard to determine *how* exactly because the change was almost imperceptible, but since I had started seeing Beverly, I was beginning to feel a slight opening or crack of light peeking through the darkness. It came as a shock to me, this new feeling of modest hopefulness. I hadn't thought it possible before, but there it was, a small bubble of air.

I think it began after that second session when she had provided suggestions for dealing with the holidays. ("Don't say yes to anything that is too overwhelming, taxing, or feels uncomfortable." "Don't feel guilty for saying no." "Don't beat yourself up if you need to spend a day or two or ten in bed sleeping or crying or doing whatever you need in order to feel all the feelings, to grieve what you've lost, to be okay with your circumstances, to be okay with yourself.") When I took her advice, I found the holiday less daunting and even almost bearable at times. Yes, I had spent more hours than I could count crying and mourning the loss, but there had also been glimmers of poignancy and life-affirming moments that took my breath away.

Case in point, following her suggestion that we include Shawn and Cole in some aspect of the holiday, Sissie and I went shopping together, to the Castleton Mall, taking our time picking out gifts. It was probably the best thing we had done in months. As we went into one shop after another, we touched the items and talked about them, wondering what Shawn or Cole would have liked. The shopping and the talking made us feel as if they were there with us, leading us to their perfect respective gifts. We found ourselves intermittently laughing, then crying, then telling stories about past Christmases, then reminiscing about Shawn's "dad humor," like when the kids were little and he would insist on donning the Santa suit on Christmas morning, saying he was too fat to fit up the chimney and that he needed a boost. We would make the kids go in the next room so they wouldn't see the "magic," and both Shawn and I would create a great ruckus pretending to shove him up the chimney, only to have Shawn reappear a few minutes later in his pajamas, saying sadly, "Aw, did I miss Santa?" Sissie told me that at some point, she and Cole figured out it was Dad but didn't want to stop the ruse, so they went along with it long after the jig was up. Sissie talked a lot about how much Cole loved Christmas because it entailed eating tons of great food, watching sports nonstop, and a guarantee of at least three brand-new video games he could master before going back to school.

At the end of the day, I bought Shawn a watch and Cole a Pacers Jersey, and Sissie bought her dad a "Best Dad Ever" coffee mug and Cole a Colts hat. We went home, wrapped them, and set them under the tree. And we cried and held each other for a while, watching the twinkle lights reflect off the wrapping paper. That was nearly two months ago, and even though I took the tree down and dragged it to the curb, those four gifts still sat in the same place on the living room floor, waiting for an unwrapping that would never come. Now as I finished my coffee and headed out the door, I glanced back at them and thought, yes, I was a little better. Just a smidge. What was a smidge anyway? A tiny bit. Like a teardrop. Yes, just a tiny teardrop better.

It turned out I had only seen Beverly twice in December and once in January because of the holiday and because she was out of town for a few weeks in the middle, so this visit was only my fourth, and it had been over a month since my last.

As I walked through the door of her office, she said, "Amanda, it's good to see you again."

I nodded with a slight smile, reading into her face the knowledge that she had speculated I might not return after so long away. I almost hadn't. It had taken every ounce of my energy and courage—oh, and that smidge. But here I was. I sat down and waited.

She began, "Let's just start with, how was your week?"

I took a deep breath and said, "Good." Then I corrected, not wanting to exaggerate, "Well, not bad anyway. Let's just say I'm glad it's Friday. Work was busy."

"What do you do for a living?"

"I'm an IT director. We launched a new HR software program this week for all employees, and there were a few issues. Nothing my team couldn't handle, but it made for a busy week nonetheless."

"So…busy is…good?" she asked.

"Well, it keeps my mind off…other things."

She nodded. "I can imagine. Sounds like a powerful job. And the fact that it's a technical job, that's even more impressive to me. I'm afraid my husband and kids think I'm stuck in the Dark Ages when it comes to technology. I'm still using a flip phone, and even with that, I can't figure out how to get my voicemails half the time." She shrugged and laughed self-consciously. Then, in a more serious tone, "But, besides work, how is your week going with regard to your emotional life?"

I stared at my hands. It was so much easier to talk about work. I began softly, "Um…I guess I'm okay. I have good days and bad days. I still cry a lot. And have trouble sleeping. There are just so many reminders, so many memories."

She nodded and said, "Okay, let's talk more about that."

Did I have to? I sat in silence for thirty seconds, wishing there was a way to blot out the thoughts that spun on a continuous loop in my mind. I said, "Sometimes in the middle of the night, I walk around the house and look at Shawn's things—his work bag, his clothes, his shoes, his bike, his photo albums from college, his yearbooks. It seems his life is all wrapped up in these items, these things…" I looked up into her kind brown eyes. "I know it sounds ridiculous. They're just *things*, after all. I know they aren't *him*, but it's as if they're a jigsaw puzzle, and if I can only fit the pieces together correctly, I can bring him back. But then as I walk around, I realize the flaw in my thinking: He'll never generate any *new* things again. He'll never dirty a dish or use the last of the shampoo in the shower, he'll never finish that bottle of whiskey he insisted on bringing out at his last poker game with the guys or leave his dirty socks on the floor of the bedroom or forget his keys in his coat pocket."

The tears were there, keeping me company during this speech. "And some of these things, these stupid *things*, remind me of the little annoyances of married life and how he would irritate me *so* much sometimes," I sobbed, shaking my head, "and how I would give anything to be irritated by him again. And how it all doesn't make sense, that I'm left here alone to deal with these things, these pieces of him like fragments of our life, by myself, and how it doesn't seem right that I should be left with these—these *ridiculous*, annoying pieces of a puzzle that can never be put back together again."

She pushed the box of tissues toward me across the low table between us, letting me take some time to cry. When the sobs died down, she was there, waiting patiently, her eyes soft and comforting. She said simply, "Amanda, *life* is a puzzle. We're *all* trying to fit the pieces together."

I nodded and sniffed.

Seeing me more composed, she asked quietly, "What else happened this week?"

How did she do that? Her insightful eyes…she knew there was something underneath that I wasn't saying. "Well, besides work, there's also been a storm brewing at home." I pressed my hand to my forehead and rubbed a stab of pain ignited there.

Beverly asked, "Oh?"

"Yeah…um…I think I told you last time that Sissie lives with Shawn's parents. Well, that's partially because her mother, Shawn's ex, she's disabled, in a wheelchair. She had an accident a few years ago and broke her back, became paralyzed."

"Whoa, okay, that's awful."

"Yes, it is."

"So, does she live alone? Is she remarried? Nearby? What happened after the accident?"

"Nope, not remarried, lives about twenty minutes from us. To summarize a few things, basically when I first met Shawn, he'd been divorced for several years, and they had worked out a pretty good custody situation where the kids spent the weekdays with their mom and the weekends with Shawn. During the summers, they alternated every other week. They split the doctor, dentist, and activity bills, so everything was fairly easy and copacetic, well, as much as any divorce can be. Unfortunately, that all changed after her accident. She had to quit her job and go on disability, and because that greatly reduced her circumstances, she wanted to change the custody arrangement and get more money from Shawn. They fought about it for a long time, and the lawyers were involved, so eventually Shawn gave in…he didn't want to go to court and put the kids through that. But what ended up happening was that the kids came to live with us full time. Luckily, Shawn's parents live right down the road, and they really stepped up. I don't know what we would have done without them."

Beverly was writing down a few notes and nodding. She asked, "How old were the kids?"

"Um, her accident was about four years ago, so Cole was, um, fourteen and Sissie eleven."

"And what happened this week?

"Well, the ex—her name is Gina—she's been calling me and leaving messages and calling Shawn's parents and sisters too."

"About what?"

"Of course, she's devastated about losing Cole, which is totally understandable—we're all grieving—but it's almost like her grief has manifested itself in wanting financial restitution for the loss. From the track and from the insurance company and from wherever she can get it."

"I'm not sure I understand...why would she be contacting you about that?" Beverly asked.

I sighed. God, it was such a complicated mess! I shook my head and spit it out as fast as I could, trying to purge it from my system. "So, when Shawn and I got married, we drew up a will saying that if anything ever happened to Shawn, a portion of his money would go to me, but the rest would be put into a trust for the kids until they turned twenty-five—split equally between Cole and Sissie. The executor of the trust is Shawn's older sister, Dinah. She's the one making the decisions about Sissie's finances right now. Well, Gina feels she should still be getting her monthly custody check, but while the estate is being worked through, everything is frozen. And Dinah has drawn up a plan with her lawyer to make sure Sissie and her parents receive the funds to sustain Sissie during this time because after all, Sissie's living with Shawn's parents, not Gina. The plan makes perfect sense to me, but Gina's freaking out because her financial situation has changed dramatically. To make matters worse, her new tactic is to pursue the Indy 500 Fund. You know, the fund they set up after the bombing? Anyway, they haven't determined how they'll divide that money yet, but she's been hounding the legal mediators, trying to see if or when she'll get her share." I shook my head and took a deep breath. "I just keep thinking, *go away!*"

I found myself breathing hard, my heart pounding. "Sorry, I know I sound bitter and irritated...after all, she did lose a son and she's had a hard life. I know I should feel more sympathy for her. Instead, I just feel like...like I don't have the energy to deal with her on top of everything else."

"I'm sorry about that. Sounds like a mess. I know this may sound cliché, but I'd like to suggest that you try to focus on the things you have control over. Obviously, you can't control Gina or her behavior—all you can do is control how you react to her."

"Right. I know," I agreed with a weak nod. "It's just so hard…I never handled the finances while Shawn was alive. I'm still trying to figure out how to get into all of our accounts. I'm so thankful that Dinah's handling the trust. I don't know what I would have done without her and Shawn's parents." I paused and scanned Beverly's mustard-colored walls, thinking about the strange, unexpected trajectory of my life and how in the blink of an eye, every single thing that felt stable and simple and natural was ripped away like the roof of a house during a tornado. I said slowly, "You know, it's funny, people always talk about the grieving process and the emotional toll it takes, which of course, it *does*, but what they don't tell you is that there's this whole other aspect of loss that has to do with logistics. It may sound silly, but we went from being a team, making decisions together, to everything now falling squarely on my shoulders. There's no one else to turn to, no one else to ask, no one else to help take out the trash, pay the mortgage and the electric and water bill, mow the yard, clean the leaves out of the gutters, put those strange bags of chips in the water softener, fix the thermostat when it stops working. I have to figure all that out on my own now. The other day the check-engine light popped up on my dashboard, and I just started to cry, you know, thinking, what do I do about that? There's no one to drop me off at the car dealership to have it looked at, so I guess I'll just continue to drive around with it, hoping nothing starts smoking under the hood or the brakes give out."

Beverly nodded kindly. "Well, I don't know if I would wait that long. Surely, a friend would be happy to help. But yes, I can see where these…let's call them 'little things'…could be just as overwhelming as the big things. Have you ever heard of that analogy of the pebbles in a jar?"

I shook my head.

"So, let's say you have an empty mason jar, and you are given a handful of big rocks, a handful of medium-sized stones, and a handful of small pebbles. The question is, which should you put in the jar first?"

I sat for a second thinking about it. I answered, "Of course, you must begin with the big rocks, otherwise you will fill up the jar with small pebbles and not have room for the big rocks."

"Exactly." She paused, letting that sink in. "Even the medium-sized stones are not a good foundation because they let the small pebbles slip through the cracks and also crowd out the big rocks. However, Amanda, I suspect those medium-sized stones and small pebbles in your life right now are much easier to deal with than the big rocks. Not that they're easy, I get that, but they're *easier*. So, I'm glad you're talking about them because they're important too, but…I wonder…would you mind if I brought up a big rock?"

I braced for impact, not moving or saying a word.

"With this tragedy, can we both agree that not only has your physical house been razed but also your emotional house? And by razed, I mean scorched earth."

"Yes," I whispered, thinking she had a way with words that hit me to the core. *My* scorched earth! *My* house razed!

"What I want us to endeavor to achieve is to build a new house, a new safe space for you. Brick by brick, taking as much time as we need. Are you open to this?"

I nodded slowly. The problem was that anything new right now made me want to cry. Every new thing reminded me of how alone I was and how Shawn wasn't with me to join in. *New* seemed like such an ugly word, such a mockery of my time with Shawn, of the fact that he was gone, and I was left (for what reason?) to pick up the pieces *by myself.*

"Okay. Before we can build the new house, I'm going to ask you a few questions about your past and present house, if you don't mind."

"Okay," I said softly, still bracing myself.

"How did you and Shawn meet?"

I took a deep breath. "We met in a bar," I began with a sheepish smile. "I was with a friend. I had just moved to Indy a few months before, and I was so excited because I finally found a friend to have drinks with, Becky. We worked in the same department, and this was our first time out together. We had both just sat down and ordered when Becky whispered to me that I had an admirer. She pointed casually, and there was a tall, dark-haired man, dressed in a blue button-down oxford and khakis, watching me with the biggest grin on his face. I was floored. I almost thought it must be someone I knew; otherwise, why would he be looking at me like that? But when I glanced again, he didn't look familiar, and since I barely knew anyone in town, it didn't make sense. I asked Becky what I should do, and she just laughed and said to go talk to him, so I did. He was with a group of guys, and they parted like the Red Sea to let me through—it was kind of funny—and I went right up to him and asked, 'Do I know you?' He just answered, 'I don't know, do you?' 'I don't think so.' 'Okay.' 'Then why are you staring at me?' His grin got even bigger at that. I think he was shocked by my bluntness. He replied, 'Let me buy you a drink and I'll explain.'

And that's how it all began. He was very charming, strong, smart, and outgoing, and we fell in love very quickly. Quicker than I thought was possible. Later I learned about the kids, and at first that put me off a bit because I was scared, being single with no kids of my own, and the thought of raising stepchildren when I felt like I was still raising myself somewhat, trying to find my own way in life, was daunting, and also because I wanted my own kids so badly. But Shawn convinced me it would be okay and that he would help me with being a stepmom."

"And how did that work out?"

Hmmm, I had to think…not a quick, easy answer. "Um, well, in the beginning there were certainly a lot of growing pains. For them. For me. For Shawn. Even for Gina. We didn't know how to interact with each other. It was all new, for all of us. Being a stepparent is so different from being a parent. Plus, they weren't babies or toddlers, but they weren't young adults either—they were somewhere in between, which made it difficult to bond. So, with Cole, he was a quiet boy—shy and timid. I always felt slightly awkward around him, especially when Shawn wasn't there. I tried to ask him questions about school or his activities or his friends, but he usually gave one-word answers. He was a great kid, always striving for excellence at school and church, on his basketball team, and with the math club. But I must admit, now that he's gone, I guess I probably never really knew him. I miss his presence, of course, and I know Sissie really misses him, even though they used to fight a lot, like siblings do. For me, it's like a gap or a shadow with him not in the house, but for Sissie it's much worse—losing her dad and becoming an only child all in one fell swoop was devastating."

"Of course. Poor girl."

"Yeah, with Sissie, we haven't always had the best of times together. She was Daddy's little girl, so in Shawn's mind she could do no wrong, and in her own mind she was above reproach. This put a strain on things. You can't have a young child thinking she has no rules or consequences. And you can imagine how that plays out as she gets older. On top of that, Sissie was very jealous of my time with Shawn. When she was younger, I would purposely go away—go home to New York or visit friends on the weekends—to allow them one-on-one time, but looking back now, I don't know if this was the right thing to do because it just made the wedge between us grow wider. It only got worse as Sissie became a teenager. Her rebellious nature really kicked in then, and we fought a lot. Shawn was stuck in the middle, so he often gravitated toward her, which I suppose was the right thing to do, but it left me on an island. To be honest, I was rather lonely."

Beverly looked at me thoughtfully as I stopped. "Okay, so things weren't a perfect bed of roses when Shawn was alive. Sounds like a normal marriage. Coming into a 'ready-made' family is never easy."

"Exactly. I'm just glad Sissie and I are getting along now. There's no longer this tension between us, and in fact we've sort of...bonded in our grief. Plus, the tragedy has matured her—she's no longer a little girl anymore, selfish or thoughtless. She's more serious...and of course, more sad. Actually, it breaks my heart to watch her, a feeble ghost of her former self. I almost wish she would give me sass like she used to—it would be better than moping around like she does now." I looked down at my hands reflectively.

Beverly said, "I'm afraid this will be something she must carry for a lifetime." She paused, then added, "But at least she has a good foundation with you still here and with Shawn's parents helping out."

"Yes, Sissie and I are *both* so lucky that Shawn's parents are here to fill in the void. Shawn's sisters and their families have been great too."

I was watching Beverly's face as she took a deep breath before beginning again, "Amanda, you mentioned that you felt like you were on an island. Was this only with the kids or...was this also related to your relationship with Shawn?"

I stopped breathing for a moment, then with an involuntary gasp, I burst into tears. Beverly dutifully held out the box of tissues. In between my sobs, I choked out, "You see—back then I thought I was lonely, but it was nothing, *nothing* in comparison to now. Yes, we struggled, as any marriage does, but in hindsight, he was so good to me, so good to all of us. And now I have to live without him. And because we fought a lot, especially in the first few years of our marriage, I probably didn't appreciate him like I should have." I sobbed and sobbed. "He *always* saw right through me...you know. He wasn't afraid of me...right from the very beginning. *He got me.* No one else ever did before, and now, no one else ever will. It makes *no sense*. Why is he gone? And why am I here? Everyone loved Shawn. He was like a magnet. The kids worshipped him. His family thought he could do no wrong. His coworkers. People watched him as he walked into a room. He was gorgeous, *magnificent*! When he smiled, everyone smiled. Everyone!"

As I put my face in my tissue-filled hands, my mind was funneling down, down, down into a familiar swirl of agony: How could something so random and awful happen to *Shawn*, of all people? He was the best dad, husband, son, coworker, boss, friend, person. And we all needed him so much. He shouldered his responsibilities like a strong ox—no fear, no hesitation, no shrinking, and no shirking.

And what was I?!

A woman without a purpose. A boat without a rudder suddenly drifting aimlessly through life's great blue sea.

It wasn't *fair*, and it made *no sense*.

None whatsoever.

And all of those innocent people! And Cole!

And me still here. *Why?*

I was sputtering a few words out loud when, from a fog-filled haze, I heard Beverly tell me to breathe. After a long, drowning gap of tortured minutes, I did. A little. And blew my nose.

She said softly, "Listen. Let's stop for today. I think it would be helpful if you would try something."

I looked up warily, weakly.

She focused in on my eyes, hers narrowing slightly. "Next time you think to yourself 'Why me?' I want you to instead think '*Why not me?*'"

I let that sink in, my brow furrowing. Dot, dot, dot...no, I couldn't do that. I couldn't get there. It was impossible.

She continued, her voice edging me toward a road that was murky and dark, with just a sliver of light at the bottom right corner like the speck of a sunrise before it peeks its head up above the horizon. "This is not a one-for-one swap. Our lives. This is not how it works. Do you think that if Shawn could switch places with you, he would? Something *evil* came into this world and took him from you. Yes, that's true. But something else is also true, and that's this: *It was just his time.* It was *his* time to go, Amanda. And it's just *not* your time. Not yet. That's just how it is. I know it's difficult, but for now I would ask that you try not to ponder these big questions that don't necessarily have clear-cut answers. Instead, I ask you to focus on this: It's not your time, Amanda. It's simply not your time."

I stared at her, my face and mind blank. It couldn't be that simple. It couldn't. My time. What was time in this context? Like a lottery ticket attached to time, to place, to purpose?

It couldn't be that arbitrary. Could it?

She got up and led me to the door, adding, "Try, okay? And we'll talk more next time."

"Okay," I said and walked away, the words still swirling in my mind: *It's simply not my time.*

Chapter VII

Canandaigua, New York
September 2018

WE TURNED AWAY FROM MAPLEWOOD and onto the main drag. I couldn't wait any longer and blurted out, "Okay, you two have to tell me where we're going. Why have you kidnapped me? What exactly am I in for?'"

Michelle answered from the back seat, "Listen, it's a surprise. The best I can do is give you a hint."

"Okaaaay," I replied suspiciously.

"We're…well, we're gonna go visit a…mutual friend."

"Who?"

"That's the surprise."

"Come on, Kelly," I turned my head to Kelly as she tried her hardest not to look back, her eyes wide and focused on the road.

Michelle answered for her, "That's all you're gonna get from us for now, so just sit back and relax. And in the meantime, Kelly, turn it up." As Kelly reached for the volume dial on the classic rock channel, I tried to block the fear and worry out of my head as we all sang along with the Eagles' "Hotel California."

When we got off the highway and started driving on country roads, I got the gist of where we were headed. I asked, "Canandaigua? Are we going boating?" I couldn't think of anyone I knew on the lake, but then it had been so long since I'd been a local, maybe one of our mutual friends had bought a place out here and I didn't know it.

"Nope. Shush," Michelle said, then even more exasperating, "All in due time."

When Kelly pulled into a parking lot filled with Jeep Wranglers, Toyota Tacomas, Ford F-150s, and Chevy Blazers, I wondered if we were lost. There was a sign, Onanda Park, and brown camp buildings scattered over several acres of land that flanked the shores of the lake.

"Oh, I know this place," I said, getting excited. "Are we going hiking?"

Kelly put the car in park and stared back silently at Michelle.

Michelle sighed for a second and looked at me with intensity and something else (worry?) and said, "We're here for a lecture. There's...um...a speaker, from our high school. Andy saw something in the Heathport newsletter about one of our classmates publishing a book, and apparently it's getting some great press, and sure enough, there's a lecture and a book signing here today, and we thought maybe we'd just pop in and say hi."

A book signing? One of our classmates? Why all the secrecy, then? I nearly growled at her as I said, "Michelle, *who?*"

"Okay, I'm just going to spit it out. Do you remember Jonathan Galway?" She didn't even pause and instead answered her own question. "Of course you remember Jonathan Galway." A nervous laugh. "It's him. He's written a book about fish."

"Wha—fish—Jona—?!" I stammered, wondering if these two had lost their minds. Jonathan Galway: my high school sweetheart, whom I hadn't seen in *twenty* years. Gathering my thoughts and sanity, not to mention my indignation and strength, I said firmly, "No. The answer is no."

They looked at each other, apparently trying to figure out who would jump in the ring first. Kelly started, "Listen, we're doing a bit of a reconnaissance mission. We're gonna see *him*, but he won't see *us*. Well, we *hope* he won't see us. Look at this parking lot—it's packed. A big crowd. No one's going to notice a few extra people sitting in the back of the room."

Michelle added, "Heck, we can be in and out in ten minutes. Tops."

I rolled my eyes and tried to calm myself. I said, "But why? What does... Jonathan Galway...and his book or his *fish* or whatever it is, what does that have to do with me?"

Michelle gave me a look, as if it was so obvious and I was being thick. Then, with a turn, she said softly, "Come on, don't be like that."

I rolled my eyes, feeling my face flush.

She went on, "I hate to bring it up, but it's been two and a half years, and you haven't even exchanged *two words* with a person of the opposite sex."

I felt my teeth clench. As if grief had an alarm clock attached to it, and all you had to do was make the buzzer sound, and boom, your heart would be healed, your unanswered questions and racing thoughts would all be resolved and quieted, your sense of closure would be achieved, and your life would go back to normal. If only it were that simple! As if I could take time and manipulate it like everyone seemed to think I could—make it bend to my will, make it a tool to take away the anguish, despair, fear, and longing. Make it do what everyone said it should: heal all wounds. Well, time must have been busy fixing everyone else's problems because I was not fully healed. I was not "back to normal," whatever that meant. Yes, certainly, I was better with each passing month in the sense that I was reconciled to my situation and trying to forge a new life, focusing on the future instead of the past, but was I totally healed? NO. Would I ever be? I didn't know.

Tears of frustration and anger welled up in my eyes. I shook my head. Kelly took my hand and said softly, "We don't want to push you, and if you really want to leave, we can, but we thought…well, we thought that as far as dipping your toe in the water, this was a pretty innocuous way of doing it."

Michelle added, "Amanda. Listen. You're young and beautiful, and we want you to find happiness again." She tilted her head and gave me a tight-lipped smile.

Just like that, my indignation and anger deflated, a spent balloon. I didn't say a word, letting a tear spill over and fall down my cheek. I looked out the window of the car at the shining waters of the lake, the dense foliage of the trees swaying in the breeze. I exhaled a big breath. I kept shaking my head no, but my mouth suddenly asked, "But—but—how do you know he isn't married or gay or mean or stupid or—or *ugly*?"

Kelly laughed out loud, and Michelle's eyes bright, she leaned forward eagerly and said, "Actually, I got the four-one-one at Oliver's soccer game last week. You remember Janice Dempsey? Well, her boy is the same age as Oliver, but she lives in Canandaigua now. I saw her on the sidelines, and I went over to chat for a while. It had been forever since I'd seen her. She's got two girls and a boy now. Anyway, she wondered if I kept in touch with any-one else from high school, and I told her just a few, and then she rattled off a bunch of familiar names, and we caught up on all the gossip. Well, wouldn't you know, one of the people she mentioned was Jonathan. She said they live three doors down from him on West Lake Road. Apparently, they hang out once in a while, and her husband says he's just about the nicest guy he knows. I asked if he was married, with kids, or anything, and she said no, he lives alone. She didn't seem to know much else, saying they had just moved into that house about six months ago and they'd only run into him sporadically."

When she paused, I blinked a few times, thinking, great, essentially, we know nothing. Oh my God, what have these women gotten me into?! But then I thought, well, maybe Kelly was right and it would be an easy in-and-out. And more importantly, if I did this thing once, in theory, I wouldn't have to hear about any future well-intentioned ideas about my love life again. That was worth something. I stared at them both and finally said with resolve, "Okay, come on. Let's get this over with."

The look that passed between them as I opened my car door—the stars were aligned to form a rainbow over their heads with a unicorn flying past in a show of unity and dazzling glory. I rolled my eyes and tried not to smile.

We walked up to the main building, and I whispered, "You know, I used to go to camp here when I was kid. This was the dining hall back then. So strange to be back. I feel just as scared now as I did then. Well, maybe more so now…yeah, *definitely* more."

Michelle, "It'll be fine. You'll be fine. We'll be right by your side. And remember, get in and get out."

The door had a sign on it: "Author Jonathan Galway. Today Only. 11:00–1:00. *A Field Guide to Fishing the Finger Lakes*." There was a photo on the book's cover: the back of a man's tall form standing in a stream, sailing a fly-fishing line into the misty morning sunrise set against a beautiful panoramic vision of green mountains, blue sky, and white clouds. It was an intriguing cover, not at all what you would expect from a field guide. It drew you in, just like I was being drawn into this building, a stranger encountering a new road, wondering where it would lead.

As we opened the door and walked inside as quietly as we could, I noticed that the long, narrow room was mostly filled with men sitting on folding metal chairs, dressed in fishing gear, all facing forward toward a podium. We went to the back row and sat down. I averted my eyes from the front of the room, too timid to look directly toward the vaguely familiar warm voice that was saying something about the effect of the zebra mussel invasion on the sensitive ecosystem of freshwater lakes.

With my head down and my entire body turned perpendicular to that voice, I whispered to Michelle sarcastically, "We don't stick out like sore thumbs at all."

"Shush," she whispered back, "and look." Her eyes flashed at me, and she raised her eyebrows just a hair, enough for me to be curious.

I turned my head and body slowly. He was partially concealed from the chest down behind the podium, but when my eyes searched his face, I felt a flame of heat rise up my neck. A rush of air escaped my lips. *Gorgeous.*

Better than I remembered. How was it possible that his jaw seemed even more chiseled, his eyes brighter and greener, his hair fuller and a deeper chestnut brown? He came out from behind the podium, still speaking with that confident, deep voice, his right hand resting casually on the platform as his other cocked with ease on his slim waist. He was wearing a light blue sailcloth fishing shirt with two breast pockets tucked into beige khaki pants, along with dark brown hiking boots.

My face must have said what I wasn't because Michelle couldn't help herself—she giggled. My head snapped to her with a frown. It was a room rapt with attention; you could have heard a pin drop, and you could certainly hear a giggle drop, along with my stomach. Absently, almost in slow motion, not skipping a beat in his speech, Jonathan's face moved toward the sound. I cowered in my chair, wrapping my arms around myself. He scanned the rows directly ahead of us, and right as I was trying my hardest to be invisible, Michelle stuck a stiff finger in my lower back, forcing me to sit up straight. A slight "oh!" escaped my lips and that was enough; Jonathan's eyes turned and then slowly, almost mechanically, focused and locked on my face. I felt the air leave my body and a tunnel form like a celestial plain connecting us across the room. His half-a-millisecond pause in speech was an acknowledgment of curiosity, surprise, speculation, followed by a slight stutter, clearly uncharacteristic, and finally, a knitting of his eyebrows in consternation.

I was hypnotized, transfixed. My face was on fire. I was padlocked to my chair with a laser focus on his eyes and movements. He swiftly broke our stare, moved back behind the podium, his right hand shaking slightly as he lifted some notes. He shifted his legs, moving his weight from one foot to the other. His Adam's apple bobbed as he swallowed uncomfortably. All the while, he was still talking about zebra mussels and some other invasive species, and maybe no one else would have noticed because he was so smooth, so well versed in what he was saying, but I could tell—I had thrown him. A little. He took a drink of water from a glass on a table behind the podium. Then, still talking, he came back out from behind the podium, this time taking possession of the full front of the room, as if to get a handle on himself and get a closer look at something…or someone…in the audience. He casually scanned the faces, taking his time getting back to mine, but then with the smallest of shy, curious hints of a raised eyebrow and crooked upturn to his mouth, he took me in, scouring my face like a man seeing an old, cherished, long-since-suspected-lost photograph for the first time in ages. It was a lightning bolt to my heart. Involuntarily, I smiled, then a second later I frowned, catching myself, realizing with confusion what I had done, what I had felt, and how much that scared me. To think that way about someone who was not Shawn and for it to have felt, even for that brief burst of a second, so right. And yet so wrong.

In the instant of our mutual smile, it was as if Jonathan Galway had erased the twenty intervening years. In my mind, I was back in high school, waiting for him to come out of calculus, grab my hand, kiss my lips, and walk me to history. All the anticipation and electricity I used to feel awaiting his presence was still there, and then some. I couldn't figure out how to balance that feeling with the overwhelming sense of guilt and confusion over my still very real, very present love for Shawn.

As if from a light-year's distance away, Kelly touched my knee and whispered, "Well?"

I pulled my eyes away reluctantly to look at her and Michelle, who were both staring at me intently. One quick glance back to Jonathan revealed he had turned his attention elsewhere but hadn't quite lost his side-smile, so I turned to the faces of the two cats who had swallowed the canary and mouthed the words, "Oh. My. God." They both grinned, but I quickly followed this statement with a curt shake of my head, indicating all was not as right with the world as they thought.

❦ CHAPTER VIII ❧

Carmel, Indiana
May 2017

As I sat down in the leather chair to face Beverly, I hoped she wouldn't ask me about the anniversary, but of course those were the first words out of her mouth.

"How are you feeling about Sunday?"

"Not great."

"Okay, let's talk about that first," she urged.

"Well," I began shakily, "they're doing a balloon release, one for each victim, and announcing their names individually, and then a moment of silence. They want us all to be there, but I—I just don't think I can. Of course, I want to honor their memories, but it's—it's just *too* hard. How can I go there? Not just physically but emotionally. Just thinking about it makes me cringe on every level."

Beverly nodded. "Right. Well, you don't have to go. I'm sure it's not mandatory. But, to clarify, when you say 'cringe,' what exactly do you mean?"

I stared at the ceiling, thinking all the thoughts, feeling all the feelings, and wanting to scream. I said, "I remember every single moment of that day and how—how *public* it all was, how it went from a scene of anticipation and excitement to mass chaos and fear in an instant. My nightmares are still filled with the images and the horror, and now I'm supposed to go to this event where yes, people will bow their heads, listen to those names, and absorb those words for about a half a millisecond, and then they'll chug their beers, hear 'Start your engines,' and forget it ever happened. You see, for them, it's like a distant, vague memory. Sure, they haven't caught who did it yet, but they're probably thinking because of that, and because of the ramped-up security, it's the safest place in the world right now. For them, it's still the 'greatest spectacle in racing,' a fun afternoon of drinking and watching cars compete. Then they'll go home and back to their lives. For me, it isn't a distant, vague memory, it isn't a nice, fun day at the track. For me, I'm still living with the horrible visions, I'm still living with the loss, wondering how to move on, how to recapture the life I used to have, thinking about what was irrevocably shattered."

As was a pattern in our sessions, I began to cry, and Beverly dutifully handed me tissues. My brave face had long since been demolished over the course of these many months of regular visits with her. At some point I realized, what was the point of trying to keep up appearances, especially for Beverly? She always saw through my façade anyway. And just as I was starting to feel a faint glimmer of hope and stability, the anniversary was here, causing me to crash again. Today, the tears were out of sadness, yes, but they were also riddled with frustration about the roller-coaster ride that was my life and also because no one at that track was walking a mile in my shoes (besides the other victims), and they never would. It wasn't as though I would wish them to, God forbid, and I didn't want to begrudge them their day of fun, but it still rankled and felt unfair on so many levels.

Beverly asked, "What about Sissie?"

I sniffed and said, "Oh, she might go with Ed and Karen, Shawn's parents, even if I don't. They want to be there for the balloon release at least. I think they feel it'll give the proceedings a sense of purpose or dignity, if not closure."

"Are you okay with them going without you?"

"Honestly, it makes me feel a little guilty. I don't know if they fully understand why I don't want to go, thinking it's somehow related to me not honoring Shawn and Cole, but it's not about that. I want to honor their lives, not their deaths. Do you know what I mean?"

"Of course. Makes sense. Have you tried to explain your feelings to them?"

"Um, no, not really."

"Well, this may be another time when you can pull from your inner resources, be strong, even though I know it's scary, and just be honest and open with them. I'm sure if you explain, they'll respect your feelings. So, do you have other plans for that day?"

"Yeah, I was thinking about going to a park, maybe get out in the woods. I used to love camping and hiking when I was younger. I remember it always brought me peace. Something about communing with nature...it's like a panacea of sorts. And I figure the less opportunity to be around people—all the hoopla and the TV—the better. Plus, then I can think about Shawn and remember him in my own way."

"Sounds like a good plan. I like that you're pursuing activities you enjoy and ones that will help with your healing." She smiled, paused, and then asked, "So, how was your weekend?"

I took a moment before answering, "I don't know…it's just hard on the weekends because, well, there's not as much to do, no work to get lost in, no friends to hang out with. I'm all alone, and I feel trapped in the house. I went to the library on Sunday to wander around, but it was so quiet, I ended up leaving after a half hour."

She nodded and asked, "I'm curious, why don't you see friends or family on the weekends?"

"Well…it's my fault. People have reached out, continue to bring me food—they're all so kind—but I must admit, it's overwhelming and I'm horrible about returning calls or writing thank-you cards or connecting in any way with anyone. Karen insisted I come down for Sunday dinner, which I did, after the library, but everyone was there, and I felt…completely claustrophobic. They always want to pull out the photo albums and talk about Shawn and Cole and plan visits to the cemetery and the tribute bench they're installing in the square. I don't know, I'm glad and thankful they're doing everything they can to keep their memories alive, but it hurts…it just hurts so much."

Beverly asked, "So, overall, how are you getting along with Shawn's family lately?"

I paused for a second, wondering if I should be fully honest. I continued tentatively, "They're very nice people, and I don't know what I would have done without them this past year. They've really stepped up with Sissie, so I can never thank them enough for that. But I have to admit, sometimes I feel like an outsider over there. When Shawn was alive, it was different. He was great at building bridges, if you know what I mean. Maybe it's because I'm from New York or because I speak my mind, but I always felt—and still do—a little awkward. I think Shawn was the buffer to my direct personality—he helped translate me to his midwestern family. Now I find myself being mostly quiet over there. It's like I don't exist in their world, don't know how to be myself with them anymore, don't know who I am to them. I was never especially close with them before, and now it's drawn the curtain even further. Am I still their daughter-in-law, their sister-in-law? The whole thing confuses me. I find myself wanting to leave almost as soon as I get there."

"Hmmm," Beverly said, nodding her head and staring at me with her understanding eyes. "What about friends?"

"Actually, Friday night, I did go out with some friends, Tim and Sandy. Shawn and I used to double-date with them."

"That's nice. Where'd you go?"

"Daddy Jacks. It used to be our regular hangout on Friday nights when we could get a babysitter. I hadn't seen them since the funeral. Anyway, I couldn't believe they actually found time on a Friday night to meet me since they have three kids who are all involved in sports and other activities. It was generous of them to take the time, not to mention with me being a third wheel...they were, well, so careful with me, you know, kind. I don't know...we talked about Shawn a lot, but it wasn't too overwhelming, and the rest of the time we focused on the live music and the food and tried to avoid anything that would make me melt into a puddle on the floor." I shrugged sheepishly. "Of course, the first words out of Sandy's mouth when she hugged me were, 'Wow, you've lost weight!' as if I didn't already know that. Then I think she instantly felt bad for calling it out, realizing it was hardly an ideal diet plan. Honestly, it's almost laughable—I mean, if it wasn't so totally *not*—I've tried to lose weight my whole adult life and wow, good for me, I've finally achieved it."

My attempt at light sarcasm wasn't lost on Beverly, but she instead noted, "So, it sounds like you *weren't* alone all weekend."

"No, that's true, of course you're right," I said, realizing that my depression sometimes put a dark bent on things. "I guess when you asked about the weekend, I was thinking about nighttime, when I'm by myself in the house, trying to sleep and not having much luck."

"I'm sorry about that. There are some great resources online—techniques to improve your sleep issues. Actually, hang on, I think I have a brochure here. Ah yes, here in this drawer...see if this helps. This may be out of left field, but do you have a pet?"

"A pet?" I said, chuckling, "Nah, it's funny because I love cats, but Shawn was allergic, and I'm not really a dog person, so we didn't have any."

"Well, I'm not suggesting that now is the best time to make major life decisions, and of course, this is not taken from my psychology degree," she said with a laugh, "but maybe in a few months, a pet might be good for you—give you something to take care of, come home to, snuggle up with." She smiled her reassuring smile and I smiled back, thinking about a little fluffy marmalade-colored kitten meowing in my ear when I laid my head on the pillow at night. That would certainly stem the tides of loneliness. But I agreed—committing to something for, say, ten or twelve years right now might not be the wisest choice.

After a moment, she changed course and asked, "And how else have you been feeling lately?"

I took a deep breath and said, "I guess I'm still thinking a lot about Shawn and the life we used to have. It's hard to see past that." I put my tightly clenched fist to my heart and cried, "I don't want to give him up or what we had together."

Beverly's kind brown eyes scrutinized my fierce gaze. "Yes, I see that. I do. And I know you want to hold on as tightly as you can for as long as you can. Of course, you will never give up those memories of Shawn or your shared love. You'll always have them. Nothing can ever take them away." She paused and added after a moment, "And my hope for you is that someday, when the timing is right, the comfort and joy you derive from those memories will overshadow the pain."

I shook my head in doubt. What good was hope? That wasn't going to bring back Shawn. That wasn't going to bring me happiness, or—heck, forget happiness—simply a day without dread, void, a cave. I was in a sort of mire, that was clear. My life was a testament to the veil of duplicity I coveted— going about my daily life as if I were dealing with my grief and learning from it, growing from it, beyond it. But I knew in my heart that I wasn't. It was all just a lie. My life was a lie. My life spoke volumes—that I was hopelessly sucked down a well with no ladder, no rope, no rescue. How would that ever change when I couldn't see past today or tomorrow?

I had a flash thought: The only way is to forge something new. But what? How?

Abruptly, as if she had read my mind, Beverly asked, "Have you ever considered moving?"

This snapped me back, as I shook my head forcefully. "Moving? From our house? No, never."

She gave a curt nod, then said, "I'm not saying anytime soon. Clearly, that would be traumatic. You've mentioned what I would call 'situationally relevant triggers'—several of them, actually—where your surroundings, your house, your things, your current physical location are all steeped in the world and life you had with Shawn. For now, I'm sure all of that is a great comfort to you, but I wonder if over time you might want to think about something different."

"I don't know…," I said skeptically.

She waited to see if I would say more, then in the ensuing silence, added, "All I'm suggesting is that maybe in the future, you may want something that is truly *yours*."

I thought, in protest, of course I already have that! I have my job…and… and…um…plenty of other things…let's see, um, what else? Good God! Oh man…nothing, nothing, nothing. Hmmm, when I married Shawn, I moved into *his* house with *his* kids, and I live down the road from *his* parents, and most of my friends were *his* friends. And as far as my job was concerned, I was basically a walking zombie, thankful for the busyness to numb my aching heart and soul, intentionally not engaging with anyone on anything personal, strict and diligent, never faltering, never letting my guard down. Was this really *mine*, this work that ruled *me*, and not the other way around? There must be *something* else, right? Something…?

Beverly broke into my racing thoughts, "Just think about it. This is your journey, and there are no right or wrong answers." Then, after a pause, she put her business face back on and redirected with, "Tell me a little bit more about your friends and family from back east."

"Oh, okay. Well, there's my mom, my sister Nikki, and my brother Dustin. Michelle and Kelly are my two best friends. They're sisters who grew up across the street from me. They've all been amazing."

"What about your dad?"

"He died when I was twenty-five. Aneurism."

"I'm sorry. That must have been awful."

"Yes, it was. He had just walked me down the aisle the month before and then, boom, he was gone. My mom was devastated. We all were."

"I bet."

"Yeah, very unexpected. When Shawn and Cole died, even though the circumstances were totally different, my mind instantly went back to the day when Mom called me and said Dad had collapsed in the backyard. I flew home right away, but by the time I got there, he was already gone." My eyes filled. I murmured, "It's hard when you can't say goodbye."

"Of course. You never get to say all the things you might have."

I sniffed. "Exactly. And you can't prepare yourself, not that there's any way to be prepared for something like that, but still…I often wonder why God takes us so unaware. It makes me skittish sometimes, now that it's happened to me twice. I'm wondering when he'll strike again and why."

"Ah yes, that is the great mystery. I'm curious why you used the word *strike*? Do you feel it's a curse or a targeting?"

I stared at her for a minute. I said, "You mean preordained? I'm not sure... honestly, I don't know what to believe. I'm always rather confused because I know the Bible speaks about how God knows every soul, before they are created, and about their time here on Earth, and forever afterward, but then my mind always goes to the question of why does he bother? I mean, if we're ultimately disembodied souls, then why do we need to be put here inside of these weak, foolish, overrated, easily breakable bodies in the first place? What's the point? Seems like a waste of time and effort. Is it some kind of joke? Let's throw the creatures down into this arena of battle and watch them flounder, fight, flee, perish. In theory, wouldn't only the strongest warriors survive to live on and rule the day? That's what confounds me. And makes me question why I'm still here while Shawn and Cole are gone. Why me? Why not me? My time? Not my time? If there's no rhyme or reason to it, if it truly is arbitrary, then what the heck are we all doing here?" My face flushed as I found my chest heaving in bitter frustration.

Beverly's eyes at that moment changed from intent listening to concerned thoughtfulness. She said, "I wonder...do you see things in mostly black and white?"

"No, I don't think so. I think...I try to look at things from all angles." Was that my voice raising?

Beverly's lips drew down a little. "Don't get me wrong. I would understand if you did. Moving things into certain buckets, let's say, in order to make them easier to manage, can be a legitimate and effective coping mechanism. But you might consider that not everything should be immediately slotted into a bucket. Maybe consider the gray."

I literally had no idea what she was talking about or what she meant. "The gray?" I asked softly, at the risk of sounding like an idiot.

"Yes, the gray. The *in between* of our world. When your mind starts to think, what's the point, why am I here, what's the purpose, how will I move beyond this, or even everything is bad right now, I'd ask that you suspend your belief or disbelief and simply *be* instead. In the gray, not everything is clear, not everything is known yet, not everything is one way or the other. Sometimes, it's the *in between* that allows our hearts to be open to all possibilities and may create a way forward that we couldn't see before."

"Oh—kay," I said slowly, still not sure I was understanding, but giving her the benefit of the doubt. She was the expert, after all, even if I didn't quite get what she was saying.

"Good," she said, now with a smile. Then turned her attention to something else. "Tell me more about your mom."

"My mom's in her sixties, lives in one of those low-maintenance condo complexes, has a ton of friends—she's the most social person I know—plays bridge and has breakfast with some high school friends once a week, plus she's in a bowling league. I mean, she makes me tired just watching her." I chuckled. "Plus, she watches my sister's kids every Friday. She's amazing. And Nikki, my sister, I must admit we were never really close growing up—she always sort of resented me for borrowing her clothes and makeup and stuff—but she's been really sweet since Shawn died, calling or texting me nearly every day to check in. Dustin, my brother, has been great too. He flew out here with his wife and two girls last summer and stayed with me for a week. He got up on the roof and fixed the gutters and took my car into the shop for maintenance and trimmed the bushes, all kinds of things. He was such a godsend, and having his girls around was great too. They got along with Sissie really well, so that was nice."

"And have you been back to New York?"

"No, not yet...I can't seem to..." I paused and swallowed, "leave."

"Even for a short trip?"

"No, it's like I'm...stuck. On the one hand, I struggle with being surrounded by reminders everywhere I look, everything I touch, but then I also feel like it's the only place where I can feel that sense of rightness within myself, like the muscle memory of our love still lingers here. I don't know, it's hard to explain, but when I'm home, I feel safe in what remains of our haven, even though it seems to bring me just as much pain as it does comfort."

She held out the tissues again as I struggled to process the conflicting thoughts, tears slipping out of my eyes. I remembered the warmth of Shawn's hugs when I'd come home from a hard day at work or when I was feeling vulnerable or scared about something. Like the time my ob/gyn found a lump in my breast and scheduled an ultrasound to rule out anything bad. In the two days between the appointment and ultrasound, I was a wreck, my mind going to the worst possible scenario, and Shawn was so calm, so rational, so reassuring. He said, "Listen, I didn't marry you for your breasts. I married you for *you*, and no matter what, we'll get through this together." I cried in his arms, and he kissed my forehead and made me laugh by saying, "Well, I should probably clarify, I didn't marry you *only* for your breasts." When the ultrasound results showed the lump was just a benign fibroadenoma, we slept in late the next morning, making love as we savored the relief and gratitude that washed over us.

Now who would hold and comfort me when the unexpected happened?

Like a medical scare.

Or a death by bombing.

❧ CHAPTER IX ❧

Canandaigua, New York
September 2018

WE SAT THROUGH THE REST OF THE LECTURE IN SILENCE, Michelle getting antsy toward the end, tapping her foot on the chair in front of her. I was in a fog, not even attempting to understand the topic or the words but instead focusing on Jonathan's face or, when I allowed myself the luxury, more pointedly on the warm feeling his voice evoked in me, followed almost immediately by a foreign hot poker of guilt and shame. It was as if I was waging a silent war within myself.

I could tell that he carefully avoided my face when scanning the crowd as he spoke, only allowing himself a quick peek when the man sitting directly in front of me asked a question. Within a second, he had trained his eye away from mine and focused on the man, never changing from his expression of neutral listening. But I knew from the slight narrowing of his eyes that he was using his best effort to focus on every word of the question and not on me.

It was like a kinetic energy swirling and forming a nexus where his essence met mine. I found myself memorizing every movement, inclination, reaction he made, like some newfangled nanotechnology developed for the sole purpose of honing attention on every detail of this man. This specimen, this beautiful, bright, shining light of a man. It felt like an explosion in my core. I was being drawn back to life from a coffin of emotions that I hadn't even realized were dead. And although I had nothing to confirm my hypothesis, I somehow *knew* he was feeling it too, was awakening too.

In my logical mind, which at the moment was a tiny blip of an insignificant ant, I knew this reaction made no sense—especially considering I was surrounded by a crowded room of people and two giddy fools sitting beside me, but there was no denying it. I was in a vortex of something new, unexpected, uncalled for, and maybe unavoidable. Much like the fish Jonathan seemed to be fascinated with and was droning on about for what seemed like an eternity. I was hooked.

And scared.

And bewildered.

After this captivity, his speech winding down, I snapped back to life quickly, my eyes wide, a warning to Michelle and Kelly. Michelle whispered, "Come on, let's sneak outside."

I nodded, and we fairly crawled away, but not before I saw Jonathan signal with one slight lifting of an index finger and a tilt of his head toward the front porch that we were to wait outside for him.

With that, my knees nearly buckled. Kelly saw and grabbed my arm. Our feet hit the wooden boards of the front porch, and Michelle whispered in a frenzy, "Quick. Down here." She walked us toward the south side of the long porch, and we plopped down on three rocking chairs that faced each other.

Michelle said, regarding my flushed face, "Okay, calm down. We said we'd be right by your side, and we are. Well…what'd you think?"

"I—I'm not sure," I said, trying to formulate a sentence when my mind was a complete mess. "Of course, he's very good looking, and I remember him like yesterday, but it's all…a bit too much for me right now, honestly."

"Perfectly natural," Kelly said with her kind, empathetic eyes. I drew some strength from them.

Then I looked at Michelle and asked in a hushed voice, "By the way, why on earth are we here?"

"Huh? Because we're setting you up," she replied, confused.

"No, ding-a-ling, quickly: what are we telling *Jonathan* about why we're here on a Saturday morning, listening to him talk about *fish*?" I spit out.

"Oh," Michelle replied blankly.

Kelly said, "We'll just tell him Michelle heard about his book from Andy, which is true, and he's a fisherman and she wants to get him a signed copy as a gift."

"That's surprisingly plausible," Michelle said to Kelly with an impressed stare. Then she turned to me, "Don't worry, I'll do all the talking—you just hang back and follow my lead."

"Okay," I said with about as much confidence as a wet noodle.

Kelly grabbed my hand and said, "Amanda, breathe."

I took a deep breath and tried to focus on her reassuring face.

We sat back and rocked quietly, watching people filter out of the hall.

A whole host of self-talk started to fill my mind: Amanda, you can handle this, just sit here quietly while Michelle talks, he's just a man after all, like any other man, he puts his pants on one leg at a time—wait—oh, speaking of pants, they fit him so well.

Good God.

Amanda!

Holy shit. I am in so much trouble.

Finally, in an attempt to purge my nerves, overactive imagination, and shame spiral, and to find focus, I broke the silence, pointing to a field surrounded by cabins off to the right and said, "We used to have bonfires over there and sing camp songs. The boys were in the cabins to the left, and the girls were up on the hill across the street."

Michelle had a revelation and asked, "Is this where you learned all those camp songs you taught us?"

I nodded and said yes.

Michelle started to sing one softly: "I know a wienie man, he owns a wienie stand, he sells me everything from hot dogs on down. Boom, boom, boom. Someday I'll be his wife, eat wienies all my life. Hotdog! I love that wienie man!" On the last note, she stretched out the word *man* and did a fist pump.

We burst out laughing.

Just then, Jonathan was upon us, and I choked on the tail end of my laugh.

He said with a broad smile, "Of course I find you three out here giggling like naughty schoolgirls—reminds me of high school." He turned directly to me and said, "I'm glad you stayed."

I was paralyzed, so Michelle jumped out of her chair, put her hand out and said, "Hi Jonathan. Michelle Jacobs, well, I used to be Michelle Abernathy and um, my sister Kelly and well, you remember Amanda Holmes." I thought to myself, leave it to Michelle to conveniently forget my married name. She remembered hers but not mine?

She looked down at me significantly with a wave of her hand as it released his, trying to get me to unfreeze. Mercifully, he shook Kelly's hand next. Then, as if in slow motion, I saw him turn to me, looking down at my face as I woke up and pushed forward in the rocking chair, extending my hand as his sent a current of heat and electricity up my fingertips.

His eyes bore a hole into me as he said significantly, "Yes, I remember."

I tried to recover and replied weakly, "Hi."

He released my hand a moment after was customary, and Michelle started speaking again. He seemed reluctant to tear his face from mine.

Kelly and I stayed suspended in our rocking chairs. I glanced over at her, and she gave me an encouraging smile. Michelle was standing next to Jonathan, going into her spiel about how she had heard he was giving a lecture here and wanted to buy her husband a signed copy of the book because he was an avid fisherman.

"Oh sure, sure, no problem. Come on inside and I'll get you one," he said, motioning toward the door.

Kelly and I got up and followed them, Michelle chatting with Jonathan the whole way about how her husband was going to be so excited, how she was so impressed when she heard about Jonathan's professional success, how they couldn't believe he was in the area doing this great lecture, and how the book would be a wonderful surprise for Andy because his birthday was coming up. I glanced at Kelly, who shook her head a little and rolled her eyes. Apparently, *not* Andy's birthday coming up. We grinned. Michelle was laying it on thick.

"Speaking of birthdays…," Michelle said abruptly, "it's Amanda's birthday today."

"Michelle!" I hissed between my teeth. I narrowed my eyes, shooting her a scowl. With a look of feigned innocence, she walked through the door, back into the assembly hall, letting Jonathan take the door from her as he held it open for Kelly and me.

Coming in behind us, he touched his hand lightly on my back, smiling, and said, "Is that so? Happy birthday, Amanda."

"Thanks," I replied, blushing. His touch was tentative, yet it still sent a spark up my spine. And another shot of shock and confusion into my soul.

"So, doing anything special for the big day?"

Kelly said, "We've kidnapped her—she has no idea what we're doing."

I confirmed with a shrug of my shoulders and an upward wave of my hands.

"Ah, I see," he said picking up a book and pen from the table.

"Andy?" he asked Michelle.

"Mm-hm," she said absently. I could tell she was scheming. As Jonathan began writing an inscription, I gave Michelle a warning look. Of course, she ignored that and proceeded, "Hey Jonathan, what do you think about joining us later? We haven't told Amanda yet, but we're going to Donny Brewer's house tonight for a bonfire. Would you like to come?"

Without a moment's hesitation, he said, "Sure," and handed Michelle the book. He asked, "What time?"

Michelle replied, "Come around eight. You remember the house? On Maplewood?" He nodded. "We'll have food, but BYOB."

"Sounds great," he said.

Michelle's face was ecstatic. She said, "What do I owe you for the book?"

He waved it off and said, "Nothing. I'll see you tonight." He gave me a small smile and said, "Can't wait."

We said our goodbyes and headed out the door. I shot a quick glance back and there he was, staring at me with curiosity. My heart beat heavily in my chest.

As soon as we were in the car and the doors were closed, we all started talking at once. I nearly screamed, "I *cannot* believe that just happened!" Michelle said, "That was wild!" and Kelly exclaimed, "Holy crap!"

We erupted in a stream of giggles. I still had a pang of guilt hanging over my head, so I said after a minute, "Don't you two count your chickens before they're hatched. This doesn't *mean* anything, and you know, well, you know…what my situation is."

Kelly drove out of the parking lot and said, suddenly sober, "We know. No chicken. We promise."

Michelle piped up, "Maybe it's just a small egg right now."

"I don't know if I can even handle an egg," I said. "You know, I appreciate the effort and planning this took, really I do. And I don't want to burst either of your bubbles, but I'm not even sure I'm ready to date. And as kind, smart, successful, and good-looking as Jonathan seems to be, we don't really know him. Think about how much you've both changed since high school. I know I have! Plus, I don't know…if I'm ready…or worthy…or whatever the right word is, to start something new."

Kelly nodded at me solemnly. Michelle was oddly silent in the back seat. After a few minutes, I looked back at her. She gave me a wary look and said, "I get it. I do. We were just hoping you'd think about it. There's no reward in this life without risk. But we'll respect your decision, whatever it is."

"Thanks. Love you guys."

Echoes of Beverly's words struck me. Even after all this time, although Shawn's death was no longer an open wound, it was still a jagged scar on my heart. And I wasn't sure if I wanted it to completely heal over or to allow the fleshy, sensitive part to stay open and unhealed. The truth was that I hadn't allowed myself to think about what I wanted because then I would have to admit that the part of my life with Shawn was over. A door closed. On him. On us. On our life together. Moving home was stripping a layer away already. Was I going to allow more to be removed? Plus, who would want my heart? I was damaged goods. My attempt at renewal and rebirth was still in progress. I should be wearing an "under construction" sign.

I added with a level of finality, "And you two seem to forget that Jonathan Galway broke my heart! I know it was twenty years ago, but I remember every single moment of that summer. It was awful."

Kelly said, "Yes, we know. But we remember when you were with him too—not just the breakup."

Michelle jumped in, "You were so in love. I remember how you used to look at each other…it was the same look I saw on his face today, Amanda! Yes, he has some explaining to do because even if it's all water under the bridge, it'd be nice to understand why he blew the bridge up in the first place, but in the meantime, maybe just keep an open mind."

"I'll try," I said, the word *try* an anvil around my neck. I remembered Beverly's advice to consider the possibilities, to keep myself open to the gray, to the universe. Then, thinking about water and bridges and bygones, I stared out the car window at the lake, allowing my swirling mind to go blank for the rest of the drive.

A while later, Michelle asked, "Don't you want to know where we're headed next?"

I sat up, turned my head with a grin, and said, "Um, yeah, 'bout time you filled me in."

"We're going to Charlotte! We're gonna hit the beach, walk out on the pier, ride the merry-go-round, and well, whatever else you want to do!"

"Charlotte? It's been *forever*. Total blast from the past!"

"Yep, I hope you brought your thong!"

We all laughed, remembering the year when bikinis got even smaller and girls with bubble butts paraded on the boardwalk with their new floss. We were never audacious enough, nor were we exhibitionists. We left that for the girls with the perfect bodies and flirty personalities.

A few minutes later, when we had all calmed down, I turned and said, "Michelle, hand me that book." I studied the photo of Jonathan on the back.

He was smiling, and his eyes held a sparkle, something knowing, like a secret. I flipped through the pages—some color, with photos, maps, and descriptions of fish. It seemed quite professional, well put together, detailed, thorough. In high school, he had hardly been the outdoorsy type. I was curious about this transformation in him. I always remembered him being more into video games than wildlife or nature. But, then again, was I anything like the girl from back then? Hardly.

I handed it back to her and said to both of them, "Interesting."

We pulled into the beach parking lot, grabbed our bags, and ducked into the public restroom to change into our suits, then took our time walking down the boardwalk that led to the beach. It was a perfect early fall day—the waters of Lake Ontario's crystal swells in motion, the sun's radiant heat absorbing into the sand, the distant cries of pleasure from children in the surf echoed in the smiles of people walking by. Off in the corner of the beach, a doubles beach volleyball game was in full swing, the players' muscles taut and glistening, and crowds of spectators drinking, cheering, enthusiastic.

"Wow," I said, "I didn't think it'd be this busy, what with school back in session and all."

"Last of the good-weather Saturdays," Michelle replied.

"Right."

We searched the horizon for a space among the congested plethora of towels, chairs, and umbrellas. Kelly pointed to a square of open sand with enough room to fit our three towels and a cooler, sandwiched between a family of four on one side and two tanned men on the other.

After we settled in, Michelle opened the cooler, reached in, and, concealing two items behind her back, said with a wicked grin, "Now, for a trip down memory lane…"

I grabbed her arm and then screamed, "Oh my God, not a Bartles and Jaymes…good gracious, where did you find that?! They still make it? And in peach too!"

"Oh yes they do," she answered triumphantly. "And this too." She flashed a Zima in her other hand, to which Kelly and I burst into unrestrained giggles. Michelle doled out the bottles, we clinked "to us" (our usual cheers), took swigs, and puckered our faces against the rush of sweetness.

Michelle continued, suddenly speaking in a French accent, "Mademoiselles, sit back and enjoy this wine pairing—oh, I mean wine *cooler* pairing—the sweet and tart notes in the Bartles and Jaymes (or Zima, if you prefer) complemented by the salty and savory Cool Ranch Doritos and Bar-B-Q Fritos." She reached into her bag ceremoniously and pulled out the chips, which we grabbed and opened, wondering with helpless and joyful awe how we had so easily slipped into a time warp.

Kelly smiled in between bites and gulps and asked, "Garçon, garçon, are there other pairings?"

Michelle, still in character, answered, "Oui, oui, mademoiselle, we just now brought up the specialty items from the cellar for our two VIP guests. A brick of cheese, what I like to call Colbay Jacques, with de l'eau crackers, and le pièce de resistance: a lovely pepperoni," She paused to hold the pepperoni up, first above her head and then perpendicular to her bikini bottoms. "Pepe makes all of our lovely pepperonis—he's rather known for the larger, fuller logs."

The two guys on the towel next to us grinned with raised eyebrows. Michelle turned to them and challenged, "Jealous?"

They both laughed, one pronouncing, "Honey, I've had plenty bigger and better salamis than that!"

We laughed out loud, our eyebrows raised.

The rest of the day followed in pretty much the same vein. I couldn't remember the last time I'd experienced such full, unbridled, unencumbered, unrelenting silliness. My face hurt from laughing, and my soul shined for the first time in a long time. After hours of baking, munching, drinking, and laughing, the sun hovered hot, blurry, and lower on the horizon, so we reluctantly got up, put on our shorts and shirts over our suits, packed up our things, and headed to the carousel.

Kelly paid our tickets, saying, "Can't leave Charlotte without taking a turn on the merry-go-round. I don't know about you two, but this is my favorite. I love how all the animals are different."

We hopped up on the platform of the ride. As we started to weave in and out of the animal shapes, I said with a groan, "My teeth feel like they're covered in a layer of moss. Those wine coolers have officially adhered to my fillings and started forming new cavities."

"We'll all need a visit to the dentist after this," Kelly said as she pulled herself up on a tawny-colored lion. Michelle hitched herself to a brown horse, and I jumped onto a large white cat with a fish in its mouth.

Without pause, both Michelle and Kelly shouted "Jonathan!" at the same time, pointing meaningfully at the fish as I straddled the cat.

"Oh, come on!" I screamed back with a laugh. "You two are too much! Enough!"

For a moment, I had a flash of the last time I had thought, "Enough." It was that first day back home again on Maplewood Avenue, only a few short months ago, when I was still addicted to Shawn's voicemail message. I smiled to myself, realizing I hadn't listened to it in weeks. Maybe these months home had begun to breathe fresh air into my cold and damaged heart, without me even knowing how or why. Maybe something was healing that scar, turning it from red to pink to clear.

❧ Chapter X ❧

Carmel, Indiana
September 2017

"Good morning. It's my birthday, and I've decided to bypass it this year," I said sarcastically as I sat down in the leather chair.

Beverly chuckled. "I see your sense of humor is back. That's a good sign. But the answer is no. And happy birthday."

"Thanks."

"How are you feeling about it?"

Knowing I couldn't lie to Beverly—she would see right through that—I said frankly, "Not great."

"This is the second without Shawn…?"

"Right," I said, nodding and looking down at my hands, holding back the tears, my bravado and sarcasm gone. I started thinking about and dreading the upcoming evening with Shawn's family. The inevitable display—Karen's German chocolate cake, French vanilla ice cream from the Schwann food delivery truck, the candles (so many candles!), the singing, the gifts, the banter and chatting about ordinary things. How could I partake of it when it seemed like such a betrayal to celebrate life when Shawn and Cole were gone? Last year, I had specifically requested to be left alone on my birthday, and they had graciously honored my request, but I knew they thought it odd. Why wouldn't I want to continue the normal tradition and make everything *seem* copacetic, even if it wasn't? But to me it hinted at hypocrisy, and I disliked that feeling. I knew for them, growing up as farmers in a harsher, less emotionally receptive environment, they were conditioned by their upbringing and were taught not to dwell on the hardships of life, but instead to move forward, move ahead, bury what was and hold up what is and what will be.

But a year ago, my philosophy was, what was the point anyway? Birthdays were such strange things—why did we celebrate them anyway? After all, I didn't give birth. I didn't request to be born. I didn't ask to be thrown into this world, only to be taken from it at some point, both acts completely outside of my control. Why am I being celebrated when I had nothing to do with the whole thing? Arbitrary, worthless, inane, illogical. Not to mention, why should I be allowed another year on this earth when Shawn and Cole didn't get one?

During the years when Shawn was alive, as I blew out the candles, my one wish had always been to get pregnant. As if birthdays weren't pointless enough, then there was *that* fruitless, rotten waste of a wish! So last year, when I began to think about going to his parents' house for the cake and candles tradition, I thought to myself, I was going to try something new: I was going to wish to *die*. Please just let me get hit by a truck or slip and fall on my head or be shot during an armed robbery. Something. Please. Not suicide—oh no, that would put too much intention behind it, and one thing I had learned in those few months after the bombing was that there was no intention, no purposeful thought, no reason behind death. I just wanted some random accident or act of violence. Was that too much to ask? I recognized the irony of this, as it was how Shawn and Cole died, but I couldn't shake the thought. My world had imploded, and I didn't know how to put it back together again. Wouldn't it be easier if I didn't have to?

So, for obvious reasons, last year I decided not to go to Shawn's parents' house to "celebrate" my birthday.

"So, do you have any plans?" Beverly asked, breaking into my thoughts.

"Well, Shawn's parents'," I said, reddening a little.

"Oh?"

I nodded, not saying a word.

She waited for a minute, regarding my face, but when I didn't speak, she redirected. "Have you been thinking a lot about Shawn around this birthday?"

"You mean more than usual? Yes, every milestone or holiday brings him back to me full force."

"In what way?"

I answered slowly, "Oh, I don't know…Shawn and I were such polar opposites, and days like today make me remember that. Just as an example, besides the cake at his parents', he also loved to have a big party on his birthday, invite everyone over, have lots of food, open up the pool, and let the kids splash around for hours with their friends. Me, I just wanted a quiet dinner alone with my husband." I stopped to smile, thinking how different we were in so many ways, but that expression about how opposites attract was true of us. I said out loud, "I've been thinking a lot lately about what Shawn would want for me, for my life, and it's hard for me to guess because we were so different. Not to mention, when I think about it too much, I feel... so...disloyal."

"Hmmm. I want to come back to the disloyal concern, but tell me about how the two of you were opposites."

"Well, as much as Shawn was loved by everyone, it wasn't so much that he was super extroverted—it was mostly because he was a great listener and because he was really fun and, more than that, fun*ny*. Everyone loved his sense of humor and his ability to pull people together. When he put his mind to something, there was no getting him out of it. And when he looked into your eyes, you really felt like you were the center of his universe. People just gravitated toward that. He had the uncanny ability to make everyone feel special. Whereas me, well, I guess I'm not as thoughtful—not that I'm mean or heartless, it's just that I was raised to take charge, be bold, make an impression, and that doesn't always translate into being in tune with others' thoughts and feelings. Now that Shawn's gone, I've noticed it more—that I needed him to balance me out. Before, I took a long time to trust people, not to mention, I was the first to speak my mind about a topic, as if I had to get my two cents in before anyone else did. Shawn would wait, listening to all angles of a story or conversation before he spoke up. He almost instantly trusted people, and he used that to be his most authentic self with everyone. That type of openness is what drew people to him. Me, I would always head people off at the pass, probably too quick to judge, to find fault, to give my opinions, and maybe it was as a means to hide my true self. Granted, these are all things I've begun to realize *now*...now that I see how much Shawn helped me with his half of our balance. I'm not sure what good it will do me, though, now that it doesn't matter..."

Beverly cut into my soliloquy. "Of course it matters. Self-reflection leads to greater understanding, and that may translate into a change in you, if that's what you wish." She paused, her eyes piercing me. "And can I just say, you are probably being too hard on yourself. In retrospect, I know it's easy to see only the good in another because, well, it's easier that way, to have that twenty-twenty hindsight and to put the other person on a pedestal. But

I would imagine that Shawn had his faults, and that the balance you speak of was equally measured on your side as well as his." She waited, but I didn't respond, not yet willing to comprehend or concede. She wrote a few notes on her notepad and continued, "So, why the comment on being disloyal?"

I shook my head. I was struggling to put my thoughts into words, and by virtue of speaking about them, I found myself cringing a little. Wasn't I betraying Shawn's memory by talking about him and our relationship so openly with someone who was, after all, a stranger? But I was in way too deep at this point. I began cautiously, "I guess I wonder what he would want for me...I know he would want me to be happy ultimately, but at what expense to his memory? He'll be in my heart forever—that's never going to change. Those memories are embedded in my soul, but then how do I move on? What does that look like? I mean, I'm dealing with all kinds of logistical concerns right now, and I keep wondering, how would Shawn want me to handle these things? I don't want to mess anything up even more than it already is with rash or foolish decisions. Then on top of that, there is the sadness and drained feeling I have most of the time, and I can't sleep, so I never quite feel refreshed or strong enough to tackle everything. Essentially, even if I wanted to move on, whatever that means, I don't have the energy to do anything about it." I stopped, taking a deep breath, pressing my hands to my temples.

Beverly's kind brown eyes held me a moment before she said softly, "One thing at a time—that's all you can do. Also, is there someone helping you?" she asked, concern on her face. "In order for you to focus on your emotional healing, I wonder if you might rely on others for these practical concerns as much as you can."

"Yes...I know," I replied, thinking through the laundry list. "Certainly, our lawyer is helping with Shawn's estate, and Shawn's family is helping with Sissie and the trust, so I'm really very grateful for that. I guess I'm just trying to figure everything else out...you know, the day-to-day, miscellaneous stuff."

"I think if you did ask for help, you'd be amazed at how much people want to help—they just don't know how. Maybe look at it like you're running a small business, and you need a few employees to assist in getting everything done. Sure, these employees aren't getting paid, but still, they're happy to help if it makes your business run more smoothly."

I nodded. I would try. It was hard to call in reinforcements when I had already received so much. I didn't want to feel like a burden any more than I already was.

Beverly paused and asked, "Is there more about the disloyalty you mentioned?"

I had to think for a minute. I looked down at my hands. I replied, "I guess the guilt."

"The guilt...?"

"Yes, I don't understand why I deserve another birthday...when—" I choked off the words with a sob, "when he doesn't get *any*, you know? It's so unfair."

She nodded and let me cry. When I looked up again, she said, "Amanda, you are deserving. Of a full life, with whatever that looks like for you, including embracing hopes and dreams for the future. No, it won't be the same future you envisioned for your life, but it could be something just as rewarding and happy. Maybe not today or anytime soon, but when you're ready. You *are* deserving."

I didn't nod or say anything, dabbing my tears with a tissue instead.

Beverly had a crease between her brows. After a minute she said, "So what *do* you think Shawn would want for you?"

"I don't know...I'm only speculating, but looking back at our relationship, we did spend the majority of our time living in his world, so I assume he'd want me to continue that way."

"Do you mean the fact that you lived in his house, with his kids, near his family...?"

"Exactly. I'm fairly certain he would think staying in his world would make me happy."

"And what do you think?"

"I think...I think...," I started hesitantly, "I'm not sure what to think. I think he would tell me to shoot for the moon, and I wonder if I'm meant to shoot for a moon on a different planet." I winced at my own stupid joke. "I've already told you how I don't feel especially tethered to Earth these days. My whole empty balloon analogy. I want to find a place to get grounded. As much as it scares me, it seems like the world I'm living in now isn't going to get me there because everywhere I turn it's Shawn, Shawn, Shawn."

"I see...Do you remember how we spoke early on about a razed house and what it might take to rebuild a new safe place for you, brick by brick? I wonder if it would be helpful for you take some time in the next few weeks to write down what that might look like. For instance, if you were to consider moving an inch out of Shawn's sphere, in whatever capacity that might be, how would you go about doing that? I'm not asking you to discard your memories or your love for Shawn, but to think of some slice of your future that can include the past along with something new and separate for you."

I nodded, trying to see how that was possible but not seeing anything clearly rise to the fore.

"Hmmm," Beverly began again, "any other ideas…?"

"Yeah," I said with a blush, "I guess I need to think about the future as it pertains to…" I gulped and looked down. How could I even say it out loud? It felt like I was saying a curse word. As I sensed Beverly studying my face, waiting for me to continue, I wrung my hands and said, "Would he want me to be happy, *in that way*, without him?"

"You mean love?" Beverly asked, more as an answer than a question, then with a firm reply, "Yes, that is something to consider, for sure…"

I thought back to my birthday wish, feeling like that was the easier, more just way out. I said quietly, "It feels so wrong."

"Focusing on the future isn't erasing the past. I'm certain Shawn is looking down on you and wanting you to live a long, full life. And Amanda, that means every aspect of life. Even love."

She paused, watching my reaction to these words. I nodded with tears in my eyes, my gut turning over.

❧ Chapter XI ❧

Charlotte Beach (Ontario Beach Park), New York
September 2018

WHEN THE CAROUSEL RIDE STOPPED, we picked up our bags and headed out through the fenced area. Kelly looked at her watch and said, "It's six ten—we should get going."

"Oh wait," Michelle interrupted. "There's one more thing we have to do before we leave, but I have to get it out of the car. Let's drop our stuff in the trunk. Come on."

When we got to the car, I was curious, even more so when Michelle pulled an unlabeled square box out of the trunk. She said, "Let's go out on the pier. I know the perfect spot." Kelly's glance at me indicated she had no idea, so we shrugged and followed.

The pier was busy with fishermen, kids with ice cream dripping down their faces, couples holding hands, and parents pushing strollers. I took in a deep breath, feeling the humidity in the air and smelling the distant scent of french fries from the snack bar. The freshwater swells of Lake Ontario were crashing against the rocks on either side of the pier, splashing up, almost to our ankles. We were all quiet, taking in the sights and sounds. At the end of the pier, off to one side, was a vacant spot above a pile of large rocks. Michelle set the box down on the ground and stood up to look at us both, her face uncharacteristically serious.

She said, holding onto my left shoulder and Kelly's right, "Before we head to the bonfire, I want to do a tribute. A sort of remembrance and a farewell and a wish." On the word *farewell*, she knitted her brows together and focused on my face as if to imprint the word on me. In response, I pushed my shoulders back, instantly feeling my throat swell with the familiar beginning of tears welling up. I frowned. We had been having such a good time, laughing nonstop, making life feel so fresh and sweet and normal again, I had almost forgotten, if just for a few hours…

She reached down and opened the box. On top of some lightweight white paper objects was a grill lighter. She grabbed the lighter and the first item, holding it up and fluffing it in the wind.

"Oh!" I gasped. It was a Chinese paper lantern.

Michelle said, "I brought three. We're going to do them one at a time. Here's the one for Shawn." She handed it to me as tears started spilling uncontrollably down my face. Kelly put her arm around me. I wiped my eyes and took the lantern tentatively from Michelle, trying to see how to start it. She helped my fumbling fingers as we adhered the wax square to the middle of the metal ring at the base. Then she handed me the lighter. We both squatted down on the ground, me holding the metal ring, her holding the top of the paper lightly, letting the air fill it as I lit the wax square. I put the lighter down on the ground and let out a slight exhale as the flame from the wax released an orange glow of hot air into the dome. For a few minutes, we stared as the heat began to build, puffing up the paper into a globe.

When the wire frame began to tug away, Michelle's face was solemn as she said, "This lantern is a symbol of the love and life shared between Amanda and Shawn. It was a life filled with warmth and light and spirit." I glanced up at Kelly, who had her hand to her nose, her eyes full like mine. Michelle continued, "This life was cut short. There are no answers, only questions, but today we will focus on the goodness that was, and we will say farewell. This isn't goodbye—it's farewell for now. Shawn, we thank you and love you for loving and supporting our friend Amanda." She paused and whispered to me, "Do you want to say anything?"

I kept my eyes on the lantern, not sure I could quite face Michelle or Kelly. I took a deep, faltering breath and muttered, "Shawn, I miss you…I will *always* miss you. It's *not fair* that you had to leave me so soon. There are so many things I wish we could have talked about, like how amazing I thought you were, such a great dad and son and husband. I wish…I wish…I don't know what I wish…because I know there's no pointing in wishing anymore, but I will always remember you, and I will always be grateful for your love, and I will always love you."

I peered around the lantern at Michelle with my tear-streaked face. She let go of her side, and as we both stood up, I released the lantern, watching it rise above the rocks and water. It was like a white incandescent snow globe against a burnt amber sky. I whispered, "So beautiful," as my right hand went to my heart and my left hand to my mouth. Michelle and Kelly came on either side of me, holding onto my waist and shoulders, looking up as I said softly, "Until we meet again, my love."

As if I were entombed in cotton, I could hear and sense mumbles from others around us on the pier, watching our proceedings and the lantern as it pushed its way toward the sunset. They were crying too, in empathy, and in remembrance of their own lost loves. The lantern stayed aloft for what seemed like a lifetime, drifting up, up, up toward a destination unknown. When I could no longer see its dot against the sky, I looked down to see Michelle kneeling with the next lantern, already lit and glowing.

She said to me, "This one is for Cole. Here."

I knelt next to her and said, "Cole, you were a sweet, kind, thoughtful, respectful soul. I'm sorry you didn't have more time here to share your unique giving heart with others. The world lost a promising young man when you were taken. May you rest in peace always."

The lantern started to rise but then lost lift and began descending slowly. There was an audible gasp from the crowd as it dropped just inches from the water but, miraculously, stayed aloft and ascended again, slowly at first and then with speed. The crowd responded with relief and a soft round of applause. It was almost otherworldly. Michelle, Kelly, and I stared at each other with small smiles of wonder.

Finally, Michelle pulled the last lantern out of the box, prepping it for flight, and said, "This one is a wish. Just for you, Amanda. You can wish anything—for the moon, if you want! And you don't have to tell us—you just have to infuse the lantern with your wish and send it off into the universe. Are you ready?" I nodded, even though I was temporarily distracted by a sudden flashback, a memory of a session with Beverly a year ago where I had said that maybe I was meant to wish for a moon on another planet. Back then, I ached to even consider any wishes for myself, let alone Shawn's wishes for me, knowing it was impossible to think of any wishes that didn't include him. But now I knew that on this day, my thirty-eighth birthday, my wish was for a future that *couldn't* include him—couldn't lead down the road I had spent years paving toward a destination that had seemed set in stone but was in fact washed away in an instant. How was I to pave a new road? What did that look like? Where would it lead?

I held the lantern up, pushing it toward the sky as I released it from my grasp, and thought my silent wish, feeling every inch of guilt and hope, a combined force of intensity in my soul: I wished for love and for a spark to grow out of nothing and become something that could never replace what was before but might just be a new, repairing flame to light and heal my fractured heart.

Shawn's lantern had long since burned out, but Cole's was still a distant beacon in the fading sunlight. We stayed, our arms around each other, silent and watching as Cole's and my wish lanterns climbed higher and higher and eventually flickered out. The sunset in the background was crimson and crisp against the darkening sky.

Chapter XII

Heathport, New York
September 2018

During the car ride, we were all quiet, lost in our own thoughts. I felt tired and introspective. The farewell lanterns felt heavy in my heart. God, I missed Shawn! But, if I was being honest with myself, the drumbeat of my anguish had muted since I had moved home, and if I was really being honest, the quieting began long before that. A twinge of guilt and shame still popped up every time I thought about it, but when I let myself linger on the past two years, I had trouble pinpointing the moment when things began to change.

Maybe it was all those sessions with Beverly where she told me life was for the living and that I might want to consider retreating from Shawn's world in order to move into my own space. She had never been forceful, never making it uncomfortable for me, rather trying to help me find my way toward a separate shard of light that might open up a larger ray of sunlight. Slowly something began to germinate and gestate in my heart. At first it was just a tiny flame that burned in the back of my mind for months, like a small flicker drawing me closer to study it, examine it, consider it. Then, as a year went by, then two, and Beverly's advice and encouragement kept coming, session after session, brick by brick, my wounds began to heal over and callus, as she had said, a little at first and then more and more over time. I slowly began to look forward instead of backward. My life began to take on a manageable quality that had been lacking since the bombing. And for the first time, I saw myself as separate and distinct from Shawn and his world. With each passing day, I made decisions and took actions that had little to no bearing on him or his family or his world. It scared me, but after a while, when I saw that the sky didn't fall, I became more comfortable and confident in my choices, made more of them, and became assertive and even, at times, defiant. And at some point, it started to feel good, and I started to feel somewhat whole again. Not fully baked, but less stymied, vulnerable, squishy on the inside, and more solid.

Then when Mom called about our childhood house being for sale, it was as though the stars had aligned for me. Before Beverly, I would never have given it a second thought, would have scoffed and turned the idea down flat. But because the drumbeat was dull and weak, but growing, I let her words sink in as I ruminated on them and eventually absorbed them into my heart and my mind. And then I moved. I said goodbye to Sissie, Shawn's family, our mutual friends, my job, coworkers, neighbors, the house, the life, the way we were, the way I was. It wasn't easy, and I cried a lot. Shawn's family tried to be supportive but were clearly reticent and disbelieving, thinking I was making the biggest mistake of my life. Why would I want to leave the safe and familiar world they had set up for me, even amidst the chaos and tragedy of Shawn's and Cole's passing? Why would I run from that? In their minds, I was a fool. And maybe I was, but I knew that staying would break my heart for good, crush it slowly into a million pieces, and as much as it hurt, I had to get away from that, had to strive for something different, something more. Yes, I still struggled with those nagging thoughts—whether I deserved to strive for anything when Shawn was cold, oh so cold, in the deep, heavy, enveloping ground and didn't have the ability to strive for anything anymore. What right did I have?

As if coming out of a deep sleep, I thought about Beverly and what she would have said to me in this moment: "Amanda, yes, Shawn is gone, but maybe this is your chance to be who you were meant to be, your time to live your life—new, tethered, strong, and deserving, as clearly as the sun shines in the sky. Your life must be charted, boarded, floated, and sailed into the bright blue sea of the future. Shawn would approve, and more importantly, regardless of anyone's approval, this is your time. Not your time to go, but instead, your time to stay. And be. And live."

I smiled with the strength of the feeling. I broke the silence suddenly with "Boy, you two are driving me all over tarnation today."

They both laughed, the solemn energy in the car dissipating.

Kelly said, "Yes, we are. Sorry about that. Are you tired?"

"Yes, a little," I admitted. "Who's coming tonight? Other than, well, other than maybe *him*. I mean, is this just one of Donny's regular bonfires?"

Michelle sensed the implications of my question, "Honey, this is your birthday bonfire. Everyone's coming, but you're going to be fine! Don't worry about a thing. Relax, have a beer, roast a hotdog on the fire. We'll have you get up in the middle and sing the 'Wienie Man' song." She shrugged with a giggle as I groaned and then added, "Let people be there to love on you. We just want you to have a good time." She reached around from the back seat and put her hand comfortingly on my shoulder.

I gulped, trying to keep the anxiety from filling my gut. Maybe I could be the center of attention for a few hours. Or maybe I would need more than one beer!

Kelly dropped me off at my house. Before they took off, I thanked them both sincerely and told them I'd see them in a little bit over at Donny's. I took a shower, inviting the hot water to calm my nerves and ease my tight muscles. My jaw hurt; I must have been clenching it in the car.

When I stepped out of the shower and saw my reflection in the mirror, I did a quick assessment. My hair was in a clip—I hadn't washed it because it would have taken too long to blow-dry. I took the clip out and watched the wavy blond curls cascading around my face and down my back. My freckles were quite pronounced after a day in the sun, and despite my slather of SPF 50, my cheeks were a shade pinker. At least I had an excuse this evening if I was self-conscious and blushed (for whatever reason, and I could think of several possible ones!).

I put on a pair of white shorts and a black top that had a pink flower detail sewn into the fabric. Then I applied my makeup and strapped on my watch. It read eight fifteen. I felt my stomach twist into a knot. As I inserted my favorite diamond stud earrings, I looked down at the glass ring holder lying on top of my dresser. Yes, I still wore it every day. *The* ring. The symbol of the love Shawn and I shared when we pledged to be together forever, for better or for worse. But I decided, right then and there—not tonight. I slipped it off my finger and placed it on the ring holder, staring at it with some trepidation, but mostly with resolve.

I took one last look at myself in the mirror, feeling satisfied with the ensemble. I slipped on my black wedge sandals and headed down the stairs and out the front door. I tried not to hesitate or think too much about anything. FDR's famous quote popped into my head: "We have nothing to fear but fear itself." Wasn't that true?! I was not going to fear. I was going to walk over there and face those people and accept their birthday wishes. Yes, even from *that* person.

As I strolled down the street, I noticed everyone's front porch lights were on. I had a feeling that Donny had invited the whole neighborhood to the bonfire. When I was within a few yards of his house, Dustin's daughter, my ten-year-old niece Yvonne, came bounding out from behind Donny's hedge and right into my arms for a big hug.

She said, "Happy birthday, Aunt Amanda!"

"Thanks, sweetie! I didn't know you were going to be here. Wow, who else is here?"

"Everyone! Well, not everyone, I guess, because Aunt Nikki isn't here. She told Dad that it was too late for the kids, but of course, she's hosting brunch tomorrow at her house, so we'll see her and Grandma and Meemaw there then. I hope Aunt Nikki makes her blueberry pancakes. They're my favorite! Yummy, yummy, yummy."

"I'm hoping for a frittata, but I'd be okay with blueberry pancakes," I said, laughing and squeezing her side. "Sorry I missed your soccer game this morning. How'd it go?"

"Good. We won. And I scored, so that was totally sweeeet!"

"You're amazing."

"Yeah, the only bad thing is that this one girl, I swear, every time I had the ball, she attacked me. You should see my shins—they're purple!"

As she rattled on, our arms around each other, we turned the corner to Donny's backyard, where the bonfire was already going strong. There were over a dozen chairs encircling the pit and three card tables set up, one with all the fixings for a campfire meal: hotdogs, potato salad, chips, cole slaw, green beans, and for later, Hershey bars, marshmallows, and graham crackers for s'mores. The next table had roasting sticks and paper plates, cups, napkins, plasticware. The final one was scattered with wrapped gifts and a "Happy Birthday" sign taped to the edge. On the ground next to the tables were several labeled coolers: beer, wine, pop, water. Wow, quite a spread, just for my birthday! And all of these people, some of whom I hadn't seen in years. I put my hand to my mouth, trying not to let the sentiment get to me. The night was just beginning, after all, so I needed to pace myself.

I quickly scanned the group of people gathered, none of whom were sitting yet. Dustin and his wife, Jenny, were talking to Donny and his wife, Danielle. Eight or nine kids were running around with sparklers, twirling them against the night sky. Kelly was talking to Mrs. O'Connor and her son, Tom, and his wife, Paula. Peter, Kelly's husband, was conversing with Donny's brother and his wife. Michelle and Kelly's parents, Mr. and Mrs. Abernathy, were there, just getting ready to sit down with two of Michelle and Kelly's older sisters, Penelope and Mariah, who were there with their husbands and kids. Michelle was standing next to her husband, Andy, who was loosely holding the head of their son, Ryan, as their other son, Oliver, weaved in and out of the crowd with a brightly lit *Star Wars* green light saber.

Good, I thought. He's not here yet. I can breathe for a few minutes.

As I walked up to Michelle, Andy released Ryan to chase after his brother, and Michelle came in for a hug and said, "Glad you didn't chicken out," then quickly added, "Don't worry. I've given Andy the full scoop about the book. He's to pretend to be an avid fisherman, if asked."

I chuckled. "Okay, I hadn't even thought of that." I shook my head, thinking Jonathan probably saw right through our ruse this morning anyway.

Andy said, "If he asks me a fish question, I'm going to plead the fifth."

"Andy!" Michelle cried, slapping his arm.

"I will not be a part of your reindeer games," he said, laughing, then turned to me, saying, "So, Jonathan Galway, eh? I haven't seen that guy since high school. I think his brother Garrett was in my class, right? I can't remember…"

Michelle answered before I could, "Yes, honey, Garrett was in your class (and Kelly's), and Jonathan was in Amanda's class. There's an older brother too, but his name escapes me…"

I said, "Jake. He was in the class four years ahead, so your sister Penelope graduated with him."

"That's right," she assented, nodding and looking toward the fire, where Penelope sat with her husband. "Well, it's a good thing he's not here yet so we can get this all straightened out first. Why don't you go say hi to everyone else before he shows up."

"Okay."

As I started to walk away, she grabbed my arm and said, "Hey, do you want a beer or something first?"

I nodded and she reached in a cooler to hand me a bottle, thinking a little fool's courage couldn't hurt. I walked around to each group, saying hello, giving greeting hugs, receiving many warm birthday wishes, and trying not to let my nerves get the better of me. I wondered if Jonathan really did know which house was Donny's. Would he even know that Donny had bought his childhood home from his parents, just as I had bought mine? But then I thought to myself, oh yeah, I almost forgot, I'm back living in

Heathport, the epitome of a small town, where everyone knows everyone's business.

Then I had a flash of dread—would he know my story? Would he know about Shawn? Would he know that I'd been in Indiana all these years? Would he know I bought my family home just a few short months ago? What had Michelle's friend said about him? That he lived on West Lake Road. That was way out in Canandaigua. So maybe he didn't know all the gossip and goings-on. I was still a little worried about it as I listened absently to Mrs. O'Connor talk about "the insidious moles" that had taken over her garden. My mind raced: What would he know? Would he feel sorry for me? Was that the only reason he was coming tonight? What had he heard? My face flushed thinking about it. And my heart started pounding. God, that would be awful! Was that why he agreed so readily? Shit, I needed to get out of here. Maybe I could feign illness. But then, all these people came out for me, for my birthday, and as far as I knew, they had no ulterior motive. Wouldn't it be rude of me to leave? What was I going to do?

Kelly, always intuitively sensing stress in the air like a lion sniffing out injured prey, came over, regarded my panicked face, and quickly cut off Mrs. O'Connor with "Now, we can't monopolize the guest of honor. Let's get her something to eat."

Mrs. O'Connor, unfazed, stood up, stretched, and said, "Sounds like a good idea. Actually, I'm pooped. Getting too old for these late-night neighborhood gigs. You young'uns enjoy yourselves. I'm headed home."

We said goodbye as Kelly guided me away toward the food table and whispered, "You alright?"

Michelle was standing there already, skewering a hotdog on a roasting stick. She asked us if we wanted one. When neither of us responded, she looked up, her face going from Kelly's to mine and then at me, "Dang girl, what's wrong?"

"Um," I muttered, not sure if I should kill the mood with my neurotic ruminations. "I'm kind of worried that maybe, I mean, I don't know…what if—what if—"

Michelle interrupted with a short, quiet, "Shush." She nodded her head.

I spun around slowly, feeling Kelly's hand on my arm.

There was Jonathan, a few feet away, shaking hands with Donny, looking even more handsome in the evening light than he had looked earlier in the bright assembly-hall fluorescents. He was wearing a white ribbed cotton

V-neck T-shirt tucked into dark green shorts, secured around his narrow waist with a brown belt. I swallowed, feeling the magnetic pull between us.

He turned from Donny and walked directly to us, swiftly shaking Michelle's and Kelly's hands and then, as I went to lift my hand, pulled me into a surprise embrace, whispering in my ear in his deep voice, "Happy birthday, Amanda." I melted into his frame, thinking only that he smelled exactly like what I would imagine a crisp walk on a snowy mountainside might smell like—clean, pure, and earthy.

He released me rather slowly and pondered my face and eyes with a crooked grin. I could tell he knew how he was affecting me. My God, I thought, he's not even nervous! That is not fair! It irritated me. I was a mess, caught off guard, not knowing how to respond. I mumbled, "Thanks for coming," my eyes never leaving his. Wide-eyed in amazement at his unfaltering confidence, I noted the flecks of yellow reflected from the fire in his forest green irises. My heart beat loudly in my chest as my mind flashed involuntarily to this thought: I could sink my soul into those eyes.

Michelle jumped in, seeing me drowning (and not in the way of the eyes), and grabbed Jonathan by the arm. "Come say hi to the others. You remember my husband, Andy, right? The one you signed the book for…"

I watched them retreat with relief, turning my attention to Kelly and saying quietly, "God, does he have to be so damned good-looking?"

Instead of disagreeing, she said, "And self-assured too."

"Thanks a bundle," I said sarcastically, and she laughed.

She added, "Don't worry about it. Just be yourself. Remember, he's on your turf now."

"I suppose," I conceded. She was right. I was here on Maplewood Avenue, surrounded by people I had known my whole life. And they were here tonight for me. Why should I be nervous, even if Jonathan was something right out of a romance novel? Besides, no matter what happened tonight, I would be no worse off than I was this morning, right?

We went to sit by the fire, near Oliver, who was roasting our hotdogs. I watched (as covertly as I could) Michelle usher Jonathan around to meet everyone. He was so polite, casual, and at ease with himself, it was truly uncanny, like someone who could walk into a room full of strangers and be perfectly comfortable. Of course, most of these people he knew from high school or were friends of friends, but still, he wasn't part of the Maplewood gang, and it impressed me that he was talking, joking, and reminiscing as if he belonged.

Once our hotdogs were done, we filled our plates at the food table and went back to our seats by the fire, balancing everything on our laps. The temperature outside had cooled down, and the fire was comforting. The fall air was crisp and dry, now infused with the sweet smell of wood smoke. The rest of the group, including the kids, started to filter in closer to the fire, skewering and roasting their own hotdogs and preparing their plates.

Conveniently, Michelle went to assist her son Ryan with his plate, thus leaving Jonathan alone. He came to find his way over to us, asking politely if he could take the seat next to mine. As he sat, he turned and smiled, saying, "So, birthday girl, did you have fun today? What did you do?"

I tried to keep my voice casual and informal, like his. "So much fun. We went to Charlotte and laid out, walked the boardwalk, rode the merry-go-round, and mostly laughed a lot. It was the perfect birth-day. And now I'm hoping for the perfect birth-night." I smiled at my little quip.

He grinned and in keeping with my joke, said bluntly, "I'm sure that can be arranged."

Again with the confidence! "Oh?" I feigned inquiry, with a slight challenge to my voice.

Instead of answering, he stared into my eyes with such intensity that it sent my knees to wobble. Then he abruptly stood up, saying, "Um…excuse me," clearing his throat, "I'm gonna grab a stick to roast a hotdog. I'll be right back."

I blinked as he walked away. Shit, what was that about?! Was I, in some unconscious (or conscious?) way, unsettling that airtight center of steel that was this man's natural state of unflappable poise and fluid gracefulness?

He came back, clearly recovered, with a loaded skewer in hand and Michelle, Andy, and Ryan following behind as they all sat down and began talking and roasting in unison. I looked over at Kelly, who was chatting with her husband, and wondered if the night would simply drift along like this, where despite my fears and agitations, it would be easy conversation, everyone talking over one other about innocuous, gossipy local chatter, with not a blip on the radar to cause me any disquiet. I took a deep breath, then a big bite of my hotdog and thought, that would be perfect. Let's just assume, yes, that will happen. I stared contentedly into the fire, swallowing my food with a swig of beer, remembering, yes, I was here in my Maplewood element, and I had nothing to worry about. Nothing at all. I ate a forkful of potato salad and sighed. The warmth of the fire felt wonderful, and it began to warm my heart, searing a gentle melting calmness into my being.

❧ Chapter XIII ❧
Heathport, New York
September 2018

About a second after I had settled into this reassuring state of mind and body, Jonathan turned to me with his full-force attention and asked, "So, what have you been doing with yourself all these years? I can't believe we've never run into each other before. Seems crazy in this small town. Of course, I'm over in Canandaigua now and don't come into town as often anymore, but still…"

"Well, um, I've been living in Indiana for the past sixteen years, so that may be why." I smiled and he nodded, his eyebrows raised slightly. He leaned forward in his chair toward the fire so his loaded skewer was closer to the coals and not the flame. I continued, "Did you know that I bought my old house in May?" I pointed in the direction of my house two doors down. "So, I'm back on Maplewood Avenue, just like old times. Kind of wild."

He said, "Hmph. That *is* wild. I suppose that's what Donny did too, with this house."

"Yep, well, you know, it is Maplewood, after all," I said, as if this explained everything, then added, "Nothing ever really changes around here. I kind of like that."

"Me too," he agreed. "Growing up on Gillian, and it being a country road, we didn't necessarily have a real neighborhood, so yeah, I've always been a little envious of this street."

I smiled and said, "Of course, there aren't any secrets either."

"No, I imagine not," he replied, then with a curious smile, "Do you have a lot of secrets?"

"I—I, well, um…," I stuttered until, thankfully, Donny appeared out of nowhere, plopping himself down next to Jonathan and saying, "Did I hear my name?"

We both looked at him, me still recovering, and Jonathan replied, "We were just talking about you living here, as an adult, with your kids growing up in the house you grew up in."

"Oh, right," he began, taking a big bite of his hotdog, at which point I noticed he was wearing a black T-shirt with the words "You wanna piece of me?" on the front. I laughed and shook my head, getting a quick glance from them both, followed by Donny continuing, "Well, after my dad died, my mom was getting kind of frail, you know, that was ten—no, nine years ago. I talked to Danielle about it, and we decided once our lease was up at our apartment, we would move in here to take care of Mom. We only had one kid then, David, but Danielle was pregnant, so we needed to find a bigger place anyway. Yeah, the timing really worked out. We helped Mom, and she helped with the kids. She passed away about three years ago, but we decided to stay. Danielle grew up in Detroit, and she didn't even think there were places like this anymore in America—you know, small-town streets like Maplewood." Danielle nodded in agreement and sat down on the other side of Donny with their daughter, Jean.

Donny stared at Jonathan, still with his mouth full, and asked, "Did I hear you're some kind of fish guy or something?" As he looked at Jonathan expectantly, I thought to myself, Donny hasn't changed a stitch since high school. Always one to monopolize the conversation, oblivious to the nuances of social decorum, but on the other hand, he was like a sweet, bumbling basset hound, friendly to everyone and great at gathering people together. I figured all chance of intimate talk with Jonathan was probably at a standstill for now, but maybe with Donny occupying him, I could sit back and listen and get a better picture of the man (Jonathan that is, not Donny). I put my empty plate down on the ground and picked up my beer, paying close attention while trying not to let it be too obvious that I was staring.

Jonathan paused to wipe his mouth before answering with a small smile, "Yes. I'm an ichthyologist. I work for the New York State Department of Environmental Conservation."

Donny frowned. "An ich—ich—what?"

Jonathan just laughed. "I study fish."

Donny asked him what types of fish he studied, and Jonathan went on for a while about that.

Then I interrupted Donny as he started to open his mouth again. "So, Jonathan, for your job, where do you work? I mean, is it an office?"

Jonathan turned to me with a calm, detached look, even as I found myself melting a little at the deep, warm quality of his voice. "I work in the field mostly. But, yes, I do have an office, well, a lab, over in Naples."

"Did you write the book in the lab? How did you find time? Or was the book considered part of your job?"

Donny spoke up before he could reply, "Wait. You have a book?"

I just stared at Donny. How had he known about Jonathan being a fish guy but not about the book? Probably only got half the story or only *listened* to half the story from whoever filled him in, most likely Michelle.

"Yes," Jonathan responded, "it was published last month. It's actually something I've been working on since college. It's a field guide—sort of a collection of photos and descriptions of the fish species native to the Finger Lakes and where to find them."

"Wow, that's awesome!" Donny exclaimed. His eyes lit up as he added, "I'd love a copy. I fish all the time. I mean, sometimes I go out with my buddy Tim, who's got a good-sized Boston Whaler over on Lake Ontario, but once in a while I hit up Keuka, Seneca, or Canandaigua by myself, in my Lund. Oh my God, two weeks ago we were on vacation in Chautauqua, and I caught the hugest muskie. It was massive—I thought it was going to take the boat down! My buddy Jared was like, dude, you better get the net out because there is no way we can get this thing off the hook otherwise. I mean, it was the ugliest son-of-a-bitch fish I'd ever seen! We got it up in the boat finally, took a photo with it, and just threw it back in. I was like…"

As Donny droned on, I stopped listening, worrying a little that poor Jonathan's time would not be his own for the rest of the night. As soon as Donny finished the story about the muskie, he started a long diatribe about the size of largemouth bass this year and how they hadn't stocked things properly. Jonathan explained the seasonal nature of the local stock and what each species relied upon for prey in order to be maintained at the right levels from year to year.

I eventually stood up, took their empty plates, and offered to get them both a refill on their beers. They nodded, and Jonathan added a wide-eyed help-me-I'm-trapped grin and winked as I took his empty from him. I walked to the card table, tossed our bottles in the recycle bin, and after grabbing two more for them, found myself a bottle of wine. I asked Danielle for a wine opener and proceeded to fill a red Solo cup with some Riesling. If I was going to spend the night watching Donny fawn all over Jonathan, I was going to need a stronger drink. Wasn't it supposed to be *me* fawning all over him? Or *him* fawning all over *me*? But, alas, I was jumping the gun with that thought, wasn't I?

My brother, Dustin, was grabbing a beer out of a cooler, so I chatted with him for a few minutes, asking how the kids were doing. As if on cue, his younger daughter, Abigail, came and gave me a hug, saying, "Aunt Amanda, is it time to open your gifts yet? Do you think…maybe…I could help?"

"Well, I couldn't do it without you, of course," I said, giving her a playful squeeze. As we talked, Dustin was denying Abigail's request for her third pop, and I suddenly felt Jonathan's eyes on me, so I looked back tentatively. He was studying me, his face inscrutable. Donny noticed him watching and touched his arm to emphasize a point he was making, causing Jonathan to turn back. Michelle came over to me then, speaking quietly and swiftly in my ear, "How's it going? Any butterflies?"

"Very funny, Michelle," I scolded. "Doesn't matter because I can barely get a word in edgewise, now that Donny has a hold of him. Apparently, unlike Andy, Donny actually *is* an avid fisherman and thinks he's on a date with Jonathan. *He's* the one with the butterflies."

"Ugh. Okay. Let me take care of that."

I went to say, "No, it's okay…," but she was off, marching toward Danielle, who was seated next to Donny, and I followed, balancing two beers in my left hand while walking back and sipping from my wine cup in my right. Jonathan took the beers from me, giving one to Donny, then looked back at me with a quick thank-you nod. I smiled and sat down. Donny kept talking all the while, not noticing a thing. I thought, poor Jonathan, here he comes to my birthday party, to be nice, or to see me, or pity me, or for whatever reason, and now he's being subjected to a new superfan. I guess it was a test of sorts—of his interest in me, or his patience anyway. At least he hadn't run away screaming yet.

Out of my periphery, I saw Michelle whisper something in Danielle's ear. Danielle promptly got up, leaned over Donny, said "Excuse us," took Donny's unsuspecting hand, and led him away for some "emergency" in the house.

Now that I had Jonathan to myself again, I said, "Where were we?"

He laughed with obvious relief and said, "Indiana."

I sighed. How to begin? "Yes, well, after I graduated from Syracuse, I got recruited to work for this insurance company in Indy, so I moved. Looking back on it now, I think I was slightly crazy." I laughed, a little embarrassed.

Jonathan just looked at me, interested and smiling. "Moving to a whole new place like that…I don't know, I was young and free, and I wanted an adventure. It was scary in the beginning, not knowing anyone, but eventually I grew to love it. It became like my second home. Anyway, fast-forward a few years, and Mom called and mentioned that our house here on Maplewood was for sale, and…um, for various reasons, I was ready for a change in my life, so I quit my job and moved home."

"Wow, just like that?" he asked incredulously.

"Yep, just like that."

"That's really cool. What did you do at the insurance company?"

Good, he was sticking to the trivialities. "Oh, I started as a lowly systems analyst, a technology role, basically a coder, then I worked my way up to IT director. I loved my job, actually, and I really miss it, especially the people… it still feels unreal that I walked away from it all." I exhaled and added, "Anyway, now I'm working on Ridge Road for this small start-up. It's strange going from a big company to a small one. I feel a little like a fish out of water, if you'll pardon the fish metaphor," I quipped, and he grinned.

He said, "Well, I think you're really brave. It's not easy starting over. I know a thing or two about that." I furrowed my brow, wondering what he meant. "Plus, I can't imagine moving that far away. My parents are still out on Gillian Road, and even though I'm in Canandaigua now, I try to stop by at least once a week."

"How are they doing?"

"Thanks for asking. They amaze me. They just had their forty-fifth wedding anniversary a few weeks ago. We offered to host a party, but they said they just wanted us kids to come over. Dad grilled steaks, and Mom was inside fussing over the grandkids while she prepped the rest of the food. They never seem to get tired, you know? It was fun, and it was nice to see them so happy…really inspirational…they're both still in love after all these years."

His eyes, as he said this last sentence, were like warm pools of light flickering in the reflection of the fire. I stared, thinking how nice it was to hear a guy talk about his parents this way. He turned to me then, asking about my parents.

I blushed a little as I said, "Oh, actually, my dad passed…about thirteen years ago."

"Oh my gosh, Amanda, I'm so sorry. I forgot." He swallowed and looked slightly mortified. "I did hear about that…I'm really sorry."

"No, no, it's okay. I still miss him, but…it's okay." I paused for a moment, thinking to myself quickly, do not go down that rabbit hole, do not. It only leads down another much deeper, much more complicated rabbit crevasse. Instead, I said, "And Mom's doing great, as busy as ever. She loves all of her activities. She puts me to shame…I swear, when she's off and running, I can't keep up." He smiled politely. I asked, "So your house in Canandaigua, is it on the water?"

"Yep, pretty much…I mean, I'm on the opposite side of the road, but you can see the water right out my front window. And I have a dock and a boat."

"That must be great."

"It is," he said, drinking some of his beer. "It's convenient for my job too." He waited a minute before giving me that intense look again as he said with a small smile, "I don't mean to be rude, but why do I feel like you've glossed over a few things?"

I didn't know what to make of that. Was he reading the reticence and trepidation on my face? How much did he already know? How much did I want to tell him? I decided to use evasive measures. I said, "Oh, sure, this and that. What about you? What have *you* been doing for the past twenty years besides fishing?"

His eyes narrowed as if he saw right through my attempt at escape. Then out of the blue, he said, "You know, I think we were both in Syracuse at the same time."

"We were? That's strange, I didn't know you went to SU. Wouldn't we have seen each other on campus?"

He laughed at my confusion, saying, "No, I didn't go to SU. I went to SUNY's College of Environmental Science and Forestry *in* Syracuse."

"Ah, okay, that makes more sense then. I don't remember…is that campus right next to SU?"

"Yeah, near the Dome."

"Oh yeah, I used to run up the hill right next to that one building. It was fairly close to my dorm, and it was a great running hill—very steep, great for the hamstrings."

"Forestry Drive. I think I saw you running there once."

"What? No way! You did?" I asked, incredulous and intrigued.

"Yep. Actually, you ran right past me. But you didn't see me there and I—well—I turned away."

His blunt confession hit me like a stab. "You did? Why?" I asked, knitting my brows, staring into his eyes, trying to decipher the reason behind such an action.

"Yeah, I know, it was sort of stupid, I guess, but I didn't want—" His sentence was cut short by the sudden rumbling of voices beginning a song, headed right for us.

We both looked up, caught off guard, as Donny and Danielle came out of the back door of the house with a candle-lit birthday cake, Donny leading everyone in singing, "Happy birthday to you…"

I quickly cleared my confused face, trying to shake off the strange twist in my gut from Jonathan's unfinished words, and smiled as Donny placed the cake on my lap, finishing the song with a rousing "Make a wish!"

I looked around at the bright, kind faces of my friends and family and felt those involuntary tears pricking my eyes again, wondering what I ever did to deserve such unmitigated kindness and care from every angle, despite the fact that I had moved away and then come back with my tail between my legs. And yet, these people didn't judge, didn't think anything of my caper, didn't hold it against me that I had left and then asked to be allowed back into the fold, a damaged, broken (and starting to heal) version of my former self. This was the power of Maplewood Avenue, and I felt it in my bones at that moment. I put my hand to my chest, feeling my heart beat, closed my eyes, and blew out the candles with a silent wish: "I want to live!" As I opened my eyes, they hooted at me, so I wiped a tear away and thought gratefully and extraordinarily, wow, what a difference two years can make!

Donny screamed, "See, we knew she was filled with hot air!" They all laughed, and I shook my head, looking over at Jonathan, who had a twinkle in his eye and something else. Curiosity? Admiration? Intrigue? I couldn't quite place it.

Danielle took the cake from my lap and cut it, doling out pieces to everyone. It was chocolate with buttercream icing, and it was delicious. Sometime later, after the paper plates had all been tossed in the fire, Michelle said it was time for gifts, which brought Yvonne and Abigail around to "assist." Bringing me the first one, a small box wrapped in black and gold. I opened the card. It was from Michelle and Andy—a pair of silver heart earrings.

Michelle said, "Do you like them?"

"Yes! Michelle, they're perfect. Thank you."

Next was a pint-sized box wrapped with a pink ribbon. The card said it was from Dustin, Jenny, and the kids. As I opened it, the general oohs and aahs around the fire were unanimous. It was a beautifully formed and detailed blown-glass bud vase with the exact colors and representation of a calla lily. With an intake of breath, I looked at Dustin and asked in awe, "Did you make this?"

"Yes. Remember that glassblowing class I took down in Corning a few months ago? Well, this is one of my first pieces…well, first pieces that didn't go right back into the fire anyway." He laughed modestly. Dustin was an artist by profession—a potter—and had his own shop in Schoen Place in Pittsford, but this was the first Amanda had heard of him branching out into other media.

"It's…exquisite. Thank you so much. I know exactly where I'll put it—on the windowsill over the kitchen sink. It'll be perfect for lilies of the valley in the spring, that patch that grows out by the shed."

Dustin smiled and nodded. He remembered.

Michelle brought over another gift, this one hidden in tissue in a green gift bag. There was no card. It was a jar, about four inches across at the mouth, with some type of cheesecloth covering it and little creatures inside, sitting on straw-like material. I held it up to the light of the fire, examining it curiously.

Jonathan took the jar lightly from my hands and said, "It's a butterfly kit."

"Oh!" I said with delight. "But you didn't have to…"

He shrugged and said, "Just a little something. Do you like it?" He scrutinized my face.

"I love it!" I replied honestly. My eyes were wide and appreciative. I asked, "So, how exactly does it work?" As he explained the process, I found myself being sucked into his eyes again. How did he know enough about me to buy me this gift, of all things? It was perfect. I had always loved nature, but my communion and obsession with all things wild was cultivated *after* high school, long after I'd fallen out of touch with him. But somehow, he knew. So strange.

A gift card from Kelly and Peter, and a makeup lip kit, hair accessories, and other miscellaneous items from others, and the gift portion of the evening was over, much to the displeasure of Yvonne and Abigail, who proceeded to ball up the tissue paper and throw it back and forth, eventually tossing it into the fire, creating a sizzling flame. After that, everyone settled into their seats—like bees humming around a flower bed. buzzing and contentedly taking in each other's company, their drinks, and the warmth of the fire.

Abigail came and asked me shyly to see the "butterfly jar." Jonathan held it up for her and walked through the process of metamorphosis as Abigail stood rapt by his side. I watched, wondering what his story was—not the butterflies, but what he meant about "starting over." He seemed so calm and patient—the perfect traits for a father. What had happened? Had he not met the right woman? Or maybe Michelle's information was wrong. Maybe he *did* have kids. There was so much I didn't know, most of all if he had changed as much as I had since we had last kissed more than twenty years ago and whether those changes made him an entirely different man from the one I remembered.

Donny came over again and sat next to Jonathan, beginning a conversation about another recent fishing trip, but Jonathan, not wanting to talk about himself anymore, changed the subject by asking him, "So, Donny, what do you do for a living?"

"Oh me? I'm a security guard. I staff the front desk and the perimeter at the Xerox Tower downtown, you know, Innovation Square. It's not very exciting, but the pay and benefits are good. And if I jump on 490, it only takes twenty or thirty minutes to get there."

Unprompted, Donny started in on a story, and because his voice was so loud, everyone around the fire seemed to get quiet and pay attention. Even Abigail stopped looking into the butterfly jar, turned her body to lean against my lap, and listened as I absently brushed her hair back with my fingers.

"So last week, all of the security guards had to do this mandatory training. We cover in shifts, you know, so there's always someone at the front desk, but for this training, a whole bunch of us got pulled into the conference room for the entire day. They had this security company guy come in, I wanna say he worked for the Department of Homeland Security, or maybe he was hired by Homeland Security…anyway, it was mostly stuff we already knew, but it was still pretty interesting.

"He first showed us all kinds of videos and PowerPoint slides with actors portraying how to handle emergency situations. You gotta love those actors. Wait, Ethel's fallen, and she can't get up!" He stopped to laugh loudly at his own joke. "We all remember those commercials. Hysterical. Well, these videos were just as bad.

"We went through all of the different fire, tornado, hurricane, and chemical spill scenarios. But then he started explaining how to handle what's called 'an active shooter situation.' Isn't it crazy, in this day and age, how we have to be prepared for some crazy, deranged psychopath to come in and shoot us?

"So anyway, this security teacher guy, he asked for a volunteer to come up to the front of the room with him, so I say sure. He said he's going to show us how to disarm a gunman from behind. I'm just standing up there, and I swear, before he even said go, he had me in some type of half nelson move. It reminded me of my wrestling days. I wanted so bad to turn around and pin him to the floor. I could have done that in a heartbeat. But I mean, I couldn't very well upstage the guy in front of the whole class. So yeah, I decided to play it cool."

He paused for a minute, making sure people were onto his brag. It was hard to miss. The atmosphere around the fire was serious and intent, but Donny was oblivious to everything except his need to be the center of attention. He was clueless about the shift in energy, the meaningful flashes of eyes upon him trying to warn him to tread lightly, to be cognizant of his audience. He plowed right through. I felt myself tense in my seat, a sinking feeling building in my gut and racing up my spine with heated sparks of pins and needles. I felt all eyes upon Donny and me, but I couldn't look away as I laser-focused my attention on the whites of Donny's eyes and the words spewing from his mouth.

He continued, "Then he showed us a few other moves…you know, he had me down on the ground with my face to the floor and his knee in my back. Finally, what seemed like an hour later, he let me jump up and go back to my seat. Anyway, he said the key to stopping something in the middle of it happening is to keep all five senses on high alert. You know, listen for anything that sounds like firecrackers or a car backfiring, because this could actually be gunfire. Watch for any details that could help you get an edge or help you escape. If you're in a fire and all of the lights are off, feel your way to the emergency exits. Always be cautious when you see suspicious packages left by themselves, anything that could potentially be a bomb—"

He stopped mid-sentence, a conscious awareness immediately (finally!) striking his face. As soon as the word *bomb* escaped his lips, all eyes instantly snapped from him to me. Except Jonathan, who was suddenly looking at everyone else looking at me, wondering what was going on. My heart started pounding, from the attention, from the shock of *that* word, from the dreadful change in energy and mood, and also from this remarkable realization: Jonathan didn't know! How was that possible? The perplexed look on his face—it was undeniable. He really didn't know. A second later I thought, well, at least he's not here out of pity, then. That was something. But what to do with this horrific situation!

Donny dug himself a bigger hole, saying, "Oh shit! Oh my God, Amanda! I am *so* sorry! I didn't think! I wasn't thinking!"

I felt horrible. How could everything go in an instant from fun and happy and light to this…this nightmare. All over again. I couldn't count the number of times it had happened when I was back in Indy, but for it to happen here, in the safety of my Maplewood bower, and so unexpectedly. What could I do? There was no going back. I said with sad, defeated eyes, "It's okay, Donny." I glanced down at Abigail and tried to pull her closer as she stared at me with curious, caring, confused eyes.

There was an awkward silence. Then Donny started apologizing again, sweat running down his forehead as he looked sheepishly at me and then at Danielle, who was giving him a wifely look of regret and disappointment. Everyone else just sat there watching me silently. To Jonathan's credit, he didn't say a word and just sat observing the scene play out with a furrowed brow.

Finally, Michelle came to the rescue, saying in a loud voice, trying hard to bring the mood back around, "So how exactly do you train your sense of *taste* to be on high alert for criminals and terrorists? What exactly do criminals and terrorists taste like anyway?"

Despite themselves, everyone burst out laughing, thankfully, breaking the tension. To continue the laugh and keep the atmosphere headed in the right direction, I interjected quietly, "Dirty pennies and gunpowder?"

That brought another round of laughter. Andy added, "No, quarter pounders and fries."

Dustin jumped in, "Donuts!

Peter added, "Nick's garbage plate!"

Jonathan was still scrutinizing me as everyone else started acting mostly normal again. Someone went to get more beers, and a few more jokes and stories followed. Eventually, the parents with kids started to pack up. I gave Abigail a kiss on the forehead, releasing her from my lap, and assisted with the cleanup, finally giving thank-you hugs to everyone as they drifted away.

Jonathan offered to walk me to my house, and I said no more sharply than I intended. How would that work? Would there be a pause under the porch light as I stood opening the front door? I had no idea how to handle that. And it had been a long day. I was too tired to try to figure out my feelings for Jonathan. Not to mention, he would obviously have questions. Questions that I was wholly unprepared to answer. But I followed my harsh no with "How about I walk you to your car?"

He said, "Sure." At least he didn't get offended or put off easily. That was reassuring.

I gave Donny a hug and thanked him for the party. He apologized again for "putting his foot in his mouth," but I told him it was fine and not to worry about it. Jonathan, clearly still in the dark, didn't say a word.

I grabbed my gifts, and Jonathan grabbed his cooler. We headed toward his car—a maroon Subaru Outback parked on the street a few houses down.

On the way to the car, he asked unexpectedly, "Will you do me a favor?"

I felt a tightening in my gut. Was this it? Was he going to ask me about the whole fiasco? I said uncertainly, like a question, "Um, sure...?"

"Will you call me Jon? No one has called me Jonathan since high school."

I breathed a sigh of relief with a little laugh. I said, "Oh, how funny. Of course, but why didn't you tell us earlier?"

"I didn't want to make a big deal about it. And technically, Jonathan *is* my name. I just decided to shorten it in college. It makes me feel like I'm in kindergarten again when I hear it."

I chuckled and said, "Right, sure...*Jon*." When we reached his car, I said, "Thank you so much for coming. It was great to see you." I suddenly felt awkward and nervous. The street was dark except for a few lamps in windows and my front porch light beaming from across the yard.

He opened the hatch to put his cooler in. As he softly closed it and turned, he unexpectedly took my gift bags from my hand and placed them on the ground. Then his eyes shifted to my face, illuminating an intensity of thoughtful query mixed with ...what? I couldn't put my finger on it. A tempered heat like the process that made Dustin's blown glass vase—soft and tender, fragile, yearning to cool and strengthen. It took my breath away.

He held out his hands in a gesture of question—could he hug me? I nodded and he drew me to him, enveloping me, and said in a husky voice, "Can I see you again?"

I found myself melting into his arms, turning my head slightly to smell him. He smelled amazing. My lips grazed the stubble along his jaw. I was so tired, and he felt so strong and reassuring. Since we had moved away from the fire, I had noticed a chill in the air, but in his arms, pressed against his warm chest, I felt nothing but protected and safe.

I mumbled weakly into his neck, "Yes." I wondered absently if he could feel my thumping heart.

We stayed like that for a good two, maybe three, minutes, neither of us saying another word that might break the spell. His hands stroked my back comfortingly while I remained still and quiet.

Slowly, like we were loosely glued together, I pulled apart from him, not allowing myself to look into his eyes. I said, "It's late. I should go."

His voice was throaty and deep as he said, "Okay." And then, "Can I have your number?"

I exhaled. Oh yeah, he didn't even have my phone number! We both laughed a little, the chill in the air coming back over us. We got our phones out and typed in each other's contact information. I noticed both our hands were shaking, and not from the cold.

"Okay, I'll call you," he said.

I let my eyes flicker up to his, and to my surprise, his attention was otherwise directed with focused concentration on my lips. I sensed a struggle within him, one that I instantly absorbed and matched.

It would be wonderful to kiss this man.

Instead, though, he said, "Happy birthday, Amanda."

I whispered back, not entirely in control of my voice, "Thanks…um… thanks."

As his eyes released me, he climbed abruptly into his car and, without another word, drove away.

❧ Chapter XIV ❧

Heathport, New York
September 1996

JONATHAN GALWAY. JUNIOR YEAR OF HIGH SCHOOL. I had just turned sixteen. I was bored, so I got a job working at the local pharmacy as a cashier. Not just a cashier—*the* cashier. It was a small pharmacy, so it was just me and Doctor Singer. He was nice. The pharmacy was within walking distance of my house, so after school I would head over there and usually work from three to eight. I worked most Saturdays too, but he would close on Sunday or only open for a few hours and handle the customers himself. It was an easy job and if it wasn't busy, Doctor Singer didn't mind if I did homework behind the counter, which made my parents happy. I was actually getting better grades than I ever had before. The busier I kept with the customers or with homework, the quicker my shift went.

One Friday afternoon, Jonathan came in with his brother Garrett. They rushed through the front door, and Garrett pointed to Jonathan's hand, which was scraped up and bleeding. I pointed to the bandage aisle, and Garrett picked up a box, started opening it before they had even made it back up to the register, and were about to put the bandage on the wound when I said, "You should probably go clean that off first. There's a bathroom in the back."

Jonathan went off as Garrett stood in front of me at the counter, awkwardly looking through the candy bar and gum display. When Jonathan came back, I asked to see his hand. He held it out, and I gingerly spread the fingers open, palm side up, in order to examine the wound. The scrapes were dark and bloody with road rash, but not deep. I asked what had happened, but before he could answer, Doctor Singer came out from behind his glass enclosure and examined the wound himself. He said, "It'll hurt for a few days, but you'll be fine." He went down the aisle for a moment and came back with an antiseptic cream, squeezing a little on the bandage before adhering it to Jonathan's palm.

Jonathan winced and said, "Thanks."

Doctor Singer said with a smile, "You'll be good as new in a few days."

I started ringing them out as Doctor Singer went back to his post. Meanwhile, Garrett walked to the back and was rifling through the pop cooler. He hollered, "You want one?"

"Sure, root beer," Jonathan replied.

When I looked up from the register, I noticed Jonathan staring at me inquisitively. He said, "You're Amanda Holmes, aren't you?"

"Yes," I said with a bit of attitude, not knowing why he was asking or how he knew my name. I was trying to figure out if he looked familiar. I realized after a second that he did, but I still couldn't quite place him.

"I'm Jonathan Galway. I've seen you in school. We have English together."

"We do? Oh yeah, sorry, I remember now." I blushed.

"I'd shake your hand, but well, I'm kind of a mess right now." He held up his hand with a smirk.

I nodded, but instead of looking at his palm, I regarded his face. It was a nice face. Nice, as in perfectly symmetrical, huge green eyes, average nose, full lips, clean, straight teeth. And nice, as in friendly and kind. I tried to remember him as he would have been in school, in my English class, among the sea of faces. Then, suddenly, I did.

I said, maybe too abruptly, "Wait, do you sit in the back next to Jeremy Thomas?"

He grinned. "Yep, that's me. And you're in the front left, next to Kim Jacobs."

"Yep." We stood there smiling at each other, and just like that, I had this strange spark fly up my spine. It was a new feeling, one I had never experienced before, and I found myself reddening even more.

Then Garrett appeared with the pop and broke up whatever strange, fresh alchemy was percolating, so I finished checking them out and they turned to leave.

Garrett was out the door, but Jonathan glanced back at me and said, "Skateboarding," with a sheepish look on his face, holding up his palm again and shrugging his shoulders. He added, "I'll see you in class, okay?"

"Okay," I answered with a smile.

At class on Monday, I noticed that Jonathan was in the seat next to mine instead of Kim Jacobs. My face lit up like a carnival. So, he had been thinking about me over the weekend just as I had been thinking about him. We both said "hey" shyly. I couldn't stop looking at his green eyes—they were so bright, but also deep, like the inside of a forest being lit by the sun. Doing small talk, me asking him about his hand and him asking me about my weekend, I felt myself blush for no reason. I wondered if he noticed. I think he did because his eyes got even bigger and his smile even larger. He was reading my face like an open book.

Kim Jacobs came in and gave Jonathan a dirty look for sitting in her seat. He laughed at her, and I shrugged, so she turned and went to sit in Jonathan's spot next to Jeremy. Mrs. Smith, our English teacher, began class, and at some point while her back was to us, Jonathan handed me a note. It read: "I think you're mint. Are you seeing anyone? Do you want to go out sometime? I have cross-country practice after school today. Do you want to come watch?" After each question, it had a Yes or No open checkbox. The note was so adorable; it felt like we were in sixth grade. I was blushing again, but when I looked over at him, he wasn't self-conscious at all, just smiling happily at me. That boy had confidence!

To the first question, I said no, the second yes, the third no. Then I wrote: "I have to work at the pharmacy after school."

I slipped it back to him when Mrs. Smith wrote something on the board. As he read it, his eyebrows knitted together. He wrote something at the bottom and handed it back. It said, "Give me your number. I'll call you later tonight and we'll figure something out."

I complied and it began.

We talked on the phone for hours that night and every night that week. He was so sweet and, as a bonus, also smart and funny. He would ask me every detail of my day, wanting to know how I liked my classes, what music I listened to, what books I read, what TV shows I watched, how the pharmacy job was going, what homework I had, what I had eaten for dinner, what my brother and sister were up to. I asked him about his parents, his house, his brothers, how fast he was at cross-country, if he liked video games, if they had a computer yet or not. It was as if we were both conducting an interrogation—not leaving any stone unturned. By the end of the week, Mom had restricted my phone time to one hour a night. She was worried I was getting too attached to "this boy Jonathan," which I was. Plus, Dustin and Nikki complained that I was hogging the phone, which I also was.

At one point, around the fourth marathon phone call, I asked him shyly, "Do you really think I'm mint?" This was our Heathport High word for hot.

He said, "Better than mint! I really like your eyes. They're so dark and mysterious. I could look into them for hours…"

I replied back in astonishment, as if this was the most coincidental thing in the world, "I like your eyes too! I love the color green. It's my favorite color! Your eyes are the exact color of pond water!"

His laugh resonated over the phone as he replied, "Oh, okay, so you're telling me my eyes look like pond scum?"

"Well, you know what I mean," I said, scolding, then trying to explain, "they're so deep and green and liquidy, like the color of pond water or well, maybe lake water. A forest? Grass? Anyway, something deep and green!"

He helped me with "It's okay. I'll take it as a compliment." He laughed and added, joking, "And yours are the color of the stain on our back deck. I'm looking out the window at it right now. Dark brown like the color of tree trunks after it rains or molasses or…hmmm…manure."

"Hey!" I protested with a laugh. Such a guy…grrrr….

"Just joshing. Speaking of hay, what are you doing this weekend?"

"I wasn't speaking of hay. I was *saying* hey. Hay is for horses, and in answer to your question, nothing. Well, working on Saturday, but that's it. Why?"

"Well, as much as I love our notes in Mrs. Smith's class and our nightly calls, I'd actually like to see you in person without an audience. What time do you work?"

"Ten to three."

"The boys' soccer team is playing Saturday night. Do you want to go with me?"

"Sure. I'll have to ask my parents, but I think it'll be fine.

"Great, we can hitch a ride. Hang on…" I heard him holler to his brother Jake in the background and ask. Then he said, "We'll pick you up at six thirty."

"Great!" I instantly felt a nervous excitement in the pit of my stomach. Wow, alone time with Jonathan (well, relatively speaking—there would be hundreds of people there watching the game). I couldn't wait. Would he hold my hand? Would he kiss me? Did I want him to? What would that feel like?

Thus far, in my nearly nonexistent love life, I had only kissed three boys and had been felt up by one. One boy's kiss, my first, was during a spin-the-bottle game, and it had been disgusting—all tongue and slobber. I hadn't kissed another boy for two years after that. If all kisses were that gross, I wanted nothing to do with them. Then my second kiss hadn't been too bad—less messy—at the ninth-grade dinner dance. I only dated that boy for a few weeks. At the dance, he said he thought I was a prude because I wouldn't let him do anything else but kiss me, so he broke up with me. The third boy was a senior, and we had gone to Durand Park and fooled around in his car for about an hour. I'd let him kiss me and touch my breasts above my sweater, but after that I shoved him away. I think I realized in that instant that I wasn't attracted to him. I didn't even like his hands, which were always cold and clammy. Was I just trying to prove that I wasn't a prude? I stopped returning his calls after that and avoided running into him in school.

I began to worry that something might not work with Jonathan either. What if we were just good over the phone and teasing each other in class, but when it came to the physical side of things, all was lost? I knew I felt a spark with him, right from that first day at the pharmacy, but was that enough? My limited experience so far showed that the odds were against us. Also, I wondered if Jonathan was more experienced than me. I didn't really know the history of his dating life. I hadn't actually noticed his existence until less than a week ago, and I hadn't gotten up the nerve to ask, so I was totally in the dark. What if he knew exactly what he was doing, and I didn't? Or worse, what if he expected me to the take the lead? But then, I was getting ahead of myself...

Why was I thinking about it? I told myself to just focus on the game and seeing friends there, and not so much on Jonathan. This helped a little. After getting home from the pharmacy, I was feeling antsy, so I went for a walk down Maplewood and across several other connected streets, making a big square. It was a lovely day and would be perfect for the game that night, although they were calling for rain. It was late September, and the leaves were starting to turn and drop. I picked up a few perfectly formed maple and sugar gum leaves, twirling the stems as I walked. I would press them into books later when I got home. I liked to use the dried, flat, colorful leaves as bookmarks. Michelle was out riding her bike with one of her friends, so I stopped to chat with them for a while. Michelle knew the whole story about Jonathan, of course, and wished me luck at the game. Her parting words were, "Remember to turn your head when he kisses you so you don't bonk noses."

I went home and watched TV for a bit to relax and then got ready. I put on a blue and gold school sweatshirt and put my hair in a ponytail. I brushed and flossed my teeth, thinking I wanted my mouth to be perfectly kissable. That got my heart racing, just thinking about it. I grabbed a jacket to bring in case it rained, said goodbye to Mom and Dad (who were sitting in front of the TV eating pie), and waited out on the front porch.

Jake pulled up to the house right at six thirty. His girlfriend was in the passenger seat, and Jonathan was in the back. When I slid in beside Jonathan, he introduced me to Emily, who looked vaguely familiar. I said hi and asked what grade she was in. She said she was a senior and knew my sister, Nikki, from show choir. Apparently, they had both been altos. Jake chimed in and said he remembered Nikki too and wondered what she was up to now. I told them she was at Geneseo getting a degree in engineering. Jake mentioned that he was at R.I.T., also for engineering. As we chatted, I could feel Jonathan turn toward me, staring intently at my face. He was quiet and seemed to be hanging on my every word. It made me self-conscious, wondering if I had messed up my mascara or something. Then I finally looked directly at him, and he smiled and grabbed my hand. It was warm and dry. He brought his knee up on the seat, touching the outside of my thigh. I blushed with pleasure and smiled back.

As we arrived at the parking lot, Jonathan scooted out behind me on my side of the car, still gripping my hand. He somehow knew not to interlace our fingers, a habit all the kids were doing but that I hated. It somehow made me feel constrained. Instead, he just held it loosely, like an old couple would do. I squeezed it as we got out of the car, and he grinned. We found a good spot on the bleachers as the game started. We hollered along with the cheerleaders doing the "P-S-Y-C-H-E-D, Psyched! Psyched!" cheer. I told Jonathan I had always loved that cheer because it was a good way to remember how to spell that word and all words that started with "p-s-y-c-h" like *psychology*, *psychiatrist*, *psychoanalysis*, and *psychopath*.

He laughed, gave me a side hug, and said, "You are too funny. I think you may need a *p-s-y-c-h*…" He paused and tried to think of the rest of the word and finally he just said, "A shrink!" I laughed as I put my arm around his back.

As the sun set, the night sky was illuminated with the field lights, but then we noticed a few drops falling. A light drizzle. Miraculously, Jonathan pulled a small umbrella out of the inside pocket of his jacket. As he opened it, he leaned into me, pulling me close with his free arm around my shoulder. Then he tilted the umbrella so there was a barrier between us and Jake and Emily.

As we watched the game, our team ahead four to two, I found myself smiling in such happy contentment with the warmth of Jonathan next to me and his glowing eyes upon me. It was a new feeling, like a flower opening its petals to drink in the summer sun.

Sometime around the third quarter, before I could even think about it, Jonathan leaned in and kissed me on the lips. It was slow, soft, and lingering. It was nothing like the other kisses I had experienced. This one sent a rocket ship into orbit in my body, like liquid nitrogen. I was high. I could barely keep from smiling during the kiss because it felt so good. As we pulled away, I could tell from the look in his eyes that this was new for him too—he was feeling the explosion as well. We smiled at each other in wonder. Within a few seconds, he came in for more, pulling me closer with his arm still around my shoulder. I moved one hand to rest on his lower back and the other on his chest. This time his kiss was pressing into my lips, separating them slightly, with a gentle exploration of my tongue. I felt myself melt. After thirty seconds or so, I felt self-conscious and pulled away, thinking of his brother and all the people packed in around us. We were still in the cocoon of his umbrella, but that didn't mean curious eyes couldn't penetrate the fortress. He loosened his grip on me and looked back at the field, breathing hard.

The rest of the next hour was like a dream and also a torture to resist him. I felt myself on fire and the pull between us like the force of a thousand magnets. Eventually, we walked to the concession stand as a ruse "to get hot cider" when we really just wanted to find a place to kiss. We ducked under the bleachers and stayed there for twenty minutes, pressed against each other, our lips and bodies like one. The way he looked at me when we broke apart was even better than the kisses.

That night, after the game, in my bedroom by myself, I couldn't sleep. Visions of Jonathan's face and mouth were seared into my mind, setting my body afire again, as if a gaping cavern I hadn't known existed opened inside me and could only be filled by Jonathan. I found myself wanting to stay awake so I could relive every moment of our time together, from the car ride to the umbrella to the kiss to the bleachers to the drop-off in my driveway, when he walked me to the front door and, instead of kissing me, whispered in my ear, "Tomorrow is only a few hours away." At that moment, I stared at him, astonished—he was feeling the same as me! He was counting the seconds until we could be together again! He wanted me as much as I wanted him!

What were we to do with this powerful, compelling, all-encompassing feeling? It seemed impossible to focus on anything else. How did people accomplish anything, get through the day, put one foot in front of the other while this fever was swirling around the body and mind like a heat-seeking missile! Lying in bed that night, I couldn't imagine, couldn't see how the world kept spinning when Earth, the moon, and the sun revolved around us, around the sensation of my lips locking with Jonathan's, my arms wrapped around his neck, my stomach and chest and groin pressed and moving against his. How would tomorrow ever come when everything stopped and centered and gravitated toward this extraordinary, explosive, yearning feeling?

But then tomorrow did come. And we talked on the phone and prayed that Sunday would pass as quickly as was humanly possible so we could see each other again. We arranged to meet before class on Monday, by the big oak tree, where we could drink in that feeling again, suctioned together under the leafy canopy until the bell rang and we ran to homeroom, not caring that we were late. We kissed quickly and parted, making sure to set our next meetup.

Then came the next meetup and the next after that. Suddenly, my life became a string of "nexts" with Jonathan, and it seemed all of the "in-betweens" were a blur that didn't stick or matter much. We spent every available hour together. I went to his cross-country and track meets, he kept me company at the pharmacy, we did our homework together, listened to music together, spent hours on our respective porches talking, holding hands, laughing, playing games. We both got our driver's licenses and took day trips to the park, beach, diner. Together. Always together. We spent so much time together that my parents sat me down on more than one occasion to express their concern that I was becoming "myopic" (whatever that meant), needing to divide my time (what? why? with who?), and getting way too serious with "this boy" (his name is Jonathan!). All of this advice and warnings were like puffs of worthless air rolling off my back. As if I would ever consider *not* spending all my free time with Jonathan. That would be preposterous! Utterly ridiculous and simply unfathomable! And when we started saying "I love you," breathing into each other's mouths the words that sealed our lips more than any other, there was no turning back. I wanted to dive into an endless canyon that contained a swirling tornado of only three things: Jonathan, Amanda, and our love.

At some point, many months in, when we were at an explosive grenade-about-to-detonate juncture, I asked my mom if I could go on the pill. She flat-out refused, again warning me against the seriousness of my relationship in light of my age, my preoccupation, my immaturity, my purity. I was crestfallen, but after talking with Jonathan about it, he suggested I try again, so I did, this time with the (true!) rationale that it would end up happening one way or the other, and wouldn't it be better if I didn't get pregnant? My mom's pinched mouth and resistant face finally fell as she relinquished the last stronghold. She wondered (almost already knowing the outcome) if grounding me would have made any difference. I said simply, "I will always find a way to Jonathan. No matter what." The look on her face and the inevitable sigh of defeat—she knew it was too late. I was already gone. And there was no going back. She could only hug me and tell me to be careful, that a girl's heart and body, once given up to a boy, couldn't be returned. It was a precious gift that should be guarded from pain and harm. She wondered if I knew that and if I was protecting it. I reassured her that I was, but then I felt a chill run down my spine.

Jonathan was gentle and loving our first time, in his own bed, his parents out of town, but I found the act itself rather painful, awkward, and unrewarding. It wasn't what I expected. For him, though, it seemed perfectly natural and pleasurable. After that, we found hidden places where we could try again. Unfortunately, for me each time became more uncomfortable and unendurable instead of improving. I was too self-conscious, inexperienced, unsure of the mechanics to derive any enjoyment other than being happy for his release. As the months slipped by, it put a strain on our relationship. How could I love this boy more than life itself and yet not know how to connect with him on this level, the most intimate of relationship builders and stabilizers?

I became insecure and doubted my place with him. I was jealous of the girls he talked to in school. I was even jealous of his time with family and friends. To make matters worse, the pill made me hormonal, which heightened my emotions. I was crying and angry, sometimes for no reason. He didn't understand it. I didn't understand it. And neither of us knew how to fix it. Somehow, subconsciously (and eventually consciously), I started to believe that Jonathan would leave me for someone else. I had to ruin it before he could ruin me. I became unnaturally obsessed with him and our relationship at the expense of what we had been in the beginning as well as everything and everyone else in my life. And I was so close to it, so I couldn't see it for what it was. Jonathan tried to reassure me, told me he loved me and that I was being paranoid and ridiculous, but I turned around every word he said to make it a mockery, a falsehood, something to be challenged and proven before it could be believed.

Finally, in June, the weekend before finals, we went to the Firemen's Carnival together, holding hands and riding the rides. Sharing a cotton candy. It was a warm and balmy night, and the banks of the Erie Canal were bustling with the sounds of amusement park games, children's laughter, and screeching ride-revelers. We chatted with the other kids who were there from school. It seemed as though everyone we knew was there. When I said I was parched, he went to fetch me a lemonade, and I saw him talking to a girl in line. Out of the blue, something in me snapped. I completely lost it, pulled him out of line, and screamed at him, right there for all to see and hear. He stomped away from me, like always, never raising his voice, never engaging in my irrational fears, but I wasn't having it. I ran after him, grabbed his arm, spun him around, yelled some more, and asked if he was leaving. He exhaled, his body rigid in restrained anger, hurt, embarrassment, and said, "I might." I had intended the question to be about the carnival, but the way he looked at me froze my blood. He might leave. For good? Staring into his eyes, which were suddenly sad, tired, and spent, I cowered like a lashed dog. He stood there breathing hard, not responding in any way. I told him I was sorry and then tried to reach for him, but he backed away, just an inch or two. It was enough, though. In that moment, I saw the writing on the wall, and at the same time I felt the floor below me plummet into oblivion.

On the drive home that night, I apologized over and over, feeling my hold on him slipping away and wondering how that could be possible. It seemed completely unimaginable to me that we would ever truly contemplate being apart. We were in love! We were meant to be together! We were perfect for each other! I said these words and more, but if Jonathan heard me, he didn't react. He didn't say a thing or look at me the whole drive. When we reached my house, he walked me to the door as usual, but when I kissed him, I noticed he didn't kiss back. There was a pause, a moment of silence between us, standing there. I asked if he was coming over tomorrow, and he said no. Then he said gently, quietly, "Amanda, I don't want to go out with you anymore."

I burst into tears. In my gut, I knew it was coming, but I thought, hope against hope, that it would not. *Could* not! And yet, here it was. Surprisingly, he started to cry too. I'd never seen a boy cry before. In my foolish mind, it made me feel a little better, as if I could find a tiny door in his heart where I could force a wedge and crank it open again.

I drew in a ragged, sniffled breath and said, "Maybe—maybe for right now, we stop, but then—then we come together—again..."

He wiped his eyes, shook his head slowly, and said, more stern now, "Amanda, *no*. I can't be with you anymore. I just can't. I'm sorry."

"But why?" I sobbed, as if I didn't already know, as if every rational thought in my mind (which were few and far between at that moment) wasn't screaming that *I* had ruined it, *I* had pushed him away with my paranoia and idiocy, *I* was the reason. For his pain. For my pain. For our breakup. Instead, adding fuel to the fire, I did just about the stupidest thing possible. Tears streaming down my face, my chest heaving, I asked, "Is there another girl? Is that why?"

His sad eyes swiftly turned angry, then resolved. Without another word, he walked away, down the front porch steps, to his car, and drove off.

He didn't look back.

That was the worst summer of my life.

Until the summer after Shawn died.

ॐ Chapter XV ॐ

Brighton, New York
September 2018

I pulled into my mom's condo complex, shaking my head at the neon pink sign that read "Tiffany Commons." It was a running joke with us that Mom had somehow found the only active Florida retirement community in the Rochester area—everything was bright and cheerful, with walking paths weaving throughout the development, easy access to the grocery, cinema, doctors' offices, pools, tennis courts, gym, and the community activities building. It was like The Villages but *way* north and covered in snow for a large portion of the year. Mom loved it. And Nikki, Dustin, and I were happy that she found this place after Dad died.

Back at our house on Maplewood when we were growing up, they had both been heavily involved in the Heathport Village goings-on—part of the Rotary Club, the Lions Club, the Kiwanis. They went on couples-only cruises, played bridge, volunteered with the local ambulance service, worked in the schools. When Dad passed, he was the superintendent of the school district, well liked and well respected by everyone (even on those winter days when all the kids expected a snow day to be called, and instead Dad had to make the unwelcome decision to keep school in session—which was most of the time—this was, after all, one of the snowiest places in the country, and he couldn't call a snow day every other day, even if he wanted to). Mom was a student aide in the elementary school and helped coach the boys from the local Boy Scout troop who went on to attempt Eagle Scout ranking.

When Dad passed, Mom was destroyed by his loss and also left without a partner, a teammate, a best friend, a wingman. She stayed in the house for three years, completely grief-stricken, trying to figure out how to live without him before finally selling the house and moving to Brighton, where she slowly established a new way of living, just as active as before but now with a community of friends by her side instead of one main champion. When Shawn died, she was such a good listener and could empathize with every one of my dreaded daily musings and dire professions of fear, unhappiness, panic, confusion, and utter annihilation, always there to provide reassurances that this too would pass and eventually life would become bearable again. Some days her words were my only lifeline, the only tether to which I clung.

She opened her orange door, adorned with a large green eucalyptus wreath, before I could knock, leaning in to give me a big hug, saying first, "Happy belated birthday, sweetheart," followed by her usual, "You're all skin and bones. Would you put on some weight, *please?*"

I reminded her, for the hundredth time, "Mom, I'm fine. According to the government weight charts, I'm probably still in the overweight category, if that makes you feel any better, so will you please stop asking?"

"Okay, okay," she assented with a wave of her hand. Her short white hair was cut in a tightly cropped pixie style, and she was wearing a yellow sweater, white pants, tall wedges, and large white hoop earrings. I wondered (not for the first time) if we were related. She had always been naturally petite, feisty, energetic, outgoing, flamboyant. I had always been curvy (even now with the weight loss), taller, quieter, shy around strangers, subdued. My hair was a big wavy blond mass on my head, never quite staying in order or bending to my will. And I was more comfortable in a pair of jeans, a T-shirt, and sneakers (which is exactly what I was wearing) than in anything fancy. She said, "Come on in. You want some coffee before we leave?"

I looked at my watch. "Um, does Nikki need us to bring anything? We can pop by the grocery..."

"Nah, you know her...everything's taken care of. Come. We have a few minutes still."

"Okay, sure."

Mom poured us each a mug, and we sat down on the couch facing each other.

"How was yesterday?"

I said, "Good. You know Michelle and Kelly. They went all out. Drove me all over—Canandaigua, Charlotte, ended up at Donny's house for a bonfire. Mrs. O'Connor was there and the Abernathys—honestly, like the whole neighborhood. It was a nice surprise." I felt a little like my sixteen-year-old self when I left out the part about Jonathan. I remembered how much she had to prop me up over that summer after we broke up—I was gutted and barely able to function. Both she and Dad blamed Jonathan for my devastation, and I didn't do anything to dispel their assumptions. I was certain if I mentioned his name now, she would recoil, and probably no amount of twenty-twenty hindsight would rescind her feelings about him. He was the first boy who broke her baby's heart. Some things, even now as my thirty-eight-year-old self, were better left unsaid, despite the twinge of guilt that always followed an omission.

"Oh, that *is* nice. I didn't know Donny had it in him," she said with a laugh.

I grinned. "Well, I assume Michelle was a bug in Danielle's ear, and she took the reins after that. I doubt Donny had much choice in the matter or took part in the preparations, but he was, as always, entertaining, if nothing else." I shrugged, then felt a slight heat rise in my face as I remembered his faux pas and the ensuing silence in the group, along with Donny's apologies, and the perplexed look on Jonathan's face.

Thankfully, Mom didn't notice and instead asked if I'd received any good gifts.

I rattled off the list, and we chatted some more about the rest of the evening and then about her week, which had been filled with her book club and shopping and a volunteer job at the local pet shelter. Then it was time to go, so she grabbed her things and we drove to Nikki's, which was five miles down the road—a beautiful red brick house built in the fifties with black shutters and a large fenced-in backyard.

On the way there, Mom said thoughtfully, "You know, I really miss Maplewood. That was the best street!"

"Still is," I agreed with a smile.

"True. All you kids growing up, running around with each other, day and night. Everyone about the same age, playing outside for hours. Sometimes I wonder about these kids nowadays with their video games and computers..."

"I know. Doesn't seem quite right that they spend so much time indoors. Although last night at Donny's, the kids who were there played tag and Frisbee and hide-and-seek, just like we used to. Maybe all is not lost," I chuckled.

"I suppose," Mom conceded. "Do you remember how Dad would be on you about your shoes?"

I laughed with my head back, saying, "Holy cow, that's right! I almost forgot. I hated shoes."

"Couldn't get you to put them on. Even on Sundays. We'd force them on your feet right as we pulled into Aunt Edna's, and two minutes later I'd see you taking them off in her foyer with that scowl on your face."

"They always seemed like such an encumbrance. Plus, by the end of summer, when I had run around barefoot for months, I could walk over the hottest pavement or on jagged gravel or over the slippery stones in the creek, and it didn't faze me one bit."

"Yes, I remember." She added with a feigned frown, "Very ladylike, as I recall."

I grinned and shrugged.

After a while, she asked, "Have you heard from Sissie lately?"

"Yeah, she called me on Friday to wish me a happy birthday. I guess she was headed to Michigan with her mom on Saturday, and she didn't think she'd have time to call then, so she called me a day early."

"How'd she sound? Is she doing alright?"

"I think so. We didn't talk for very long. She was excited about seeing her cousins up at the lake."

Mom nodded, then asked curiously, "How does her mom drive?"

"Oh, she doesn't, actually. I think when they go to her parents' house up in Michigan, Gina's brother comes and gets the van, and they ride together in that."

"Must be so hard," Mom said, shaking her head.

I nodded silently. "Yeah."

"But, really, how is Sissie?"

"Um, I guess I don't really know," I answered thoughtfully. "After the bombing, we got so close…I guess because we were both so destroyed, and grieving together helped us…we both needed a shoulder to cry on. But then when she went to live with Ed and Karen, and I stayed in the house, I felt a distance growing between us again, sort of like it was when I first married Shawn and I was the third wheel in their relationship. Fast-forward two years to when I sold the house, and well…that kind of put an even bigger wedge between us. She didn't think it was fair that I should sell the family home, as if I was somehow trying to erase the memories of Shawn and Cole and our time there. I don't know…she still holds resentment toward me. I think it's misdirected, but what can I do? It probably doesn't help that Ed and Karen aren't happy with me about it either. I really believe in my heart they wanted me to keep living there, under their domain, for the rest of my life."

Mom raised an eyebrow but didn't say anything.

"I—I couldn't, though, you know," I said with finality. "I couldn't do it anymore. It was just *too* hard. Everywhere I looked, everything I touched, *everything...*"

Mom put her hand on my knee. "I know, sweetie, I know."

A quietness fell over us in the car. We pulled into Nikki's driveway, and before we could get out, Mom said, "Listen to me, Amanda." I looked at her, my thoughts sober and slightly sad. "You did what you had to do. For *you.* You know that, right? And that's okay. It's *okay.*"

I took a deep breath and nodded.

As we walked through the door, my dark thoughts were instantly buoyed by three lovely whippersnapper nieces rushing into my arms. First, the little one, Nikki's three-year-old girl, Wendy, then Dustin's girls, Yvonne and Abigail. Finally, a shy five-year-old, David, Nikki's boy, came up to me and stared with wide eyes, handed me a gift, and ran away to hide behind his mother's pant leg. I thanked him, but he was long gone, with only one eye peeking out at me suspiciously as Nikki scooted him backward with a laugh so she could pull the bacon and egg frittata out of the oven.

Abigail whispered in my ear, "Aunt Nikki made both!"

"Pancakes *and* frittata?! Whoa!"

Yvonne added, "And bacon and cut-up fruit and toast and orange juice and...um, something else, I can't remember."

Mom glanced at the table and chimed in, "Skillet potatoes." She went around to help Nikki, giving her a hug in the process, and said, "Nikki, there's enough here to feed an army." Mom scooped up David in her arms and tickled him until a cheery giggle escaped his lips. She said, "That's more like it, little tiddly widdly."

Nikki just smiled and shrugged. I gave her a hug, as well as her husband Doug, thanking them both for the spread, and then Doug handed me a stack of plates, napkins, and silverware to place around the table. The girls started bringing empty glasses, and Dustin and his wife, Jenny, each carried a pitcher of orange juice and water.

I asked Nikki, "Am I supposed to open this gift now?"

"Naw, sorry...he was so looking forward to helping you with the gifts, well, with *opening* the gifts, haha, I think he jumped the gun. You can set it over there. Come on everyone, let's eat."

Meemaw Holmes was there too. Both of my mom's parents had been gone since the nineties, as well as my dad's dad. Meemaw was my dad's mom, and even though she was eighty-eight, rather frail, and lived in a nursing home, we still tried to include her in family events. Doug must have picked her up. I went over to her, gave her a kiss on the cheek, and helped her out of the rocking chair and to the table.

As we passed around the food and dug in, everyone made small talk about the weather, which had turned even chillier overnight, making it feel as though fall was in the air. I asked the girls how school was going, and they rattled on about various subjects and what they were learning. Doug and Dustin talked about work and about some new gutter guards Doug had just installed. Mom engaged Meemaw in a dialogue about the new director at the nursing home.

At some point Nikki looked over from Wendy's high chair, where she had just placed a scattering of blueberries, and asked me how yesterday was. "You ladies paint the town red?"

I smiled. "Hardly, but we did have fun." I repeated the same breakdown of details I had given Mom earlier. I concluded with, "It was good to see everyone and catch up."

She was nodding her head throughout my speech, tending to David and Wendy at the same time, but at this last sentence, she turned to me and said with a knowing smirk, "Oh yeah, I *heard*."

Oh shit. Dustin and his big mouth.

I shook my head. "Very funny. No, nothing like that."

Nikki, not even batting an eye, asked matter-of-factly, "Why not?"

"Nikki," I started, trying to keep my voice down, "you know why not. I'm not...sure...I'm ready for that."

"Ready for what?" Mom jumped in, catching the tail end of my sentence despite my lowered voice.

My eyes big, I stared at Nikki, willing her not to spill.

She didn't even look our way, too absorbed in feeding the kids, and said nonchalantly, "Amanda dating."

"What?!" Mom said, slightly aghast.

"Nikki!" I cried, scolding.

Nikki, unfazed, added, "Yeah, dipping your foot, eh, Amanda?"

Finally, she turned to see the hole I was searing right between her eyes. She choked a little and tried to correct, "Oh! Sorry, I didn't know, I mean, I wasn't there, I mean, I just heard...and didn't think."

"No, you didn't think," I agreed definitively. I turned to Mom. "It was nothing. We ran into someone from high school yesterday. Michelle and Kelly invited him to Donny's bonfire."

"Who?"

When I froze, Nikki answered simply, "Jonathan Galway" and got up to grab Wendy's sippy cup from the kitchen. Chickenshit. I could have strangled her as she dropped the name so casually and walked away.

"Oh," Mom replied, somewhat vague in her expression, not sure she remembered the name, then slowly, as it dawned on her, she said with a thud, "Oh."

Dustin, the snitch, inserted himself, "He's really a cool guy. I talked to him for a while last night. He does some kind of job with fish. Wrote a book about it. He really knows his stuff."

Mom just nodded and said, "Huh."

He continued, "I mean, you should have seen Donny—he was in heaven, thought he was talking to a rock star or something."

Mercifully, Nikki sat back down and changed the subject. Mom threw several fleeting glances my way throughout the rest of the meal, her questioning eyes wanting answers that I was not about to share with the audience at hand.

Eventually we all finished and helped clean up. David, somehow no longer shy, grabbed my hand and pulled me into the living room where the "chair of honor" (as he called it) resided for me to sit and open my gifts. Not to be outdone, Wendy came to assist as well. Within what seemed like five minutes, all of the gifts were opened, wrapping paper and tissue scattered all over the floor, and Nikki directing the kids to help consolidate the remains in a trash bag. I sat in my special chair smiling and running my fingers over a beautiful swirly gray scarf from Mom, a plum-colored sweater from Doug and Nikki, and a book from Meemaw. The kids supplied handmade cards with their original artwork, which I loved and which would be dutifully magnetized to the fridge when I got home.

Our stomachs full, as well as my heart, we retired to the backyard, where we watched the kids climb around the jungle gym and scream in delighted squeals while asking to go "higher and higher" on the swing set. It was a deliciously lovely, sweet afternoon. A few hours later, Meemaw was getting tired, so I offered to drop her off on the way to Mom's. We packed up and headed out, thanking everyone for the wonderful birthday celebration. After we dropped off Meemaw, I turned to Mom, analyzing her face and wondering if she was going to bring up Jonathan. Yes, there it was, her curious look, expectant and waiting.

A few minutes from her house, she said softly, "Um…hey…I noticed you took off your ring."

I held my hand away from the steering wheel and regarded the unadorned finger. I nodded and said, "Yeah, it seemed to be about the right time." Then I murmured, "I think."

"Well, I'm glad. And this boy, I mean, this *man*, Jonathan…you—you *enjoyed* seeing him…?" Her brow was furrowed, and she seemed to be waiting for me to reply before she breathed.

I said, "It was a *surprise* to see him, after all this time, and it kind of threw me. I mean, emotionally, it was confusing, as was to be expected, I suppose, but yes, overall, I did enjoy his company. He seems like a really nice guy."

Mom finally breathed and asked, "But—but sweetie, wasn't he the boy who hurt you so badly? I would think you'd never want to see him again."

I said, "Sure, if you'd asked me last week, I probably would have agreed with you. And not just because of our history, but because we've both lived a *lifetime* in these past twenty years. Or at least I know I have," I frowned a moment before adding, "but then when I saw him…I don't know, Mom, it was like the first time we met at Doc Singer's. All the old butterflies were still there." As I said this, I glanced over, somewhat abashedly, and shook my head. "Believe me, I couldn't have been more astonished myself. But it was almost like some type of witchery or magic, I swear." I laughed a little, thinking about it in this way. "It's hard to describe, but he sort of melted me… just with his eyes." I paused as I approached her driveway and put the car in park. "I know, I know it sounds crazy, and I probably shouldn't think of him in this way—for so many reasons right now—but I couldn't help it. It had a force of its own, in a way."

Mom took all this in without a word, and I began to wonder if she was going to warn me like she did back then, and like she had with other boys along the way as well—ones where she could see the writing on the wall before I could. I didn't know how I would react to that. Would I take her advice and give it up before it began? That would certainly be the wiser, more practical choice.

I waited.

Finally, she regarded me closely and said, "You know, sweetie, you *have* lived a lifetime, especially in these past couple of years, but on the other hand, you're still quite young, with your whole life ahead of you." She said this softly with an encouraging smile, and I could see what she meant. She didn't want me to waste my life pining over a high school heartbreak *or* the life I left behind in Indiana. Neither would serve me well or lead to a future worthy of pursuing, especially in light of my recent birthday wish. She placed her hand on my cheek, and I leaned into it.

Her next words surprised me. "You were both kids then, you and Jonathan. I would suspect you both have regrets. And truly, who holds someone accountable for something they did at sixteen? Let bygones be bygones and see where this magic, as you call it, takes you. It's not so common, this thing you sense with him. I know what I speak of—I had it with your father—and I wouldn't brush it off before you've had a chance to explore it. I know you don't want to let go of Shawn, and I don't want that for you either, but maybe…just maybe you can keep him close while also leaving yourself open to something new."

I said skeptically, "Maybe." I felt my throat swell. If only it was that easy! Would Jonathan, or Jon, as I had to keep reminding myself, want to see me as the woman I was today, with a world of baggage and mixed thoughts, feelings, and ideas about love and relationships? And what about me? I had so many questions. About him. About us. About our past. About the twenty years in between. What baggage did he have, if any?

I was scared. And a part of me, if only a tiny part right now, was also (dare I think it?) almost *hopeful*. That scared me more than anything.

❧ CHAPTER XVI ❧

Heathport, New York
October 2018

FOR THE NEXT FEW WEEKS, I had trouble sleeping, my mind still agitated over my birthday weekend. I would sit out on the front porch in the wicker rocking chair, wrapped in a cardigan, sipping hot cider or tea under the stars. Some nights I'd hear Mr. Hawthorne let his dog out or someone over at the Abernathys' bring a trash bag out to the garbage cans, but otherwise, the nights were soft and still.

One Sunday in early October, I knew I had to work in the morning and that I should go to bed, but instead I sat on the porch, looking up at the stars and chatting with Shawn for a bit (not out loud, but in my mind). I told him I missed him. Like when we walked into a crowded room together or church or a family gathering, and he always took the lead. I was the one who voiced my opinions, but he was the one who set the tone. He relished coming into a room and making an impression. And he was great at working through conflict—whether in a political conversation or a fight between the kids. He calmed the raging storms, worked through complexities like a master nego-tiator. He was always an adult, never backing down from a challenge, and I told him how much I appreciated and missed that. It was the little things as much as the big ones. I told him with a laugh how I still struggled with the stupidest things—like when I hit the wrong button on the remote control the other day and couldn't figure out how to get the TV working again and eventually gave up. *See,* I told him, *if you were here, you would have laughed at my cursing and inept fumbling and simply taken the evil contraption from my hands and boom, within twenty seconds it would have been fixed, with an indul-gent smile at me.* Now, I would have to wait a few days until I calmed down enough and had the patience to tackle it again. Now, I had to think before I took something on (big or small) because this time, there was no backup plan, no one else to turn to in the event that something didn't work or if help was needed. Now, I was alone.

I began to think about that word: *Alone. Al-one. All. One.* That's what I was right now. All me. No one else. Just me. Just one. When I was younger, I never thought, even for one minute, that at the age of thirty-eight, I would be alone. It seemed like a bad dream, and of course, it was. Yes, I had friends. *Amazing* friends and family. And yes, I was truly blessed because when push came to shove, they were there for me, they had my back. But somehow that wasn't the same as being *with* someone. Being tied to someone, one other person, a partner, a soulmate.

And I couldn't help but wonder: Was I meant to be alone? Did Shawn want me to be alone? Did *I* want to be alone?

At that exact moment, my phone chirped. Jon!

A text: "Hi." After I verified that my heart was still in my chest, I looked at the time: ten forty-two. Before I could reply, another text: "Sorry it's so late." Then a moment after that: "Is this a bad time? Are you asleep?"

I laughed. Clearly, if I had been asleep, I wouldn't be *now*. I wrote: "Hi. It's okay, I'm awake. How are you?"

"Good. Can I call you? Easier than typing."

Before I replied, I got up from the rocking chair and went into the house, closing and locking the door behind me. I brought my empty mug to the sink and rinsed it out, took my cardigan off and hung it in the closet, lay down on the couch with a throw pillow and a blanket, and wrote back: "Yes."

As the phone rang, I felt my heart ascend from my chest into my throat. "Hey," I said.

"Hey," he echoed, a smile in his voice. "Took you long enough to reply. I was beginning to wonder, well, if you were debating...about it."

"Talking?" I asked, thinking about it myself. I *had* taken my time...was it subconscious? Fear, nerves, anxiety? Then I said, "Nah, I'm glad you called. I'm sorry. I wasn't sleeping, but I admit I *was* in another world, out on the porch, watching the stars." His text certainly brought me back down to earth in a flash. And suddenly, I began to think about that tether I used to talk about with Beverly.

"Oh," he said slowly, not understanding, but acknowledging. "It *is* a clear, starry night out, isn't it?" He paused tentatively. "Um, hey," he cleared his throat, "sorry it's taken me so long to call. I…I was kind of…unsure about the whole thing." He laughed nervously, which seemed so unlike him that it made me laugh a little too. *He* was unsure!

I gave him the understatement of the year: "It's okay—I know how you feel."

A puff of air came through the phone, an exhale of relief. He said, more upbeat now, "Okay, good. You're not mad?"

"What? No, don't be silly."

He stammered a bit as he attempted to explain, "Not…not about you, I wasn't unsure—about…*that*, just the whole *thing*, you know? Not…not that it's a *thing*…yet, or even will be, but still—"

"Jon," I cut in, "listen, it's fine. It's okay. Let's just talk. No worries." Oh my God, I couldn't believe *I* was having to talk *him* off the ledge! This is *not* how I expected our first conversation to go! For whatever reason, it made me smile.

Again with the exhale. After a pause, he asked tentatively, "So, how have you been? How was the rest of your birthday weekend?"

"Oh good…thanks for asking. We had a brunch at Nikki's on Sunday, so I got lots of time with the nieces and nephew. And saw my Meemaw, so that was great. Makes me appreciate being home again. When I lived in Indiana, I would fly home once or twice a year and try to fit ten visits into a four- or five-day period, effectively shortchanging everyone. I always felt rushed and slightly guilty. Anyway, now when I'm with people, I can take my time and let the visits happen more organically. Better quality time. It's been wonderful."

"So, tell me again, how long did you live in Indiana, and when did you move home? I'm sorry, um, is it weird that I'm having to ask you the most basic questions?"

"Of course not," I replied, thinking, this is like finding your favorite board game from childhood again and trying to remember how to play it. Oh, and the way the board game works has completely changed in the meantime. And all of the players are different. And the rules. And the game itself. I said, "Well, I moved to Indiana right after Syracuse, for a job, back in 2001, and I just moved home in May."

"Wow, that's a long time to be away."

"Yes, it was," I said softly, with sixteen years of thoughts and memories popping into my mind.

He paused, maybe wanting to launch into more questions, but sensing my reticence to expound, he instead said, "Well, I'd love to hear more, but I didn't want to keep you up, I just wanted to see if you were, um, available... to get together sometime. Maybe Friday, if that would work?"

I paused for the merest instant because my mind was still caught up in a swirl about those sixteen years, but then I pulled myself out of it and said, "Sure, Friday would be great. Do you have something in mind?"

"Yes, actually. If you're open to it, I wondered if you wouldn't mind me coming over to cook for you."

"Cook? For me? Here?" I asked, taken aback.

He clarified, "Yes, well, you see, I'd have you over here, but I've been retiling the backsplash in my kitchen, and it's a bit of a mess right now. And I was thinking that if we went out to a restaurant or bar, it would be loud and hard to hear, and anyway, I just figured—um, that I'd invite myself over to your place instead. Do you mind?"

"No, it's not that—of course, you're totally welcome, it's just...well, I'm happy to do the cooking, or we could get takeout. I'd hate to have you feel obligated to cook." My mind was racing—he cooked! All those years with Shawn, and never once had he cooked for me. Actually, he barely lifted a finger to do anything domestic around the house. Sure, he was spectacular with yard work and fixing things, not to mention very mechanical with the cars and power tools, and with building things, but when it came to the traditional "woman's work" (what we used to jokingly call it as I smacked him on the butt with a dish towel), I knew to stay in my lane and let him stay in his.

"It's no problem at all," he said easily, causing my heart to speed up because I believed him. "So, is six o'clock okay?"

Still stunned and processing, I said, "Uh-huh, sure, yes, okay."

"Okay, see you then."

"Okay, bye," I said and hung up, staring at the phone.

Wow! Something new and different. And yet somehow also old and unknown.

My next thought: Holy crap! He's coming *here*. My house. My space. My safe haven. My sanctuary.

I hit the panic button. It was five days away, and yet my mind went something like this: Was my house clean? Would he like what I had done with it? What if he hated my paint colors or my furniture or my renovations? Did I have enough pots and pans? Would he like cooking in my kitchen? When was the last time I had cleaned the bathrooms? Had I hung all the pictures back up on the walls in the bedrooms after painting? What was I going to wear? Should I pull my hair back or leave it down? What if I didn't like what he cooked? Would I eat it anyway? Would I look funny chewing in front of him? What if it was wings or sloppy joes? How would I keep from being messy? What if I got food stuck in my teeth and didn't realize it? Would he tell me or just look away?

Then I stared around the living room as I lay on the couch. There were two built-in bookshelves completely covered with framed photographs of my life in Indiana. The entire Morgan family posing in front of our favorite restaurant, a selfie of Shawn and me at Spring Mill State Park, Shawn and Cole biking the Hilly Hundred, Sissie and her cousins posing together in front of the roller coaster at Holiday World, everyone standing behind us on the steps of the church at our wedding, and countless others. I lay there feeling the heat rise in my face.

There were other photos too—of my family, with Mom, Dad, Nikki, Dustin, the nieces and nephew, and the funny ones of Michelle, Kelly, and me from high school and many from the years since them. But still. What would Jon think? What would *I* think if I walked into his house and it was filled with photos of him with his arms around another woman? Photographic evidence of an entire life lived apart? I stood up from the couch and pulled half the frames down, quickly shoving them onto the top shelf of the coat closet. I would figure out where they belonged more permanently later. After that was done and the shelves were rearranged, I spent the next hour cleaning, organizing, vacuuming, scrubbing. Finally, a little after midnight, exhausted, I brushed my teeth, changed into my pajamas, and went to bed.

The next morning, I woke up, still tired, with a raging headache and raging guilt, and pulled all the frames out of the closet and put them back up again, crying my eyes out the whole time. I repeated the process about seven times that week, finally settling on leaving the less intimate ones up and hiding the rest away.

That week at work was a blur. I knew I was in trouble on Friday at two o'clock when one of the software engineers asked me why I added a critical chain resource buffer onto the project timeline with an end date three months *in the past*. Oops. I may have been distracted.

I went back to my cube and texted Michelle and Kelly: "Red alert. Jonathan, who wants to be called Jon, btw, is coming over to my house tonight to cook for me!"

Kelly wrote back first: "He is?! How are you feeling about it?"

Then Michelle wrote: "OMG! 'Bout time. But why didn't you tell us? Jon not Jonathan? Hmmm, alrighty then."

Me: "I didn't want you to make me nervous (more than I already am). Plus, I didn't want you to read too much into it. I'm feeling very anxious and confused about it."

Kelly: "Just be yourself. No expectations. What time?"

Michelle: "What's he making?"

Me: "Six. I have no idea. I was too shocked to ask."

Michelle: "Well, whatever it is, send him over to my place when you're done. The boys are always ravenous beasts after soccer."

Me: "Lol."

Michelle: "I'm serious. It would be on his way home…"

Me: "Michelle!"

Michelle: "Fine."

Kelly: "It's okay to feel confused, but try to have a good time too. We love you."

Me: "Thanks, love you guys too."

Michelle: "Worst comes to worst, drink. That always helps me."

Me: "Right. Thanks. I'll text you tomorrow and let you know how it goes."

Kelly: "Okay, good luck, semester."

Michelle: "Love ya, semester."

Me: "Xoxo semesters."

When I got home from work, I quickly changed into a pair of black jeans and a cream-colored sweater. I left my hair down, fixing a few stray curls, and touched up my makeup. Down in the kitchen, I sat on a barstool and scrolled through my phone, trying to keep my mind occupied in an attempt to calm my overwrought nerves.

When the doorbell rang, I jumped. Then, I took a long, deep breath before walking as casually as I could through the foyer and up to the doorknob, which somehow seemed as big as a basketball. I turned it slowly and there he was. Jonathan Galway! His green eyes flashing on me, a studied, admiring look, seemingly taking me in from head to toe. I blushed a little, then motioned him through the threshold. He was holding two grocery bags stuffed with supplies, wearing a dark green Henley, blue jeans, and hiking boots, which he promptly took off (even though I told him it was fine). I took the bags from his hands and brought them into the kitchen, and he followed a few seconds later, all the while looking around and commenting, "Wow, the place looks great."

"Thanks. I spent the first month or two painting and updating everything. It's still not perfect, but it's getting there."

He went right to the bags and began unpacking them, saying, "I hear ya. I've been redoing the kitchen in my house for—well, for a long time. I'm doing all the work myself, so that could be part of the problem." He laughed.

"Well, that's very brave," I said with a smile. "I did all the painting, but I've hired everything else out."

"At some point, I may resort to that. I was hoping to have my backsplash done a few weeks ago, but with the book coming out and these speaking tours I've been doing on the weekends, I haven't had much free time."

"Doesn't sound like it. I have a great tile guy if you need a recommendation. He did the work in both bathrooms."

"Thanks…I may take you up on that."

The first thing out of the bags was a bottle of wine. He asked, "Do you have a corkscrew?"

"Sure," I said, grabbing one out of the drawer. As I handed it to him, his thumb grazed my hand, and an electric current ran up my arm. He noticed it too, looking directly at me and then quickly away, focusing on the bottle. I stepped back from him, not realizing until that moment how close we had been in my U-shaped kitchen, inadvertently in each other's space as a natural state of being, the years washed away, our habit of being comfortable with each other still potently familiar.

I turned, somewhat abruptly, to pull two glasses out of the cupboard, and as he poured wine into them, I noticed his hands were shaking. We clinked and said, "Cheers." I swallowed, hard, staring into his warm, inviting eyes.

A long second later, he was inquiring where the pots and pans were, and I was lifting them out and arranging them on the counter and stove for him. He turned the oven on, pushed up the sleeves of his shirt (oh, those toned, tanned forearms!), and started filling the large pot with water from the faucet, asking politely, "You're not allergic to anything or on a low-carb diet, are you?"

"Nope. I love everything. Especially carbs," I said with a chuckle.

"Good. Me too," he said, grinning over at me.

"Please, can I help you…in some way?" I asked, looking around helplessly.

"Nope. I've got this. Feel free to take your glass of wine and have a nice long swing on the front porch. I'll let you know if I need anything."

"But—but—I'm happy to—"

"Shoo," he cut me off.

I laughed. "Did you just 'shoo' me?"

"Yes, I did. Would 'get out' have been better?" he asked with a wicked grin.

I scoffed with an even bigger grin and answered, "Um, no. But really. You don't want me to stick around, show you where everything is?"

"I'm sure I can figure it out. Go ahead…I'll be out in a minute—just let me get things started in here first."

"Okay," I finally assented, wondering if I had landed on another planet.

A moment later, there I was swinging away, watching the sun descend in the sky as Mrs. O'Connor raked leaves, Mrs. Roberts snubbed out a cigarette with one hand, holding a *Reader's Digest* in her other, and Mr. Abernathy pulled his Buick into the driveway, grabbing a briefcase out of the back seat and heading into his house. And I was thinking to myself with wonder, there is a man in my kitchen cooking dinner for me. And I'm out here, drinking a glass of wine, watching the world go by. I shook my head, trying to remove the look of utter astonishment from my face ten minutes later when Jon stepped outside and sat down next to me on the swing, our thighs nearly touching.

I said with a smile, "I could get used to this."

He laughed and clinked my glass.

The swing swayed and we drank our wine in silence, enjoying the green vista of trees that lined the street and the light breeze against our backs. Finally, Jon broke the silence. "You know, it's strange being back here. Feels so familiar, like old times."

I gulped. This was the first acknowledgment he had made, if only loosely, of our shared history. I didn't want to presume anything, though, so I said, "Yeah, I've been feeling that way for months. It was especially strong when I first moved in. It seemed like every place I looked held a memory from my childhood. Not just in the house either—I mean the whole neighborhood, in town, at the grocery store, driving by our old school and the soccer field, not to mention the ice cream parlor, that big old horse barn down by the canal, the oak trees on Merchant we used to climb. You name it. Just about anything could set me off. And still does."

"I bet," he said, looking around the yard and up the porch steps before he came back to my face. "We used to sit out here and swing all the time. I remember Dustin would come out after a while and interrupt us. He was so annoying back then, wasn't he?" He chuckled as I stared, my breathing stopped. "I sometimes wondered if your dad put him up to it." While he said this, my mind was screaming, of course he did! We spent nearly every minute on this swing either making out or fiddling around with each other as best we could (above the clothes) without getting caught.

Oddly, he didn't seem to notice my distress, nor was he openly bothered by the acknowledgment of our shared failed relationship. He asked casually, "Did you have a nice day at work today? Explain to me again what it is you do?"

Hmm, okay, shifting gears. "I'm an IT project manager. I'm sort of like the person who keeps track of everyone's work throughout the lifecycle of a project. Everything you might do to launch or change a software program, from development to testing to production to maintenance to support to termination."

He looked impressed. "Wow, that sounds like a very important job. You do all of that on a computer?"

"Yep, with help from the developers and engineers. I also use a software tool that helps me build out the plan, but essentially I'm in charge of keeping everyone on target with their tasks, capacity, workload, and timing."

"How did you learn to do this? I mean, were you always this technical? I guess I don't remember that about you in high school." He looked a little sheepish, and I thought (but was too afraid to say), and I don't remember you liking nature or fish either! Then I thought, we're both so different (and the same!) from our high school selves, aren't we? It was all so confusing.

Instead, I said, "Well, when I was at Syracuse, I was a computer science major, and I took a class on this new programming language—it was the big coding tool back then for business systems. Anyway, I was really good at it, and during the class I coded a fairly concrete functioning application for booking travel, and during my senior year when companies came to SU for recruiting, I described what I had done, and before I knew it, I was being courted by several big firms. So, I took the best offer, in Indianapolis, and moved. Later, as I worked my way up the ladder, I became well versed in a whole bunch of other coding languages as well as the project management software and process." I noticed suddenly that he wasn't necessarily understanding a word I said, but his eyes were studying me as if a light had been turned on in a dark room. I found myself reddening and quickly stopped talking.

I blinked a few times as he suddenly frowned, abruptly stood up, and said, "I have to go check the food. I'll be right back."

I stared after him. So strange. I began to think back on my words, and I couldn't think of anything that would have offended him. Was I talking too much about myself? I would ask him a few questions when he returned, draw him out a bit…maybe that would change the vibe.

When he came back, he was all smiles, and I was more perplexed than ever. I asked quickly as he sat down, "What about you? How was your day? Do you like your job? You said you have a lab, was it, in Naples? Where exactly is it located? Right in town?"

He smiled, an indulgent smile as if he had read my mind. He began, "Yes, right in town, actually. It's a converted house. I share it with my partner, Brian. We both use it for our studies, but when we're not there, we spend most of our time working in the field."

"When you say 'in the field', what do you mean? Sorry, it's hard for me to picture, having spent my entire career inside of a ten-by-ten-foot cube."

He raised his eyebrows and then frowned. "God, that would be awful," he voiced.

I shrugged and didn't deny it, but said, "Meh, I burn easily, in the sun." I grinned.

He grinned back. "Yeah, thank goodness I don't. We spend a lot of time on boats. Fishing, taking samples, analyzing the water quality, stuff like that. I hate to bore you."

"You're not boring me," I said simply.

He went on for a while, talking about the joy he found in his job and in writing his book, and I found myself memorizing his face, the curve of his jaw when he smiled, the flicker of light in his green eyes when he mentioned something he was passionate about, the fullness of his lips, which made me remember back to that first kiss under the umbrella. I wondered if it would feel the same to kiss him now. I felt a blush creep up my neck, and I took a long sip of my wine to cover it.

He went to check on the food again, and I sat back and let the buzz from the wine spin through my veins, making me feel loose and fuzzy. My nerves were gone, replaced with something new—a heady, cozy warmth, as if I were floating on a sea of summer clouds. Yes, of course there was still a hint of that guilty storm brewing behind the breezy clouds, but I pushed it back, not letting it invade this new, quiet, careful, fresh space.

When he returned, I asked him, "Do you still run?" trying to concentrate on his answer as my eyes drifted back to his mouth.

"Yes. Well, not as much as I'd like, and I'm certainly not as good as I was in high school, but yes, I try to get a run in at least a couple of times a week." He paused for a minute, then held out a piece of paper and asked, "Speaking of running, what is this?" The paper was a list I had created and stuck to the fridge, alongside magnetized photos of friends and family. I was kicking myself internally—of course, after all that cleaning and clearing out, I had forgotten to hide the list! It had one item marked off so far, but he was pointing to the one that said: "Run a marathon."

I grabbed the list from his hand and said dismissively, "Oh that. Well, I like to make lists." I stared down at it with a shrug, not wanting to look him in the eye. Finally, when he didn't reply, I looked up and said, "This particular list is things I'd like to accomplish in the next few months or year." I hesitated, not knowing how much I should tell him and how he would react. There were things on the list that I didn't want to explain. I decided to focus on this one. "Yeah, I'd really like to run a marathon, maybe this coming spring."

"Have you started training yet?" he asked.

"No, not yet. I looked online last week, and there's a *half*-marathon in January. The Winter Warrior at Rochester Tech Park. I thought I'd see if I could do that before I tried a full."

"Have you done any others?"

"Yeah, back in Indy, there's this huge half called the Mini, and I did that one a few years ago. I didn't really train, though, so I ended up walking most of it. I'd like to see if I could run one, and then join a program or something to train for a full. Have you done any?"

"No, never. I've always wanted to, though…maybe we could train together for this one in January."

"Maybe…," I said with a small smile, wondering about his open and enthusiastic face. He was talking about something that was *three months* away! My stomach did a somersault. Then I had a sudden thought about that offhand comment he made the other night. I said, "Speaking of running…at the bonfire, you mentioned you saw me running up Forestry Drive when I was going to Syracuse. You never really explained why you didn't say hello."

He looked away, saying, "Oh that. Yeah, um, listen, before we get into that, can we go inside and have dinner? I think the food should be just about ready."

"Okay, sure," I said, getting up with him and walking back inside. I folded the list up and shoved it into my pocket. He seemed suddenly more serious, so I tried to lighten the mood. "What are we having anyway?" I asked, sitting down at the dining room table, where he had set two place settings, turned the dimmer down on the lights, and lit two candles (how did he know where to find my crystal candlesticks hidden in the back of my sideboard?).

He brought the food in from the kitchen. "Caesar salad. Penne con Gamberi. Freshly grated parmesan. French loaf with olive oil and seasoning. Buon appetito!"

"Wow! I feel like I've slipped through a wormhole and landed in Florence. This smells and looks amazing. Thank you so much."

He smiled and sat down beside me, doling out the salad and pasta. "Well, I hope it's a delicious wormhole. Dig in."

"Please. Pasta is one of my all-time favorites. Where did the sauce come from?"

"My garden. Well, partially…it's store-bought, but I've doctored it up with some of my own tomatoes."

I took a bite and let my face express my appreciation. It was spectacular!

We ate silently for a few minutes, and then I prompted, "So, Syracuse…?"

"Yes, Syracuse," he said with an exhale and a thoughtful glance.

The air between us was suddenly thick. As he sat there, staring into my eyes, the candlelight dancing in his forest-colored irises, I started to sink into the aura of him, feeling as if we were on a precipice together, about to go over the edge with our hands clasped together. It was an unnerving feeling—restrained, ponderous, expansive, invigorating. But mostly, it was terrifying.

❧ Chapter XVII ❧

Heathport, New York
October 2018

He began, "Yeah, so that day, I had just come from my apartment, and I was late for class, but when I saw you there, running up that huge hill, looking so…so athletic and, well, beautiful, I was staggered. I—I couldn't get up the nerve to stop you, to talk to you, to say a word, so I just turned and walked away." When he said the word *beautiful*, I felt my knees throb under the table. He was staring down at a piece of bread in his hand. He went on, "I hadn't seen you in so long, and all I could remember was that horrid last time we'd talked, under that beaming spotlight of a front porch light." He looked toward the front door even now, his face reflecting the tortured memory. "And I was simply—too ashamed to stop you. I'm sorry. I was a coward."

It was then that he regarded my face with something akin to regret and bashfulness, like a child thinking of a past infraction, not sure if he would be understood or forgiven.

I felt every hair on the back of my neck stand up.

He felt *he* was in the wrong!

I put my fork down and placed my hand on his arm. He looked at it, not sure what to make of it, then back at my face, expectant, uncertain. I said, "Jon. Listen to me. You were not a coward. You were brave. You broke up with me because it was the *right* thing to do." I sighed, then smirked a little as I added, "Oh, don't get me wrong, I hated you and wished you dead with the force of a thousand angry hornets." He laughed and squeezed my hand. I went on, "But then, later, much later…," I paused to figure out how to formulate my tangled thoughts into words, "I realized it was what needed to happen…to make me grow up, to make me become the woman I was meant to be. You see, I was so young—we were *both* so young. We were having these strong, complex, impassioned, *powerful* feelings toward each other, but the timing was off. I don't know about you, but in hindsight I think I wasn't ready for the seriousness of our relationship. I didn't know how to handle the sheer *magnitude* of it. I became twisted, tortured, tempted by my baser instincts, my petty insecurities and jealousies, my immaturity. *I* was the coward. I was the one who took what was good between us and ruined it. And I'm sorry about that. I'm truly sorry. Will you forgive me?" I held my breath.

Oh, the slowly creeping ray of sunshine in his eyes at that moment!

He said flatly, "There's nothing to forgive."

I exhaled, feeling his thumb rubbing my hand like a shim cracking open a door—only a sliver, but what light came through that sliver! A door that had been closed, sealed, padlocked, barred, forgotten, and erased. I nodded to him—in acknowledgment of his words and the intent behind them, for both of us. A profound second or two passed, the momentous quality of the matter reverberating into our pores. Then we quietly went back to eating, sipping our wine and regarding each other with a newfound curiosity and attentiveness, now no longer loaded with misgivings or misunderstanding. It was a relief. And frightening.

We talked about trivial things for the rest of the meal—how he had come to write a book about fish, what his brothers and parents were up to, the friends he still saw from our high school, other hobbies and interests we shared (surprisingly, there were quite a few, causing us both to beam in unexpected delight). We were merely scratching the surface with each other, being overly cautious and patient, somehow knowing not to dig too deep too soon.

But then at one point he asked, "So, you're not on Facebook? I mean, I don't recall seeing your profile come up on my list of friend requests."

I flinched a little and said, "No. I was a while ago, but I deleted everything." Then I paused and said quietly, "It wasn't—healthy—for me anymore." Jon looked at me, puzzled. How could I explain to him about the constant inquiries from Shawn's long-lost friends, wondering where he was, why his profile was stuck forever on May 29, 2016. Or the people, well-intentioned or not, who wanted to provide sympathy to me for my husband's death over social media. It always seemed superficial and unnatural to me. I wanted to honor him in my real life, in my real heart, and for me personally, this did not include the fake "reality" world that lived inside a phone. Plus, how could I move on when, every time I tried to heal, there was more fodder for pain right there at my fingertips. Beverly gave me sound advice, which I prompted and gratefully took: delete my account.

Jon, studying me and filling in the blanks himself, said casually, "Yes, it can be rather addictive. That's smart. What you did."

I gave a curt nod, not correcting his assumption, and said, "Thanks."

We finished eating, and he suggested we clean up and head back out to the porch. He brought the plates and bowls in from the dining room as I did the dishes. Once everything was straightened up, he poured the last of the wine into our glasses and we stepped outside. The night had turned dark, and there was a brisk chill in the air.

I said, "Whoa, chilly. I'm gonna grab my fleece. I'll be right back."

"Good idea. I have a jacket in the car…see you in a sec."

We set our glasses down with a laugh and went our different directions.

When I came back out, zipping my fleece over my thin sweater, I noticed he had grabbed the candles and placed them on the porch table alongside our wine glasses. There was a circular glow radiating up onto the wainscoted wood ceiling above, and I was glad I hadn't turned on the "beaming spotlight" of a front porch light. I hugged my arms around myself, sitting beside Jon on the swing, feeling the lovely crisp fall surroundings suffused with a delicious tingle of electricity between us. Unlike earlier, this time he put his arm loosely around the back of the swing, only an inch above my shoulder. I felt the magnetic pull of him entice my body toward that encircling cocoon, but I held back and stayed ensconced in my own wrapped bubble.

I began to wonder about him, on a physical level. He was so warm and inviting. And so close. What would it be like to kiss him again? Would it be like that first kiss at the soccer game in the cave of the umbrella's cover? Would it set my heart and body on fire, as it did back then? Did I want that? Right here? Right now? OMG, it was so scary! And tempting.

We listened to the sound of the swing and the crickets chirping, each of us lost in our own thoughts.

Finally, he asked, "Why do you make lists?"

"Lists?" This caught me off guard. But then I realized what he meant. He was probing, continuing our earlier conversation. "Oh, you mean the one from the fridge? Well," I started hesitantly, not sure how much to reveal or how to reveal it, but then screwing up my courage, I forged ahead, "when I was back in Indiana, I had started to see…um, a grief counselor." As these words escaped my lips, I couldn't look at him to gauge his reaction. I simply stared straight ahead at the inky night sky beyond the candle's glow. "She was really helpful, and at some point she suggested I try to organize my thoughts and feelings into lists, I guess in order to better process what I was going through. In a way, this mundane, innocuous thing…it made me have something future-minded, something to keep me grounded, to provide structure. Anyway, as you can see, I'm still using these lists to help me."

The "e-ew, e-ew, e-ew" cadence of the swing seemed to engulf the ensuing silence as the minutes ticked by, my breathing coming in low, shallow puffs.

His voice was soft and gentle, like a whisper in the night, as he asked, "Amanda, why were you seeing a grief counselor?"

His arm that had been hovering an inch above my shoulder was now on it, forcing me to look up. It was like a dam letting loose. My breath came out with a sob. Then in a rush, like a cannon being launched, I said quickly, shakily, with anguish, "My husband—Shawn. He was at the Indy 500—the bombing there—he and his son, they were both killed." I felt the tears coming now, running down my face. I was stumbling over my words. "It was—two years ago May and—and it's one of the reasons—I decided to—to move home." It had been so long since I'd been forced to say these words out loud. After moving back to New York a few months, I'd been shielded from the constant reminders, the condolences, the news reports, the FBI visits, the shared mourning, the family and friends whose only thought was of me as a widow and all that entailed. Here, everyone seemed to already know my story and, more importantly, knew enough not to ask me about it. When we did talk about it, it was at my prompting and my pace, which worked out perfectly, allowing me to process the words and feelings in my own way. Now, I was fumbling, stuttering, my explanation and emotional reaction rusty, jagged, raw.

Jon stayed very still, his hand still loosely resting on my shoulder as I buried my face in my hands. After a few minutes of silence, he said, "Amanda, I'm sorry. I didn't know. I am *so* sorry."

I was cognizant of the fact that his sorry encompassed his sympathy for me but was probably also mixed with regret because he hadn't known and because he was just now putting two and two together from the bonfire, not to mention his feelings for me muddying the scope and tenor of sympathy. I was feeling all of this as well and, unsure how to proceed, stayed tucked within myself, tears still streaming down my face.

He murmured, "Were you there…?"

I shook my head.

He mumbled, more to himself, "Wow."

We didn't say anything for a while.

He rubbed my back lightly with his hand. It felt comforting, and we let the rhythm of the swing provide the background for the minutes that ticked with the tender drum of the night.

When the tears finally stopped and I was able to sit up, compose myself, and wipe them from my eyes and cheeks, he said again how sorry he was and then said more softly, "You don't have to talk about it if you don't want to…"

I sniffed with a grim smile and said, "No, no, it's okay. I'm okay now. Really. Feel free to ask me anything. Although it hurts, I realize it's only natural that you would be…curious. People usually are…"

"You sure? We could wait, for another day…?"

"Actually," I said with resolve, "I'd rather get it all out in the open, sooner rather than later. If that's okay with you."

"Yes, of course."

I set my jaw, trying to figure out what to say and how to say it. I began simply, "We were married just shy of eleven years. He was a *good* man. When I met him, he had two children from a prior marriage, a son and a daughter, so I was thrown into a ready-made family, which had its difficulties as well as rewards. We—we had our routine, you know, a way we lived our life where, even when we struggled, we came back to each other and made it work. No matter what."

I glanced over at him and he nodded, a hint of something behind his eyes, a hidden story or pain being triggered or unearthed by my recounting. He kept listening mutely, so I pressed on.

"His son, Cole, he was seventeen when it happened. He was such a sweet boy. It seems like a special kind of torment when a kid that young, his whole life ahead of him, dies unexpectedly, without warning or preparation—not that there is any valid preparation for such a thing! And the way it occurred— a random bombing by forces or people who didn't know Shawn or Cole, didn't know or even think about any of the people who died that day or were injured. I don't think I'll ever understand it. It's so *unfair*. You always think these things happen to someone else, and then when they happen to you, you can't believe it. You think it's some type of nightmare that you'll wake up from, but then…you never do. And—and Sissie, Shawn's daughter, is now without a father *or* a brother. Nothing can ever change that for her, ever."

"Is she…?"

"Back in Indiana? Yes," I answered, "with Shawn's parents. Her mom is there as well."

He nodded, still with that indecipherable look on his face. "And did they ever figure out who caused the—"

"No, it's still officially under investigation, according to the FBI."

"Amanda…"

"It's okay. You don't have to say anything. I know, it's hard for people…to know what to say." I smiled a little and added, "I know it may not seem like it, but I'm actually doing a lot better now. My counselor back in Indy helped me with the grief and also with the forward-thinking part, the lists and action steps…everything, really. She was the one who first suggested I think about moving, and then, coincidentally, I heard about this house being for sale, so I, well, I bought it and the rest just followed."

"What's this counselor's name?" he asked unexpectedly. I looked at him, baffled. I opened my mouth to answer, but he stopped me, chuckling and squeezing me to him gently, saying, "I'd like to thank her because, well, because you're *here*. Now. With me."

I smiled and leaned gratefully into his warm, broad chest. "Beverly. Her name is Beverly."

After a long while, as our hearts kept beat with the swing's pendulum movements, he finally broke the silence with, "I hate to say it, but I should be leaving. It's getting late, and I have a long drive."

I cleared my throat, sitting up a little, and said, "Sure, I understand." Despite asking for Beverly's name, I knew he had a lot to think about, and maybe that meant I wouldn't hear from him for a while, or ever, but regardless, I felt better, maybe even a little stronger, for having told him everything.

He lifted off the swing, pulling me up with him. He gave me a hug, and I murmured into his neck, "Thank you for tonight."

He squeezed me harder and said, "You don't have to say thank-you. It was great to see you again."

"For me too," I whispered. I drank in the smell of him for a moment, then thinking I'd end the night on a lighter note, I drew back with a grin, "So, do you still think I'm mint?"

He laughed out loud, craning his neck back in a big belly laugh. Then he held me away from him, a hand on each shoulder, shrinking his height down so we were eye to eye, and said with feigned seriousness, "The mintiest."

I slapped his arm, saying, "Great, now I sound like toothpaste."

We both laughed and drifted down to his car, arm in arm. He gave me one last hug, and I said, "Thank you again for cooking. It was amazing. I'd offer you the leftovers, but I'm going to hoard them for myself and stretch them out for at least two more meals. You are quite the Renaissance man."

He shrugged and smiled down at me, not quite wanting to let go. Finally, he said with a husky voice, "My pleasure." I wondered if he was talking about the food.

As he drove away, I walked back up the porch steps and into the house, a feeling of elation filling some of the cracks that were part and parcel of who I had been since Shawn died. I wasn't quite sure if the feeling was as real and palpable as it seemed in this moment, but I was hoping it would stay for a while and try to tender a tiny welcome, an invitation, a promise, even a hope-filled thimble. It felt *so good*.

As I got ready for bed, I thought to myself, don't get ahead of yourself, Amanda—there are still so many mysteries, so many unanswered questions, including that perplexing treasure trove waiting to be extracted from behind his eyes. There *is* a story there. I'm not sure what it is or how (or if) it relates to him or to me or to us, but I know that full steam ahead isn't the way to uncover it.

And that isn't the way to heal my fractured heart either.

Chapter XVIII

Heathport, New York
October 2018

A week later, I was out for drinks with Michelle and Kelly at Lock 32, our favorite brewery in Pittsford. We had just sat down with our beers when Michelle spit out, "Okay, I can't wait any longer. What happened with Jonathan—er—Jon?"

"Um, well, let's see," I began, as a tease, "he made me the best pasta and shrimp dish—even cooked the sauce with tomatoes from his own garden. We sipped on wine, ate an amazing Caesar salad with these really crisp croutons, and then pulled apart this amazing crusty bread, which we dipped in olive oil and these super-flavorful seasonings—"

Michelle cut me off with a snort. "Amanda! You're torturing us! What happened?"

"Nothing happened, you ninny," I answered flatly, tilting my head at her.

"Nothing?" Kelly said, disappointed.

"Well, not *nothing*. I mean, we talked about our breakup. That was interesting! And I told him about Shawn. We ate, we sat on the front porch swing, we hugged. And then he left. Haven't heard from him since."

"He hasn't called?" Michelle asked, appalled.

"Nope," I said with a shrug. "I didn't think he would."

Kelly looked at me with concern. "I'm sorry. But—but why? Did anything go wrong?"

I waved offhandedly. "No—we had a great time together, but honestly, guys, did you really think he'd dive right in after I told him everything? Who would?"

Michelle pressed, "He seemed so into you, though. I didn't think he'd be put off by that."

"Well, who knows? For all I know, he might not want the baggage or drama, or he might already be dating someone else. I didn't ask him very much about his personal life because he seemed reluctant to share."

Kelly asked, "Are you, I mean, are you okay? Hurt?"

"Nah, I'm fine. As I said earlier, I wasn't even sure I was ready to date anyway. Maybe he sensed that."

Michelle asked, "Maybe…so, weren't there *any* sparks?"

I closed my eyes for a second, thinking about his arms around me, and I knew I couldn't lie. I said, "Well, of course there were sparks. Those sensations, that magnetism, doesn't just go away, apparently not even after twenty years. But that doesn't mean we have to act on it."

"Right," Michelle said hesitantly, not buying it.

"Well," Kelly reasoned, "just because he hasn't called doesn't necessarily mean he isn't interested. Maybe he's just taking it slow or thinking it through first. We really don't know what the cause is, so let's not jump to conclusions."

"Right, exactly," Michelle agreed, this time with conviction. Then she asked, "So, what about the breakup?"

"Oh, just that he was sorry for the way it all went down too, just like me. Water under the bridge. We were young. We didn't know how to deal with the heavy, serious nature of our relationship. We both said and did foolish things, and the timing was off, so we broke up, and that ultimately was the best thing for us. We each went on to live another life, and that was okay."

Michelle said, "Speaking of that, so you didn't get any info about him, about where *he's* been these past twenty years?"

"Not much, other than work stuff and his house in Canandaigua." I paused, thinking back to our conversation. He had definitely steered clear of anything personal, which was a bit disconcerting and also somehow intriguing. I wanted to know more, and now I wondered if I would ever find out. I continued, "It's so strange because there were a few points during our conversation, especially when I was talking about Shawn, that he seemed to be thinking about something in his own life."

"Like what?" Kelly asked.

"I'm not sure. I just sensed that he could somehow relate to my relationship with Shawn. I still don't exactly understand how or if I was maybe just overinterpreting his face, but regardless, I sensed that he had his own story to tell and wasn't ready to reveal it."

"Hmpf, well, not yet anyway," Michelle said.

Kelly and I nodded, sipping our beers.

I began to think about all the forms of baggage in this world and how some were heavier than others, but we all had it, in every shape and size.

The next couple of weeks at work were busy. It was a nice distraction. I kept my head down and worked extra hours, wondering absently if my supervisor thought I was crazy being a salaried employee with no overtime pay, yet staying late when not asked or expected to. I'm sure he wondered about me—why I had taken a job like this when I was overqualified and all of my work experience on my resume was from Indiana. It probably didn't help that I had been less than friendly and forthcoming about my personal life with my coworkers. I tried to stay in my cube as much as possible, eating my lunch in there while reading a book and rarely taking breaks. At the beginning of meetings, when everyone was chatting, I stayed quiet, and if anyone asked how my weekend was or what I had been up to the night before, I always answered with a standard (vague) "good" or "not much." I sometimes wondered what they thought about me. It was a small office, maybe only forty employees, and they often went out for drinks after work, but I always politely refused. I don't know why the idea of sharing my history with them scared me so much. They were nice enough people. A great mix of technical, geeky types and outgoing, friendly sales reps and software engineers. I just couldn't bring myself to say the words as to why I was no longer living in Indiana, why I had taken a job that paid half of what I used to make, why I never socialized with them, why I wore a wedding ring but never talked about my husband.

Sometimes I wondered if I should go find a better job, one that was more like my previous position and utilized all of my skills, knowledge, and experience. But for some reason I stayed, coasting a bit. Ever since I was sixteen, I'd been working, working, working. Even during college, I'd worked thirty hours a week, in the dining hall and as a cashier at the university bookstore, on top of the fifteen or eighteen credit hours of classes I was taking. Summers in between semesters, I waitressed at the local diner during the day and bartended at night. And I was recruited to work for the insurance company back in Indy right out of college, my first day less than two weeks after the graduation ceremony—just enough time to find an apartment, pack up my entire life, and drive six hundred miles to a new city where I knew no one. I remembered feeling envious of kids whose parents paid for a "summer off" trip after college, allowing them to backpack their way around Europe, traveling on trains and staying in hostels. Now that I had the means to do something like that if I really wanted to, I felt too old and alone and scared to even consider it.

I'd never had a reason or the financial stability to take off work for that long. Shawn and I made a pretty good income together. And neither of us were big spenders, always buying used cars instead of new, staying in the same house, and limiting our vacations. But with the house maintenance and the kids' activities, child custody, and everything else life brings, we were never flush with cash either. We had a substantial mortgage left on the house, and it took some time for me to pay off my student loans. Then as friends from church and coworkers at the office became pregnant and decided to give up their careers for motherhood or take six months or a year of maternity leave, I wondered if that would finally be the reason I would get a break from work for a while. But of course, that never happened. Whenever I heard about a coworker getting pregnant, I would go home and cry myself to sleep. Not only were they getting to experience the wonders of being pregnant and the joys of a newborn baby, but they also didn't have to even *think* about work for months or ever again. I knew I was being petty and ungrateful, but I found it all so unfair.

Even after the bombing, I went back to work right away, thinking it would keep my mind off everything. Which it did, for the most part. If only I could work twenty-four seven and not have to face the nights and weekends alone with my thoughts and fears and feelings. When I made the decision to leave, I packed up and sold my house in Carmel, Indiana, before I told anyone at work. Then I handed in my notice on a Friday and moved the following day. I knew it was wrong of me to sneak away like that, not give two weeks' notice, not say goodbye to those kind, good people. People who had been my friends, who had been in the trenches with me on many a project, problem, and crisis over the sixteen years I'd been with the company, and in the trenches when Shawn died too, but I knew I couldn't handle a long, lingering goodbye. There had already been too many goodbyes for me, and I couldn't stomach any more. So, I took the cowardly way out and didn't look back.

And now I was being just as heartless to my new coworkers. I knew it wasn't right—that I should be more engaged and engaging, a more outgoing, talkative, friendly, nice kind of colleague. But it was so much easier to focus inward, to look at my computer screen instead of into their curious, inviting, interested eyes.

The ironic thing was that I didn't even have to work now if I didn't want to. Shawn's life insurance, the Indy 500 Fund, selling the house, and liquidating most of our assets allowed me to pay cash for my Maplewood house, and I still had plenty in the bank—in fact, I was basically set for life. One of my original discussions with Beverly was about my fear of not having financial security, and I'd had no clue that it would end up like this. Oddly, instead of assuaging my fears and anxiety, in some ways having financial security scared me half to death. No one in my sphere, no one I had ever met before, was *set* for life. What did these people do with their time? How did they fill their hours if not with work? How did they find purpose? If money wasn't the main motivator for working and building a fulfilling career, what was? Ever since I could remember, I had worked to eat, to live, to pay the bills. Now I had to turn all of that on its head and think about my job as something I could potentially do if money wasn't a factor. I found myself astonished to think that I could embody that saying people always quoted but rarely acted on: Work to live, not live to work.

I was pondering all of this on a Tuesday night as I made dinner for myself at home alone. I fashioned a boat out of aluminum foil with a piece of salmon in the middle, drizzled with olive oil and sprinkled with lemon pepper seasoning, and placed it on the grill. Then I set jasmine rice to boil on the stovetop alongside a bag of frozen vegetables cooking in the wok. I sat down on the couch to wait right as Michelle called.

She spent the first few minutes talking about her boys and then asked (coincidentally) about the thing I had just been thinking about. "How's your job going lately?"

"Meh," I said unenthusiastically.

"Really? I thought you liked it there. Didn't you just tell us a few weeks ago that you were going to ride it out?"

"Yeah, I know. It's so weird because when I told Jon about it, I suddenly realized how foreign it probably sounded to him, me spending all my days inside, typing on a computer for eight hours in a little cube. On the one hand, he was impressed, but on the other, he clearly thought it sounded...I don't know...constrictive or *re*strictive or something. These are my words, not his."

"But is that how you feel too?" Michelle asked. "I've always thought you were like this super-supreme IT goddess and your job was so amazing that when people asked me what you did, I always just said, 'I have no idea.'"

I laughed. "Well, thanks for that. I still love the technical stuff, but it just feels like I should be doing something else with my time or maybe using my technical skills for something more meaningful. When I listened to the passion in Jon's voice as he described his job, it was so inspiring. I mean, I never thought about fish for even two seconds before he started rattling off the amount of research and hands-on work and analysis required for his job, and he loves being able to make this impact (however small) on the planet for future generations. I began to think about how awesome it would be to feel that way about my job and my career." I sighed and added, "Don't get me wrong—I'm very grateful to have a job at all and that everyone there is nice. Not to mention, it doesn't keep me awake at night from the stress, doesn't cause me any heartburn, but I've been wondering lately if I should start looking into something more...I don't know, *fulfilling*."

"Sure, why not? What type of stuff do you like?"

"That's the thing...I'm not sure. I've always been so focused on computer-related work because, well, that's what I got my degree in and what I've always been so good at, not to mention that it comes easily to me, and from what I can tell, compared to others, I'm quick at it—you know, easily adaptable to the ever-changing aspect of technology and what it entails to stay on top of it. But, when I stop and think about the work I do, I don't see how it's really making a contribution to the world, not long-term anyway. Do you ever wonder about stuff like that?"

"God, no," Michelle answered with a laugh. "You know me—I'm a mom, it's what I do and who I am. My biggest contribution to this life is those two boys, Lord help me and Lord help us all. I probably put all my eggs in the wrong basket, but there it is. Just kidding—I love those boys and I'm proud of them, but in the grand scheme of things, I live to feed, shuttle, launder, cook, clean, teach, gripe, moan, scrape, scurry, rinse, and repeat. That's my career, so to speak."

"And you're great at it."

"Thanks," she said. "Well, speaking of the Tasmanian devils, I need to scoot. I've got burgers on the grill and mac 'n' cheese in the Crock Pot. Let's plan to get together this weekend, okay?"

"Sure, I'll text."

"You better. Later, gator."

"Bye."

I finished cooking and sat down at the dining room table to eat with my computer off to the side, typing into Google: "Career advice for a midlife crisis."

The results ranged from career tests to appointments with online psychologists to college applications to vacation planning. I decided to complete one of the free career quizzes. There were a lot of yes/no and multiple-choice questions, not to mention a lot of distracting banner ads for job search websites. Luckily, I could eat with one hand and answer the questions with the other. A few short minutes later, and my future life and happiness could be decided with the click of a mouse! I smiled to myself, thinking this has to be just about the stupidest thing I'd ever done. But oh well. It was a start.

In the end, when I pressed the "Your Future Career Awaits" button, my life goals appeared as: math teacher, nurse, artist, police officer.

WHAT? I literally laughed out loud, letting my voice reverberate off the dining room walls that maybe should have been padded. I thought, that's what I get for trying to figure out my life with a computer. I ought to know better. Aren't computers what got me into this conundrum in the first place? Ugh.

The only one that sounded remotely appealing was the math teacher. Not really the "math" part so much as the "teacher" part. Would I be a good teacher? I had never thought about it before. What did teachers do anyway? Molded the minds of future generations? Or expanded their minds anyway. That sounded kind of cool. But what would I teach? Certainly not math. That sounded about as exciting as dirt. Maybe I should instead think about what I *could* teach. Something with technology. Maybe a programming class. Or project management. Or straight computer science.

But the thought of standing up in front of a room full of people frightened me to death. I had never been a great public speaker, even when I was the head of the IT department back in Indy. I dreaded those big town hall meetings where I had to get up and speak for forty-five minutes about the state of our work using a laser pointer directed at the large-screen PowerPoint presentation. My only saving grace was the fact that those big assembly rooms had fairly dim lighting so the slides would project to best advantage, and that allowed me to slip into the background so *I* could project to best advantage. Otherwise, my red cheeks always gave me away. It was bad enough that my voice would wobble until I hit a rhythm about halfway through. Then there was always the dreaded question-and-answer segment at the end where I never knew what people would ask and I would have to pull something out of my head, not always the most eloquent response nor probably the most accurate. Afterward, I would keep myself up at night going back through every word, spinning, ruminating, obsessing over every flawed expression, every missed opportunity to clarify or impart the words in a better, more concise way. In reality, these presentations probably landed with ninety-nine percent accuracy, positivity, and completeness, as evidenced by my year-after-year excellent performance reviews, promotions, and bonuses, but in my warped mind I couldn't see past my inability to conquer this frustrating thing: public speaking.

At any rate, as I did the dishes and put the rest of the food away, I thought, in the grand scheme of things, none of that mattered now. I wasn't in Indiana anymore. And all those promotions and great reviews amounted to nothing in the end. Here I was sitting in a house by myself, trying to figure out what to do with my life and thinking how ridiculous it was that I couldn't be a teacher because I hated to get up in front of people and talk. Well, so I wouldn't be a teacher.

But then what?

I watched a little TV and went to bed, thinking as I fell asleep that I'm a thirty-eight-year-old/eighteen-year-old. I have to go back to that feeling of being a senior in high school and not knowing what college to go to and what major to pick and what to do with my life. In the next thought, I said to myself, or you can just take the easy way out and stick with what you have: a good job that uses some of your skills, comes easily to you, pays fairly well, and that most people would be happy to have. Maybe the answer right now was settling for simple gratitude and ease. Maybe…

On Wednesday morning, I was in the middle of a meeting in a small conference room with four people, and one of the analysts was explaining how the throughput converter tool wasn't working properly when I heard my phone chirp. I glanced down. It was a text from Jon! Oddly, I felt myself blushing. Here I was at work, where not a single person knew anything about my personal life, let alone about Jon, and yet his text still made me blush. Lord help me, that man had power over me! I turned the phone facedown and tried to disappear into the wall.

When the meeting was over, I went back to the sanctity of my cube and texted back: "Hello. How are you?"

"Good. How's it going?"

"Good. Hump day. Working. Fun, fun."

"Oh, sorry to interrupt. I just wondered if you'd be open to getting together next week sometime."

My heart sped up. So, he hadn't disappeared into the ether after all! "Sure, that would be great. What did you have in mind?"

"What time do you usually get going in the morning?"

"I'm an early riser. Ready and out the door by 6:30 a.m. You?"

"Me too. Great. I thought I could bring you with me on a research outing."

"Fish?"

"Yep. Maybe grab some breakfast beforehand?"

"Sounds great."

"Okay, Patty's Place is right on Main Street in Canandaigua. 7:30?"

"That works."

"Say, Thursday?"

"I'll have to ask for a day off work, but it shouldn't be a problem."

"Sorry, I didn't think of that. It's okay?"

"Of course. No worries. What do I wear? Do I need to bring anything?"

"Something to hike in and some warm layers. It might be cold. That's about it. I'll pack some sandwiches for us."

"No, please let me do that. I'd like to contribute."

"Okay, perfect, something that can easily fit in a backpack."

"Got it."

"Looking forward to seeing you again."

"Me too."

"And marking something off your list."

My mind went blank for a minute. Huh? Then it hit me—the list from my fridge! God, he must have memorized it! I was quickly trying to remember… OH! There were several rather private (Shawn-related) items on that list, so he certainly didn't mean those. Then, for a split second, I thought about the marathon thing again. That didn't make sense—why would I need hiking gear? Not to mention that had nothing to do with fish. Finally, it came to me: I had written something about hiking—where…?

Before I had finished my thought, he texted, "It won't be Watkins Glen, but another place almost as beautiful."

"Oh! Wonderful," I typed, relief washing over me that he hadn't touched on the Shawn items.

"See you Thursday then."

"Okay, bye."

Chapter XIX

Canandaigua, New York
November 2018

Sleep eluded me the Wednesday night before our outing. I'd done a preemptive strike and asked for both Thursday and Friday off work, thinking I could take Friday to sleep and recuperate from the date. Of course, thinking the word *recuperate* implied that I would be knocked out by the experience, and maybe I would. I honestly wasn't sure. God, I hoped not, but it had been more years than I could count since I'd been on a formal date. If, in fact, this was a date. Maybe I would only need Friday to process. Wouldn't there be so much to think about, so much to absorb and analyze and rehash? I was already on overdrive just anticipating every possible thing that could go wrong—or right—on the date.

First, I thought about the logistics. We would both drive to Patty's Place, but then who would drive after that? Would he jump in my car or I in his? I didn't even know where we were going. Were there roads leading there, or was it off the beaten path? If he came in my car, would I be nervous trying to drive and talk at the same time? What about all that kinetic energy that always seemed to be swirling around us—would it be heightened in that small space, regardless of who drove? I assumed we were going hiking, and I was looking forward to that, but I also assumed we were going fishing, and I didn't know anything about that. What if he wanted me to fish with him? How would I know what to do, how to act, what was expected of me? Would I look like a fool? Even with the hiking, I was a bit nervous. Although I used to hike and camp quite a bit in my twenties, it had been years since I'd done either one extensively. I was hardly a rugged outdoorswoman, even though I longed for that and aspired to it (thus, the item on the list). Would he find me horribly slow, inept, clumsy? What if I slipped on a rock and fell? Would he laugh? Help me up? Would *I* laugh, cry, die of mortification?

Second, I began to wonder what we would talk about. Would he ask me more about Shawn? Would that be awkward? What about his life? I needed to find out about the past twenty years. He hadn't mentioned anything about his prior dating life. Had he been single, married, divorced, widowed? Did he have kids? Was he really living in that house on West Lake Road by himself and, if so, for how long? Were any of these personal topics off-limits? What about his job—how had he become an ichthyologist? Was that the word? How did he get into that field? And how did he come to write a book about it? There was so much I wanted to know, and I didn't know if he would think I was prying. Would he even want to reveal anything to me? I had put so much of my life out there for him to consider. Would he be hesitant to do the same?

Third, because we had been so close and intimate in our youth, I felt this overwhelming comfort and ease with him, but then I remembered I needed to be careful with that. Of course, it was only right that I told him about Shawn our first night, but I also felt a bit uneasy about the fact that I'd made myself vulnerable and an open book so soon, crying on his shoulder. Did he find that weird? Did that scare him away? Is that why it took him a few weeks to reach out again? I would completely understand if he had contemplated running for the hills when he heard about what I had been through.

Finally, my thoughts raced through the scariest option: What if everything went well? Like *really* well. What if we got along perfectly? What if I loved every minute of my time with him? What if I felt feelings for him that I hadn't felt since Shawn? What if I felt feelings for him that I hadn't felt *for* Shawn? What would I do? What would he do? How would I handle that?

Of course, I spent the week before the date running through many of these worries with Michelle and Kelly (over the phone) and even a little bit with Mom (in person, at lunch on Saturday), but no amount of speculation could predict the future, so they continued to tell me to take it as it came, relax, be myself, and enjoy it, no matter what happened.

The night before the date, at three fifteen in the morning, I gave up on sleep and got up. I went downstairs, got a glass of water, plopped down on the couch, and scanned the TV. *The Tonight Show Starring Jimmy Fallon.* No, not in the mood right now. *Halt and Catch Fire.* No, too intense and techie for this early in the morning. *The Maltese Falcon.* No, too dark. *Pride and Prejudice*, the BBC version with Jennifer Ehle as Elizabeth Bennett. Yes, absolutely—one of my favorites.

By the time episode two ended, I was relaxed and feeling confident about the day, although still both tired and wired. I showered and got ready, digging through my closet for the required clothes. Luckily, I quickly found my hiking boots and thick socks. Then I pulled on insulated yoga pants, a long-sleeve kelly green T-shirt, a purple fleece, and a quilted down vest. I put an extra shirt and a pair of socks in my backpack, along with gloves and a hat. I threw together our lunches and headed out the door. On the drive there, I turned the music up, singing along to keep my nerves at bay.

When I arrived and walked in the door of Patty's Place, he was already there at a table, sipping coffee. He smiled and everything inside me melted. I sat down and smiled back. The waitress came over, and I ordered coffee. We sat for a minute, staring at each other with our smiles, not speaking. It was so odd but somehow not out of the ordinary for us. We slipped right into that comfort zone. So hard to define, yet palpable. I finally looked down at the menu. After a minute, he asked if I knew what I wanted, and I said yes.

A moment later, the waitress came with my coffee and we ordered. I noted that he called her by her first name, Janet, and she called him Jon, so I guess he was a regular. As she walked away, she gave me a sidelong glance, with genuine curiosity, so I stared back at her and then at Jon with a slight frown.

He whispered across the table, "Janet's not used to seeing me in here with a…woman. Or anyone, for that matter. I think I'm giving her palpitations." He grinned and I smiled back. Janet was about seventy years old and looked as though she had seen just about everything, so I supposed it was a monumental occurrence that I had set her to wondering.

"Well, my weather app says it's going to be fifty-six and sunny," I began, figuring the weather was a universally neutral topic for an icebreaker.

"Yeah, can't ask for anything better this time of year. And it'll be perfect for the fish."

"So, where exactly are we headed today anyway?"

"A gorge out near Hi Tor. Have you been, off 245?"

I shook my head. "No, I don't think so. I mean, well, maybe. Is that near Naples?"

"A few miles away."

"And what will we do there?" I asked.

"We'll hike up it. I have to take a few samples and catch a few fish."

"Can we see your lab? Didn't you say it was in Naples?"

"Sure—I'd love to show it to you. Besides, if I collect samples, I'll need to drop them off."

She wondered, "Are you allowed to be out and about like this in the middle of a workday?"

He laughed. "Amanda, this *is* my workday. What we're doing today is what I do most days. The only difference is that today, it'll be a much more interesting trek."

He smiled shyly, and I blushed a little, taking a sip of my coffee.

Our food arrived, and we turned our attention to local gossip. I asked, "Did you hear that rumor about Thendara?"

"About Tim McGraw and Faith Hill buying it? Yeah, I think it was just that, though—a rumor."

"Too bad. Not that they didn't buy, but the part about it closing. We used to go there all the time as kids. It was such a perfect location for a restaurant, overlooking the lake and all, but I guess it was just too hard to keep it going when they were only busy for three or four months a year. At least the people who own it now kept the original house and boathouse."

He agreed, "Yeah, I think they renovated it but kept the original charm. Seems like there are so many houses being torn down and rebuilt on the lake now. I kind of miss the old days when there were only small, unique lake cottages. I mean, there are still a bunch of those, but seems like every day a new mansion goes up. I guess I miss some of the historic places."

"Me too. Do you remember my grandparents had a cottage out on Granger Point? It's still in the family, but we don't go there much anymore. Aunt Edna's kids use it during the summer, and I met them out there once in August, but otherwise it sits empty much of the time."

He nodded. "Yeah, I remember that place. Built with cobblestones, right? I think you took me there a few times back in high school. I loved the bonfire pit. I remember it was surrounded by geodes, right?"

"Yep, that's the place. It's amazing that you remember the geodes. Maybe you and I can check it out sometime. I believe the key's still hidden in the flowerpot in the shed."

"That would be great. I bet I could catch some great fish off that dock."

I laughed, thinking, of course he was thinking about the fish. "Probably."

We munched on our food quietly for a bit and then talked about some of the other local restaurants, places, and people we knew.

After we finished, Janet came and took our plates and refilled our coffee. We sipped in silence until I began softly, a little scared, "Jon, do you mind if we talk about something more…serious?"

He looked up with surprise, followed by, "Sure, yeah, okay."

I put my fork down and gulped. "I know, well, that you're probably wondering about me, after what I told you a few weeks ago. And I must admit that I'm kind of…struggling with some conflicting feelings." I was starting to breathe hard, the coffee and nerves kicking in. "I wanted to be up front with you. I don't know…what to feel or how to act. I'm a bit of a wreck." I laughed self-consciously and he shook his head, a furrow forming between his eyebrows, but I continued, not wanting my momentum or resolve to be lost. "It's been great…reconnecting with you, and I can't wait to spend the day with you, but I also have these other feelings that are more difficult to process…including guilt and confusion." I paused and left it at that, thinking I simply can't say Shawn's name in front of him because it's so wrapped up in my sadness and I don't want to bring that up today, but then I also don't want to set the wrong tone or expectations. I finally added, "I guess what I'm trying to say is that I want to be here with you today, but I hope you understand that this is new, uncharted territory for me and it might take me a while to…adjust."

He regarded my face with such unabashed care, concern, and understanding that it took my breath away. He waited a full minute, during which my heart never stopped pounding like a drum in my chest. Then, ever so softly, ever so calmly, ever so gently, he took my hand and turned it palm side up, saying tenderly, "You know, one thing you don't know about me is that I'm a palm reader."

I could not have been more flabbergasted if he had told me he was a unicorn. I inhaled, staring at his face incredulously, feeling the heat of his fingers.

He smiled for a moment—a soft, genuine smile—then lowered his head over my hand, serious. "Let's see here," he murmured, peeking up at me from under his brows, "I see…a long life…robust, healthy, full," he said, pointing to the two horizontal lines toward the top of my palm. "This top line is your heart line—it's a little jagged and frayed around the edges, but still long and deep. Now this line, the one below it, this is your head line, your intellect and work life—steady, smooth, successful. Then we see your life line," he traced the line leading down perpendicular from the horizon lines with his finger, and I felt his fingertip in the heat of my cheeks. "Strong, straight, solid. But wait, what is this other line? Ahhh, uh-huh, I see, this is your fate line. It has a large break in the middle." I gasped. He was right—it did! I held my breath, feeling a tightening in my throat. He looked up from my palm at that moment, his eyes radiating a shiny, penetrating glow as he said, "But look: a new line forms and picks up where the other broke off."

I stared at the broken line in astonishment, noticing it did start up again, trailing down longer than the first, almost all the way to the base of my wrist. As I looked from my palm to his face, he was still serious, all traces of the earlier smile gone, his eyes slightly narrowed, studying my reaction. I looked back steadily with a mixture of wonder and fear.

Without another word, he opened the palm of his free hand in front of me and said, "Amanda, look—I have the same broken line."

He did! My eyes widened and I felt my heart lurch. There it was, clear as day—the perpendicular curved line shooting toward his wrist, severed in the middle just as mine was.

A severed fate line! Slashed straight through. Amputated with the force of an ax. What was, gone. Only to be taken up again with what was to come.

Chapter XX

Canandaigua, New York
November 2018

Janet brought our check, and I pulled my hand away, blinking several times. Neither of us looked at her as we said thanks, but instead locked eyes, trying to read a lifetime into that stare. I noticed that the glow that had been flickering in his irises just a moment ago was suddenly dimmed. A shadow had passed over his face, like an eclipse of the sun. It made me grieve for him, even not yet knowing why. And it made me strangely mad. Who or what would dare cause there to be a shadow over that strong, noble, confident, sweet face?

We paid the bill and drove in his car toward the lake, both of us quiet with our own thoughts. I looked out the window at the nearly barren trees and rolling farm fields zooming by. The sun was just starting to shine in the morning sky, reflected off the harvested corn and wheat stubble. I concentrated on the houses we passed—the old green-shuttered white wooden cottages and the cobblestoned, wraparound front porch Victorians. Then the huge, modern, wall-of-glass assortment. The deep history of the lake somehow always stayed the same and, conversely, seemed to change every year. I guess that was the way of the world.

I broke the silence with, "So, is your house near here?"

He flinched for a second, then said, "Oh, thank God you spoke. I was beginning to think you were going to ask me to take you back." He gave me a wary smile.

"What? Why?" I asked, puzzled.

"Well, I don't know…what we talked about back there. I wondered if I scared you off."

I gave him a reassuring glance. "No, of course not. I *would* like to hear more about you and your life, whenever you're willing to share. But whatever happened in your past, and in my past, has made us who we are today and has led us to this place, right?"

"Right," he agreed readily, giving me a grateful smile. He answered my earlier question, "So, my house is on the other side of the lake, West Lake Road, fairly close to town. We can drive by it on the way back this afternoon. It's just a small 1940s bungalow, but it has a good-sized backyard, and obviously, the lake access is nice."

I nodded and smiled.

He went on in a different vein, clearing his throat and glancing over at me, "I want you to know that whatever we decide we're doing here, you and I, with this, with us," he stared, and I nodded, catching his drift, "let's just take it slow. Better yet, let's just take it at *your* pace, and I'll try not to get ahead of myself." He grinned. "I want you to feel...safe and ready, for whatever will come. I think that would be best for me too."

I nodded again, in mute agreement. I tried not to show the relief that washed over me, thinking he would interpret it as a rebuff, which wasn't the case. I was just scared and unsure, and the reprieve he was offering gave me breathing room to process and explore my feelings.

We drove for miles along the country roads and then through a little town with a pretty white church, finally turning a few miles later onto a road that was lined with a forested mountain to the right and a valley filled with the remains of grapevines and wildflowers to the left. It was breathtaking.

I said, "Back in Indiana, and I imagine everywhere else, they think New York is just New York City. You know—dirty, loud, crowded, fast-paced. They don't realize *this* is here." I pointed at the spectacular vista. "This is the *real* New York."

He agreed, "I know—we're so lucky, right in our backyard."

After a mile or so, he pulled over onto a gravel shoulder and put the car in park. There was no indication that this was a legitimate place to park—no signs, no trailheads, no placards. All I could see was the field on one side of us and the sloped forest on the other.

I asked, "This is it?"

"Yep, come on. You'll see." He smiled conspiratorially.

As we stepped out of the car, I pulled my hat and gloves out of my backpack, put them on, and zipped up my jacket. Then I put the backpack on, looking at Jon, who was grabbing all kinds of gear, fishing poles, and packs out of the hatch, strapping most of it to his back. We started on our way, trekking through the forest on a path that appeared out of nowhere, clearly a secret that only the locals knew about. He smiled at me, in his element, and I felt grateful that he wanted to share his world with me.

"God, what a beautiful morning!" he said radiantly. It made me laugh because it was cold, our feet crunching on the frosted undergrowth, the sun not yet reaching down into the forest. He added, "It's a bit of a hike to get where we're going, and you'll be surprised how quickly you heat up. You'll be taking off layers in no time."

"I hope so," I said with a shiver.

He laughed, and just like that, with completely natural ease, he took my gloved hand in his and we walked side by side as the trail permitted for the next couple of miles. I tried not to think too much and just enjoyed the comfort of being in his presence.

At some point he said, "I'm glad we got all that rain last week. The falls should be remarkable."

"Oh! That's where we're going? To a waterfall?"

"Yes, the lower falls. There are upper falls too, but you have to hit them from the top, and it's a much more rigorous climb down, so I figured we'd start with this easier hike first, for today, going up."

The "for today" made me think with a slight thrill that he was intending more outings in the future.

The forest was thickly wooded with maple, birch, poplar, and pine. As we made our way deeper into the woods, I was amazed at how peaceful and quiet it was, not another soul or car or human-made object to be heard or seen. It felt wonderful to be away from all that technology and the hustle and bustle of my normal life. Besides our footsteps, the only sound was the caws of the blue jays and crows in the distance. When the trail became narrow in a few spots, Jon let go of my hand and let me pass first—such a gentleman. As he helped me crawl over a fallen tree stump and then followed me, I watched his careful, thoughtful movements, thinking he was lithe and agile like a panther.

I asked abruptly, slightly out of breath, "How is it that you're single?"

He laughed, startled, then said quietly, "Um, actually, I'm divorced."

"Oh," I said, my eyes wide at his revelation. Suddenly I realized how rude and out of line my delivery was, so I added, "I'm sorry, I didn't mean to...pry."

"It's okay. You told me some pretty heavy stuff the other week. I suppose it's my turn."

I regarded his face, which had a grim smile but seemed open to the dialogue. I asked, "Was it…a long time ago?"

"Three years ago. Well, she moved out three years ago."

I nodded, processing, thinking how it was only slightly longer than I'd been without Shawn. And wondering about the fact that she had moved out of their shared house, which I assumed was the West Lake Road house. I don't know why, but this struck me, maybe because I knew of so many breakups where the husband moved out and left the house to the wife. But maybe those cases involved children. I asked quickly, trying to keep the panic out of my voice, "Kids?"

He glanced over and said swiftly, almost angrily, "No."

I nodded, looking down at the ground, as I had clearly, though unintentionally, upset him.

We walked on in silence for a while.

When I sensed he had cooled down, squeezing my hand at one point, probably because I was so quiet, I asked shyly but determinedly, "So, you haven't…dated since?"

"Oh yes," he said sarcastically, with a grin. "Haven't you seen my profiles on Tinder, Match, and eHarmony? Different girl every night."

"Haha. Very funny. Come on, you haven't…tried?" To me, it seemed impossible that this wildly handsome, kind, smart, well-employed, seemingly sane man was just happily single, the consummate bachelor, and that no woman had tried to snatch him up in the past three years.

He walked on, not answering for a bit, but then stopped us in our tracks, staring at me with suddenly sober eyes. He explained, "I didn't want to date. The divorce felt like…a slow death, in a way. I was mourning the loss of what was and what could have been. And well, I still loved her. I still love her, even now." He shrugged his shoulders and looked at me with open candor.

A shot of jealousy pierced me as my eyes widened in surprise. He still loved her! A cold chill ran through my veins as my heart froze in place. I dropped his hand.

Seeing my response, he pulled me to him in the middle of the trail. "Amanda, don't look at me that way! I'm sorry." I stood stiffly in his embrace, the shock still seeping into me. I couldn't see his face, but his voice was suddenly fierce as he said, "I want to be totally honest with you. I *need* to be totally honest with you. The way it was with her, well, it was always a game of deception and manipulation. With you, I want things to be direct, open, real. I *have* to have that." His voice softer now, he said, "Even when the words hurt."

I didn't understand, but I nodded slowly into his chest, understanding the sentiment despite not knowing the details. I could relate—my life had been torn apart in an instant, and after that, I could no longer live in a world that was built on superficialities or innuendos, let alone dishonesty. The absolute truth, I had learned from Beverly, gut-wrenching as it may be, was the way forward and led to deeper and healthier relationships.

He kept me in his embrace for a moment or two more, and I eventually wrapped my arms awkwardly around the lower part of his back, which was the only space not covered by his gear. After a minute or two when we didn't say a word, he released me and stared into my eyes as I looked up at him warily. He said, gently but firmly, "Although I still love her, it's completely and utterly hopeless. There's nothing between us now and never will be. Do you understand?"

I nodded, a crease in my brow. I didn't understand a thing about what happened to him, but I *could* understand the feelings he was conveying. They were much the same as mine for Shawn—I would always love him, even though we would never be together again.

He went on, stuttering a little with fear, confusion, trepidation, "And then there you were—in that room with all of those people—so out of place, so unexpected, so beautiful. It hit me like a ton of bricks. *You* hit me like a ton of bricks." He was breathing hard, a couple of inches from my face, and I found myself gripped in the clutch of his deep, burning eyes. He added simply, "It was something I hadn't expected to ever feel again."

Suddenly, with passion, he kissed me, sending me spiraling down a vortex, a dark, sensuous path covered with twilight, obscurity, and focus. A shot of heat blasted into my core like a bullet, and without a thought, I gave in, kissing him back, sinking into him, my heart beating out of my chest, hungry to drink every inch of him into me. It threw me back to that kiss under the umbrella all those years ago, but this kiss was so much more powerful. Something I had never experienced before—a punch that encased every raw, animal, potent, need-driven urge grown from years of pent-up anguish, restraint, and deprivation—as if it was meant to fill a yearning, yawning cavern.

After what seemed like an hour but was only a few minutes, he abruptly drew apart, exhaling in exasperated release, his eyes narrow and smoldering. He turned and marched away down the trail with angry, unthinking strides. I stood bewildered, catching my breath and pinching my hot, wet lips together.

Chapter XXI

Canandaigua, New York
November 2018

IN A STUPOR, I FOLLOWED, suddenly feeling rejected, separate, blind.

I heard the river ahead and saw the end of the trail as it came to a large opening. He filed out ahead of me, going directly to a large rock and stepping up onto it. I looked from him to the river's rushing current, momentarily distracted by the crystal-clear water and fish swimming underneath, as well as the way the river's shale-filled basin cut through the terrain like a snake. It was a sight to see and took my breath away, despite my distress.

Jon was peering down into the water intently, avoiding eye contact with me.

I stayed on the edge of the river, walking along the grassy bank carefully, glancing toward him, puzzled and hurt.

For several minutes he pulled a few things out of his pack, vials of some sort, coming off the rock to dip them into the water and seal them up again, never once looking at me. His mouth was a tight, crisp, straight line. I took my gloves and hat off and put them in my backpack, trying to seem occupied.

He put the vials away. Slowly, his face a mask, he came to me and stood a safe few feet away.

He asked cryptically, "Why are *you* single?"

I released a dark, abrupt laugh, wondering why he would echo my question now, when I had so many other thoughts in my head. *That* was what he wanted to know? After that kiss? Plus, he *knew* my story, so why such a question?

I replied, reluctantly but honestly, "I guess I've been struggling over the last couple of years. I've been trying to understand my place in this world without Shawn and without the life I had with him." I looked down at the

rushing river and added, "I don't know if I deserve to be happy, to have...
love...again. At least, I don't yet know how to accept it. It seems like a betrayal or a trick of the fates, and it scares me."

He didn't say anything, so I finally looked up at him. His eyes were piercing me as I stood self-conscious under his gaze. He seemed annoyed and
angry. I didn't understand it. Why wasn't he speaking? Were my words too
open for him? Did he understand me? Did he hate my reference to Shawn as
much as I hated the sparse words he said about his ex? Did he regret asking
me here? Did he judge me? What did he think?

Finally, trying to hide the hurt in my voice, I asked, "Are you...mad at
me?" I paused, trying to give him the benefit of the doubt, rephrasing, "Did
I do something to upset you?" I held my breath.

He exhaled derisively and said through clenched teeth, "Mad?! I'm not
mad at *you*, Amanda. I'm mad at *me*!" His frustration was evident as he
turned away from me and kicked a stone into the water. He regarded me, his
face awash with regret, saying, "Here *I just told you* that I would go at *your*
pace, and yet, when I'm close to you, alone, like this..." His arms swept the
glorious landscape as if to envelope us in its embrace. "I can't help myself. I'm
so sorry. God, can you ever forgive me? I know how—how fragile you are. It's
just that it's been *so long* since I've felt this way, and I guess—I guess I don't
know how to rein myself in. Please forgive me. Please."

I watched his tortured face and immediately felt several things at once—
mostly relief (he wasn't judging me!), then wonder (I had the same effect on
him that he had on me!), guilt (why hadn't *I* noticed that the kiss was too much
or too soon or too anything other than amazing?!), and finally, gratitude (once
again, like our breakup in high school, he was taking it all on the chin himself!).

I said quickly, "Jon, yes, of course. Like you said to me before, there's nothing to forgive." I closed the distance between us and took his hand in mine,
touching the palm and looking up into his face. I said, "These broken lines,
they're part of what made us who we are, but that doesn't mean their jagged
edges won't prick and tear at us from time to time, especially now that we're
trying to draw a new line." He was watching me, the light in his eyes turning from frustration to sadness to slow understanding. I continued, "It may
not be easy. It may feel awful and wrong at times. It may even feel like we
shouldn't...*try*." At this, the tears began to well in my eyes because the grief
and guilt were boiling up in my veins. I whispered, "I want so much not to
feel conflicted, but I don't know how."

He pulled me into an embrace, his hand stroking my hair, and said, "I know. I know. I don't have any answers either. Not yet. But once again, I'm sorry…for before. I promise you, it will never happen again. You lead the way. You set the pace. I mean it this time. And Amanda?"

I drew back to look up into his face.

He said softly, "Thank you for being honest with me. For telling me your thoughts and feelings. For every single word you said. I know from experience that it isn't easy to be…so vulnerable, and I want you to know I appreciate it." He paused and I waited, regarding his serious eyes with their warmth shedding a glow into my heart. He added thoughtfully, "The deserving part—I'm struggling with that myself, so I won't offer the canned words that everyone else does because I personally find them repugnant. Just know that I hear you. I see you. I'm taking in everything you say."

I nodded, more grateful for his tact than I cared to admit. It was nice to know *I* didn't have to make *him* feel comfortable with *my* feelings.

In the next second, as I pulled him closer for one last hug, I thought to myself, wow, it was going to be difficult to figure out what my pace was, especially when he felt so good in my arms and when the effects of that kiss were still coursing through me.

"Come on," he said, pulling away softly, picking up his gear, taking my hand, and directing me farther toward the river's mouth. "We have a bit more hiking to do."

As we started walking, using the stream rocks as stepping-stones when the banks were too steep, I asked, "So, do you normally wear waders or water shoes when you're fishing?"

"Depends on how deep and wide the water is. Today, the spot I'm taking you to has a good area off to the side where I can stand and cast into the water from the land."

I nodded. A few seconds later, I asked with a grin, "And where's your facial hair? Don't all fishermen have beards?"

He laughed, looking back at me ruefully. "Well, actually, I had a goatee until a few months ago, but I shaved it off. Do you like facial hair?"

"Not particularly."

"No beard it is." He smiled.

I continued, "Is this a river or creek or stream or what?" I had to talk above the sound of the water that rushed past us in slick, driven force, carrying rubbery-looking leaves in a fluid flow.

"It's a branch of the West River. You've never been?"

"Nope," I replied, "I don't think so. When we were kids, Grandpa used to take us to another place, closer to the north end of the lake, a big gorge. I remember, for some reason, finding golf balls at the top by the waterfall."

"Oh yeah, by Bristol Harbor? I fish up there quite often too. It butts up to the golf course."

"I wonder how many of these hidden glens and gorges we have around here," I said, looking at the magnificent, seemingly untouched scenery.

"Near Canandaigua? Hmmm, I don't know, but a lot. It makes my job easy. Of course, there are days when I have to drive over to Skaneateles or Cayuga or Onondaga. Those days are longer, but Canandaigua offers a lot of what I need, which is nice."

"Right, I bet." We were silent for a while as we hiked up a steeper section. Then I asked above the din of water cascading over a ridge, "Are you always so…alone when you fish?"

"Well, not today!" he said with a smile. "But usually yes." He wondered, "Haven't you ever fished?"

I shook my head. "Not unless you count fishing for perch and sunfish off Grandpa's dock on Granger Point, and that was about thirty years ago."

He looked back at me, shaking his head a little, and said, "Um sure, that's something. But I'm glad you came today. I'll show you. Of course, for my job, it's not just fishing. There's also a lot of assessing the water quality and conditions, the season, the various species, even the air. Fish are a great barometer of the environment."

When we came to a large opening in the river, we stopped as Jon said, "This is it," with a wave of his hand and a broad grin. I took in the view, my eyes wide, awestruck. The gorge's massive half-domed bowl rose like a phoenix out of the river's clearing, edged on both sides by a wall of shale stacked in tightly bound layers. At the head of the dome was a huge waterfall releasing a torrent of water step-by-step down into an enormous reservoir, like the colossal mouth of a whale.

I let out a whoop and exclaimed, "Wow!"

"Yes!" he said in response. He pinched his index finger and thumb together in his mouth and whistled loudly, and the dome echoed back its high-pitched, assenting answer. The acoustics were amazing.

I pointed to the reservoir and asked, "How deep is that water?"

"Ten, twenty feet and very cold." He shouted back above the cacophony.

He directed me toward the side of the gorge to a section of flat shale where we could lay down our things. "This whole area's called Clark Gully. It's where the Senecas first settled hundreds of years ago, on this hill, surrounded by these waters and trees. You can see why, can't you?"

"Totally," I agreed. Then I asked him, "What are you fishing for?"

"Whatever I can catch," he said with a wry grin. "No, actually this time of year, it's kind of hit or miss. I'm going to start with the fly. Hoping for some trout, rainbow, or lake, or maybe brown, if I'm lucky. Certain times of year, there's also salmon, but not today."

"No kidding? Salmon, in the Finger Lakes? I had no idea!"

He smiled. "Common misconception. Only from Alaska?"

"Uh-huh," I admitted sheepishly.

"There are all kinds of salmon. We get landlocked salmon here in this region, but it depends on the alewife population, which is their main food source. Sometimes they stock alewife to make it work, from year to year, but other times it just happens naturally."

"Who stocks? You mean planting the fish?"

"Yes, most lakes and rivers are stocked at some point with various species. By the state. To keep the populations of both predators and their prey healthy. That's part of my job—to determine what's out there during any given season, what's thriving and what needs a little help."

As I sat on the flat shale ledge, he came over to show me how he prepared his gear, saying, "Okay, so this is the fly rod. And this is the line. The whole thing is really light. Feel it. Compared to a regular fishing pole, it's longer and thinner." Out of his pack, he produced a spongy-looking mat with little insects attached. "I make my own flies." He handed me one, and I was astonished at the detail—intricate, colorful, realistic.

"Jon, these are spectacular! You made these?"

"Mm-hmm." He nodded. I put the one back on the mat and picked up another. It was a dark green bundle of wings and wiry threaded pieces woven together in a perfect pattern of mimicry. The hook was so well disguised, it was difficult to see, hidden in its camouflage.

As I handed it back with a smile, he said, "Great selection. So, you just tie this on the end of the line, like this." I sat studying his strong, masculine hands tying this delicate work of art to the line, which seemed more difficult than pulling thread through a needle. I had to marvel at the skill with which he performed this act of dexterity in less than half a minute.

"With traditional fishing, the weight of the lure sends the line through the air and into the water. With fly fishing, because the fly is so light, the weight of the line carries the hook and fly through the air, and you just lightly tap it against the surface of the water. Like this." He pulled the line in lightly with his hand, then cast once, twice, three, four times quickly and skillfully. "Ten and two, ten and two. See, like the hours on a clock. That's usually the best placement."

I sat watching, fascinated and in a trance. It was very rhythmic, like a pendulum, but also somehow paced and beating, like a drum. In the beginning, I tried to watch the fly as it touched down tentatively on the water, but it was almost too fast to catch it at the proper moment, so I moved my eyes up to the line, watching its rainbow arc reach back into Jon's competent hands, moving in a symphony of perfectly harmonious notes.

He looked back at me after a few minutes, and I shifted my gaze from his hands to his face, smiling up at him in wonder. He smiled back, keeping the rhythm in his hands steady, not missing a beat.

He stood, then walked cautiously from stone to stone, casting into the water's abyss. I was in a state of blissful silence, drinking in the surroundings, mesmerized by his movements and the thought that I couldn't possibly be any farther away from the coffin that was my normal computer/cube space than this and how fantastic that felt. I slowly closed my eyes to breathe in the unadulterated air and leaned my head back, listening to the rushing water and Jon's whizzing line. My elbows were locked behind me, propping up my body as I sat cross-legged on the ledge, my hands pressed against the flat surface of the rock, which felt cool and chalky. The smell of the forest's leaves and mossy undergrowth hit my nostrils in a wave of encapsulated earthiness. Off in the distance, I heard a woodpecker's staccato knocks. The sun had risen in the sky and was kissing my cheeks with its warm hands as I breathed in and out, in and out, in and out.

Five minutes later (or was it ten?), I slowly opened my eyes, taking in another deep breath. Jon was still casting absently but, to my surprise, he wasn't watching what he was doing. Instead, he was studying me. He quickly looked away, caught. There had been a flicker of something there, though. Not admiration or joy. More like consternation, fear, and a bit of longing. I blushed and blinked, glad he was busy with his task again so I could regard him in return, noting how able his hands were, how confident his footing, how easy and smooth his movements. I couldn't help but think about our kiss and wonder how his masterful and effortless skills would translate—would he be as able in *that* way as well? More so than in high school? I blushed thinking about how much I had matured in that area and suspected he had as well.

This time, when he looked back, he read my eyes and took them in, not speaking but offering a small smile that I gradually, luxuriously mirrored. Words were superfluous. Time ticked by languidly, both of us lost in our thoughts and the motion of the fly tapping with perfect precision upon the water's surface.

At one point, Jon had a hit and I started, my eyes focused in fascination on the process. He reeled against the fish quickly at first, then slowly. It flipped and flopped in protest, bobbing above the current and then back down again. I was no judge of fish size, but it appeared quite large. When he had it close enough, he reached down and held it up by the lip, being careful of the fly. It was still struggling, but he kept a firm grasp. I got up and walked over. It looked to be about a foot long, with sleek, slim lines of pink and green drawn down its side.

I exclaimed, "Wow! It's beautiful! What is it?"

"A rainbow trout." He smiled at my captivation. I touched it with my fingertip. Its skin stiff and cold, it bucked in dissent. Still holding the fish in one hand, he put his rod down, reached in his pack, and pulled out his weight and measurement tools. He said, "Fifteen inches, one pound three ounces."

"Will you keep it?"

"No," he said, shaking his head, removing the fly swiftly with his fingers and laying the fish back down lightly in the water. He let go and I watched it swim away, slinking through the inky water, back upstream toward the gully. He recorded the fish's stats in a notebook.

"Does it hurt them?" I asked.

"Maybe. I mean, I don't know for sure, not being a fish," he said with a sideways smirk. "I try to be as humane with them as I can, just in case. Sometimes they swallow the hook, and it can be difficult to retrieve, so I'm extra careful when that happens."

"Do you ever keep them and eat them?"

"Not when I'm working. But I go to Canada once a year, in June, with my lab partner, Brian, and some other friends to fish for two weeks. It's very remote—we have to fly in on a floatplane and stay in the only cabin on a lake that's connected by straits to a string of other lakes. We catch hundreds of fish a day, and we usually bring several full coolers back with us. Mostly steelhead and pike, and my favorite, walleye. I have some in my freezer right now. I'll fry you up a batch sometime, if you like."

"That would be great. Is your kitchen backsplash done, then?"

As he answered, he began casting, starting the pendulum again. "Yep, finally finished it last weekend. The kitchen is back in working order."

I smiled. Was that an invite? I asked him, "Which do you like better, fly fishing or the other fishing…what is the other fishing called?"

"Just plain fishing," he said, grinning. "I like them both. Fly fishing is better in rivers, creeks, and streams. Regular fishing is for open water."

"What do you use to bring them in?"

"Oh, lures or nightcrawlers—worms."

"What's the biggest fish you ever caught?"

"Biggest? Here? In the Finger Lakes, or where?"

"Yes, here."

"Hmmm, well, for trout, I caught a thirty-two-pound lake trout in Chautauqua a few years ago. I've caught several fish larger than that, carp and muskie, but that lake trout was amazing, so I guess I remember that one the best."

"Wow. Did you use a lure for that? Did you have to use a net?"

He laughed. "Yes, a lure. Yes, a net too. It gave me quite a fight."

"I bet," I said, finding myself unexpectedly fascinated by this odd sport I had never once thought about before.

We fell into a comfortable silence again. I stayed sitting on the ledge for a while and eventually got up and walked around, carefully navigating the stones to keep my feet dry. Jon moved around as well but kept his eyes on his work and, more often than not, on me. I was amazed at how many times I glanced his way and found his attention diverted toward me at the same moment. Sometimes we smiled, sometimes not, still navigating the waters of this novelty much like my feet along the gorge's slippery path.

I found it remarkable that we felt so comfortable being quiet in each other's presence. There was no need to fill up the silence with words or actions. We could just be. I thought to myself, this was one of the many benefits of having known him so young and dated him then. I didn't have to worry about being alone with him in the woods. I didn't have to spend time asking about his background or family or where he grew up. We both knew the essentials already, and we both knew there was plenty of time to mine the rest—the deeper, more intimate treasures yet to be revealed.

I came up behind Jon's back and was a foot away from him now, standing on a rock on his left side. He turned and said, "What are you thinking about?"

"Oh, just how life is so strange. And that we're both so lucky to have found each other again."

"Yes," he said simply, stopping his work, and leaning in to kiss me. His hands were both occupied, and I left mine at my sides, but the connection of our lips sent my heart soaring. As he drew away, his eyes were glowing, and it made me feel warm all over to see that I had the same effect on him that he had on me and that we needn't act further on it now, that we needn't rush or take any drastic measures with that pace he had granted me, but that we could still kiss, like this, and know that we were both safe and sweet and okay.

He went back to his work, and I went back to my backpack, pulling out my phone and taking photos of the beautiful scenery and a video of Jon fishing. It had been, well, forever since I'd used my phone for photos and videos, having gotten out of the habit when I felt guilty and unworthy knowing my life's memories continued on while Shawn's and Cole's photos were forever frozen on that awful date. It felt good, healthy, welcome to begin again.

He caught one more fish, smaller than the first—a black crappie, he called it. I took photos of him holding it. I told him I didn't think it was as "pretty" as the rainbow trout but that it was still "very pleasant" with its speckled black spots. He said with a grin, "You're such a girl."

After another hour or so, we sat next to each other on the ledge to eat lunch. From my backpack, I pulled out two brown paper bags that contained peanut butter and jelly sandwiches, snack packs of Fritos, Ziplocked grapes, Famous Amos chocolate chip cookies, and Capri Sun pouches.

Jon held up his pouch and said, "Perfect. I feel like I'm in kindergarten all over again."

I grinned and said, "What can I say? At least I didn't cut the crusts off the bread, Jon*athan*."

"Great, now I'm in trouble."

I chuckled and added, "Don't judge. I *can* cook, despite how this looks, and grill, and I'm an expert crock-potter, not to mention baker. I'll make *you* dinner sometime."

"It's a date," he agreed readily.

"What's your favorite dish?"

"Hmmm, a good steak or burger probably. But obviously I love fish too. And pizza and pasta and Mexican and Chinese and sushi and soup. Um," he laughed, "I guess I love everything."

"Good—me too. Well, I'll make you one of my Indiana specialties sometime."

"Pork tenderloin?"

"Oh, um, no, I don't know how to make that, actually, although yes, agree, *so* good. But I can whip up a mean batch of chicken and noodles."

"That sounds wonderful, especially on a cold winter day."

"Exactly."

"Was your boss upset that you had to take the day off?"

"Nah, it was the first day off I've asked for since I started there in July."

"You haven't asked for *any* vacation since July?" he echoed, incredulous.

"Nope."

"Well, I'm glad I gave you a reason to take a day off, then."

"I'm glad too," I said, blushing a little. "I've been working a lot of extra hours lately, so yeah, it was time. I took tomorrow off as well."

"Oh? Why are you working so much?"

I looked down at my bag of cookies, eating one before I responded. "I don't know…I guess it keeps my mind off things. But honestly, lately I've been having a bit of a dilemma with my job."

"Oh?" he asked, concern knitting his brow.

"Yeah. Don't get me wrong—the job itself is fine, but I've been thinking about doing something different. More meaningful or impactful or, I don't know, something *more*. Do you ever feel that way about your job?" I asked, reaching.

His eyebrows rose a little, then came back down as he thought about it for a split second and said, "No, not really. I love my job."

I frowned a bit. "Of course you do. Who wouldn't love this?" I glanced around to appreciate the splendor of the gorge and falls.

"Yeah, I'm spoiled," he agreed, taking it all in. "But no job is perfect. During the winter months, we get stuck in the lab for days, or worse, we have to trek through the ice and snow or sit out on a freezing lake for hours ice fishing. It's not all glitz and glory, I can tell you that."

"Sounds like heaven to me," I whispered, still frowning. I continued, "Back in my office in Indy, there were so many people resigned to the daily grind, you know? It was just what you did. Get up, get ready, drive a half hour to work in rush-hour traffic, plop down in front of a computer in a tiny cube for eight hours, then back home for a short time before you have to get back up and start the whole routine all over again. And no matter what, keep your head down, keep your job, don't rock the boat, get the salary, get the bonus, get the pension, one day after the other after the other until you retire or die." I sighed. "Now that I'm home again, I just want to feel…closer to the true meaning of my job—not just be a small cog in a big wheel. It's so hard to understand or feel the impact of a job when your work is buried at the bottom of a colossal machine."

He didn't say anything—just listened quietly.

I went on, "You'll laugh at me…I did one of those online career questionnaires, and it told me I should be a nurse or a cop."

He laughed on cue. "Well…sure, why not?"

"No," I replied with big eyes and a shake of my head.

"Or an artist or teacher."

"Oh, well, those are better, aren't they? Can you paint?"

"Not at all. And I hate getting up in front of people."

"Hmmm, back to square one."

"Uh-huh, pretty much." I started crumpling up the remains of our meal, putting the trash into my pack. I added, "I suppose I'll figure it out eventually."

"Right. Of course you will." He stood up and grabbed his pole. "Are you okay for another half hour or so?"

"Yep, sounds good to me."

He began casting again and, not having any luck, finally took some samples from the water and packed up his gear. We headed back through the forest toward the road, and I found myself watching him hike. He was so confident in his steps, even over the bumpy roots and loose ground and down the descent of the slippery shale glen. Even with all his gear, he was graceful and sure, grabbing my hand and leading the way. I knew it was only his physicality, his strong legs and athletic movements, but for whatever reason, I drew strength and reassurance from his presence, not wondering or questioning a thing like I thought I would in the days leading up to the outing. Everything seemed so peaceful and easy despite my earlier fears and worry. Oh sure, there were still those nagging questions about his divorce and how wide the cavern of his broken line was compared to mine, or compared to a straight, unbroken line, but I just figured that would come with time. With patience, study, and the steady, rhythmic beating of our hearts.

❧ CHAPTER XXII ❧

Naples, New York
November 2018

WE GOT TO THE CAR and placed our packs and gear in the hatch. He said, "I have to drop off these samples at my lab."

"Great," I said with a little flutter in my chest. He was so open to sharing his workplace with me. I thought back to that week of back-and-forth ridiculousness with those picture frames, and I wondered what he would think of my scattered indecision and attempt at subterfuge. Then again, I hadn't seen *his* house yet, and maybe I would find a wall-sized oil painting of his wedding portrait. Yeesh, that tightened a vise in my gut just thinking about it.

As we turned onto Main Street in Naples at the corner where Bob and Ruth's Diner stood, I thought what a quaint little town Naples was. I hadn't been through it in years, but so many of the amazing old houses remained, restored and well maintained, plus a whole new batch of wineries and shops, not to mention the same old cemetery and school, all nestled into the rolling hills. We opened the windows to smell the few remaining grapes that hadn't yet been harvested. The vineyards were planted in perfectly spaced rows, and the smell was fantastic.

"Wow, you get to smell this every day?"

"Uh-huh, during the fall anyway. Just about done for the season, though. Have you ever been to the Grape Festival?"

"No, but it sounds amazing."

"It's a lot of fun. In September. Sometimes we set up a booth to show the kids the different species of fish with this interactive display that Brian built. It's fun to watch their faces when they guess the right answer."

I smiled, imagining Jon engaging with the kids and how great he would be at that—fun, patient, charming, witty. My mind went back to the firm *no* he had uttered when I asked whether he had kids. There must be a story there. Yet another thing I would need to uncover. Did he not like kids? Had there been fertility issues? Had *she* not wanted any? A moment later, I realized he may have been wondering the same things about me.

We pulled into the driveway of an old house painted light blue with white trim. A Blazer was parked in the driveway ahead of us. That must be his lab partner's car. So, I was finally going to meet someone he knew. Payback for all of those people he was subjected to at Donny's bonfire. Well, I guess I had already met Janet, the waitress, but I didn't think that counted.

He said, "This is it."

As we got out of the car, I said, "This house is a lab? Doesn't seem possible, at least from the outside."

"Yeah, it used to be a law office, but we converted it. We received a grant from the state about ten years ago for some research we were working on, so we moved out of the state office we were using in Rochester and set up this lab. It's a lot more convenient for the fieldwork we do."

Jon grabbed his pack out of the trunk. We walked up to the front porch, and he held the door open for me. As I walked into the front hallway, I looked around. It was the strangest-looking place. It still had all of the old oak wood moldings around the entrances to the rooms, hardwood floors, and antique light fixtures on the ceilings, but the rest was what I would imagine a mad scientist's lab would look like. My mind flashed to an image of Dr. Jekyll and Mr. Hyde. An entire wall in what I presumed was the old dining room had built-in bookshelves filled with what appeared to be textbooks about fish and fishing. To the left was the old living room, with several metal lab tables supporting four larger tanks of water and live fish, and next to those a stand-alone metal shelf unit holding five neat rows of fifty or so smaller full tanks. In the dining room, Jon's lab partner was standing at a metal surgical table in a white coat with plastic gloves, dissecting a medium-sized fish, taking pieces to inspect under a microscope.

The whole scene was so foreign to me. But fascinating. Do people really work like this? I was so used to nondescript computer server rooms, generic cube farms, and administrative offices. This was something I'd never seen before.

Jon's lab partner looked up from under thick glasses with strange sides—safety glasses, I presumed. He seemed a little startled to see a guest coming through the door with Jon.

Jon came around from behind me, putting his hand lightly on my back, and said, "Hey, Brian. This is Amanda Holmes."

I corrected awkwardly, "M—Morgan, actually."

Jon turned to me with a "whoops" face and said, "Sorry, Amanda Morgan."

Brian said, "Hi, nice to meet you. I'd shake your hand, but…" he held up his scalpel as explanation.

I smiled and said, "No worries—nice to meet you."

Brian asked Jon, "Been out?"

"Yeah, Hi Tor, Clark Gully."

"Any luck?"

"A rainbow and crappie."

"Nice."

"Meh, something."

Brian went back to his work without another word, and Jon pulled out his samples and started organizing, noting, and doing several other work-related tasks as I sat down on a metal stool and watched. Every once in a while, he would look up at me and smile. He knew I was checking him out. I couldn't help it—watching him in his own environment was like watching a master chef in a well-organized kitchen—fluid, natural, competent. Along with my fascination and admiration, I also felt a bit envious. I really needed to get my career back on track. Yes, I was sure I looked just as capable as Jon in my own work world (at the computer or at a meeting or presenting), but could I say I was as engaged, enthralled, determined as he was? I mean, he had taken me, a woman on a date with him, to his lab—maybe out of necessity (to drop off the samples), but I couldn't help but wonder if it was more like "bring your kid to work day," where he wanted to show me the tricks of his trade because he was proud of them. And why wouldn't he be? His job was interesting, tactile, a slice of nature wrapped up in an occupation. I tried to imagine the situation in reverse and nearly laughed out loud, thinking about how awkward Jon would be sitting in on one of our technical meetings, listening to us debate whether we could consolidate our user test cases from fifty to forty-five in order to shave one day off the project plan. Even thinking of it now made me cringe and want to let out a big "snoooore" on his behalf.

After about ten minutes, he was done, so he walked me around the rest of the place. The next room, which was the kitchen, wasn't very big, but otherwise fairly standard. Older cabinets and countertops, but fully functional.

I opened a few cupboards—there were plates and glasses and bowls, just like any other kitchen. He mentioned that they stayed overnight sometimes for early outings the next day or because some lab tests needed more time. The fridge had some food, drinks, and condiments. He grabbed us both bottled waters.

The downstairs bathroom was a rather dated orange powder room, which I debated about using but opted to see what was upstairs first, which was the right move, as there was a fully functional and renovated bathroom there, flanked by two tiny bedrooms, each with a twin bed and nightstand (and nothing else). Everything was surprisingly clean. While I was in the bathroom, he went back downstairs and I snooped a little, opening the medicine cabinet above the bathroom sink—it was empty except for a bottle of aspirin. I went back downstairs and he showed me the basement. He flipped on the light switch and I followed him down the cement steps, which led to a cold, hard floor and walls, the light just a bulb hanging from the ceiling. A few shelving units held various garden and yard equipment and tools, gloves, and other miscellaneous items. It was a little creepy and spidery, so we headed back upstairs.

When we got back to the living room, Brian looked up, smiled, and said, "Did you meet Sebastian?"

"Who?" I asked, perplexed.

"Our ghost—Sebastian. He lives in the basement."

I shivered and opened my eyes wide, but then he laughed and said, "Oh, don't worry, he's a friendly ghost. We usually only hear him down there when we stay overnight by ourselves."

"Seriously?" I asked, turning to Jon.

"Yep, we've both heard him." He glanced over at Brian, and they nodded at each other and at me with grins on their faces. Jon shrugged and continued, "Just part of the charm of the house."

"Uh-huh. Sure. I bet," I said, sarcastically.

Jon laughed and said, "Well, on that note, you ready to go?"

"Yes, on that note, definitely," I said, my eyes wide.

I looked at my watch. It was five. We nodded, said goodbye, and left.

As he started the car, he said, "Well, what'd you think?"

"Very cool. Wish my office was like that."

He smiled and pulled out of the driveway, asking, "You want to do anything else? We could stop at Bob and Ruth's for a burger if you like…"

I looked down and said, "Naw, um, as good as that sounds, I guess we should call it a day." I kept thinking back to that "my pace" debacle earlier with the kiss. I didn't want to push my luck, or his, or *ours*.

He nodded easily, thankfully not taking offense. "Righty-o, Canandaigua it is."

I began to calculate, realizing we had been together for nearly ten hours. That was a long date! And yet, if I was being honest with myself, I only wanted more. It was probably the most time I had spent with any one person since Shawn died. That realization, coupled with my desire for yet more, made me feel all kinds of emotions—and I wasn't exactly sure how to untangle them at the moment while I was still in the presence of his bright green eyes watching me, gauging my face when I glanced his way.

He pulled up to my car outside of Patty's Place and put the car in park.

I said simply, "Thank you for the perfect day."

"It was, wasn't it?" he agreed, then added, "But—but sorry about earlier." He frowned a little.

I took his hand in mine and said, "It's okay. There's no road map, no GPS for...what we're doing, and maybe that's okay."

He nodded in agreement, his eyes warm soft pools of light.

Then, with a combined force of fear and bravery, I asked, "Want to do something next week...or, um, the week after?"

I could see his eyes light up, but instead of an instant affirmative, he asked, "Are you sure?"

"Yes," I said with a curt nod. More was more, and that was something to lean into, wasn't it? Plus, a week or two would give me time to sort through the cobwebs that had spun an intricate web in my confused psyche. Hopefully that would be enough time because I was trying my hardest, as Jon got out of the car and helped me with my pack, not to reach my arms around his neck, clutch his whole body to me, and draw a kiss from his sweet lips.

Chapter XXIII

Indianapolis, Indiana
December 2018

As the pilot came on the loudspeaker to say we were beginning our descent, I felt a lurch in my stomach. I looked out the window and took a deep breath as the cars going by on 465 came into view. We flew over the Indianapolis Motor Speedway, plain as day, and I hated the sight. Of course, they had built it all back up again so it looked the same as before the bombing, although it was now accompanied by a monument to the victims in the middle of the grassy interior, a tall, thin tower like a steeple beckoning toward the heavens. All the old feelings of horror, anger, and sadness came rushing back, and I put my hand to my face, wiping away the tears before my seat neighbor could notice my distress.

It had been five months since I'd been back. And I'd only come based on a summons.

It had been hard to leave Heathport. Jon and I had met for drinks a week after our outing, just for a few hours, and it had ended with a rather chaste kiss, him leaving me to my "pace" and me proceeding cautiously, still feeling the tug of Shawn's unspoken pull. It was so difficult to describe my jumbled thoughts and feelings (to myself, let alone to Jon). On the one hand, I wanted so much to fall into his arms and throw caution to the wind, but on the other hand, there was something holding me back that I couldn't quite put my finger on. And he wasn't pushing either, which I suspected was related to his divorce, the details of which he had yet to reveal.

But what had changed over the past few weeks, which was the part that made it hard to leave, was the fact that we had started talking on the phone. Every night. Before bed. About our days or our work or miscellaneous things.

We were both now heavily training (separately) for the half-marathon in January, so a lot of our discussion was about our running stats for the day. We had both downloaded an app to record our distance, time, splits, miles per minutes, and so on, and we went through the information together to glean potential improvements or ideas for the next day. He was much faster than I was, so we would never be able to run together, but somehow this daily breakdown about our individual goals and each other's progress was motivation enough to strive for something better. And it felt almost like a metaphor for our relationship. By talking with him every night (and not seeing him, which apparently sent me down the confusion spiral), I was able to take small steps toward intimacy with him, the kind of intimacy I needed to feel safe and to move forward, if only with words and thoughts and encouragement.

It was even to the point of me wanting very badly to see him in person. We had arranged that I would go over to his house for dinner (that promised fish fry) the next Friday night when, unfortunately, I got the summons and had to leave on a flight, everything put on hold for the time being.

Of course, I hadn't told anyone back in Indy about him and didn't intend to, which caused me some agita as I grabbed my carry-on, walked toward the terminal and through the security gates, and saw Shawn's parents and Sissie waiting there for me with open arms. Clearly now wasn't the time, and as I gulped down my guilt, I wondered if it ever would be. I gave them each a big hug and handed Ed my carry-on upon his insistence. I put my arm around Sissie, telling her with honesty that she looked great—taller with longer hair and her lovely face growing more into maturity. I left out the part that I thought she also looked surprisingly happier, with the dark circles under her eyes gone and that weary look that used to linger there now no longer apparent. And she was eager to talk, which seemed also unlike her, in a promising, uplifting way I hadn't expected.

It was like an out-of-body experience to go from New York, where everyone around me was so careful not to talk about Shawn, Cole, and the bombings, to here in Indiana, where the first words out of Sissie's mouth were, "Can you believe they caught the bastard?"

"No, I can't," I said, laughing ironically at her turn of phrase and the fact that she used a swear word right in front of her grandparents. They didn't flinch, though. I knew they were thinking the same thing. Finally, the monster was behind bars.

I said, "I really thought this day would never come. I'd given up on it ever happening."

Sissie continued as we headed toward the short-term parking. "Yeah, totally. I mean, what are the chances, after all this time? And the FBI combing through everything a thousand times—all those interviews and videos, and still nothing—until boom! Got him!"

"So, what exactly do you know?" I asked them as we got in the car and Ed drove us out of the airport, trying to see if we were given the same information by the FBI. "All I had was a quick call with Agent Thompson on Thursday where he said they got him and that I should get out here for a meeting Monday at nine."

Karen said, "That's all he told us as well. The meeting is with all the survivors and kin. I suppose we'll get more details then. I noticed they've also scheduled a press conference at noon, right after our meeting. They mentioned it on the news this morning."

As I watched the old familiar sights and sounds out the car window, Karen asked how my flight was and I told her fine. I told them the flight out of Rochester had been delayed an hour, so I was lucky to make my connection in Chicago. Thankfully, the gates had been in the same terminal, so I hadn't had to run, which often happened during these layovers in the winter when the weather was unpredictable and deicing caused frequent delays and snarls in the scheduled flights.

I thought about the fact that I wouldn't be staying in my old house, the one I had shared with Shawn and the kids. It was so odd to think about complete strangers living there now. And even odder to think I would be staying at Shawn's parents' house—a house I had only been upstairs in maybe two other times in my life.

Ed broke into my thoughts with "Wait until you see your house. We'll drive by on the way. The new owners have painted it! You'll never guess what color."

Before I could reply, Sissie jumped in, her nose wrinkled in disgust. "Oh my God, wait till you see! It's hideous!"

"Oh, come on. It can't be that bad."

Karen looked into the back seat with her eyebrows raised and said, "Yes, it's that bad."

Sissie continued, "And they took down the front porch swing. Totally stupid. Why would they do that? And replaced our fence with a chain-link one. I guess it's for their dogs, but still, it looks awful, if you ask me."

"My goodness, how many dogs do they have?" I was thinking about the pristine wood floors that we'd just had re-sanded and re-stained not too many years ago.

"Five! They're big too—some type of retrievers or something. I rode my bike by the other day, and they were loading all five in the back of their SUV. Who the heck has that many big dogs? Imagine the amount of dog food you'd have to buy? And all that poop! Eww, gross!"

Karen said, "Now, now. Ed went down and talked to them one day and said they're perfectly nice people. They don't have any kids, so maybe the dogs are like kids to them."

"I suppose," Sissie conceded. She looked over at me and changed the subject. "So Amanda, what have you been up to? We've missed you."

"Thanks. I've missed you too. Well, let's see, I've been working for a small software company—*much* different from where I worked here, but the same tech skills and workload and all that. And I've been hanging out with friends and family, which has been really nice, you know, to see everyone anytime I want as opposed to once every six months. I feel like my nieces and nephew really *know* me now. I'm not just that weird aunt who appears out of nowhere once in a while."

Karen said, "Oh, that's nice, dear. And how is your mom doing? I bet she loves having you home."

"Yeah, that's been great too. We have breakfast or lunch nearly every week, and she fills me in on all of her activities. Her latest venture is some new sport called pickleball."

Ed asked, "What on earth is that?"

"I gather it's sort of like tennis but with a smaller court. Anyway, it seems to be all the rage in her neighborhood."

Karen said, "Wonderful. She puts us to shame, Ed. We're lucky if we get our weekly walk in, and that's usually only around the block to visit with the neighbors."

I laughed and said, "Oh don't feel bad, she puts *me* to shame. I can only hope to be as active as her someday."

I turned to Sissie and inquired, "How have *you* been doing? How's your junior year going?"

"Fine, I guess." She looked down at her hands. "Most of my classes are fine. But I really hate my English teacher. He's making us read *Ethan Frome* right now. Total snorefest." She made an exaggerated snoring sound.

"Come on, I liked that book. Edith Wharton, right? Something about sledding? Well, if you don't like that one, try *House of Mirth*. Much more interesting, although kind of the opposite of the title, a little depressing, but still a good read. And I really liked *The Glimpses of the Moon*, which has a much happier ending."

"I can barely handle *Ethan Frome* right now, thank you very much. I swear, every two days Mr. Wolfe wants us to write a synopsis of every other chapter. As if I don't have any other classes. Who has time for that?"

"Well, maybe I can help you with it while I'm here."

"That would be great. How long are you here for anyway?"

"Only until Wednesday. But still, you can show me what you have, and we can go through it together."

"Okay, cool."

"How's your mom doing?"

"Oh, mostly fine. I was over there this morning. She's been having some difficulties with her pee or kidneys lately, a UTI or something, but I guess that's fairly common with her condition. The nurse who was there this morning checked on her and gave her some meds."

I nodded. I wondered how much Sissie had witnessed with her mom's treatments and how hard that must be on her. But maybe in a way, it would make her more empathetic with others who were different from her in the future. Or at least have greater patience when trying to understand them.

I asked Sissie if she was still dating Tyler, and she looked at me as though I had two heads. He was the boy she had been "totally in love with" just a few months ago, but apparently that was over. She said she was happy being single right now, which cracked me up, spoken like a thirty-five-year-old.

Ed slowed down when we drove by my old house.

I cried, "NO!" involuntarily when I saw it.

Sissie laughed and exclaimed, "Oh, YES! Isn't it *awful?*" It was *purple* with *navy* shutters. I didn't know if they were going for country charm or a tribute to Barney the Dinosaur. I gagged. Why would they do that? It made me want to cry or throw up…I wasn't sure. And our beautiful white picket fence was gone. The chain-link was so tacky. I guess it served a purpose, but still…*yuck*.

It made me think of Maplewood. I said, "Sissie, I'm going to have you come out and visit me sometime at my New York house. It's much better than what's left of our old house. You would love it. The village is right on the Erie Canal and only a short drive from Lake Ontario and a little farther to Canandaigua Lake. Maybe next summer when you're out of school."

"Sure, that sounds great!"

Karen added, "That would be wonderful."

We pulled into their driveway, and Karen showed me to my bedroom "to get settled in before dinner." After a visit to the restroom, I unpacked a few things from my carry-on and went downstairs to the most delicious smell of Karen's homemade chicken strata casserole, yeast rolls, green beans, mashed potatoes, and apple dumpling. It was all I could do to keep my mouth from watering as I stared at the overfull kitchen stove top and counter. A few minutes later, Shawn's sisters showed up with their kids, and we hugged and talked all at once and then laughed because we couldn't understand what everyone was saying in the ensuing chaos. It was funny—somehow all of that awkwardness I used to feel coming over here with Shawn, surrounded by his family and his world, was simply…gone. I could just be me. I had somehow gained that inner strength, a feeling of being settled within myself now that I had five months under my belt encased in the healing world of Maplewood and my new independent home life there. Plus, we had Shawn and Cole's loss in common and the shared pain that elicited, but we also had the happy memories to pull from and bond over. We ate and talked and laughed and cried. Even though the grief and sadness still hovered around the edges, we could now reminisce about them with tears of laughter mixed with the tears of grief.

I realized the difference: we talked about their lives now—and not their deaths.

The evening was spent peacefully, getting caught up and drinking in the warm, cozy feeling that the company, Karen's Christmas decorations, and after-dinner eggnog provided. Finally, around ten, we all said goodnight. Shawn's sisters and their husbands and kids left, and Sissie and I headed up to our rooms while Ed and Karen turned off the lights.

Walking up the stairs, I laughed, whispering to Sissie, "Isn't it weird sleeping in Dinah's old room?"

"Yes!" she whispered back. "The bed is right out of the 1970s, I swear." She giggled. "I think your room is worse being Dad's old room. The comforter has baseball bats and mitts on it! And wait until you see the photos on the wall—like a scrapbook of Dad's entire childhood."

Her eyes were big. She wasn't sure how I'd react, so I just grinned and said, "Well, I hope I won't find any photos or letters from old girlfriends."

"Whoa, hopefully not."

We hugged, and she went into the bathroom as I flipped the light on and shut the door to Shawn's room before getting into my pajamas. I texted Jon quickly and told him I was tired and would call him tomorrow. He texted back the thumbs-up sign.

Then I looked around the room and felt a lump form in my throat. All of these photos of Shawn: sitting with his sisters on a big rock next to a creek, taking a swing with a baseball bat, formal Christmas photos of the three of them in their Sunday best, the obligatory cap-and-gown high school graduation photo, him standing next to his first car, a Datsun, and finally, on the dresser, an eight-by-ten of him hugging Sissie and Cole to him with the waters of Siesta Key in the background.

That photo was only five years old. I had taken it with my phone and printed a copy and framed it as a gift to Ed and Karen for Christmas one year. That was the day we had rented kayaks and spotted manatees in the intercoastal. Sissie and I had been in the same kayak, and we'd paddled up to them slowly. They'd let us come right next to them in the water, docile and quiet, but by accident, the front end of our kayak drifted over one of them, and much to our surprise, it tail-butted our kayak with a big tha-rump! We'd been so shocked that we'd screamed and laughed in delight. It had been a truly enchanting moment. Shawn and Cole had stayed safely away, watching and laughing with us (or was it *at* us?). And there was the photo from a few hours later, on the beach, frozen in time, commemorating our magical day.

I held the frame in my hands and cried. There would be no more family trips. No more magical moments. No more shared memories. No more photos. No more hugs for Sissie. No more hugs for me.

Chapter XXIV

Indianapolis, Indiana
December 2018

I WENT TO BED SAD and woke up angry. When my alarm went off at seven Monday morning, my first thought was, who is this guy who stole my husband from me? Who made this room and bed that I have just cried and slept in be a cemetery, a tomb, a tribute to my husband instead of a living, breathing, symbolic image of a future for him? Why was this man still alive and my husband dead? How could the balance of good and evil be so off-kilter?

I got up and peeked in on Sissie in her room, saying good morning just as she was pulling the covers off and getting out of bed. Ed and Karen were already downstairs brewing coffee, if my sense of smell was right. I stood in the shower, letting the hot water burn my chest and back, thinking how I wished it would burn the thoughts of this horrid man out of my mind. The picture I had of him in my head was still of the Grim Reaper in the cape with the scythe. I thought those images would have gone away by now, but they were still there, strong and dark, reemerging from the recesses of my mind. I wondered if, after today, that image would be replaced by the face of a real man. I certainly didn't want that. How would I ever get *that* image out of my mind?!

I got dressed, quickly put on some makeup to cover the red speckles that had formed under my eyes from crying, and headed downstairs. While Sissie was in the shower, I asked Karen about Sissie missing school, and she said she had talked to the office about their meeting, and they had given her an excuse for the day. I nodded and we drank coffee and ate breakfast in silence.

I was thinking about that word *closure*. My mom, Michelle, and Kelly had all said coming back here to Indy for this was a good way to get some closure. I had agreed, mostly to placate them, but in my mind (then and now) I could only think, there is NO closure! No matter what happens to-day, I still don't have Shawn! I hadn't been able to say goodbye to him, hug him, or tell him I loved him and that I would always love him. I hadn't been able to talk about what an amazing life we had together. I hadn't been able to thank him for all the ways he had been there for me. How he had made me a better person. How he had rescued me from my loneliness. I hadn't been able to cry and tell him how much he had meant to me and how I would never forget him.

We would never watch Sissie graduate from high school or walk down the aisle at her wedding or hold her first child in her arms. We would never kiss, hold hands, hug, laugh, sleep, cuddle, or make love again. We would never sit out on the back porch watching a rainstorm come in from the south. We would never swim in the ocean, share a margarita, play a game of backgam-mon, talk about work. Again. We would never grow old together. We would never have *together* or *again*.

So how could there be closure?

As Ed drove us downtown to the Federal Building, I reached out across the back seat to grab Sissie's hand. We were both nervous, not knowing what to expect. She looked at me gratefully, with anxious concern on her face. As Ed parked the car, I began to think how familiar it was being in downtown Indy again, a few blocks from where I used to work, but it was also strange, as though I was an outsider in a foreign land. And how could I ever have predicted it would be under these circumstances, a dark cloud hanging over my déjà vu and my nostalgic memories?

We headed soberly toward the entrance. The security guard took our names and pointed us to an auditorium off the lobby. When we walked in, there were already about fifty people mingling about and finding seats. I recognized some of the injured victims—a woman with a prosthetic arm and leg, a boy in a wheelchair, two men limping to their seats, one with a cane, and a little girl with a walnut-sized pink indentation on her forehead and a patch over the socket that used to be her eye. And many more. I looked away, toward the floor.

An elderly couple walked up to us, saying hi and shaking hands with Ed and Karen. The Robersons. We had met them at the funeral for their son, who was the same age as Shawn. They were from Noblesville. David had been their only son. He was survived by his twenty-year-old daughter, Rachel, who also came up and shook our hands and gave Sissie a hug. It was nice to see them, but we wished our mutual connection, this macabre tragedy, was not the reason we had met in the first place or were meeting again now.

Mr. Roberson said, looking at Ed and Karen, "Well, we're meeting under somewhat better circumstances this time at least."

They all nodded with grim smiles. Ed said, "Yes, that we are."

Not much else needed to be said, so we took our seats.

More people filtered in until the auditorium was full, groups talking in murmurs. Rachel was sitting next to Sissie and talking about her junior year at IU. Ed and Karen were talking about the weather with the Robersons. I sat there and looked around at the scene. There was a nervous energy, no one sure what was to come, and there was also that same feeling of deep, unendurable sadness that always lingered and permeated the air when in the presence of these people who shared this unbreakable, unwarranted, unwanted, and unbearable bond of tragedy.

Thirteen dead and eighteen injured.

And these were just some of the survivors, friends, and family. Many who weren't here were from other countries. On that day, they had come to Indianapolis to see the greatest spectacle in racing, thinking it was a safe and serene city, a jewel in the heart of America's Midwest. And they had left in shock and horror, thinking, like the rest of us, was there nowhere safe left in the world?

Huddled in tight conference, in anticipation of the truth, the reason, the whys behind the loss, pain, and suffering, in anticipation of having someone to blame, accuse, tie the noose around, in anticipation of the all-encompassing and ever-elusive *closure*, we waited with bated breath.

A man in a formal business suit and tie and reading glasses perched on the end of his nose went up to the podium and cleared his throat into the microphone. Then he said, "Welcome. Welcome, everyone. I'm Special Agent George Thompson of the FBI. I appreciate your coming today. We wanted to get the victims, friends, and family members together this morning, in advance of our press conference at noon, to let you know that we have, in fact, captured the person we believe is the alleged perpetrator of the Indy 500 bombing. We have been working diligently and extensively with the Office of Homeland Security and other federal and local agencies to get to this point in our investigation. We want to state right up front that, based on the information we have at present, we've ruled out any and all terrorist organizations. Let me be clear: the suspect we have in custody is a homegrown Indiana man with no religious affiliations or ties to terrorism."

There was a hushed gasp. Following this astonishing statement, a silence fell over the crowd in anticipation of the agent's next words.

"We would like to thank our local law enforcement, who were able to apprehend the alleged suspect rapidly and without incident. So now, today, I would like to provide you with some information about the man as well as our process of discovery and capture. We will be sharing various details with you this morning—more than with the public—out of respect for your loss and suffering. However, in light of the fact that this is an ongoing investigation, be aware that certain aspects of the case and prosecution will continue to remain confidential.

"So, without further ado…" He cleared his throat again, tipping his head down to assess the audience from above his reading glasses. At our wide-eyed looks, on the edges of our seats, he seemed satisfied enough to continue, peering through his glasses at a sheet of paper on the podium. "We apprehended the suspect at his parents' home in Lebanon, Indiana, on Wednesday, December fifth at 0900 hours. He is currently incarcerated at the maximum federal security prison in Terre Haute. His name is Devon Austin Wade. He is twenty-nine years old. He was living with his parents and his younger brother, Thomas, on a farm in Lebanon upon his apprehension. From what we know so far, Mr. Wade is a man with a history of mental illness. Two months ago, we received an anonymous tip to look into Mr. Wade as a potential suspect. We began to investigate and gather evidence. Finally, when we interviewed Mr. Wade, his parents, and their other son, a picture began to appear of Mr. Wade's obsession with perpetrating certain experiments and crimes, including arson, inhumane treatment of animals, and particularly the inappropriate use of explosive devices."

He proceeded as we all sat in rapt attention. "Since the anonymous tip, we have validated that Mr. Wade matches the profile in the surveillance videos from the day of the bombing, although he has since made changes to his appearance, probably in an attempt to conceal his identity, as you will see from the interrogation video. In addition, his alibi for that day does not check out and we believe is completely fabricated. We have also found bomb-making materials at the Wade farm. We have seized the Wades' computer, which contains evidence related to the bombing. From what we can tell, from a young age the suspect has used his parents' farm, including a large barn in the back, as a testing ground for unlawful activity, including setting fires, torturing and killing animals, and experimenting with various types of explosive devices, including pipe bombs like the one used at the Indy 500. His parents admitted that they have even feared for their own lives during Mr. Wade's exploits. Based on the anonymous tip, local law enforcement have gathered and are continuing to gather evidence from the Wade home in an attempt to tie the bombing as well several other incidents in the Lebanon and Indianapolis areas to Mr. Wade.

"Right now, I would like to show you a video of our interrogation of the suspect. Although the interrogation lasted over twenty hours in total, in the interest of time, we'll be showing just a brief section that we believe illustrates the thought process of the suspect and his intentions in conducting these crimes. Please stay put after the video and we'll take the rest of the morning to field your questions.

"Miss Watson, can you roll the video? Thank you. I'll dim the lights."

Mr. Thompson stepped down to the light switch, and the video played on the screen behind the podium. I glanced over at Sissie. The realization that we were both about to see the man who murdered Shawn and Cole was making us both nauseous, but we held hands and swallowed, staring blankly at the screen.

The video was grainy and had a yellow hue to it. There was one barren bulb hanging from the ceiling in the small interrogation room, which also had one metal table and two hard plastic chairs. The video started with one man, an officer in plain clothes, sitting across from the suspect, who was leaning back in his chair, defiant and almost cocky in his posture. Mr. Wade had short, messy blond hair and no beard. He was heavy, bloated, and unkempt, with a dirty gray hooded sweatshirt, black jeans, and dark high-top sneakers. His appearance was in stark contrast to the man in the videos from the day of the bombing, who had long dark hair, a full beard, a baseball cap, white T-shirt, and navy basketball shorts.

The detective was asking him questions about the day of the race. Where he had been, who he had been with, what he had been doing. Devon Austin Wade's body language on the video was one of avoidance and anger. Part of the time, he would shoot daggers at the detective's face, his mouth pinched and insolent, and the rest of the time he slouched down in his chair, studying his fingernails and mumbling under his breath. He couldn't seem to sit still, moving from one position to another, clearly irritated and wishing to be gone. The detective asked him several times to sit up, look at him, and answer, but he was trying every possible means to avoid complying. His erratic behavior was antsy, manic, almost deranged.

Finally, after multiple promptings, he answered the detective in one-word grunts. The detective said Mr. Wade had indicated earlier that he'd been riding his motorbike out in the fields. But then the detective countered that information, saying Mr. Wade's parents confirmed they hadn't seen him all day. So, the detective asked if he had any other proof he'd been out riding. Did anyone see him on his motorbike? Could anyone confirm that he was in the fields? Did anyone drive by and notice him? No answer. The detective then asked him about the online purchase of the Indy 500 ticket they were able to trace to the Wades' computer.

The detective wanted to know why he had purchased a ticket when he knew he would be out riding. Mr. Wade just grunted that he went out riding every day and it was no big deal. The detective pressed him about the ticket, and Mr. Wade just remained silent. The detective asked him again to tell him everything he remembered about that day, where he slept that night, what time he woke up, what he had for breakfast, who he saw. Had he heard about the bombing? Did he watch it on TV? What did he think about it? Was he shocked, concerned, horrified? At this point Mr. Wade leaned forward in his chair, his head in his hands, pressing his fingers into the sides of his skull and shaking back and forth.

Finally, the detective stopped and tried a different tactic. He told Mr. Wade he was going to take a break and got up and walked out of the room. The video was still on and showed Mr. Wade glance up to watch the detective walk out the room, then lay his head down on his arm on the table. After a few minutes, it looked as if he had gone to sleep, completely immobile and quiet. Then another detective came in who immediately seemed less stern than the previous one. He opened the door forcefully, waking Mr. Wade up, and went directly over to him and shook his hand, saying, "Nice to meet you, Mr. Wade. I'm Detective Bentley." Then, "Is there anything I can get for you? A coffee? A glass of water? Cigarettes? A Coke?"

Mr. Wade just looked at him strangely for a few minutes and then said, "Can I go home now?"

"Well, no, Mr. Wade. We have a few more questions for you."

"Can I see my parents?"

"Well, now, they are actually coming down to the station shortly, but in the meantime, we need to talk to you privately first."

The detective cleared his throat and began again in a friendly, open, welcoming voice. "So, I know Detective Jelecki has already filled you in on why we have you here today and has mentioned that you have the right to seek an attorney at any time, correct?"

"Yes," Mr. Wade replied warily.

"Yeah, well, we're really just here to have a conversation with you. That's all. The sooner we can get this conversation over with, the sooner you'll be done, okay? How does that sound? Are you sure you don't want a water or anything?"

Mr. Wade shook his head. He seemed to be listening, although he still wasn't looking the detective in the eye and was instead staring down at the table with a deep crease in his forehead.

"Mr. Wade. Do you mind if I call you Devon?"

He shrugged his shoulders.

"Great, so Devon, I wanted to hear a little about your childhood. How was it growing up on a farm? I grew up on a farm myself, up in Noblesville."

This piqued his interest slightly. Devon looked up at the detective and said, "It was alright."

"We mostly farmed corn and wheat and soybeans, but we also had animals. Goats and chickens and pigs, you know, some barn cats, the usual. Do you have any animals on your farm?"

"Yeah, some," he answered suspiciously.

"What kind of animals do you have?" Detective Bentley asked innocently.

"I don't know…same as you had, I guess."

"So, have you had any dogs on the farm, Devon?"

Devon's face changed—it twitched with some type of realization, but then was quickly replaced by feigned indifference.

"No."

"No, Devon? No dogs? You know, I've talked with your parents and your brother already—we had a long talk yesterday. I thought they said you've had quite a few dogs over the years. Wasn't there a dog named Ranger?"

Devon shook his head in response, looking down at his hands.

"No, Devon? No dog named Ranger? What about Toby? Did you have a dog named Toby?"

Devon, his head in his hands, shook back and forth, saying in a low voice, "No, no, no."

"Devon, look at me. Devon." He waited until he looked up. "Devon, what happened to Ranger and Toby?"

Devon paused but then finally said, "They died."

"Ah, I see. Okay, so they died. How did they die, Devon?"

He shrugged his shoulders.

"Devon, did you kill those dogs? Did you kill them? Why would you kill your own dogs? Why would you do that?"

Devon looked up at the detective with hateful eyes, shaking his head and saying adamantly in denial, "I didn't kill them. I didn't kill them." Then a moment later, softer, "I didn't mean to kill them."

Detective Bentley interjected quickly, pushing him, but still with a soft, open voice, "Oh, okay, so you didn't *mean* to kill them? Devon, what did you *mean* to do to them?"

"I don't know…I didn't mean it…I didn't mean it…."

"Devon, didn't you take Ranger out back behind your barn and pour gasoline on him and set him on fire…didn't you *mean* to do that, Devon?"

"No, I didn't mean to. I didn't mean it. I was just trying to see something, to see something…."

"What were you trying to see, Devon?"

"I don't know…I just wanted to see if he would burn. I didn't know it would kill him." He was holding his head in his hands, his whole body shaking back and forth.

"Come on, Devon. You want me to believe that? I know you like fire and playing with fire—right, Devon? So, why would you think that Ranger wouldn't burn? Didn't you *know* that Ranger would be hurt and probably killed?"

"No, I didn't know…I just wanted to see if he would catch fire."

"Uh-huh. You like to set fires, don't you, Devon?"

He shook his head in response to this, looking at the detective as if he knew he was setting a trap.

"And what about Toby? What happened to Toby, Devon?"

"He died."

"Yes, well, we've already established that he died, Devon. How did he die?"

No response.

"So, we know you like fire, Devon. It seems like you also like blowing things up. Isn't that true, Devon?"

No response.

"I've been out to your farm, Devon. I've been in that back room of the barn, you know. I've seen all of those interesting books you've been reading and all of those interesting parts you've been putting together, Devon. Do you want to tell me about that room and those devices you have lined up on that big wooden table? What are all of those parts for, Devon?"

No response.

"Are those the parts you put together to blow things up? To blow Toby up, Devon?"

"NO!"

"They're not?" Detective Bentley's eyebrows went up incredulously and he repeated, "They're not? Whose room is that? Is that your dad's room? Was he out there putting those parts together? Was that your dad's stuff out there?"

"NO!"

"Then whose? Was that your room, Devon?"

"I don't know."

"That was your room, wasn't it, Devon?"

No response.

"Devon, you know I've already spoken to your brother. He told me all about Toby. How Toby was such a great dog. A border collie, right? So loyal, so smart, so kind. Very protective. They'll pretty much do anything you ask, won't they? Is that how you got Toby to obey when you strapped that bomb to his back? Is that how you got him out in the field that day?"

"NO, NO, NO," he cried, shaking his head.

"Why would you do that, Devon? Why would you kill that sweet, innocent, loyal dog?"

"I didn't know...I don't know," he replied weakly.

Detective Bentley's demeanor changed in an instant. He leaned in, a foot from Devon's face, and spoke bluntly, "Yes, you DO know, Devon! Explain to me what you did to those two innocent, pitiful creatures."

Devon looked up at him with horror on his face. Then slowly there was a shift in him. Still staring, his mask came down like a veil, uncovering a diabolical evil darkness, pooled in the deep wells of his eyes, directed at the detective. He screamed into his face, "YES! I DID IT! And I LIKED it! I liked to see them follow me and do what I asked. I liked to watch Ranger burn, to hear his cries of agony, to watch his pleading eyes. I liked it! And Toby was even better because he was in front of me one minute and poof, gone the next! I obliterated him! In an instant, I obliterated him! I made him disappear! I did magic!"

Both Devon and the detective were breathing hard, the detective staring at Devon in shocked silence. A moment passed, then two, a stare-down between them. Then the detective, in the gentlest, most reserved voice, asked simply, "And is that how you felt that day at the track, Devon?"

Devon's eyes narrowed, all hints of pleading or sympathetic confusion gone from his eyes. He said with raised, challenging eyebrows, "I don't know *nothing* about those people."

Detective Bentley abruptly lifted himself up straight, his mouth a thin line, and walked out of the room. Devon looked at the door, his hands in tight, insolent fists on his knees, his chin up and proud.

✣ Chapter XXV ✣

Indianapolis, Indiana
December 2018

In the Federal Building assembly hall, the video stopped in the hushed, horrified silence. The lights flipped on, bright and harsh, and they were like a defibrillator to the audience. Agent Thompson stepped back up to the podium. I felt a cold chill run down my spine. I looked around; every eye was narrow with anger or swollen and large with shock and revulsion, every face twisted in a grimace of disgust. Some were crying. That—that man—that *thing*—that's who killed our loved ones? He seemed to have no remorse, no conscience, no scruples. He wasn't even remorseful about the dogs—what on earth did he feel about our loved ones, if anything? They were just his little experiment? *Bodies* on which to test his bomb-making skills?

One thing I hadn't thought of before this second was the actual way a bomb destroys and pulverizes a body. He made a bomb and put it next to hundreds of people because he wanted to see how their bodies would react, how their limbs would be pulled apart and mutilated, how their heads would collapse on their brains and skulls, how their faces would be torn off, how their insides would be blown to their outsides, how they would cease being a body at all, and maybe even how they would cease being a human to him.

It made my stomach lurch. I wanted to vomit and had to clench my teeth to keep from running for the door. That was how and why my Shawn died? And Cole? For this man to witness the mechanics of a death by bombing? It was resecting the spirit and soul of a person and thinking of them only as the physical collection of their molecules—that they were only a vestibule with an empty core. How could you not also see the soul, the heart, the mind, the spirit? What kind of monster couldn't see, know, feel that?

As Agent Thompson started to talk, I glanced over at Sissie. She had the same look of sickness and disgust on her face. He said, "So we believe this brief excerpt of the interrogation of Mr. Wade gives you a sense of the type of man we're dealing with. The complete interrogation took place over several days, along with our conversations with his family. As we mentioned earlier, Mr. Wade has been detained, and during the arraignment, we believe the judge will rule that no bail be set in this case. We will be cooperating fully with the prosecutor and defense attorney in the coming weeks and hope to provide more information as it becomes available." He looked down at his watch and said, "It's almost ten now. I'd like to take about an hour to answer any questions you may have. Detective Bentley and Detective Jelecki are standing by as well." He waved his hand toward the uniformed men standing next to the wall as they came forward toward the podium.

Many of us were still sitting in shock. Finally, after a few minutes, an older gentleman stood up and asked, "Why did it take so long to catch him?"

Agent Thompson paused and sighed for a second before answering. "Yes, well, until we received the anonymous call, we were unaware of Mr. Wade's existence. The suspect grew up in a very rural setting and had no job or friends. In addition, his parents homeschooled him, so his suspicious and frankly illegal behavior was only observed by a handful of close family members. When we canvassed the neighborhood, the farms to the east and west were miles away, and the families there were not familiar with the Wades. In addition, according to his parents, Mr. Wade changed his appearance quite frequently, losing weight, then gaining weight, growing a beard, then shaving it, growing his hair out, then cropping and dying it, adding tattoos. They said they didn't think anything of it when he changed his look right after the Indy 500. They didn't know he had purchased a ticket or had gone. The Wades don't have a television. Devon had one out in the barn, and we believe that's where he watched the replay of the bombing and the aftermath. The only way his parents even found out about the bombing was the coverage in the newspaper in subsequent days, but the photos of the suspect were blurry and grainy in the paper, as you may recall, and did not raise their suspicions or trigger them to recognize their son.

"As you are aware, we've followed up on thousands of tips. We've had over a dozen agents assigned and working actively on this case. However, many of the tips unfortunately led to dead ends. It wasn't until we contacted Mr. Wade's parents and searched the home that we could confirm the tip and our suspicions, which ultimately led to his arrest." He paused and added, "We recognize that these past two-plus years have been very difficult, and we want to thank you for your patience during this process."

After a moment, another question came from an angry-faced twenty-something man, "Is this guy going to fry or what?"

Agent Thompson cleared his throat and responded with a calm voice, "Of course, Mr. Wade will be afforded a full trial in due course, following the usual penal process. But, in answer to your question, although this will be handled as a federal case, the trial will most likely take place in Indiana, and yes, we are a capital punishment state, so that is a possibility. The judge and the jury have the right to determine Mr. Wade's sentence, including all available options."

Someone in the crowd screamed out, "Let him fry!"

Applause broke out.

I didn't clap but sat listening quietly, looking over at Sissie thoughtfully. She wasn't clapping or smiling either. Neither were Shawn's parents. We all knew killing this guy wouldn't bring Shawn or Cole back. I wasn't sure what I thought about the whole capital punishment piece, let alone the months of trial that were sure to be a long, drawn-out public spectacle filled with drama and rancor. But for me personally, vengeance didn't seem like the answer. Then I thought to myself, ultimately, what did it matter? Regardless of whatever fate was in store for him, it couldn't compare to the audience's forever-changed lives, our ongoing torture. It was a bitter pill with no promise of closure. Thirteen lives lost. Gone forever.

That night, alone in Shawn's childhood bedroom in the wee hours when everyone was asleep, I stayed up and talked to him and cried. I talked about all the amazing times we had together. That first moment when I met him in the bar when he was so handsome and strong and bold. Those months afterward getting to know each other, the subtle ins and outs of becoming a couple and diving deeper into each other's worlds. Then the marriage and ready-made family, the daily grind made easier knowing he was waiting for me at home, the vacations, the holidays, the family time, the years of love, support, and friendship. I talked about the rough times too. The times I had felt lonely, even as I was surrounded by people, often *his* people, and he hadn't been there for me or maybe I hadn't been there for him. The times we fought over stupid things, like the laundry and dishes. And over big things, like having children together and when we didn't see eye to eye about raising his kids.

I talked about how sorry I was that he had to die so soon. About how it wasn't fair that so many years were stolen from him. I cried and cried, telling him how sorry I was that he wasn't here and that somehow, by some sick, twisted turn of fate, I was. I told him how I didn't understand it. How I still asked myself sometimes (despite Beverly's instructions), why me? Why was I still here and he was gone? I talked about how he should have been the one to stay and raise Sissie and be there for his aging parents and continue his amazing career. Cole should have gone to college and been a sports commentator or a statistician on a sports team. He should have gone on to marry a sweet, sassy, cute girl and to have shy, pudgy, adorable babies together. Cole's kids should have been able to play with Sissie's kids—cousins who were also best friends.

When there were no more tears left, I admitted finally to Shawn and to myself: I know there's no going back. Regardless of the whys, regardless of the what ifs, regardless of the hows. I know I must move on. It won't be easy, and it won't *feel* good, at least not right away, but it's the only way. Almost at the instant when I thought the word *only*, I felt an overwhelming sense of calmness and reassurance pass over me, as if a warm, soft blanket had been placed on me, and I sank into the bed, wiping my eyes and allowing the comfort to seep into my being as I drifted swiftly off to sleep.

For the next day and a half, I spent as much quality time as I could with Shawn's family. I helped Sissie with her homework and chatted with Ed and Karen over old baby photos of Shawn and school pictures of Cole. After the meeting and press conference, we didn't say another word about Devon Austin Wade. We weren't going to devote another ounce of energy on that person, or rather, that *excuse* for a person. Instead, we spent our remaining time together reminiscing about Shawn and Cole and talking about the future—Sissie's goal of becoming a nurse someday, Ed and Karen's latest trip they had planned to Ireland, Shawn's sisters and their kids' ambitions. It was as if my visit (and maybe the capture of the killer too) released something in all of us. No closure, but maybe freedom. To allow ourselves the privilege to be happy again, free of guilt, free of confusion, free of the weight of what was lost and could never be again. It felt good.

My flight home to New York was so different from my flight to Indianapolis. Instead of brandishing my proverbial fist at the track, I stared down at the lights of the Christmas tree on Monument Circle rushing by below our plane, lit up as if to say farewell to me, a cozy reminder of a past well lived and the hope for a future yet to come. The entire flight, I found myself thinking about Jon and wondering what he was doing and if his patience had worn thin over the past few days when I had been basically radio silent. I could only hope he would understand.

As soon as the plane landed and I got out of the Rochester airport, I called Jon on my hands-free car phone. It was Wednesday, a little after seven o'clock. He picked up on the first ring.

"Amanda, hi," he said with his wonderful deep, kind voice. My heart tingled a little with the warmth of it.

"Hey."

"You back?"

"Yep, driving home right now."

"How—how are you? I, um, I saw the press conference…"

"Yeah, it was pretty awful. But if nothing else, I'm glad they got the guy, and now we can all…well, not think about *that* aspect of the tragedy as much anymore, at least not until the trial, which I'm sure will be a zoo, but I'm planning on disengaging, for my own sanity if nothing else."

"Right. Makes sense. And how was everything else…?"

I took a deep breath before I answered, knowing he probably heard that. I said, "You know, it was…really…good. So hard to be back in that world and to be surrounded by those memories, but it helped me process some things that I had been, honestly, avoiding, so I'm thankful for that."

"I'm glad. Well, if you want to talk about it, let me know."

"Thanks. But you know what?"

"What?"

"I'm okay. I'm really okay now. And you know what else?"

"What?"

"I thought about you. A lot."

Silence. Tick-tock, tick-tock, tick-tock.

"And I wondered…is that invite for a fish fry still available?"

Whoosh of air on the line.

"Is that a yes?" I asked with a laugh.

"Yes, that's a definite yes."

"Will Saturday work for you?"

"Yes."

"Do you want me to come early? Maybe we could get a run in together beforehand?"

"Yes."

"Will I get that promised walleye you said was the best?"

"Yes."

"Do you need me to bring anything? I make a mean macaroni salad."

"Yes."

"Are you able to give me more than one-syllable answers at this point?"

"Yes," he said with a laugh, finally snapping out of it, saying, "Are—are you sure?"

"Yes," I answered definitively.

"Okay, then come by as soon as you like. I'm usually up by six."

I laughed. "Well, I might wait a little bit longer before I head over there, but sounds good." Then I asked, "How's your training going? I only ran one day, yesterday morning, and only six miles. They have this trail called the Monon that goes for miles and miles, but I didn't have any gels with me, so I only did three miles down and turned around. How far did you end up going? What were your splits? I haven't had a chance to check the app yet…"

We talked the whole drive home, and before we hung up, we both mentioned looking forward to Saturday. I also asked what he thought was the "quintessentially most important question at the beginning of a relationship." (I think I heard him gulp over the phone before saying, "Um, I'm not sure…") I followed with, "Cake, pie, candy, or cookies?" The laugh of relief and breezy answer—cookies—made me smile from ear to ear as I said, "Same. Get ready then."

"Oh…I *will* be ready."

That night, back in my Maplewood home, lying in my Maplewood bed, looking out my Maplewood window at the soft snowflakes falling, I felt a contentment I hadn't known or felt in a long time. I even got up from my bed and walked over to my ring holder and picked up my wedding ring. After looking at it for a while, I put it on my finger one last time, holding up my hand to see it there and remember what it had meant to me. I lifted my jewelry box lid, pulling out the velvet inside layer to open a small box underneath. I slipped the ring into the box and put it back inside, closing and sealing it.

Now for the hard part. The voicemail. I went back to my bed, tucking myself up under the covers. I listened, for the ten thousandth time. "Hi, it's me. Where are you? Give me a call…or I'll try you later, bye." Shawn, where are you? Are you with me now? Will you be with me forever? Sometimes, lately, I have trouble remembering your face, and I have to go to our photos to remember the details. If I delete this voicemail, how will I remember your voice? Then, as if someone was speaking softly in my ear, I heard a whisper. It said, "I'm with you always." I started. It had been clear as day. Like a voice in the room. I looked around, but it was empty. Then I burst into tears. They were tears of joy. And love. And awakening. And realization. *He was with me.* Forever. I didn't need the voicemail, I didn't need the ring, I didn't need the photos. He was with me. Here, with me, always, in my heart and in my memories. Nothing would ever take him away from me.

I pressed the delete button on the voicemail, putting the phone down on the pillow next to me. Then I fell into a deep, dreamless sleep.

❧ Chapter XXVI ❧

Heathport, New York
December 2018

It was Friday, and I was feeling a strange mixture of guilt and elation. Not because of the upcoming date with Jon but because on that flight back from Indy, I had made another decision that I needed to execute today, and I felt my palms sweating, realizing it was now or never. I marched into my supervisor's office and told him I was quitting. I felt awful because he had been so supportive, especially when I had just taken three days off for a "family emergency," which was actually my visit to Indy. Of course, I hadn't told him the truth, but he had readily agreed, seeing me as a valuable asset who barely ever asked for anything, let alone time off. I sat across from him and explained that I appreciated everything he had done for me, hiring me as an "unknown quantity" when I needed a job, and how I would always remember the experience I had gained working in a start-up like this—the energy and enthusiasm it took to launch a new software program—but I said that if I was being honest, my heart wasn't in it like it should be and that I had decided to pursue other opportunities instead. I asked if he needed me to give two weeks' notice, and he said no since it was the end of the year anyway. He was very gracious, stood and took my hand, saying it was okay and he wished me all the best.

What I didn't tell him was that I had spent the previous evening scanning the online hiring sites for jobs that were completely out of my comfort zone. For instance, I had applied to the following four openings: Natural History Museum Docent, Adjunct Professor (Learning and Leadership Development), Orchid Garden Curator, and Trail Run Field Organizer. Each of these jobs sounded fascinating to me but also completely and utterly foreign to every molecule of muscle-memory career experience I had formed over the past sixteen years. I figured I had about as much chance of a callback as I had of winning the lottery. But this was my new take-charge stance in life, and I figured, what did I have to lose? I wasn't going to sit around the house staring at the four walls all day. I wanted a new adventure, one where money wasn't the object, so, as Beverly would say, why not shoot for the moon?

And speaking of Beverly, it was Friday night, and I had several items to mark off the list on my fridge. In between making macaroni salad and oatmeal chocolate chip cookies and figuring out what to wear and what to bring for my date with Jon, I took down the crumpled and re-flattened list and stared at it. Wow, quite a few things could be crossed off now, and instead of that making me sad, like I thought it would, it felt wonderful, like I was finally making progress toward…what? I wasn't sure yet, but the forward movement of striking through some of the words was enough to make me giddy.

Goals:

~~*Finish House Renovations*~~
Plant a Garden
Run a Marathon
Hike Watkins Glen
~~*Remove and Store Ring*~~
~~*Delete Voicemail*~~
Send Letter to Beverly
~~*Seal and Store Wedding Dress*~~
Find New Job
Get a Kitten
Visit a National Park
Go Camping and Horseback Riding
Learn a Musical Instrument

As I drifted off to sleep that night, I thought about how my sleep and emotional life had improved. Yes, there was still some anxiety about every new situation, especially when I felt my heart tripping on the memories from my past, but with each new day I was moving in the right direction, integrating those past memories with fresh, new ones, and I could feel the wholeness of it in my bones. I was even surprised and impressed at how smoothly my "quitting" discussion had gone (despite my sweaty palms!). Now I was feeling even more free and clear for my date with Jon.

The next morning, bundled up in layers of running gear and packed with a bag of clothes to change into (several options, not knowing where we would end up or what we would do besides running and a fish fry), I texted him saying I was on my way and found myself grinning like a kid on Christmas morning, driving to his house, wondering about a thousand things all at once: how his house would look, how *he* would look, how it would feel being in his space, if he would finally tell me about the ex (and how I would react to that), if he would like the food I brought, if I would like the fried walleye, and more than anything, if we would kiss again. Or...more...?

When I pulled into his driveway, I instantly liked his house. It was a bungalow-style 1940s model, two stories, painted cream with blue shutters. It had a blue front door that matched the shutters and a small hill for a front yard, with cement steps leading up to the entrance. The front yard wasn't very large, but it had a great view of the lake, which was right across West Lake Road. A floating dock had been removed from the water and placed on a slight strip of land on the lakeside. That must be where he moored his fishing boat during the season. Today, though, the water was swirling in angry, white-capped waves under a dark gray sky. I pulled up to a detached garage and put my car in park, taking a deep breath as I got out with my bag and food items.

He was there, opening a side door that was covered by an overhang leading from the garage to the house.

"Good morning!" he said. I felt slightly nervous as he held the door open for me, but he was cool as a cucumber, like always, which calmed my nerves. He took the macaroni salad and cookies from me, saying, "Ohhhh, yum."

I smiled.

As we stepped into the little mudroom just inside the side entrance, he said, "Well, this is it. My house. Not much to speak of, but it works."

"It's nice. I like it!" I said.

"Well, it's no Maplewood Avenue."

"Hey, Maplewood Avenue doesn't have a lake, so yeah, I think you're good."

"True," he assented.

I laid my bag on the floor in the corner, and he pointed to the hooks on the left for me to hang my jacket. I noticed there was a dog leash hanging

there. I thought, did he mention a dog? And my second thought was, what
else would I find that he had forgotten to mention? Gulp. The mudroom
had one set of stairs that went down to what looked like an unfinished basement, where I noticed a washer and dryer off to the side. And as we ascended
the stairs, I found myself immediately in a beautiful, brand-new, granite-
countered, subway-tile-backsplashed kitchen.

My eyes wide, I exclaimed, "Wow! You did this? This is great!"

He smiled and said, "Yep. Well, I had someone else sand and refinish the
hardwood floors throughout the whole house, including the kitchen, but everything else I did myself. It took a year, so I wasn't too speedy about it, but I
like how it turned out." Then he set my food on the counter, reached around
the corner, on the other side of the refrigerator, and handed me a huge bouquet of red roses. He looked into my shocked eyes and said, "Thank you for
coming here. I know you were probably…anxious about it."

"Oh, Jon, they're beautiful! Thank you!" I took them in my arms and
smelled their sweet perfume, then reached up to pull him to me for a kiss.
His lips were soft and warm and minty flavored, and they felt wonderful on
mine.

When we drew apart, he was looking down into my eyes with amused
surprise. He said, "Remind me to get you flowers more often."

I grinned and kissed him again for that.

He found a vase in one of the cupboards, and as I cut the stems and arranged the roses, he asked if I wanted coffee, to which I said sure, and he
poured us each a mug. Then he walked me through the rest of the house,
which was traditional (no open-floor plan here) and bachelor-friendly. Quite
a few pictures and items relating to ducks and fish and other man-cave-
worthy decor. It was cozy and pleasant. A nice living room with a big navy
couch and recliner across from a large flat-screen TV. Upstairs, there were
three bedrooms, each rather small. One was set up as an office with a large
bookcase filled with books in one corner. His bedroom looked out onto the
backyard, just as mine did, and I was surprised to see that the yard appeared
to be quite large. It was surrounded by a wooden fence, and I could clearly
see the remains of his vegetable garden, the wire cages for his tomato plants
still staked and leaning against each other. The rest of the yard was speckled
with mature trees and bushes.

I asked, "Did I see a dog collar downstairs? Is that why the yard is fenced
in?"

He nodded grimly and answered, "Yeah, Angus, my black Lab. Sadly, he died back in April. I miss him. He was a great dog, but he was getting up in years and had arthritis in his legs, so he was having trouble getting around. He fell down the basement stairs when I was at work one day, and I found him lying down there not moving, so I took him to the vet, who put him down."

"I'm so sorry…that must have been awful," I said sympathetically.

"Yes, it was," he replied briefly.

As we went back downstairs to the living room area, I noted that there was no trace of his ex in photos or in anything else, as far as I could tell, so that was a relief. I was also happy to see a live Christmas tree modestly decorated with white lights and a large star on top, which added a cozy holiday vibe to the room and which I thought was a nice touch for a bachelor pad.

We sat down on the couch facing each other, our knees not quite touching, sipping our coffee. I asked, "What have you been up to?"

"Oh, the usual. Work, groceries, cleaning. Really exciting stuff."

"How are your parents doing?" I asked. He had called me earlier than normal the night before because he was headed to his parents' house for dinner and didn't know how late he would be. I had told him about quitting my job, and he'd been supportive of my decision, asking me more details about the job openings I had applied for, laughing at the orchid garden one ("That's a job? Sounds interesting!").

In answer to my question, he said, "Parents are good, same as always. They never seem to change, which I appreciate. I hung out with my nieces quite a bit. They made me play hide-and-seek for, um, let's see, like twenty minutes, so that was exhausting," he said with a grin, "but otherwise, very nice."

He asked more about my trip, and I filled him in, dancing a little bit around the more intimate nuggets like my late-night conversations with Shawn in his childhood bedroom. Jon was very respectful, sitting and listening with those intense green eyes on my face, sipping his coffee and letting me skim over the subjects that were more difficult.

After a half hour or forty-five minutes, we got up and put on our gear, and he drove us to a country road nearby that would be good for our run. It was a beautiful, open, slightly hilly area with enough trees to block the wind. As we got out of the car, putting our hats and gloves on, I began to wonder how it would work, so I asked, "Are you going to walk beside me?"

He laughed. "Very funny. I know you're not that slow, but don't worry about me—I'll just slow my pace to stay close."

"You don't have to."

"It's okay," he said with a smile, "I want to."

He stayed true to his word and ran at my pace for most of the run, talking with ease as I huffed and puffed, trying not to look as if the frosty air in my lungs created a massive deterrent to my breathing and talking, which it did. He would string together sentence after sentence while I answered in one-word grunts. Sometimes he would break into a sprint, go ahead, then turn around and come back to me, slapping my hand with a high five, as though we were in a race. I enjoyed watching him go—he really had beautiful form. I tried to straighten up to mimic him, feeling inadequate in my speed. But he didn't seem to mind or notice and kept chatting with me about how great it was that we could run together like this and what a pretty day it was (even though it was snowy, gray, and cold). He made me smile and feel good with his optimism and carefree attitude. It made me wish we *could* run the Winter Warrior half-marathon together, but of course, I would kill his time. Plus, as much as I loved running with him, I knew being with him and talking was not a routine I was used to and would probably hurt my usual steady breathing and pace.

Most days, I ran alone with my earbuds piping in my best running playlist, the beat of the songs keeping my legs in lockstep with my pace. Today was a treat but not something I would repeat during a race. But it certainly felt amazing! In fact, the reason I was huffing and puffing was not just because of the freezing air, but because Jon's presence, sweet glances my way, and handsome form sent my heart beating faster than normal and my breath catching in my throat.

Seven miles later, we finished, but before we got back in his car, he gave me a cold, sweaty hug, saying, "We did it! Good job!" We both laughed at our contrasting outer frigid layers and inner hot, wet layers. Then he pulled back and looked at me in all seriousness, much to my surprise, and said, "God, you even smell good like this!"

"Oh, come on! Get outta here!" I said, pushing him back from me toward his driver's side door.

He said, "No, I swear. I love the way you smell. Even your sweat smells good."

"Whatever." I rolled my eyes and smiled, going around to my side and getting in. I thought he smelled good too. I wasn't about to tell him that, though. So strange—I guess those oddly curious pheromones were real.

"So, what are we doing the rest of the day?" I asked as we drove down the road back toward his house.

"Well, we can shower and eat some lunch. I have some deli meat if that's okay. After that, we're wide open. We can sit around and talk, take a nap, read a book, watch a movie, whatever you want to do."

"Sounds perfect," I sighed. It did sound perfect! It was nice to just be with him...to not feel the need to entertain each other and do something all the time.

He let me take a shower first. His bedroom adjoined the bathroom, so I changed in there. For some reason, I swear I felt the electrical charge coming off his bed as I stood naked, taking my clothes out of my bag. I knew from a logical standpoint that he was downstairs waiting for me, but from an energy standpoint, it was as if he was in the room with me, seeing me without clothes, setting my pulse on fire, as he always did, making me wonder what it would be like to be in this bed with him right now.

I got dressed as quickly as I could, putting on a thin maroon sweater and jeans, and headed downstairs. He looked up from the recliner, startled as I gave him a deep kiss and said with a smile, "Your turn."

He asked with a twinkle in his eye, "So I take it you didn't find any skeletons in my closet up there?"

I laughed and said, "Not yet."

"Phew. Okay, I'll be quick. I set the fixings for the sandwiches out on the counter. Feel free to make yourself one." He gave me a peck on the cheek before heading upstairs.

When he came back down, his hair still wet, his face cleanly shaven, looking like something out of GQ magazine, I tried not to stare. He pulled out two TV trays and set them in front of the couch so we could eat side by side. I told him the true story of how Michelle, Kelly, and I ended up at his book lecture on my birthday, which now seemed like a lifetime ago. I told him how Michelle ran into Janice Dempsey at their sons' soccer game. He laughed and pointed toward the house a few doors down and said he had wondered if it was something like that.

"Janice and Tony. They're really nice. That's funny that Janice talked about me to Michelle. I didn't realize my life was such an open book or that I was such a charity case." He smiled with chagrin.

"Oh, I don't think she was saying that—just that you were living alone, as far as she knew. That was all Michelle needed, though, to get a bee in her bonnet or a bug in her ear or whatever it took to give her an excuse to set me up."

"Right. Well, in retrospect, I'm glad she did."

"Me too," I said with a smile. A moment later, as I was chewing and thinking, I finally put my sandwich down and wiped my mouth, saying softly, "I *am* glad we reconnected when we did, and there's no other place I'd rather be than with you right here, right now." I paused to let that sink in, and he stopped to regard my face, noting the seriousness in my voice. He didn't say anything, simply taking in my words, and I continued, "But I've been wondering lately, if it would be okay with you, if…you wouldn't mind telling me your story. About your life…before we reconnected. I feel like I've told you so much about me, and yet I'm in the dark about you." I waited as he put his sandwich down, a shadow coming over his face. I added, "I'm sorry, because I know from experience how hard it is to talk about something painful that you'd rather forget…something you can't change and that will never go away…something that is etched on your heart forever. I know—believe me, I know. But I also know, like you said to me once before, that it's best to build the foundation of a relationship on openness and honesty. Absolute truth. Remember?"

He sighed and said, "Yes, I do. It's what I want, more than anything." He nodded with grim pursed lips and said, "Let's finish lunch and I'll tell you everything." We ate in silence after that, him ruminating, me feeling the jitters, wondering what was to come. I almost felt my back stiffen, physically and figuratively, as I braced myself to hear about the woman he had said he was still in love with. After he put the lunch things away, including the TV trays, he sat back down beside me on the couch, turning to face me, sitting several inches away, not allowing any parts of us to touch. I wrapped my arms around myself and waited.

CHAPTER XXVII

Canandaigua, New York
December 2018

HE BEGAN SLOWLY, "Her name was—is—Melanie. I don't know where she is now, but we were married for thirteen years."

I nodded slowly and asked, "How did you meet?"

He sighed and began, "After I graduated from SUNY, I spent a few years in Wyoming, working for the Fish and Wildlife Service. She was traveling around the country to different parks and nature preserves in a Volkswagen bus she'd inherited from her grandfather. She was so interesting, a big adventurer, filled with wanderlust, up for anything. She loved the outdoors and wanted to experience life at the core, you know, just like I did. I found her fascinating and exciting."

As he spoke, his eyes filled with the glow that up until this point I had only associated with his regard for me. It stung and I had to steel myself, not allowing the tears that pricked my eyes to fall, gulping them down with a burning in my throat. Luckily, he was lost in his own story, staring out the window toward the raging lake waters across the street as if he were beginning a great sea adventure on a pirate ship and hadn't noticed my eyes or my face or anything else besides his clearly still-poignant memories of that novel and enthralling exploration on which he was about to embark with *her*.

He went on, "We hung out for a while that first year, off and on, but right about the time we would settle into a routine, she would be off again, onto the next state or park or festival or concert or whatever or *who*ever. Then, about halfway through year two, she started to stay longer with me—for several months at a time. I suggested that she simply move in with me, but she said she didn't want to be tied down and insisted on breaking away, leaving in her bus when I brought up anything more permanent or serious.

Looking back now, I think I overlooked or chose not to see some of her erratic, unsteady behavior. But I was young and thrilled by whatever moments
I could get with her. She was exciting, outspoken, beautiful, brave, and unpredictable, and back then, everything about her appealed to me. She had
no fear and no need for the stability and security that most people seek. She
rarely worked and instead lived off whatever she could make with her own
hands—tie-dyes, jewelry, dreamcatchers, paintings, headbands, you name it.
She would sell these items at concerts and festivals and use the proceeds for
gas and food money.

"By the third year, I was feeling a little homesick, and I heard about the
ichthyology job from Brian—who, by the way, had been my roommate in
college. I applied, interviewed over the phone, and got it. As I packed up my
stuff to move back to New York, Melanie was gone on one of her adventures,
so I wasn't able to say goodbye properly. I told her over the phone that I was
leaving and that if she ever needed anything from me, she could look me up,
but I was also very clear that she would need to decide to put down some
roots before I would consider dating her again. As much as I loved spending
time with her, I had grown tired of the hot-and-cold aspect of our relationship. What was hard for me was the fact that I liked her more than anyone
else I had ever met, but not knowing where she was or who she was with
during those off times was difficult for me. I told her I wasn't wired that way,
couldn't pretend ignorance when she disappeared or was evasive with me. I
needed more to hang my hat on, and what she was giving me wasn't enough
anymore.

"She wasn't particularly happy with my decision, and I didn't hear from
her for several months after that, but then out of the blue one Saturday afternoon, she showed up on my doorstep—this doorstep, actually," he pointed,
giving me a chill as I stared wide-eyed at the offending door. "And just like
that, she was back in my life, this time with promises to settle down and make
it work with me because I was the only man for her." He put up his fingers
in quote symbols around "only man" and wore a look on his face I had never
seen before—a scowl. He went on, "I wanted so much to believe her because
of the way I felt about her that I let her reel me in, let her dupe me, and there
I was, setting up a home for us, doing everything I could to keep her around,
including planning weekend hiking trips and romantic getaways and visits
to the Adirondacks and the Catskills, not to mention skiing, snowboarding,
and ice-skating in the winter and boating, cliff jumping, skydiving in the

summer. We were always out there, making new plans, trying new things, being daredevils, adrenaline junkies. It was like a lifestyle for us."

As he spoke, I sat quietly, watching his face as it displayed mixed emotions. Soon, a strong feeling of nausea percolated in my stomach, and I had to stop focusing on his words for a moment. At first, I couldn't tell what I was feeling. It seemed almost like jealousy, but then I also began to stew, worried about him, *for* him, and angry at her, this woman I didn't know. It was like reading a book where you already knew the ending was sad, but you had to keep reading to see how the characters progressed to their inevitable end, all the while agonizing over their hurt and the injustice of it all. That's the way this felt, and I hated it. Every single word he was saying was written in his eyes, like an anchor weighing down his soul. I wanted to take him in my arms and protect him from what was to come, from the sadness that was clearly still brewing there.

He continued, "Then, a few months later, she told me she was pregnant. I was completely shocked, assuming she had been using birth control, as she'd told me all along. But you see, I was such a young fool, and I didn't even realize it. I was so taken in by her, believing everything she told me. She was a master at making me feel like the center of her universe, and when she was like that, I believed anything she said. Of course, the flip side was that she could also make me feel small, insignificant, utterly worthless, but I'll spare you the details. Just know that one wrong word or action could set her off, and when that happened, there was no stopping the volcano. Ultimately, sometimes days, sometimes weeks later, we'd make up and everything would be good again for a while, and I found that the roller coaster was part of the rush, the thrill of the ride that was who we were and what made us exciting and so intensely in love.

"We were married, the whole shebang, her family here from Canada and my family meeting them for the first time, and everyone getting along swimmingly. We had a big ceremony and planned it fairly quickly so she wouldn't be showing. It was over in Geneva at Belhurst Castle with Seneca Lake in the background, a full moon, the rolling hills scattered with grapevines. It was a truly magical night, and all I kept thinking was our troubles were in the past, and I finally got the girl, and she was exactly what I'd always wanted, and now we were having a baby together, and how I couldn't have planned my life any better."

At this, he paused, not for effect but clearly because what he was about to say was excruciating. His face went from almost whimsical to tortured in an instant, and my heart squeezed a little tighter.

"In the beginning, everything seemed great. We were getting along and super excited about the baby, so we started nesting, redecorating one of the bedrooms as a baby room, and shopping for a stroller and crib. Since Melanie was from Canada and didn't have many friends in the area, my brother Garrett's wife, Lora, planned the baby shower, to be hosted at their house. They sent out invites, and Melanie's mom and grandma and a few of her aunts and cousins were planning to drive down for the event.

"But then Melanie started acting…off. I knew she took prescription medications for some of her emotional issues, but I just figured they were for anxiety or ADHD. Heck, I knew tons of people needed meds for all kinds of things, and I never thought very much about it, assuming most everyone needed a little help once in a while. Then, about six months into Melanie's pregnancy, she became completely paranoid that her meds were hurting the baby. She would wake up in the middle of the night in a panic, screaming that the baby was going to be deformed. The doctor had assured her that everything was fine and that the meds wouldn't harm the baby. No matter how many times we talked about it or talked to the doctor, though, she still seemed to doubt it. Finally, without telling me or her doctor, she went off her meds."

He paused for a minute, looking down at his hands, trying to control the emotion in his voice. All I could do was watch his pain, feeling helpless to push these thoughts and words away. It was as if he knew they had to be said, but he wished they could just be wiped from his mind and his memory. I knew exactly what that felt like.

He took a breath and continued, "She was about seven months along, a week away from her shower, when she started to unravel. Of course, I didn't understand, thinking it was hormones from the baby. She would sleep for twenty-four hours at a time, then follow that by staying up and cleaning or cooking or building something, completely forgetting to sleep for two or three days. We were fighting all the time. I tried to reason with her, get her to maintain a more regimented schedule for the baby's sake and for hers. Plus, I didn't understand where all the rage was coming from. She would lash out at me for no reason, and I couldn't calm her down, no matter what I tried. Sometimes she would leave the house, going God knows where, disappearing for a few days at a time. I was totally unable to reach her by phone or by any other means. She would just be gone. It was beginning to feel like Wyoming again, where I couldn't rely on her, couldn't trust her, except this time she was my wife and she was carrying my child." As he said this, his eyes were fierce, his lips set.

"Then the Friday before her shower, when I hadn't seen her in three days, she showed up at our house, and she looked...different. I couldn't explain exactly how, but she looked...less full somehow and oddly, less healthy. I asked her what was going on and she refused to explain, saying nothing and that everything was fine, going off to bed early. The next morning, I asked her if she was ready for the shower. She didn't say anything, looking a bit paler than usual, and left without a word to meet her relatives at a local hotel before heading to the shower. She was gone all day and came back late, the car loaded with gifts, saying very little other than the shower 'went well.'

"The next few days were strange, almost as if she was in a deep depression, barely leaving the bedroom, sleeping a lot and not wanting to participate in normal daily activities. I figured she was tired, being in her third trimester. Even when her family came over to hang out for a few hours before leaving to head back to Canada, she only came downstairs for twenty minutes in her pajamas and said almost nothing. Her mother seemed concerned, and when I walked them out to their car, she pulled me aside and said something to the effect of 'Melanie goes through spells like this sometimes, but she'll snap out of it in no time.' She thanked me for taking care of her and for being patient with her. I wasn't exactly sure what to make of that. Of course I knew what she was referring to—I had experienced those spells firsthand—but for her mom to act as though they were a regular occurrence, I began to wonder if this was a long-standing pattern throughout Melanie's life and I was just now finding out the extent of it. Like I mentioned earlier, I guess I swept a lot under the rug back then, choosing to focus on the love I felt for her and how amazing she was and not on her...quirks...or her faults.

"As Melanie slept or remained immobile over those few days, I unpacked the shower gifts and arranged the nursery, filling myself up with hopeful anticipation of the joy to come and trying not to think too much about the state of Melanie's moods. We hadn't found out the gender of the baby, so the colors in the nursery and the baby outfits were mostly shades of green. We had a local artist paint a rainforest jungle scene on the walls. It looked adorable, and I spent a lot of time in there, sitting on the rocking chair and touching the clothes and baby books and toys. It was all so new to me, but I reveled in it, could barely contain my excitement."

He paused, looking away from me, almost trying to gain some strength from the floor, then continued shakily, "When she 'snapped' out of it, as her mother called it, she was out of bed like a jackrabbit and told me she was going to visit a friend in Buffalo for the weekend. I asked if that was wise, traveling in her condition, and something about the way she answered me sent a chill down my spine. She said, 'Oh, I'm not worried.' She kissed me and left with a smile on her face, but I sat up that night, anxious. I tried to call and text her, but she was unreachable. Finally, days after she said she would return, she came back through the door one snowy night, chipper as can be, grabbing me in a bear hug, but the moment I held her and pulled away, I wanted to die. Her bump—the place where our baby used to be—was simply not there anymore."

As he said this, his face awash with anguish, I gasped, putting my hand to my mouth. "Oh Jon!" I cried.

He nodded flatly and said, "I screamed at her, 'Melanie, what happened? Why are you smaller?! Where's the baby?' She narrowed her eyes at me, as if I was crazy, and said, confused, 'What baby?'" His voice cracked on the word *baby*, and he looked down at his hands, a tear slipping down his cheek, which he promptly wiped away angrily. "I have no idea where she'd gone or how she'd done it, but it was all over, and there was nothing I could do about it."

I shook my head, still with my hand at my mouth, not knowing what to say or how to console him. He shook his head too, knowing no words were adequate anyway.

When he didn't go on, I asked him softly, my voice getting stuck along the way in disbelief, "You—you stayed with her—after *that*? But—how?"

He leaned his head back onto the couch and sighed. At first, he answered simply, "It wasn't easy." Then, after a pause of a few minutes, his eyes closed, he finally sat up and stared at me. "She was ill. I mean, she was mentally ill. And although there were times when I was angry with her—more than angry—I knew it wasn't her fault. She was sick and needed my help. What followed was a two-week manic frenzy where I couldn't reason with her or calm her down. Then it turned on a dime and she crashed down a deep spiral, with a suicide attempt. She realized what she had done. I eventually had to check her into a treatment center. She got back on her meds, and they were able to stabilize her, and after a while she came home. While she was away, I packed up the baby room and painted over the jungle mural, which was just about the hardest thing I'd ever done in my life. Garrett and Lora came over and took the gifts away and sent them all back.

"When she was on her meds, life was good. We slowly resumed our routine, hanging out here during the week and taking adventures on weekends.

Clearly, trying to have another child was out of the question, so I made sure that would never happen again. And for her part, she did her best to settle into a more conventional relationship with me, staying close by for the most part, no longer slipping away for days. We had many good times—many *great* times, actually—but it was always the case that just when everything seemed to be going perfectly, she would equate that in her mind with a chance to go off her meds, and then all that stability and routine would be gone, usually without any warning, and the erratic behavior, the absences, the sleeping—it would all begin again."

He paused, breathing hard, staring into my eyes, hoping to draw forth understanding and the possibility of forgiveness for something that was clearly not mine to forgive. With defeat and heartbreaking agony in his voice, he said, "It got to the point where I couldn't do it anymore. I had to let go or I'd go down with her—you know, *drown* with her. I had to come up for air and take my life back, as best I could, without her. It was the hardest decision I'd ever made."

"Oh Jon, I'm so sorry" was all I could say as I took his hand in mine. He squeezed it, still with that look of pleading intensity in his eyes. A few seconds later, he stood up, dropping my hand and excusing himself abruptly. I watched him walk toward the bathroom, wondering what tortured guilt he was probably feeling as he regarded himself in the mirror. And yet, on my part, I felt nothing but admiration for this man who stuck to the hard road despite all the odds, even if in the end, it wasn't enough.

When he came back into the room, he stood above me, his palms upward, and said, "Yeah, so that's my story." He waited a second and added with a sad smile, his voice trailing off, "You sure you want to stick around…?"

In answer, I stood up and took him in my arms, cradling his head into my shoulder as he held me close, relief in his hands as they gripped my back. I said softly, "Yes, I do."

CHAPTER XXVIII

Rochester, New York
January 2019

As I came across the finish line, there he was, his smile huge, his medal swaying around his neck. He picked me up into a bear hug that swept my aching feet off the ground, our bib tags crinkling against each other. I kept saying in amazement, "I did it! I did it!"

He breathed into my ear, "Great job!"

In a blur, he put me down and someone handed me a medal and a banana, and we walked to the side, out of the way of the crowd. I looked down at the app on my phone and exclaimed in pure joy, "Two twenty-three!"

He laughed and nodded.

"What was yours?" I asked.

"One fifty-seven."

"Oh my gosh, that is so good, Jon! You're amazing!"

He hugged me to his side and echoed, "No, *you're* amazing!"

The whole thing had gone so smoothly, I couldn't wipe the smile off my face. The rush of endorphins was like a high I'd never felt before. As we walked slowly to his car, I felt every joint in my body ache, but I didn't care. I kept grinning over at him like a crazy fool.

He grinned back and said, "There's one to mark off your list, eh?"

"Woot! Woot!"

Of course, he seemed fine, walking as if he'd just finished a summer jaunt on the beach. I punched his arm lightly, and said, "You don't hurt?"

He shrugged. "I'm tired, but otherwise okay."

"A hot shower and a nap sound good to me right now."

He smiled. "Sounds like a perfect plan for the rest of our day."

I munched on my banana, and he asked, "Do you mind if we stop at

DiBella's on the way home? Grab a few subs? I feel like I could eat a house."

"Um, hell yes, please."

We got in the car, taking our bibs and gear off and throwing everything in the back seat, driving to the nearest DiBella's, still grinning as we ordered with our arms around each other the whole time. There was something so special about sharing this feat with him—both of us having trained these many months together and run the half-marathon with great finish times (even though separate paces). It was like another new bond that had formed between us, one to add to the list of bonds we had been building slowly ever since my birthday back in September. I could never have predicted back then where I would be on this cold January day, and yet here I was, my face hurting from smiling so much, and my body hurting with a good kind of pain that made me feel with every ache that I had done something I never thought possible.

For the rest of the drive back to his house, we compared notes about our running stats and everything we remembered along the course (water stops, funny signs people held up, the long stretch that was really windy and cold, when we felt the most exhilarated, and so on). We both laughed at the three best signs: "Run like your mom just used your full name," "Always give 100% (except when giving blood)," "You run better than the government."

When we got to his house, we ate our subs on the TV trays while we watched the playback of the race, which Jon had recorded from the morning news. We didn't see ourselves in any of the clips, but it was still fun to see everyone else who was there. They interviewed three women about my age who I remembered vividly because they were wearing bright pink tutus over their highlighter-yellow tops and running leggings. Then they interviewed the winners, which was interesting.

After eating, I took a hot shower, which felt like a luxurious spa treatment on my cold, achy joints. When I was done, I came downstairs in a pair of baggy sweats and said to Jon, "My body has officially turned to mush."

He smiled. "Good." He stood up and kissed me lightly on the lips, saying, "Feel free to stretch out on the couch or…wherever. I'll be done in a few."

As I watched his retreating form head gracefully up the stairs (seriously, he wasn't sore at all?), I began to wonder about that "wherever" comment. We had now been dating (somewhat officially, although never specifically stated) for four months, but Jon had been true to his word about leaving me to 'my pace,' and although we had kissed about a thousand times since that first intense vortex in the woods by the glen, we had never gone any further. When I thought about the physical aspect of our relationship, I was both eager and frightened. It was a strange dichotomy. Of course I was attracted to him—he was gorgeous! But more than anything, I was attracted to the calm, patient, kind, caring, smart, wonderful person he was. That turned me on more than any physical feature. The fear came into play when I let myself think about the fact that it had been *years* since I'd had sex, and that was with my *husband*. Oh, and the fact that I'd already done it with Jon, twenty-plus years ago, and that hadn't ended well.

On top of that, I wasn't sure if his mind was mixed up, like mine, with the thought of what had been and how that might affect what would be. Since he'd told me about his marriage to Melanie, we only talked about her once, and that was when he asked me out of the blue what Shawn had looked like. I stared at him strangely, thinking it odd that he hadn't noticed the photos in my house and wondering why he wanted to know. I answered, "Tall, dark, handsome, with broad shoulders and black eyes." He only said, "Ugh," which made me laugh because in my mind, there was no comparison. Jon was equally handsome, but in a different way, and that was just fine with me. But when he asked about Shawn, it made me think back to the way Jon had lit up when he talked about the early years with Melanie and how much he had loved her, so I followed suit and asked, "And Melanie?" His eyes got that look again, and I cringed but held myself steady as he answered, "Petite, long dark hair, dark eyes, cute little nose, athletic." I said, "Of course." He took me in his arms then, without another word, and kissed me in response.

So yeah, I guess I had been procrastinating, letting the fear consume me. We had never slept over at each other's houses, never even been in each other's bedrooms together. Our goodnight kisses lasted for thirty minutes at times, but in the end I had always pulled away, my knees wobbly, my head in the clouds. If I was gauging his reaction correctly, it was as much of a sweet form of torture for him as it was for me.

But today I'd run a half-marathon, and I was on top of the world. I felt as though I could conquer anything, even Mount Saint Jonathan. While he was still in the shower, I snuck into his bedroom, took off all my clothes, got under the covers, and waited. His sheets and pillow smelled like him—that wonderful earthy, clean smell—and I snuggled down deeper, feeling his essence permeate me. I was hidden under the bedding so tightly that a few minutes later, when he came into the bedroom, a towel tucked around his waist, his hair dripping, he didn't notice me and closed the door, opened the top drawer of his dresser, and swiftly dropped the towel, causing me to gasp. He spun around, momentarily shocked by the sound and by the fact that he was naked, grabbing the towel back to cover himself. But then as he stared at me, my big, wide eyes the only thing peeking out from under the covers, he gave me a slow, wonderful, glorious smile. It was filled with understanding, and that was exactly what I needed.

He said softly, "May I?" and pointed at the bed, and I nodded wordlessly. He shut the drawer, but not before he grabbed something out of it, placing it on the nightstand.

My eyes darted from his face to the towel in his hand, which immediately came away, leaving me breathless. Then he lifted the covers that I was still gripping to my body and slipped in beside me. At first our bodies didn't touch at all, and we faced each other on the two pillows. He kissed me, and as with all his kisses, I began to feel the warmth of his lips and tongue radiating into my core. With this kiss, though, he stayed gentle at first, pulling away at one point to check on me, still not sure of my full intentions. My body was wrapped in a cocoon of covers, and I hadn't let him near enough to notice that I was naked. But when he pulled away with that amazing kind and caring look, the one I had just been thinking earlier was part of what I found most attractive in him, I untucked the crease in the blanket that separated us and wrapped my entire body, full length, around his. The groan that escaped both our lips at that moment, and the depth of the kiss that followed, were like nothing I had ever experienced before. It was as if the buildup that had been percolating and gaining force over the past few months exploded the instant our bodies connected.

A crash of heat detonated in my chest, sending a surging pulse into every corner of my body and most especially into my groin. As his mouth moved from my lips to my neck to my breasts to my stomach to below, I felt as if he had awakened a sleeping dragon. I had forgotten how this felt. And maybe it wasn't a forgetting as much as a completely new discovery, one that had its origins in muscle memory but was now gaining traction as a whole new beast. I couldn't get enough of it, as I made obvious with the sounds emanating from deep in my throat. With my eyes closed, drinking in every single thing he did, I lost all sense of time and reality.

We stayed in that transcendent space for what seemed like a lifetime, him drawing out my pleasure in a way that I hadn't known was possible or that could be orchestrated by the will of a man's expert mouth and movements. It was an awakening for me—this level of attunement that had the power to evoke such freedom and release in the center of my being. When I eventually opened my eyes, he was there, watching me and waiting for his own release, finally taking it with several swift and hearty strokes, causing me to smile as he surrendered and then laid his head down on the soft spot between my neck and shoulder. When it was over and our breathing had become normal again, we took separate quick trips to the bathroom and then lay back down, spent, finally falling asleep in each other's arms. I was tranquil and content beyond anything I could remember or fathom.

I woke up first, and it was dark outside. I was on my side, and he was lying spooned up against my back, so I slowly turned and watched him sleep. He looked…peaceful. As his naked chest heaved rhythmically up and down in smooth, steady intervals, I laid my hand on his heart, feeling the strong thumping there. Then I trailed my hand down his waist to his stomach, caressing the muscles and soft skin until my hand lay flat on his hipbone, at which point he opened his eyes, smiled, and kissed me.

He said quietly, with a scratchy voice, "Hi there."

"Hi," I answered with a smile.

"I think that may have been the best sleep I've had in…forever."

"Me too." Then I grinned and added, "Wait, are you telling me I put you to sleep?"

He replied with a chuckle, "Let's just say you can tuck me into bed like that anytime you want."

I raised my eyebrows and kissed him.

We drew apart and he said, "As much as I'd like to explore that, um, napping technique a bit more, I have to admit, I'm starved. You?"

"Famished."

"Great. I have some leftover chili—how does that sound? With some good crusty bread?"

"Like perfection."

"Okay, let me get that going."

He kissed me quickly, jumped up, not self-conscious in the slightest, completely naked, still talking, saying, "I've got a growler of IPA in the fridge from Naked Dove too…maybe we can stay in tonight and veg out, watch a movie or something…"

"You had me at *chili*," I said with a laugh, staring openly at his spectacular physique as he threw on a pair of boxer briefs, sweatpants, and a long-sleeve T-shirt. His movements were so graceful and fluid for such a taut, muscular body. I marveled at him and wondered absently if I would ever feel as free with him as he was with me. Of course, under the darkness of the covers, he seemed to relish what I was offering, but still, even with Shawn, when I was much chunkier, I had always been afraid to show myself fully, choosing to dress in the closet or the bathroom and hide under the covers during lovemaking. But I reminded myself about being on top of the world today and how I had actually conquered not only a half-marathon, but also Mount Saint Jonathan. Everything in me was feeling confident and strong, and it had nothing to do with my weight. I threw the covers off, just as he had, standing up in full view of him as he was about to exit the room. He turned, stopped mid-sentence, and stared, saying only one simple word: "Wow."

I giggled and picked my clothes up off the floor, tiptoed over to him, giving him a peck on the cheek, my breasts skimming his chest as he tried to grab hold of me while I slinked away into the bathroom, the whole time laughing at the look on his face, which was something akin to ravenous.

"Oh my God, woman, you'll drive me to drink!"

"More?" I laughed through the bathroom door.

"Yes, and then some!"

"Well, you better crack that growler then."

"I might need something stronger," he chuckled, then with an exaggerated sigh, "Okay, I guess I'll see you downstairs."

"I won't be long."

"Good."

❧ Chapter XXIX ❧

Heathport, New York
February 2019

"You two are never gonna believe it—I got a job!" I screamed, my hands in the air for double high fives and hugs all around.

Michelle and Kelly complied and squealed in unison, "Woot! Woot!" and "Awesome!"

Kelly asked, "Where? When? How?"

"Come on in and I'll explain," I answered, holding the front door open for them. "By the way, happy birthday," I said, giving Kelly an extra squeeze.

"Thanks," she said with a sweet smile, closing the door behind her.

"Did you guys run into any issues on the roads? It looks pretty nasty out there."

Michelle shrugged and said, "490 was fine, but these side roads are a mess. I made Andy do the driving. He's over having a snowball fight with the boys in the yard."

I laughed as I peeked across the road at the Abernathys, and sure enough, Michelle's husband and boys, barely visible behind a wall of falling snow, were lobbing huge orbs at each other, screaming in protest and then laughing as they slipped and dodged and fell in the blanket of white, clearly having a wonderful time.

"That looks like fun!" I exclaimed. "We should join them."

Michelle gave me an *Are-you-crazy?* look and said, "Um…no."

"Oh, look at that. There's Mrs. O'Connor shoveling her porch and front stoop."

They peeked out the door with me, and Kelly said, "Wow, nothing keeps her down. I hope I'm like that at her age."

Michelle shook her head and said, "I hope *my boys* are like that when I'm her age so they can come over and shovel my drive."

Kelly and I laughed as I took their coats, hanging them in the closet, saying, "You know, when we were kids, we used to spend all of our waking hours out there in the snow. Remember?"

Michelle said, "Yeah, I remember, but we probably also had shit for brains back then." Then with a grin, she conceded, "How come we never felt cold? It was like we were insulated with our own stupidity, or was it sheer determination? We thought if we played hard enough, we wouldn't freeze, and wouldn't you know it? It was true."

Kelly smiled and said, "Do you remember when Donny Brewer ice-skated over Dustin's hand?"

"Yes," I said, my eyes big. "That was awful. I remember Dad grabbing a chunk of snow from the side of Derrys' pond and packing it right onto his bloody fingers, then rushing him to the emergency room."

"Ew," Michelle offered with a grimace.

"He still has the scars," I added as we came into the kitchen and sat on the barstools. "What's your poison? I have red or white wine, beer, pop, water…? I've made us fettuccine Alfredo, if that influences your decision."

"Oh, yummy. What are you drinking?" Kelly asked.

"Red."

"Perfect," they both agreed.

When I finished pouring, Michelle said, "Okay, now we need to know everything about the job."

I took a big, excited breath and said, "It's at MCC. They just called and told me. I start in two weeks!" I exclaimed, still in disbelief. "So, as you know, I've been doing phone interviews over the past couple of months for all kinds of jobs, and I was beginning to think I wasn't going to find anything, especially because every job I was interested in was so different from anything I had ever done before. I mean, there were quite a few places I never heard back from because frankly, I had no qualifications. But I got a call back about the adjunct professor position at MCC, and during the interview they said they really liked my real-world professional experience, but they couldn't hire me because I didn't have a master's degree or a teaching background. I figured, oh well, that was that—I'll just keep looking. Plus, as you know, I'm not the best public speaker, so I was actually somewhat relieved to not get that one. Then a few weeks later, the woman who interviewed me called back and said they had a new position opening up soon that she thought I would be a better fit for. We talked for forty-five minutes about the premise of the job, and it was as if I instantly knew what it was about and how I could tackle it and make it amazing. I couldn't believe it."

"Well, what is it already? Are you trying to tease us?" Michelle asked with a chuckle.

"Okay, I'll try to describe it, but like I said, it's new, so I'm sort of making it up as I go along, which is exactly what I think they want me to do. They have this new department called Professional Learning and Leadership Development, where they offer classes to the college's staff, including professors, to teach them certain aspects of the real-life working world—not just university or college theoretical knowledge, but real-world knowledge. These teach-the-teacher classes will help supplement the professors' existing experience and education with more practical hands-on instruction that they can then apply to their own programs and future curricula. For instance, they want me to start with a class that shows the step-by-step instructions, tasks, people, and skills needed to execute an end-to-end technical project. Like soup to nuts, everything it takes to develop and launch a new website initiative or an interactive HR program or an internal employee-only collaboration site. I'm not exactly sure what example I'll use yet, but the good news is that I have a ton of ideas just based on my work background. Of course, I won't use anything proprietary—everything will be simulation—but my brain is already flooded with ideas."

"Wow, that sounds right up your alley," Kelly said. "But won't you still have to get up in front of these people?"

"Yeah, at first that's what I was a little afraid of, but the women assured me that I can make the class as interactive as I want, meaning I don't have to stand up front at all if I don't want to. Instead, I can use the computer lab as my classroom or, better yet, have everyone bring their own laptop into an open classroom, and we'll work side by side, hands-on, developing the structure and implementation of the simulation together. This may sound cheesy, but I think with this job, I'll really be able to make an impact, giving my students something practical that they can use in their professional lives—say, setting up a teaching project or website or app or blog—or some extra edge to help their business or students get ahead. I'm hoping it'll feel much closer to the final outcome or reward at the end of the day. No longer will I be a small cog in a big wheel."

"Awesome," Michelle said. "I can't even imagine where I would begin with a job like that, and here you are, jumping right in, knowing exactly where to start and what to do. Very impressive."

I blushed a little, thinking how it was rare to receive Michelle's thoughts without her usual good-natured but sarcastic humor, and that made me appreciate her comment all the more. I said, "Thanks," then turning to Kelly, "As a matter of fact, I do need some help getting started, from you, my teacher friend, pretty-pretty-please, to figure out exactly what a 'curriculum' or 'course schedule' looks like. And anything else you can tell me about organizing and shaping a semester's worth of classes. I'm not even sure what materials to provide or if I should use a textbook or a syllabus or worksheets or what. I have no clue what I'm doing as far as that goes."

Kelly said, "No problem—happy to help. My music classes have always been at the high school level, but you could probably look them over and adjust accordingly."

"That would be great. Thank you both so much for your encouragement." I smiled. "Now how about some birthday dinner?"

I had the pasta done already and warming on the stove top, so we filled our pasta bowls and headed to the dining room table, along with our wine, salad bowls, a loaf of bread that I'd warmed in the oven, and a plate of seasoned olive oil. As we began eating, I said, "The best part of this new job is that I can set my own hours. They said I don't have to follow the normal semester schedule because the target audience isn't students—it's professors. In fact, because the professors are normally teaching their own classes during the morning and early afternoon, they suggested I pick a later time slot, like three or four in the afternoon. And I can make my own rules for what's required as far as quizzes, tests, exercises, grades, and all that."

Michelle had a knowing look on her face. She said, "Does this mean you'll still have plenty of quality time with, um, wait, what's his name again?"

"Ah," I said with a smirk, "I was wondering how long it would take you to ask about Jon. I'm amazed that you lasted a full, let's see, twenty minutes this time."

"Well, can you blame me?" she asked with fake irritation. "You haven't been exactly forthright lately."

I stared down at my fettucine and replied softly, "I know...I'm sorry."

Kelly inquired kindly, "So what *is* going on?"

I exhaled and looked at her and then Michelle. I said with a smile, "To tell the truth, I think I love him."

"Holy crap, Amanda!" Michelle cried, her fork falling out of her hand onto the side of the bowl with a crash.

"You do?!" Kelly exclaimed.

I nodded, my cheeks turning red, my heart beating, a smile washing over my face. "Yep."

"That's wonderful," Michelle said. "Have you told him?"

"Nope, not yet. I guess that's why I haven't talked about it with you two. He hasn't said it yet either. I think we're both feeling it, but we're also both a little scared…mostly because of our pasts and also maybe because things are going so well that, I don't know, I guess neither of us want to jinx it. He was here last night for a few hours, before the snow came, and we cuddled on the couch and watched a movie together. I just love the way I feel with him, so safe and secure. I never thought I'd feel that way again." I paused, with a small sigh. "Is it weird that sometimes I almost feel like it's too good to be true…or like I don't deserve to be this happy again after already having had one deep, loving relationship? Many people don't even get that." I stared at them guiltily with my confession.

Kelly took my hand and said, "No, it's not weird to feel that way, but I think what you have with Jon is exactly what you both *do* deserve, *especially* because of your pasts. It's what Michelle and I had hoped and prayed for, and exactly why we reintroduced you to Jon in the first place."

I squeezed her hand back, swallowing down the tears that had begun to well up. I said with a smile, "Thank you—I definitely owe you guys."

"Nah. We couldn't have asked for a better outcome, and we're so happy for you both," Michelle added sincerely. She lifted a glass, and we tapped them together in appreciation. As we went back to eating, a few minutes went by, then Michelle, back to her usual levity, confused us both for a second by asking, "Do you remember in the *Sex and the City* movie where Charlotte had, well, an *accident* in Mexico?"

I nearly spit out my wine as Kelly and I burst out laughing. I said, "Um, yes. *Why*, for goodness' sake?"

"Well, I was thinking, you're kind of like that."

"Oh my God, Michelle, in what way am I like *that*?"

"Charlotte was worried about being so happy with Harry after adopting Lily and getting pregnant that she gave up running because she thought it might jinx the baby, but Carrie says something to her like, 'Um, sweetie, you shit your pants this year, you're good.' Remember?"

I answered, shaking my head, "Yes, I remember…but once again, failing to see…?"

"You're like Charlotte, thinking you'll jinx your happiness with Jon, but you were subjected to a massive bout of crap a few years ago, and in my mind, sweetie, for the rest of this life, you're *good*. You're about due for the other side of the coin. If anyone is due, it's *you*. That's all I'm saying."

It cracked me up because this admission of Michelle's may not have been as elegant or understated as Kelly's, but it made me cry too. I nodded and smiled through my tears. I muttered with a shaky voice, "Okay...okay..."

After that, I sniffed and said thoughtfully, "You know, that was another reason I took the job. At first, I didn't want to have another job that revolved around technology, but because I can set my own schedule, I'm free most of the day to get outside, go running, enjoy nature, check out the local museums, start some new hobbies. Maybe I'll even go out in the field with Jon once in a while. He said he would teach me how to fish, and I said I'd teach him how to use his computer, and between the two of us, we'll both be learning and growing. Crazily enough, we're planning to ice fish next week on the lake, assuming it's fully frozen by then, and I'm going to show him how to track his fish stats on this computer program I wrote. It'll be fun."

"Ice fishing? Count me in, um, *never*," Michelle said.

I laughed and said, "He assures me it's not as cold as you might think, but I'll believe it when I see it."

Kelly changed the subject and asked, "Did he ever say anything more about his ex?"

"Nope. That day when he told me everything, I felt so awful for him— what he went through—it's almost like a wound I couldn't ask him to open again."

"So, you don't know how they ended—I mean, the divorce?"

"Nothing. He said once that she moved out about three years ago, but I never asked the details of why or how. Do you think I should? I guess it really doesn't matter, but then sometimes I wish I knew a little more, like where she moved to and if he ever talked to her again."

"You don't think they're still in touch, do you?" Michelle asked, slightly concerned.

"I have no idea. I've never had any indication that they are, but it's not like I'm with him twenty-four seven, so who knows?"

Kelly wondered, "Would you...be worried if he was?"

"Hmm," I murmured, thinking about that, "I'm honestly not sure. I should probably just say flat out no, but then I keep thinking about that first time he told me about her and how he said he still loves her. I mean, I still love Shawn, so I get what it feels like to love someone you're never going to be with again, but the difference in this situation is that she's still flesh and blood and…well, there's always the possibility that just by virtue of that, she could still be in the back of his mind—or worse, in the back of his heart."

Michelle said, as a statement instead of a question, "But you trust him."

"Yes, I do," I said with a nod. "It's more like a nagging thing, and I'm probably just being completely ridiculous even thinking or talking about it."

Kelly said, "No, not really, I mean, I think you should just be open and say that you know it hurts him to bring it up, but you'd like to understand how they ended and where they stand today."

"Right, I will," I agreed, but wondered in my mind if I really would. "I'm going there tomorrow. We're running in the morning—"

Michelle cut in, "You crazies are still running? In this weather? I thought that was just for the Winter Warrior."

"We decided to keep it up. There's a full marathon in September that we might enter, but that's a long way off, so in the meantime we've been running several times a week. It takes months to get in shape for a race, and then if you stop training, you could lose it all so quickly. I'd rather just continue. But anyway, after our run, he's taking me to meet a friend of his who lives up in the hills over Canandaigua—some kind of artist. And maybe after that, I'll get up the nerve to talk about the ex. We'll see…but hey, I feel like I'm monopolizing the conversation here, and if I'm not mistaken, there's a bit of a major milestone that we seem to be ignoring. Here, give me your plates—I have a surprise."

I smiled and started grabbing the empty dishes off the table. As Kelly stood up to help, Michelle shoved her lightly back down, saying, "We've got this. You sit. Relax. Have another glass of wine." She poured more into her glass, and Kelly sat down gratefully, grinning at both of us.

Michelle and I quickly rinsed everything off, leaving piles in the sink, as we heard Kelly in the dining room chiding us, "I hope you two didn't go to too much trouble. It's not like a big birthday—just another year older."

I quickly opened a bakery box with three perfect red velvet cupcakes, placing them on a pretty serving dish and lighting a candle on one as I said, "*Every* birthday is a big birthday!" I began singing the happy birthday song, and Michelle dried off her hands and followed suit, coming behind me with some gifts in her hands. Kelly made her wish and blew out the candle, and we spent the next two hours doing what we always do—laughing, crying, teasing, catching up, telling stories, reminiscing, and generally being silly, wacky, loving best friends.

✣ Chapter XXX ✣

Canandaigua, New York
February 2019

I arrived at Jon's by eight the next morning. After a lingering kiss, we chugged some coffee, bundled up, and headed out for a run. The snow was still coming down, which made it rather dicey, as the roads were not yet cleared, and our feet sank into the white piles of fluffy marshmallow-like matter. Jon stayed close by, slowing his pace to make sure I didn't slip. We laughed, noting how our stats would be abysmal, as we were basically navigating a minefield of snow and ice and sloshy treads the whole way. But we didn't care—we were happy to be together. That was how it always was with us now, peaceful and content to simply be in each other's presence.

Afterward, back at his house, we tore off the outer layer of our icy clothes, leaving them in his mudroom. Before our run, I had left a pot of my homemade chicken noodle soup on the stove, so we sat down at our TV trays and ate two heaping bowls full while we watched an episode of *The Big Bang Theory*.

At some point he said, "This is good. Thanks for cooking."

"Sure. I cooked it the other night, but it's one of those soups that reheats really well. I realize it's not as good as your deep-fried walleye, but still pretty tasty, if I do say so myself."

"It's perfect—warmed me right up." He leaned over and gave me a kiss. "And *you're* warming me right up too."

I smiled with a slightly raised eyebrow. "So, that old adage is true?"

"What old adage?"

"The best way to a man's heart is through his stomach."

He laughed, kissing me again and saying, "No doubt," then with a coy grin, "I can think of a few other places as well, but more about that later…"

He took another spoonful of soup while I glowed under his hint, which made me think (for maybe the millionth time) about his mouth and the mastery of his lovemaking skills, which were still a marvel to me every time. So different from high school! But then so was I—the girl who couldn't have found an orgasm if it struck her in the face back then was now a woman who had full command of that domain when given the proper expert administration.

I hated to compare, and mostly I didn't, but it was hard not to think about my years of intimacy with Shawn and then to be astonished that two men could be so different in bed. It wasn't that Shawn was bad and Jon was good. It was just that they were different. Shawn was mostly busy and rushed and thinking about a means to an end. Luckily for both of us, we hadn't needed much time for our mutual pleasure, which was convenient because there always seemed to be kids waiting for rides or food or activities, or his work calling, or my work calling, or his parents stopping by, or laundry or cleaning or house repairs, or something to interrupt us or at least to make us feel as though we needed to get it done and out of the way quickly. Not exactly an indulgence, let alone a proper physical expression of our love for each other, but certainly enough to keep us adequately satisfied.

Whereas with Jon, I felt as though I was on a slow, meandering trip down pleasure lane. It reminded me of that ride at the water park where you lie on an inner tube and drift along the lazy river for hours, touching lightly against the edge of the stream, then rushing back into the swift water's current, then paddling along at your own pace for a while, only to stop and exit at the very point when you're waterlogged and you've reached your limit on sun and fun.

There was no other way to put it: Jon liked to take his time.

And even more interesting, he told me on more than one occasion his philosophy on the whole thing, which was rather a revelation. He said, "You know, in the end, no matter what, I'm going to get mine, so let's not focus on me. I'd rather focus on you."

Whoa.

It was as if his goal was to find pockets of pleasure in my body that had been buried so deep that I never knew they existed before, let alone that they could be unearthed, explored, and tapped at any time, without warning, and often in a variety of ways over the course of many encounters.

We finished our soup and headed up the stairs together, him grabbing at my bottom, me giggling and dashing away as I stripped off my shirt on the landing, then danced quickly from one leg to the other, peeling off my leggings. He was out of his clothes in an instant, leaving them on the floor of the hallway. He came up from behind me in the bathroom and bent down to turn on the shower. Waiting for the water to heat, we were wedged together between the toilet and the sink as he kissed me feverishly and reached around to undo my bra, tracing his fingers around from the back strap to the front and slowly lifting the cups to reveal my breasts, which he promptly held up to his mouth, tossing the bra to the side. I leaned back against the sink and closed my eyes, feeling his mouth and tongue directing jolts of passion into my core, my fingers weaving into his hair. He went lower then, removing my panties and kissing me down there for a moment before removing each of my socks and leading me by the hand into the hot shower, the steamy cascades falling over us like a waterfall. We kissed and pressed against each other, our hands exploring the wet, hot, glossy skin of each other's shoulders and backs. Eventually I squeezed his backside to me so I could feel him against my inner thigh.

At the moment I felt that and wanted more than anything to take him in my hands, he pulled away and picked up the soap, rubbing it between his hands to build up a lather and using his soapy fingers to wash me. He began with my arms and back (turning me around to make sure he "got everything," he said with a smile). Then ducking down to my feet (using his fingers between every toe, which was the strangest and most intimate feeling), he moved up to my calves and thighs, then to my stomach and the area between my thighs, and finally to my breasts, spending an inordinate amount of time on each breast, needing to re-lather and reapply as he orchestrated an exercise of hide-and-seek, nipples disappearing under the soapy suds only to reappear when the water and his fingers swept over them like a light rain washing over two freshly bloomed spring flowers.

When I tried to touch him, he wouldn't let me and kept the center of our bodies an inch or two apart during this process, me feeling an opening that wanted more than anything to be filled but being held back in a most delightfully frustrating way. Finally, once I was clean, he handed me the soap with a lingering kiss and a smile, and I mirrored the ministrations on him in an equally delicate and drawn-out way, enough so that in the end, when I was just about to place my lathered hands on the main attraction, he stopped me, swiftly turning the shower off, grabbing me up in his arms, snagging a towel from the rack along the way, plopping it down on the bed before laying me gently upon it and saying in a husky, rushed voice, "I think we're just about clean enough."

I giggled and nodded as his mouth found mine and his wet, naked body found everything else. Despite his normal routine of waiting for me to reach climax several times before he would proceed, this time was different in that he made sure I was fully satisfied once (and goodly satisfied at that!) before wasting not a moment longer to put on protection and claim his own pleasure. I could do nothing but marvel at him with honest admiration that he had lasted that long.

When we were done, breathing hard and still dripping wet on top of the towel covering his bed, he wrapped me in his arms, kissed me, and said without a second's hesitation, his eyes blazing, "God, Amanda, I love you. Period. Full stop. I freaking *love* you."

I smiled and felt my eyes prick unexpectedly. It had been so easy, so open, so clear, just like that for him. And I knew it was for me too. I hadn't asked for it, nor expected it, not in a million years, not after what I'd been through, not after the moments and days and months and years that I'd suffered the pain and regret and confusion and bitterness and death. And here I was, in this bed with this glorious man telling me he loved me.

I echoed simply, letting the tears fall, "I love you too."

We hugged then, our wet bodies still warm, cheek to cheek, chest to chest, and I felt as though the world had opened up a bubble of perfection and had placed us in it together to see how we could remain in that suspended space forever. So we did.

Chapter XXXI

Canandaigua, New York
February 2019

Back to reality a few hours later, after we had crawled under the covers and napped, we awoke to say those three words over and over again to each other, as if to get used to the sound on our tongues. Then we dressed and headed out the door to his friend's house.

On the drive there, I asked, "What's his name again? And how do you know him?"

"Ryan Coxswain. I met him, let's see, maybe fifteen years ago when he walked into our lab. He thought we were a shop. He was going door-to-door to find a place to sell his woodworking items. They're truly amazing pieces. You'll see. Anyway, he's a really interesting guy. He lives way up in the hills above Canandaigua, away from everything, and, you know, he's an artist, so he's a little eccentric, but I think you'll like him. He comes down to Naples once in a while, so Brian and I will meet him for lunch or drinks, or we'll go to his house for bonfires on the weekends. He's also one of the guys on my annual Canada fishing trip."

"Sounds…interesting," I said, laughing. "I'm glad I wore my flannel. Do I need a shotgun?"

"Maybe," Jon replied, laughing back. "No, he's really cool. He lives on a hundred acres and has a woodworking shop in his barn."

"Well, I can't wait to meet him and see his place."

Jon kept a steady, warm hand on mine across the seat, lifting my fingers to his lips on occasion and then looking at me with those loving green eyes. They melted me every time. After fifteen minutes, my ears started popping as the car ascended the hilly bypass overlooking Canandaigua Lake. We were certainly out in the country now. I had no idea where exactly—these roads were completely unfamiliar to me. Finally, Jon turned down a gravel path with a sign reading "Slippery Elm Shoot Road."

I pointed and said, "That's the street name? Funny."

"Backwoods, baby. You're not in Kansas anymore, Dorothy."

"No, I guess not," I said with a chuckle.

The forest bordering the gravel road parted onto a driveway of sorts, mostly just two ruts dug into the dirt. We pulled up next to a black pickup truck in the driveway and got out of the car. To the left was a large two-story red barn that backed up to a creek running down from a steep hill gouged into a ravine lining the forest perimeter. Beside the barn was a full-size grist mill waterwheel fed by the creek, the wheel not running at this time because of the weather, I assumed. Off to the right was a log home and beyond that a row of evergreen trees atop an embankment that sloped down past the house. It was like a scene on a Vermont postcard, except we were in rural Western New York. It was surprising and resplendently beautiful.

Ryan must have heard our car because he came out the front door of the house and waved. Behind him came two large brown dogs, wagging their tails and barking.

Jon said, "Don't worry—the dogs are nice."

I just said, "Okay," then added with an incredulous whisper, "The man has a grist mill?"

"Sawmill, actually. But yes. Wild, isn't it?"

The dogs got to us first, both coming to me and sniffing my hands and jeans. I patted their heads as Jon greeted Ryan.

Jon turned to me and said, "Ryan Coxswain, this is Amanda Morgan."

"Nice to meet you, Amanda," he said, shaking my hand genially.

He was about Jon's height, with soft dark brown eyes, dark hair pulled back into a ponytail, and a full beard and mustache. Underneath all that hair, he had a very nice smile with perfect straight white teeth. He was handsome in a rugged, outdoorsy kind of way.

"So, you ventured up the mountain, old man," he said, grinning at Jon.

"I thought Amanda might want to see your little piece of paradise."

Jon laid his hand loosely on my shoulder, and I blushed as I saw Ryan scrutinize my face. I was clearly an anomaly. It reminded me of the look that waitress gave me at Patty's Place.

Trying to get the attention away from me, I said, "Your property is beautiful," then pointed and asked, "Was the mill here when you bought it?"

He cleared his throat, looked toward the wheel, and said, "Heck no. This place was a zoo when I bought it twenty years ago."

"Oh," I said with a little laugh, thinking he meant the term figuratively. But then a second later, based on his serious face, I frowned, wondering how there could be a zoo up here in the middle of nowhere. There weren't any people or houses or much of anything.

He saw my confusion and clarified, "Yes, I mean an actual zoo. With animals. The previous owners had been running a sort of makeshift caging facility here, believe it or not. Right over there on the other side of the house. Want to see?"

"Sure," I said and looked over at Jon as if to say, "What the—?" He just laughed and grabbed my hand, leaning over to pat one of the dogs as we followed Ryan.

As we crossed the snowy front yard of Ryan's house, he asked, "You want a beer for the tour?"

"Sounds good to me," Jon answered, and I nodded. We stood on the front porch as he went in to get the beers. I turned to face the scenic landscape— the babbling creek off to the side, the rolling hills for miles ahead of us, the forest thick all around. I exhaled in awestruck wonder.

Jon scanned the horizon and said, "Yeah, I thought you might like it." He squeezed my hand.

When Ryan came out with our beers, we clinked them together and said, "Cheers." The beers were encased in Yeti koozies (thankfully, because it was cold out, and my gloves were thin), and as I took a sip, I found the cold liquid deliciously refreshing and hoppy.

Ryan led us back down the steps and around the side of the front yard. He looked back at us as he began, "So, yeah, this couple, they were probably oh, I don't know, sixty-five when I bought the place. They'd been living here since the fifties. Somehow or other, back in the seventies, they acquired a tiger that had been bred in captivity but no longer had a home. Right when it was about to be euthanized, they saved it and brought it back here. They'd been using this huge pole barn to store tractors and farm equipment, but they cleared it out and constructed a large cage for the tiger."

As he continued talking, we went around to the back of the house, over a small bridge covering the creek, and through a path cut between the evergreens. Traipsing along the path, we came out the other side into a glorious, wide-open hillside—a pasture with an endless blanket of white snow. Off in the distance was another field that looked as though it had been harvested in the fall and had ten-foot-high hay bales scattered like chess pieces on a chess board. To the left, bordering the evergreens at the top of the hill, was a massive tan pole barn. Parked on the other side, I could see a trailer—one used for transporting horses—and also a midsize enclosed box truck.

Ryan continued, "So after a while, they heard of other animals needing homes, and before long they had an elephant, a bear, a monkey, several lions, a few ostriches, and well, anyway, you get the idea—they had a zoo."

"Wow, that's amazing," I said, still in disbelief. "I've never even heard of it! My grandparents owned a cottage out on Granger Point, but they never said anything about a zoo up here."

"Yeah, well, as you might imagine, it wasn't exactly up to code, so they kept it on the down-low. I mean, they didn't advertise or anything, but still, just by word of mouth, the kids in the neighborhood would come pay like five bucks to see the animals. It was called Morana Ridge Zoo. In fact, besides the zoo, this road—Slipper Elm Shoot Road—has actually been here for almost two hundred years. There's a property about a mile down the road that's been a working farm owned by the same family for at least a hundred years. And half a mile past that is a one-room schoolhouse that's on the National Historic Register."

"Very cool," I said, thinking how crazy that so much history lived in these country hills. I added, "I'll have to ask my mom and Meemaw if they remember."

"If they've been coming down to the lake a long time, they probably will." Then he asked, "So, Granger Point...does that mean you're from Canandaigua?"

"Um, not exactly. I grew up in Heathport with Jon. We graduated in the same class in high school, but yeah, when I was little, I would come down to my grandparents' place on weekends during the summer, so I consider Canandaigua sort of like a second home."

Ryan nodded.

I asked, "So, I take it the zoo's no longer operational?"

"Yeah, it's been closed a long time."

I inquired, "How did you ever come to buy the property?"

"I'm originally from Chicago, but I went to Cornell for art, and on the weekends I would drive around, mostly to peddle my sculptures, but also to get ideas for my next project. One day during my senior year, I saw a "for sale" sign and decided to stop. I talked to the old couple for a while and then headed on my way. Well, three years later, after I had graduated and moved to New York City, I took a trip and drove by the same "for sale" sign. Apparently, it wasn't easy to sell the remains of a zoo on a hundred acres. Anyway, by then I was ready to get away from the city and find a more rural location in which to make my art. I had recently sold a few big pieces, so I had cash to burn, and I really liked the community here—loose and friendly and sort of granola, if you know what I mean. So, I bought the place and moved here."

"Wow, just like that?" I smiled at him, thinking that's what I had done when I moved to Indiana—relocated to a completely new place where I didn't know anyone. Well, maybe not quite the same—I hadn't moved to a zoo!

"Yep, just like that," he replied with a smile.

Ryan led us up the hill to the pole barn, continuing, "As you can see, this land is pretty remote, so the officials kind of looked the other way for many of the infractions. Finally, though, the place was getting run-down and on its last leg. The couple didn't have enough money to keep it going. The only animal they had left when I bought it was an old elephant, so they transported him to an elephant sanctuary out near the Southern Tier, and then they moved to Florida. There was a rumor for a while that they let some of the animals loose in the Montezuma National Wildlife Refuge, but I asked them, and they said no—the rest of the animals had died of old age."

He opened a side door of the barn and let us into the massive space. It was filled with the remains of the tiger cage as well as various other cages and enclosures. Toward the back were two horse stalls.

"It smells like elephants!" I cried in amazement.

"Yep, it still does, doesn't it?" Ryan said and laughed.

"So, do you have horses?" I pointed at the stalls.

"Yep, they're out in the pasture. Dubber and Sally. A couple of old Appaloosas I bought a few years ago. They keep me company up here in the sticks. Along with these guys." The dogs had followed us into the side door of the barn and went right back out again through the back door and into the pasture, probably looking for the horses.

Ryan led us through the barn, pointing out and explaining the miscellaneous items stored there. I thought, wow, how does this guy afford this place? It must take a bit of money to maintain the acreage and a mill and all the outbuildings. Does he work a regular job in addition to the art? Jon hadn't mentioned anything other than he created "woodworking pieces." I did see quite a few large power tools off in the corner of the barn as well as various tree parts—roughhewn planks and branches. It would be interesting to see what he did with such raw materials.

Back outside, Ryan leaned over the fence of the pasture, calling the horses. One came over right away, and Ryan pulled a carrot out of the pocket of his barn jacket to place in the happy horse's mouth. He kissed the horse between the eyes and said, "There you go, sweet Sally." Jon and I tentatively rubbed her side. She flicked her tail in response. Dubber came over after a while, wanting his treat too. We stood out there drinking our beers, talking, petting the horses, and watching the dogs run around for twenty minutes until my booted feet started to feel the cold. At more than one point, I noticed Jon's gaze resting on me, especially when Ryan told stories about some of their past adventures, times when Ryan went fishing with Jon or Jon went with Ryan on some of his road trips to sell his art. I just listened quietly, laughing at their gentle razzing and friendly rapport. As if I needed a reason to love Jon more, I could see that he was well-loved and admired by his friends, or at least this friend anyway—someone I could tell was just as nice and kind as he was.

We walked back toward his log home, and Ryan led us inside, where there was a huge cathedral ceiling, a stone fireplace flanked by two couches and a lounge chair, a simple kitchen, and a wooden ladder leading up to a loft. Jon pointed to his book, which was prominently featured on the coffee table, and I smiled. Ryan offered us hot chocolate or coffee, but we politely declined and instead sat on the couches and warmed up, still chatting.

Ryan was curious about us and asked, "So, you two met in high school then?"

"We actually *dated* in high school," Jon corrected. "But, for various reasons, it wasn't meant to be back then. But Amanda showed up at one of my book lectures in September, and well, we got reacquainted." He gave my knee a squeeze, and I shrugged at Ryan with a grin.

Ryan said, "You must be a big fisherwoman."

I laughed and said, "Um, no, not at all. My friends kind of bamboozled me into the book lecture—I had no idea what I was getting myself into. And I guess they didn't really either."

"Well, it looks like it all worked out for the best in the end," Ryan said, looking from me to Jon with a knowing smile.

Jon agreed, "Yes. Remind me again, Amanda, to buy Michelle and Kelly a drink the next time we see them."

"I will," I said.

Ryan seemed to let that sink in and then inquired, "So, how's the book doing anyway?" turning to Jon.

"Great, actually," Jon replied, slowly taking his eyes off mine to look over at Ryan. "I mean, I'm not selling millions or anything. It's kind of a select audience. But I've sold several thousand online and in bookstores. Amanda and I drove around a couple of weeks ago to hand-deliver a box full to every shop that would take one in Naples, Canandaigua, and Watkins Glen. We're thinking about hitting up Keuka, Honeoye, Seneca, Skaneateles, and Onondaga next."

"Well, that's the way to do it. Good for you."

Ryan asked me about my job, my family, and my background. I gave him a lot of details about my new job, partly because it was so new that I was still getting used to describing it to people properly, but also because I thought, better to talk about the job than get too into the weeds about my past life in Indy. To his credit, he seemed interested in everything, but not in a prying way. It was comforting to think my relationship with Jon would include excursions like this where I would get to meet his friends and learn about his world, just as he had already begun to tap into my Maplewood community.

Finally warmed up, we made one last stop before leaving, heading back outside toward the red barn we had seen next to the creek. As we walked, I asked Ryan about the mill wheel, wondering where it came from.

He said, "I bought it down in Alfred and transported it up here in pieces. It was from an old grist mill, but it was all torn up and broken. It took me almost three months to restore it and get it working again. I use it as a sawmill now, to cut wood, but mostly I just like the way it looks next to my barn."

I laughed and said, "Me too. It's stunning, like a postcard."

When he opened the door of the barn, I gasped in awe. My eyes couldn't take it all in—there were at least fifty of the most brilliant wood sculptures I'd ever seen, dotting the whole front interior room of the barn. They were all shapes and sizes, some darker woods, like cherry and mahogany, and some lighter, like maple and oak. They were hard to describe—smooth figures, almost like ghosts or nymphs, enticingly cryptic and intricate. I was blown away by their exquisiteness and the unusual aspect of having found them here in the middle of nowhere, in a red barn, up in the hills above Canandaigua Lake. So this was how he made a living! I could see people paying good money for one of these masterpieces.

Both Jon and Ryan were watching me as I reacted physically to the sculptures, holding my hand over my mouth and opening my eyes wide in wonder. I looked over at them, and they both smiled and laughed at me as if I were a child. I asked if I could touch one of them and Ryan nodded, so I went over to a large sculpture made of yellowish wood, as tall as me and nearly as wide, and ran my hand along its side—it was smooth as silk. It felt like a piece of washed marble. "Amazing!" popped out of my mouth involuntarily, and I heard another chuckle from my audience. Then I walked toward the back of the barn, careful not to brush against any of the other pieces as I went, to examine one that looked to me like a cubist version of a tree—the brown and red branches and limbs were all akimbo and directed away from the flat, rich cherry base. It was like a tree that had been caught in a tornado or a blender. I loved it. It reminded me of the trees on Maplewood Avenue after an ice storm hit in 1991 and how they had initially looked as if they had been dipped in sparkling liquid glass, but when the ice stayed for days, the weaker branches tore off in jagged chunks and pieces. It was devastating, and many of the maples died after that, but what remained, like this sculpture, was as unique and striking as what had been before, just in a different, more defiant and radical way.

I asked Ryan, "Do you sell these pieces?" and not waiting for him to answer, I said, "I want to buy this piece."

Ryan came over to me as he laughed, with Jon in tow. "Whoa there, Nelly! Don't you want to know the price first? I think you might change your mind…"

"Oh, really? Sorry, I'm not good at estimating the cost of art. Is it a lot?" I asked innocently, not taking my eyes off the sculpture.

"Well, I just sold two pieces last week, which netted me eighteen thousand dollars. That little number you're looking at is twelve thousand, but for you…let's see, would ten thousand work?"

"Ohhhhh…" A whoosh of air escaped my lips. "Wow, I didn't realize—I had no idea—I—I—" I stuttered.

Ryan laughed heartily and said, "Don't worry, I won't hold you to it."

Jon put his arm over my shoulder, grinning and said, "Oh yeah, I may have failed to mention that Ryan here, well, he's kind of famous."

I was standing there, mute, my foot still in my mouth.

Jon went on, "He's been featured in big magazines and everything."

Ryan shrugged, a grin on his face, and said in a singsong way, "Nice work if you can get it…"

I could only manage to say, "Wow."

He continued, as if to downplay Jon's praise, "I mean, it wasn't always that way. When I met this bloke, I used to peddle my wares practically door-to-door, so I was certainly not what you would call an overnight success."

We walked into the back room of the barn, where the axle of the mill wheel came in through a hole and attached to some type of machine that Ryan pantomimed to illustrate how he forced a board through, slicing it into thinner sheets. He also showed us his lathe. I didn't quite understand the mechanics of everything, but observing his passion for the process was interesting.

Finally, we said our goodbyes, promising to come again soon when the weather broke so we could enjoy an evening bonfire, which seemed as though it would be quite spectacular as Ryan pointed with a grin to a pit filled with a pile of limbs, scraps, and branches rising forty feet in the air. He gave us both a hug and said again how nice it was to meet me, sending an extra glance of approval at Jon and a thumbs-up as if to say, "You done good, boy." He was really a sweet guy, not to mention an amazing artist. As we drove away, I thought about how nice it was to get a fuller sense of Jon's world through his friend. Ryan was a reflection on Jon's character and how well Jon interacted with the people closest to him. It made me smile—right when I thought I couldn't find more to like about him, I was astonished that there was, in fact, more.

We went back to Jon's house, and he grilled some chicken while I made salads. We stayed in, ate, and cuddled on the couch, watching *Forest Gump*. At the end of the night, we slipped into his bed to crash, and I thought about how lucky I was to have found love again and with someone so good (in and of himself) and someone so good for *me*. I still had a few lingering questions, but I figured we had a lifetime to sort through all that. Tonight, right before I drifted off to sleep in his warm embrace, I wasn't going to let anything mar our perfect day or the feeling of absolute happiness that had settled in my soul.

Chapter XXXII

Canandaigua, New York
February 2019

The next morning, as we sat at his kitchen table eating a breakfast he prepared of eggs, bacon, toast, and coffee, I decided to ease into a conversation about his ex by talking about other things first. Yes, I admitted to myself, I was a bit of a chicken. I asked if he would be open to hanging out with my family the following weekend. Nikki had invited us both to her house in Brighton for her son David's sixth birthday. He said sure and added that it was just about time I made an appearance at one of his family's Friday night dinners, so I said sure back. We grinned, thinking about how everything seemed to be coming together all at once and how, oddly enough, that didn't scare or intimidate me at all, nor him, based on his easy glance at me as if chilling with my family was a no-brainer.

I said as a false warning, "You may have to watch out for Mom. She'll try to rope you into playing pickleball. She's completely obsessed, already top of her league for her age group, and now she tells me she wants to start playing younger players so she can quote 'up her game.'"

He laughed. "Well, that's impressive. Should I be worried?" He eyed me, wondering if I was serious.

"Naw," I said, reassuring him. "Just say the same thing we all have—that pickleball's not your thing."

He nodded.

"Hey, on another note, but also related because this is so not *my* thing… remember how the last thing on my fridge list is learning a musical instrument?"

"Uh-huh," he said, chomping on a piece of bacon.

"Well, so the other night with Michelle and Kelly, as we talked about my new job and how I needed to pick Kelly's brain about teaching techniques, I realized that she's a music teacher. I know, totally duh-to-me-Amanda. So, I asked her if she would be willing to teach me a musical instrument, and she asked which one, so I said maybe piano. She said she would but also warned me that it wouldn't be easy."

"Do you even have a piano?"

"No, but the Abernathys do," I answered with a grin. "We're going to meet over there once a week, maybe on a Wednesday or Thursday night for an hour or two. Michelle said she would come over with the boys to harass us when she could, and then we could go out for drinks or dinner afterward. I told Kelly I insisted on paying her, despite her protests. I'm like losing-my-mind excited about it, even after she warned me how hard it is to learn. I told her I wasn't trying to be Bach or anything—I just wanted to learn a few tunes so I could say I'd done it and so at the next party I go to with a piano present, I can sit down at it and *pretend* like I'm Bach."

He shook his head with a smile. "You're quite the trooper, that's for sure."

We ate in silence for a few minutes, still smiling, as I tried to figure out how to broach the topic I was avoiding. I cleared my throat, swiping my mouth with a napkin, sipped my coffee, and said with a change in tone, more serious now, "Hey, um, I wanted to talk to you about a few things, but I'm not exactly sure how to start."

He caught my shift and immediately asked, "What?"

"I—I don't know if bringing this up again is too painful for you, but I wondered if we could talk a few minutes about your—your life before, and your, um, marriage."

He put his fork down, taking my hand, and said, "Of course. Amanda—you can always talk to me about anything, and I will try to always be an open book to you. Remember, my goal is to have complete and absolute honesty between us."

I exhaled in relief. "Okay. Good." I paused, gearing up for my first question—the one that had been eating me up inside the most, the one I hadn't even mentioned to Michelle and Kelly because it hurt me to even contemplate the ramifications of the answer. I began, "Well, so—so, you mentioned once that after you…lost the baby, you made sure that Melanie would never get pregnant again." I felt a heat rise up my neck and into my face, but there was no way to stop what I had begun. I continued, "I didn't know exactly what you meant by that…" I let my voice trail off, my breath held in suspension.

He stared at me, confused, then replied slowly, "Um, yeah, so I just meant that I always made sure to be the one responsible for birth control." His forehead creased and he added, "Why?"

"So, you didn't…get snipped?" I asked, trying to hide my eagerness.

He shook his head and said, "Nope."

I tried to look into his eyes, but with my next words, I just couldn't. I stared down at my plate of food, gulped hard, and said quietly, "Because, well, I wondered what you thought about having kids in general…if you were opposed to it because of what happened, which I would totally understand, or if you had ever thought about the possibility since then…"

The silence that followed felt like a time bomb waiting to detonate. I kept my eyes down and my breath in check. Then, like the wisp of a butterfly's wing, he let go of my hand and used his index finger to lift my chin, and I saw the dawning understanding on his face. He said, "Amanda, yes, I've thought about it—in fact, quite a bit lately."

"And…?" I whispered.

"I think next to wanting you, it's the thing I want the most."

"It is?" I replied, astonished.

He gave me a soft smile, pulled me from my chair onto his lap, and said, "Yes, it is."

We kissed and I felt the weight of the world leave my shoulders and drift off into the ether. After a few minutes, his hands resting lightly on my knees, his face grinning, he said, "So I take it you've thought about it too?"

I nodded with a smile. Trying to stay calm, despite the heartbeat drumming in my chest, I leaned into him for a moment or two, then pulled back and said, "Okay, so not to put a damper on this conversation, because, by the way, you have just blasted me off like a rocket ship into space, but I want to be realistic. I realize that a whole lot of other stuff probably needs to happen first before, well, *before*, including more time getting settled into our relationship. But also, I must state unequivocally that I'm no spring chicken and I, well, I had some troubles in this department in the past."

He waited, not saying anything.

I let out an exasperated sigh and continued, "I always wanted kids, but well, Shawn already had two, so he wasn't exactly keen to start all over again. I'll admit that…," I looked down at my hands, both of which he now held in his, "I was rather sneaky about my use of birth control, or as the case may be, lack thereof."

When I glanced up, he'd raised his eyebrows but stayed mute.

"In retrospect, I know it was wrong of me, but you have to understand—I was *twenty-five* when we got married and I'd just lost my dad, and I wanted so much to have my own children, thinking about Dad's legacy and how many times he told me before he died that he was proud of me and how I would someday be a wonderful mother. The thought of that never happening just devastated me every time I considered it. So, not right away, but a few years into our marriage, I stopped taking any precautions."

"And?"

I shook my head, trying not to focus on the ten thousand tears I shed back then when absolutely nothing happened.

Jon squeezed me to him and said softly in my ear, "I'm sorry."

I shrugged one shoulder and let myself be hugged. After a minute, I pulled away and added, "I want to say that this was the one deception in my marriage, not something I took lightly, and afterward I felt awful about it. I never told him, but instead simply went back on the pill and reconciled myself to being the best stepmom I could be."

He nodded, his understanding green eyes making me feel slightly better. He said, "Well, I think…a lot of factors go into making a baby, and you know, maybe something was just off during that time. It doesn't necessarily mean you *can't* have a baby."

"Right, I suppose," I agreed, allowing a tiny twinge of hope to percolate in my veins.

He grinned as he kissed me on the cheek and said, "And I would certainly like to give it the old college try—whenever, as you say, we're fully *settled* in our relationship."

I chuckled. "I'll tell you one thing: with you, there is no *settling*—only reaching and being appreciative."

"For me too, baby—total gratitude."

We kissed for several minutes, and then I went back to my chair to finish breakfast. Toward the end, our bellies and hearts full, I said offhandedly, "You know, you never really explained to me how you and Melanie broke up. You mentioned that she moved out, but what preceded that?"

He answered unemotionally, "She disappeared again, and that was the last straw."

"Oh," I said, somewhat taken aback. "You mean you never fought or had a conversation about it?"

The moment the words were out of my mouth, they hung there for a second like a bubble waiting to be burst. Then they were abruptly shattered by the unexpected sound of Jon's side door opening and slamming shut. Someone's footsteps came bounding up the stairs to the kitchen, followed closely by a woman's voice crying out, "Yoohoo! Hey, Jonny! Hi sweetie! I'm home! What'cha doin'?"

Instantly I started, my eyes wide, my heart pounding in shock. Jon's face went white. Before either of us could speak, move, or react in any way, a short, dark-haired woman with black jeans, a black T-shirt, tattoos on both arms, a lip ring, and coal-black makeup emphasizing her big black eyes entered the kitchen in a cloud of energy. I heard her Doc Martens screech to a halt as she recoiled at the sight of us. Although she paused for less than a second to adjust, her next movement seemed without break, thought, or reason. She punched me in the face and screamed at the top of her lungs, "WHO THE FUCK ARE YOU?" sending me to the floor, my legs sprawled and entangled under the table. My empty plate crashed violently to the floor beside me, shattering.

Jon was up as if he had been shot out of a cannon, restraining her and screaming, "Melanie, no!"

I felt sick, shocked, scared, and red with anger. I detangled myself and stood up, breathing hard, reaching for my face while holding myself steady with the back of the chair. My hand to my nose, I pulled it away for a second and saw that it was covered with blood. My knees nearly buckled and Jon, still holding Melanie back, reached for me reflexively, but I stepped back from his hand, looking at it with horror. I was shaking all over with rage, adrenaline pumping like a galloping racehorse.

She was lurching at me now, Jon restraining her arms behind her the way a cop would do during an arrest. He pulled her body away from me toward the sink. I watched in a daze, trying to process what was happening as if I had been dropped in the middle of a movie set where I knew nothing about the plot, but somehow I was the main attraction.

She was still screaming, "WHAT the FUCK, Jon! Who is this woman in OUR house? With MY husband? What the FUCK is going on here?"

Jon was talking to her the whole time, trying to calm her down, his biceps and forearms taut with the restraint. "Melanie, calm down. Look at me. I said, *look at me*. Focus on *me*, not her. Breathe. Take a breath. Come on. In and out, in and out, in and out."

She wasn't really listening to him and was still staring at me, wide-eyed and livid, but eventually she turned to see his face as if noticing him for the first time and asked with venom, "Who is she, Jon?"

Jon's jaw was set as he responded in a growled whisper, "*None* of your goddamn business, Melanie. Come on, let's go outside and get you calmed down."

As he began to lead her away, she was writhing against him, trying to break free, saying, "What do you mean, it's none of my business, you motherfucker?"

He said to me out of the side of his mouth, "Don't move. I'll be right back." His face was a restrained mask as he pulled her down the stairs. Underneath the mask, I saw the years of ancient conflict, patience, and sorrow. Her tirade of profanities continued as I heard him open the door with difficulty, still holding her in restraints, then slamming it closed behind them and taking her out into the snowy yard.

Chapter XXXIII
Canandaigua, New York
February 2019

As soon as they were both out of the house, my flight instinct kicked in, and I ran upstairs to get my things, shoving everything haphazardly into my bag and racing back down the stairs, holding my bloody nose to my sleeve. The gushing blood was mixed with a stream of tears that came together in a flowing river down my face and onto my chest, staining the front of my flannel shirt. I stared absently at the dark rivulets, momentarily struck by how much they looked like that wax they used to seal letters. It felt like some type of sign that these thick drips were replicating that ancient action, sealing something shut in my heart.

I stopped at the top of the stairs leading down to the mudroom. My purse and jacket were there, and I was at a momentary loss about how to proceed without being seen by them, just outside the windowed door, still screaming at each other. I also hesitated because I had never known of any other egress from this house other than the side door. The front door seemed to be shut up or unused, at any rate, but I tiptoed like a bandit down to the mudroom, ducking and grabbing my things and heading swiftly back up the stairs to test the front doorknob. It was locked, so my shaking hands wrestled with the deadbolt until it turned and I was able to get the door to creak heavily open. I escaped down the snowy steps and ran out into the front yard. Now I could really hear them. I had a feeling the whole street could hear them. She was still protesting and throwing insults and demands like a street fighter.

I had to get out of there—now. They would definitely see me as I escaped to my car, but there was no other option, so I ran as fast I could across the yard, unlocking the car door with the keys in my bloody hands. I jumped in, closed the door, and immediately locked it just as I heard Jon off in the distance hollering, "Amanda, don't go!" I started the car and screeched out of the driveway in a blast of tires onto West Lake Road toward Canandaigua.

I drove a couple of miles down the road, then pulled into the parking lot of an assisted living facility, putting the car in park. I stared in my rearview mirror as if I was afraid someone had followed me, but no one had. I sat there, utterly devoid of coherent thought, breathing hard and allowing the adrenaline to slowly drain away, leaving me shaking uncontrollably. My fingers felt oddly frozen and numb, and I stared down at them as if they were gray Popsicles detached from my body. Then, like the releasing of a dam, the tears came hard with great big gasps of air, sobbing and panting, and sucking blood and snot through my swollen nose. I rubbed my knuckles into my aching, wet eyes and cried into them as if the world had ended. And in a way, for a moment, it felt as though it had.

There was this overwhelming feeling of, holy crap, what do I do? What on earth do I do? Right this minute. I could not see a way forward, not just in a practical sense, as in, do I drive home or go back to Jon's house or to Mom's or Michelle's or Kelly's, or *what*? But also in every possible sense, from the standpoint of "This is my life, right here, right now, and this just happened." Holy crap, what do I do?

I sat in a state of absolute shock, immobile, disbelieving, with no clear picture or answers about anything, for at least twenty minutes. Then, finally, I put my hand up to my nose, testing it very carefully to see if it was broken. It seemed solid but excruciatingly sore and still draining a light amount of blood. The inner part of my eye near the base of my nose was sore too. My contact lens felt strange, like it wasn't quite in my eye correctly, and I had trouble seeing out of that eye.

My mind was racing—how could a weekend that had been so perfect, life-altering, and life-affirming have gone so horribly, toxically, inexorably wrong?

At that moment, my phone rang. Jon. I didn't answer. He tried several more times, leaving voicemails that I didn't listen to. A few minutes later, I glanced down at the beginning of a text he sent. "Amanda, I'm SO sorry. Where are you? Are you okay? Please call me. I have to know that you're okay." I put my phone in airplane mode and threw it down on the passenger seat.

I didn't respond because I didn't know if I was okay. I didn't know anything.

After a few more minutes, I felt stable enough to drive again, so I headed home, thinking all I wanted to do was go to sleep in my own bed, for maybe a hundred years. When I turned onto Maplewood, I felt a stab. I had moved here, moved home, to heal my heart. And now my heart was sliced open with a machete, raw and burning. My Maplewood, my panacea, my deliverance. Was it still?

I put the car in the garage and walked up the porch steps slowly, disconsolately. I struggled to get the key in the lock and enter the house, finally going directly to the bathroom to look at my face, which was covered in blood. My eye was already turning a pinkish-purple color, the lid droopy, my nose swollen with dried blood encrusted inside my nostrils. I looked as though I'd been in a boxing match. I grabbed a washcloth from the cupboard, put it under the hot water, and began wiping the blood away, trying not to press too hard. Then I grabbed another clean washcloth, let it run for a few minutes under the hot water, which made my hands tingle. I sat down on the toilet and put my whole face into the warm, comforting cloth as I sobbed and sobbed and sobbed.

A while later, I went up to my bedroom, still holding the washcloth. I threw my clothes, including the bloody flannel shirt, into the hamper (thinking I should just toss it in the trash), took my one remaining contact out of my eye (the other was mysteriously gone), and went to bed and slept, feeling as if all energy had been drained from my body by a razor-sharp angry sieve.

When I awoke, it was dark out, so I looked at my phone, still in airplane mode, which said seven sixteen. My throat was raw from crying, and my eyes were nearly swollen shut, the punched eye tender and sore. I got up and went to the bathroom, noticing that my face looked even worse than it had this morning. I came back to the bedroom and debated leaving my phone off for another day. But then a flash thought popped into my mind, something from Beverly about facing the music, even when it was the thing you wanted most to avoid. She had mentioned a quote from a famous missionary who also happened to be a poet, Amy Carmichael, relaying one poem's title that contained this philosophy: "In Acceptance Lieth Peace." This struck me as a last straw to clamber and yearn toward. If I could get through the loss of my husband to the likes of a devil in the form of a man, I could get through this, whatever *this* was.

I touched the airplane mode button to release it, and immediately my phone started chirping. So many missed calls and texts from Jon, oddly stopping about an hour ago, which made sense about ten seconds later when I heard a knock on my door. I sat up stiff and paused in indecision. God, he'd probably stand out there all night if I didn't go down there. I stood up and sighed, throwing on a robe and my glasses. I slowly opened the door, and he came through like a shot, gripping my shoulders and staring intently into my face. His strangled voice shook as he cried, "Oh my God, Amanda, are you okay? Please tell me you're okay."

An odd mixture of feelings raced through me—love, relief, fear, betrayal, anger, confusion. His mere presence sent me into a spiral of savage bewilderment. I wondered absently, as if my body was not my own, how should I react? Should I tell him to get out? Should I let him hug me and comfort me? Should I scream? Cry? Rage? Puke? Faint? I wasn't sure what to do and stood rooted to the spot, staring into his frantic eyes.

Beyond worry, recognition was dawning in him. He stepped back from me as he deciphered my wasted, deprived, and depraved state of mind. Taking my hand and leading me into the living room, he said softly, "Come."

I let myself be led like a whipped dog and sat on the couch beside him, his hands now holding both of mine. When the lamp reflected the horror of my bruised face, he said, involuntarily and in despair, "Oh, Amanda...," then a moment later, touching my cheek lightly with his fingers, "Amanda, I know you probably hate me, and I must admit, I hate myself right now, knowing what I've just put you through—you, who have," his voice broke then, and he cleared his throat before continuing, "who have been through so much already. I need to explain, though, not as an excuse, because there is no excuse, but because I want you to understand *what* actually happened this morning. After I explain, I promise, I'll leave and never contact you again if that's what you wish."

I didn't say a word, thinking his word *never* made my stomach hurt.

"I want you to know that before tonight I hadn't talked to or heard from Melanie in years. I had no idea she would show up or that she would do and say those horrible things as if we were still together. It's a complete lie. As you might imagine, when she's not on her meds, she's irrational, and her mind doesn't necessarily process reality in the same way that our minds do. She also self-medicates on occasion, using whatever drugs she can find, and that can lead her to becoming delusional. When I try to reason with her in this state, she can't see the truth for the lies. I've learned over the years to placate her for the time being, until she comes down and realizes what's real. But obviously, if I'd had *any* idea that she might come back to the house—that there was even the slightest chance of it—I would never have had you over. Oh Amanda, I'm so sorry! I've seen her violent before, but I guess I didn't think she was capable of this." He paused, his eyes filling with tears, scouring my face. He whimpered, "If only I had locked the door, or grabbed her in time, or—or—something…"

He paused, sinking his head down, then continued, "I guess I foolishly thought she was out of my life forever, *finally*, after all the years of total… *agony*. There's no other way to describe it. When she was stable, she was great, but when she wasn't, life was a living hell. But I hadn't heard from her in so long. When you asked this morning about how we ended, I never had the chance to explain. I came home from work one day, and all of her stuff was gone, and she was gone. I tried to get in touch with her, just like I'd always tried, but she was unreachable. This time was kind of odd, though, because she'd never cleaned out the house like that before. When I didn't hear from her for six months, I had a lawyer draw up divorce papers and send them to her parents' house in Canada. I thought maybe that would prompt her to come back and mend things, but instead, a few months later, the papers came back signed. I couldn't believe it, but I had no other choice but to believe and to reconcile myself to the fact that she wasn't coming back. I found it a rather stoic and tidy way to end a marriage that had been fraught with drama and anguish and that had brought my heart to the brink. It's taken me these past few years to get over it, and the exhaustion I felt in the end took time to unwind and detangle from my fried and twisted soul. It was a horribly difficult time."

As I watched him talk, I ached for him, this man who clearly tried so hard to keep the pieces of the puzzle together with the force of his love, but had failed miserably despite his maddening and unflappable commitment.

I said gently, "I see. I see it all, Jon, I do. And I'm sorry. There are no words."

"No, there aren't," he agreed, his eyes and shoulders so tired.

I asked softly, "Where is she now?"

He looked up with surprise and said in earnestness, "Oh, Amanda, don't worry, she's gone! Back to Canada. I drove her to Niagara Falls, and her parents met me. They told me she'd been on a bender for weeks because they'd threatened to check her back into rehab. That's probably why she drove down here—a last-ditch effort to avoid going. It wasn't easy for me to persuade her to go back, but underneath she knows it's what's best for her. She's still very mad about seeing you in the house. I guess it took her by surprise in her confused, disjointed drug haze. Anyway, by the time I turned her over to her parents, she was subdued and willing to go, so I can only hope this time will stick for her."

He put his head down again with a tired sigh, then regarded me as he said, "I don't know if you need to hear this, but on the drive up there, I explained to her again that we were divorced and that what I do now is *my* business and that *my* house is no longer *her* house and that she can't just show up like that *ever again*." He shook his head in disgust and remorse.

When he looked up again, his eyes were pleading, swimming, filled with guilt and pain. He gripped my hands as if they would keep him from falling off the edge of a cliff and said, "Amanda, can you forgive me? Being with you has been the first *really good thing* in my life since—since I can't remember when, but *a long time*. Not just since the divorce, but since way before the divorce. You can never know what a godsend you've been. I didn't even know I was only half alive until you came to me, just how you are—sweet, kind, funny, beautiful—I didn't even know that I was like a desert, a dead piece of land, a wasteland! To be able to get up every morning and have something to look *forward* to, to know I'm going to see you or be with you—it's given me purpose, hope, joy in a way I didn't think possible."

I felt myself starting to melt into his beseeching eyes, but I couldn't let myself fall quite yet. I asked cautiously, "But you told me once that—that you still loved her."

He took a deep breath and replied, "Yes, but as a family member who is ill and hurting and needs my compassion, *not* as a wife. Never again as a wife, I can promise you that."

I paused and continued, "But—but I feel like I should confess to you, if you maybe didn't already realize it, that I'm basically a stable, steady, drama-free kind of person. In fact, I've probably had enough drama already to fill a lifetime, and I never asked or wanted it in the first place. Underneath, I'm actually rather boring, and I'm also kind of fragile—not a big risk-taker or adventurer. I'm mostly a homebody who likes to be near her friends and family and do little things like share a meal at a picnic table or watch the kids in the neighborhood skateboard down the street or read a book on the front porch. I mostly want to feel stable and secure and loved and to share my love with someone special who values what I have to offer. There are no bells and whistles here. Just me. What you see is what you get."

"Amanda!" He put his face in his hands, shaking his head. When he looked up again, his eyes were shining, and he was grinning ironically. I frowned, confused.

He cried, "Don't you see, don't you know, Amanda? *Boring* sounds like *heaven* to me! First of all, though, you are *not* boring. You are fascinating and beautiful and unique and deep, and I can't imagine ever getting enough of you! Second, if by boring, you mean you'll be the *same person* from one day to the next, and you won't use all your powers of manipulation to *crush my soul*, then that is exactly what I want from you. Can't you see that? You are *exactly* what I want! I want you to be Amanda and to stay Amanda—that's all I ask of you—that is to say, I want us to face this crazy, ever-changing world together using all the power of our *love* and perseverance to conquer whatever may come, *together*.

"And as far as you being fragile, don't you think I know that? I could see that the moment I laid eyes on you in that room, surrounded by that crowd of people, looking larger than life but also so small. And I've been trying *hard* to be cautious and to give you your space so that *you* would lead us down the right path at the right time. And I know you won't believe this, especially after what happened this morning, but what I want more than anything is to help you heal and to protect you from any more pain in your life. I'm trying, Amanda, *I'm trying*, but I guess I can't protect you from everything, and I'm truly sorry for that."

We sat staring at each other, and I found myself breathing hard as I listened to his words. I wanted so much to believe them and to jump into his arms and abandon all sense and reason, but something held me back.

Watching me hesitate, he suddenly stood up and went toward the kitchen, coming back an instant later with the list from the fridge in his hand. He sat back down on the couch, leaning toward me, holding the paper out and saying, "Amanda, this list—you never explained all these items to me, and I never asked because I was reluctant to cause you pain of any kind, but can't you see? Just like me, you had something in your past that was burning there, in your heart." He pointed at some of the items and started reciting them: "*Remove and store ring, delete voicemail, seal and store wedding dress.* I'm not an idiot—I knew that first night when I came here that these items were related to Shawn and the longing you *still* had for him. And in a twisted way, I understood your predicament because I was in the same situation: loving someone I could never be with again. And being here, in this house with you so close and so real, I was scared half out of my wits to start anything with you because of how much I knew, in my heart, about *that* kind of pain and what it does to a human soul. And I knew how you had to let so much go— your hopes and dreams and plans—despite your best efforts to keep them alive and real."

The look I gave him was filled with bubbling anger, as he had touched on hallowed ground.

He said, "I know you think your situation is different—"

"Yes!" I cut him off. "For one thing, Shawn isn't coming back to punch *you* in the face!" I was fuming, my chest heaving as I stood up, pushing his hand and my list out of the way.

He followed me determinedly into the kitchen.

I stopped by the counter and turned around to face him, still angry and accusing.

His voice was calmer now as he continued, "But I also know that the memory of Shawn might just be stronger and more powerful than the real-life version of my ex. I'm not saying I was totally blameless for my divorce— there are two sides to every story—but at least you're not competing with a ghost—a ghost with no flaws, no errors, no mistakes. And I know you're thinking, how *dare* I bring him up to you like this." I pursed my lips with a curt nod. "I get that. And I'm sorry, because I don't say these things to hurt you, I really don't. But don't you see? We must admit that we're *human* and that we've *both* lived a life before *us* in order for our future to matter and to remain real. The only way I can see it working is that, despite our fears, despite obstacles, despite any *new* pain that may come our way, we take a risk and decide the risk is worth it. And Amanda, even with what I know of heartache, you are worth it—I believe *we* are worth it."

I knew it. I hated that he had to spell it out for me, this invisible wall of fear causing me not to see or assimilate it at first, but now—I knew he was right. I felt the tears well up in my eyes. I said, shaking my head, "I'm still afraid. There are so many things that could go wrong, like this morning—so many unknowns. Wouldn't it be easier to stop before we've dug in too deep…?" I was grasping at straws, my resolve crumbling, the tears now falling down my face.

Seeing me break down, he came in for a hug then, and I let him wrap his arms around me. I cried into his shoulder. He said with the first glimmer of a lighter tone, "Oh sweetie, we're deeper than the deepest ocean already."

I sniffed and nodded mutely into his chest as I sank into him like the heaviest stone being thrown into the deepest ocean.

❧ Chapter XXXIV ❧
Heathport, New York
March 2019

It was a Friday afternoon in March, and although there was still snow on the ground in spots, for the most part it had melted, leaving behind slushy green patches of lawn and massive gritty soot-covered snow mountains in the parking lots of the village grocery store, bank, and post office. I remembered that, as kids, we loved this time of year because spring was on its way and because we would walk into town and pretend we were mountain climbers rushing and jumping up and down these crusty black mountains left behind by the snowplows.

It was nearly fifty degrees out, so I sat on the front porch swing with a light jacket, waiting for Jon to pick me up. When he pulled into the driveway, I smiled and raced down to his car as he stepped out and pulled me into a bear hug, only to draw away a moment later in order to kiss me on the lips.

He took my hand and said, "God, that never gets old."

I grinned and agreed, "No, it doesn't."

We sat down together on the swing, and he put his arm around the back of the swing the way he'd done the first time he came over and cooked for me, except this time I snuggled against him and his arm came around my back, pulling me into his chest. He sighed and said, "Wow, what a glorious day. So warm, and the sun is shining. Feels almost like May instead of March."

I nodded and said, "It does."

He asked, "How was work?"

"Good. I had fourteen people in class today. I showed them how to use Microsoft Project to develop a critical path engineering project plan to build a new environmentally safe drainage system in a chemical lab. It was fascinating, and they really seemed to get into it. There was actually one engineer in the group who used to work for Kodak, so he was really helpful in creating realistic tasks and timelines."

Jon shook his head with a smile. He said simply, "You're a wonder, my dear."

I smiled a little, knocking against him in my modesty.

"How was your day?"

"Oh, fine. Brian and I went to Keuka together, but the fish weren't biting, so we took a few samples and went back to the lab."

I nodded mutely. We sat in silence for a bit, contently swinging, watching the robins thump around in the yard, rooting for worms. Mrs. O'Connor came out to grab her mail and waved hello. We smiled and waved back.

I asked, "What time are they expecting us?"

"Six-ish."

"Okay, I made macaroni salad. I hope that's enough."

"That's fine. Mom won't care—she probably has enough food to feed an army, like always."

I grinned. "No doubt."

"How was piano last night?" he asked.

"Dreadful," I said with a sigh. "I had no idea how hard it would be, even though Kelly warned me. I mean, you have to play the top part at the same time as the bottom part and do the foot-control thingy too. My brain doesn't work that way. I nearly cried a few times. Of course, Michelle was right there to provide comic relief. When I was at my most frustrated, she came and scooched in front of me, sitting directly on the keys, and then wrapped her legs around me, plopping on my lap and said, 'I can't watch this a moment longer, and I certainly can't *listen* either. Let's go get a drink.' I said, 'Oh alright,' pushing her off me, and we went to McCarty's for beer while her parents watched her boys."

Jon squeezed me and said, "You'll get there. I'm sure it takes time. You've only been at it for a month or so."

"I know…that's what Kelly says." I shrugged. "Anyway, speaking of beer, do you want one?"

"Nah, this feels pretty good just sitting here with you. I don't need a thing."

I sighed. "Me either." I tilted my head back, and he kissed me tenderly as I melted into him.

When we pulled apart, I said simply, "I love you."

His glowing green eyes took me in as he echoed, "I love you too."

As we went back to swinging, I began to think about this past month and marveled at the one-eighty since that horrific morning at his house. We had both been in such a state of shock that our world could have come crashing down with that one fateful punch, but for whatever reason, instead it had brought us closer together. Sometimes I shivered at the notion that I may not have let Jon into my house that night when he came pleading at my door. Where would we both be then? But he had come and I had let him in, not just into my house but also my heart, and we had figured out a way forward that was about us, not our pasts—yes, integrated with our pasts—but under a new world order. One where we would reconcile every aspect of our lives—past, present, and future—together as a team.

We talked on the phone or saw each other every day now. We were still running and comparing stats in preparation for the marathon in September, but now when we talked, we delved into the deeper things, like stories from our past and our hopes and dreams for the future. And we'd begun to widen our circle as well. He'd come to my nephew David's birthday party and charmed the pants off my mom and everyone else there—not with anything overt…more in his polite, gentlemanly, curious, and kind manner, and according to Nikki, simply in the way he looked at me as though I was his everything. And I had already gone to one of his parents' weekly dinners, and we were headed there tonight as well. They were the nicest people, and I detected such a cautiousness, feeling they didn't want to break the spell between Jon and me, as if they had been through so much with Melanie over the years, and me seeming so stable in comparison, they feared rocking the boat in the slightest and scaring me away. I tried my utmost, in my interactions with them and with Jon in their presence, to show that there was no chance of me going anywhere and that I was here to stay, through thick and thin.

We'd had one raucous Saturday evening here at the house with Kelly and Peter, Michelle and Andy, Donny and Danielle, where I'd made a big vat of creamy mushroom chicken soup with a side salad and homemade biscuits and apple butter, and we'd stayed up late playing the boardgame Taboo. It was the most fun and we laughed so hard, we cried. Later that evening, as Jon and I made love under the warm covers, all I could think was how happy and lucky I was.

I'd met his lab partner Brian's wife at a dinner in Naples one weeknight, and we'd been up to visit with Ryan at the mill one Sunday afternoon for a while. Our time with friends and family, getting to know each other on a more intimate level, cleaved me to Jon in a way I never thought possible. To see him interact with those he was close to—how much they respected, admired, and loved him—was like icing on the cake. I could see it in the way they talked to him and talked about him to me. And the way he looked at me—like I had changed his world as much as he had changed mine—this was what, more than anything, set my heart healing, warming, and soaring. I think we both finally felt whole again, individually and together.

And thankfully, not a peep from Melanie. Jon talked to her parents a few times, and they said she was still in rehab, but only during the day now. She would come home and stay with them at night, and so far she'd been sticking with her regimen. In the intervening weeks, I asked Jon a lot about Melanie. About their life together. I wanted to know everything, so he told me about the good times with her and the bad. Sometimes the stories made me jealous, but mostly they made me sad. When I expressed my thoughts, he explained matter-of-factly that their bad times were a symptom of her disease, not a failing of her as a person. I really ruminated on that. He was such a good man. If the situation had been reversed, I didn't know if I would have been as generous or understanding. He taught me a lot about who he was, the deep well of his soul, and how a soul can be brought to the brink and yet come out the other side more thoughtful, introspective, and humble. It was a testament to who he was, and I thought for the millionth time how lucky I was to have found him again. Oh, I wasn't so naive as to think that there wouldn't come a day when Melanie would show up and disturb our life again, but now I knew every morsel of meaning in these interactions from their past, and therefore I knew that we could tackle anything that came our way together, including a visit from Melanie.

We also talked a lot about my former life in Indy. About Shawn and his family. I told him how Shawn took me into his world when I was at my most vulnerable and alone. And how he showed me unconditional love in a way I had never known before. I relayed some light stories, like the time Cole and Sissie were jumping on the trampoline in our backyard and Sissie's hair got caught in the springs. We had to cut a huge chunk out, and she cried for days, but when I took her to the hair salon to get a new cut, despite her torment at the time, she eventually liked it so much that she kept it that way for years afterward. And I told Jon about the time we all dressed up as characters from *Harry Potter* for Halloween. Cole was Harry, and Sissie Hermione, and

Shawn and I Draco and Bellatrix. We were quite the sight in the neighborhood, and it was one of many happy times when I felt completely full of motherly pride and love, even though they weren't my biological children. We also talked about the times when Shawn and I didn't get along. When we fought over the kids or his ex or his family or work or whatever couples fight over. The times when I cried by myself for hours in my car after learning that yet another month had gone by without getting pregnant.

So yeah, we talked and shared, and we listened and learned. We looked into each other's eyes and understood. We sorted out the past and sorted out each other's place in the present. And we kissed and faced each other, knowing the future between us was not going to be perfect, but that it would be *our* future.

ᛘ Chapter XXXV ᛘ

Heathport, New York
June 2019

Maplewood. Summer. Hot and balmy. The crickets were chirping, and the fireflies were beaming their little glowing orbs into the grassy haze like tiny dancing nymphs in the night. The "e-ew, e-ew, e-ew" of the front porch swing sent its vibrating pendulum cry out into the darkness, and I sighed in blissful peace, laying my head on Jon's lap, his arm across my stomach and his hand in mine, my legs sprawled out between the chains at one end of the swing. Donny and Danielle's daughter, Jean, strolled by with their dog, Tandy, and we both waved as she hastily waved back with a "hi there" and a "weeee" as the big dog led her down the sidewalk in a rushed sniffing frenzy.

We laughed and Jon said, "God, I love this street. And what a beautiful night."

"I know," I agreed and added softly, "Sometimes I think I feel the impact of Maplewood in my bones, like I was always meant to come back here, but I got lost for a while, pieces of me cut off from what was always supposed to make me whole."

In response, he leaned down and kissed me, and I felt his lips touching my soul in the way they always did, repairing those pieces that had broken off and making the puzzle come together again.

When he pulled away, I asked him curiously, "What took you so long to get here tonight?" It was a random Wednesday in June, and he had texted me earlier in the day that he would be late and not to wait on him for dinner. So, I'd made myself a salad and eaten it at the kitchen counter, reading a book and wondering what time he would arrive. As soon as he got there, he wanted to swing on the porch with a glass of wine, so here we were, sipping and swinging in happy unison.

He hesitated with the question, clearing his throat and acting slightly nervous, which was *so* not like him. I sat up quickly, turning myself toward him, and saying, "What? What's wrong?"

He grabbed my hand and smiled. "It's okay, sweetie—nothing's wrong. But I do have a surprise for you. Do you mind wearing this?" He pulled a bandanna out of his back pocket and held it up.

"Come on, a *blindfold*? You're kidding me." My eyes narrowed at him.

He said, "Nope. No joke."

I exhaled and complied like the dutiful girlfriend I was as he wrapped the bandanna around my head. Then I sat there blindly listening to him get something from his car, my heartbeat beginning to strum. When his footsteps were back on the porch and he was a foot away, he said, "Hold out your hands."

I held them out before me, palms down, but he turned them so they were faceup and together, as if I they were a chalice for drinking water from a stream. He seemed to be opening something up, like a metal door or latch, and then placed something warm and fuzzy in my hands. I screamed, "OH!" and heard the cutest, most precious sound—"Mew, mew, mew"—and I felt the tiniest tongue lap against my thumb.

He untied the bandanna, and I looked back and forth between him and my hands, my eyes wide, my heart banging out of my chest. "Oh, Jon, a *kitten*!"

He smiled at my expression of utter surprise, wonder, and joy. He petted the little darling's head, and I grabbed Jon by the neck and pulled him to me for a kiss, nearly screaming, "Jon, I love it!"

He laughed at my crazy outburst, and then my attention was back on the peach-colored, longhaired ball of fur in my hands. I lifted the kitten to my face and kissed it, snuggling its fluffy head into my neck, watching its huge eyes survey me and its surroundings curiously, feeling its baby purr build and resonate in my chest.

I was literally beside myself, besotted beyond reason, and could barely speak for shock and gratitude, but I managed to ask, "Where—where did you get it?"

"Remain calm," he said, laughing at my excitement. "I got her today at the humane society. Yes, she's a girl. She was number five in a litter of six. She's about eight weeks old. She's had her shots and was just cleared for taking home. They hadn't given her a name yet, so you're welcome to do that."

"I love her!" I cried again now that I had a pronoun to use. Then I held her back up to my face and said definitively, "Her name will be Marmie, short for Marmalade because she's the exact same color, and she's just as yummy, aren't you, Marmie, my little baby?!" I squished her into my cheek and kissed her, and she mewed like a confused and slightly distressed child, but I didn't care—she was mine and I loved her.

"Marmie sounds perfect," he said with a laugh, leaning in to pet her and kiss me again.

I shook my head at Jon, starting to cry involuntarily as I said, "Such a sweet surprise, Jon, really…!

"Yeah, well…," he started, looking down at his hands and then continued tentatively, "I've been thinking lately about that list on your fridge and wondering how to knock another thing off, so…yeah…this was one."

I nodded and smiled, distracted by Marmie as Jon went into the kitchen and came back with the list.

"Can we?" he asked, holding it out to me.

"Can we *what*?" I replied, not listening.

"Can we…maybe tear up the list now?"

"Oh!" I cried in surprise. Then looking up at his big, calm, pleading green eyes, I said with a sigh and a laugh, "Sure, we can! Let's see, yes, I've already planted a garden, got a new job, learned piano—well, sort of—hiked Watkins Glen with you, um, twice, and I've been horseback riding three times (by the way, when are you coming with me?). But I haven't been camping yet, and wait, what about the national park and the marathon?"

"Please. Do you really think we'd forget about the marathon? We just ran fifteen miles on Sunday."

"True."

"And as far as camping, maybe we'll plan a trip this fall to a park, bring the camping gear, kill two birds with one stone."

"Yay!" I cried, excited. "I'd really love to go to Yellowstone. That's been a dream of mine."

"Sure—your wish is my command, my love," he said with a grand bow.

I looked at the list, still a little undecided. "It always feels so good to cross things off …but…," I sighed again, snuggling Marmie in my lap, "it's time. Okay, hand it over." I grabbed it from him and tore it up triumphantly, throwing the pieces on the ground.

He smiled and said, "Well, good. I was hoping we could start a new list tonight. I'll be right back."

He picked up the torn pieces and took them inside, coming back out with a pen and a small notebook in hand. He sat down beside me on the swing and wrote:

Goals for Jon and Amanda:
Name New Kitten

He handed me the pen and said, "There you go—cross it off," so I did, looking down at Marmie with a laugh.

Then he turned the notebook toward his chest so I couldn't see and scribbled something quickly.

"What are you writing? Let me see," I said, reaching for his hand, but he pulled away, grinning mutely and shaking his head teasingly.

While he was doing this, I continued to stroke Marmie and then suddenly noticed that she had a thin collar, buried in the fur around her neck. I said, "Oh, is this for fleas—" I stopped mid-sentence as I felt something small, hard, and inverted on the inside strap of the collar, tied into the buckle. I pulled my hand away as if I'd been shocked with a jolt of electricity. Then the tears started, welling up in my eyes, as I looked at Jon with a fixed, startled stare.

Jon regarded me closely with his intense, glowing eyes, laying the notebook facedown on the wicker table next to the swing and gently taking the kitten from my hands and unbuckling her collar. Then, in his slow, thoughtful way, he was down on one knee before me, holding Marmie in one hand and a ring in the other, displaying it to me between his finger and thumb, and saying in his clear, confident voice, "Amanda, I love you. You are everything to me. You are *home* to me. Will you marry me?"

My eyes as round as saucers, my hands trembling as they flew to my mouth, I cried, "YES!" and swiftly knelt beside him, taking his face in my hands and noting how his tears mirrored mine as I kissed him and pulled him to me while Marmie mewed in protest, wondering what all the fuss was about.

When we drew away, awash with love in our eyes, he gently returned Marmie to her crate and took my left hand softly in his, kissing the palm with his lips and saying, "Remember our fate lines?" I smiled behind my tears and nodded. Then he placed the ring on my finger, and I held it up to the light. A circular, clear blue sapphire set in a halo of diamonds.

I stammered, "Oh Jon—it's beautiful! And it's my birthstone, how did you know? It's...*perfect!*"

He smiled mysteriously and stood up, bringing me with him. As soon as we were up and no longer encumbered by the kitten, I threw my arms around his neck as we both laughed and kissed, his body taut against me, his heart beating in rhythm with mine.

We stayed with our arms around each other, hugging and crying. We said, "I love you" at the same time and laughed. He reached down to grab the notebook, which said:

<u>*Goals for Jon and Amanda:*</u>

Name New Kitten
Get Engaged
Run a Marathon
Get Married
Love Each Other Always
Live a Long and Happy Life Together

I smiled and crossed off "Get Engaged." I gave him a long, deep kiss, telling him how happy I was. We brought Marmie inside, leaving her in the crate in the living room as I whispered through the metal door, "We'll be right back, sweetie—you wait right here. Mommy and Daddy have some business upstairs." I grinned at Jon as his eyebrows rose and he allowed me to lead him to my bedroom, loving the feel of my newly weighted finger pressed against his hand.

❧ Epilogue ❧

Heathport, New York
December 2019

Dear Beverly,

Please forgive me because this letter is way overdue. I hope you're doing well in Indy. I was reminded to write because I'm sure you've seen the news stories about the conviction of Devon Austin Wade and his life sentence. Well, I don't want to dwell on how hearing that made me feel, but just know that the best form of justice in this world, I believe, is living my best life, despite what evil came and tried to take it away. And to that end, I feel that I have succeeded, despite all the odds stacked against me.

So, now you're probably wondering what I mean, and I'm going to explain and give you as many details as I can in this short letter, which can never fully describe this one true fact: my heart is bursting.

I recently got married. Yes, married! Imagine that! After all those tearful sessions with you when I thought I couldn't go on, and here I am, happier than I've ever been. And I just want to say thank-you from the bottom of my heart because I know I couldn't have had the strength or courage to move forward without your guidance or to become the person I am today. I'll never forget that, and I'll never forget you.

I still miss Shawn and Cole and think about them every day. I suppose that will never change. And I'm glad because that part of my life and those memories will live in my heart forever and will continue to make me grateful for what I have and who I am today.

I thought I'd give you a quick recap. As you know, in July of 2018, I moved back to New York, into my childhood home. In fact, at this exact moment, I'm

snuggled on the couch with a blanket and our kitty, Marmie, watching my amazing, strong, handsome husband out the window as he shovels the snow off the
driveway so I'll be able to get my car out tomorrow for work. Oh yeah, the reason
I need the driveway cleared is because I have a great job as a teacher at the
local community college. Apparently, I have an aptitude for explaining real-world
business acumen to academic types—who knew? I love it, and the best part is
that the hours are flexible, so I can spend my free time pursuing other passions
(for instance, this summer I planted a garden and took up horseback riding!).
Once in a while, I even tag along with Jon at his job. By the way, he's this sort
of master fisherman by trade—I know, I didn't get it at first either, but now I'm
completely hooked, if you'll forgive the pun, haha. Don't get me wrong—I mostly
leave him to do the casting and reeling, but I do love spending time outside and
communing with nature. No longer am I stuck in an office cube all day, and I
couldn't be happier!

I should probably also explain how we met back in September over a year
ago—on my birthday actually—or rather, we remet. We dated in high school,
but the timing (and just about everything else) was off, so we went our separate
ways. But lo and behold, twenty years later, I saw him, and the sparks were still
there, just as bright and just as scary. There were a lot of ups and downs in
our first few months together, as you might imagine, and not just because I was
still steeped in grief over Shawn, but also because Jon had a few demons of
his own that needed to be rooted out before we could set a new course for our
relationship. Slow and steady wins the race (which, by the way, was my motto
this past September when I completed my first full marathon!).

Well, we worked through everything together, Jon proposed back in June,
and I accepted. We decided to get married on the anniversary of our recon-
nection—my birthday—right here on the front porch of my Maplewood Avenue
house, surrounded by the whole neighborhood and all our friends and family.
We arranged the reception as a huge barbecue in the backyard, complete with
fireworks and a mariachi band! It was the happiest day of my life. I'm enclosing
a photo of us at the wedding standing next to the sculpture that his friend Ryan
made for us as a wedding gift—isn't it extraordinary? Jon is such a great guy
that he naturally draws the most interesting, loyal, and kind people to him. It's
been a wonder just becoming a part of his world. And he tells me the same
about me and my world. In fact, guess who came to the wedding? Shawn's

parents and Sissie! It was the most emotional and gratifying thing to have them here. Essentially, between spending time with them (and seeing their joy for me), reciting our vows, and getting married in my childhood home surrounded by everyone and everything I love more than life itself, I was a weepy puddle of tears the entire weekend.

Anyway, the whole wedding and honeymoon (we went camping, hiking, and horseback riding in Yellowstone) was spectacular, and I wouldn't change a thing. So, we're living in the Maplewood house together now, but we're keeping Jon's house, which is on Canandaigua Lake, so we can still go boating on the weekends. And also so that Jon can teach our child how to fish off the dock, the same way he learned as a boy. Oh yeah, did I mention that I'm pregnant? Yes, it's true, and I'm still so shocked and grateful that you could knock me over with a feather every time I rub my belly and think how this crazy life is so unpredictable and wonderful.

On that note, I'll conclude. Once again, I'm sorry it's taken me this long to write and to say thank-you, but better late than never, right? I just wanted you to know that I'm okay (better than okay!), and even though I don't know what the future holds, I know that I'm strong enough and thankful enough, not to mention fully equipped, to tackle anything that comes my way!

Sincerely,
Amanda (Morgan) Galway

The End

Acknowledgments

Maplewood was the first book I wrote. Back in 2016, I had no idea what I was doing but felt an absolute compulsion (almost a fevered yearning obsession) to get the words out as fast as I could. I finished the 130,000-word monstrosity in two months and cried like a baby when I typed "The End." I had achieved my lifelong dream of writing a book. I had fallen in love with my characters and my story and wanted more than anything to share them with the world. Little did I know that it would be five years (and hundreds of rejection letters and rewrites) later before I would become a published author, and in fact, three other books came out first (*Rue*, *Punk*, and *Bibliointuitive*).

I know this will sound crazy, but looking back now, I'm grateful for those rejection letters. Writing is like a muscle that needs to be exercised and stretched and perfected in order to become strong. In the beginning, my writing was mechanical and mystical but lacked finesse. I have since learned (through the course of daily writing, struggling, and growing) how to make a story come together and click. And I'm still learning.

The other reason I took so long to publish *Maplewood* is because it made me sad. In 2016, when I started writing, I didn't tell anyone except my husband (who wondered why I was getting up at four o'clock in the morning—before heading to my day job—to pound away on my computer like a deranged gerbil). I kept it quiet because I was afraid that people would judge me—who is she to think she can be an author? I struggled with my self-confidence. But in March of 2017, my best friend, Bobbi, came into town for a work conference, and we met for dinner. With my hands shaking, I handed her an envelope with a thumb drive and a set of instructions, telling her I had written a novel and wanted her to read it but not to share it or tell anyone. As I held my breath and wondered if someone's heart could actually fall out of their chest from pounding so hard, she took the envelope and said, "Amy, that's really cool. You wrote a book? Wow, I didn't even know you liked to write." She was so gracious, and when she returned home and read it, I was even more grateful because she didn't pan it (even though she probably should have—that first version was really rough!). She could have said, "Amy, this is a great little hobby, but really, you probably need to quit because to be honest, your writing is awful." If she had said that, I would have walked away and never written another word (and probably cried myself to sleep for a year). But instead, she said, "I had trouble separating the 'real Amy' from the words in the book, and maybe you could shorten some of the descriptions, but otherwise it's a good story, and you should keep going." The blue sky opened up and my heart soared right up into the heavens!

Now, here's the sad part: a couple of years later, Bobbi got an aggressive form of colon cancer and passed away at the age of forty-nine. It was awful. It's still awful. She was an amazing best friend and an amazing human. She was also the first person who read my writing and told me to keep going. Much like Michelle and Kelly in *Maplewood*, she grew up in a house full of girls kitty-corner across the street from me on Maplewood Avenue. And because this story is a tribute to her and to our happy childhood growing up on Maplewood, it makes me sad that she isn't here to finally see it come to fruition.

I dedicated *Rue* to her, even though she never read it, because back when I gave her *Maplewood*, she was the one person who could have crushed my soul but didn't. Instead, she selflessly handed me the moon with her encouragement, and I will be forever grateful. So, even though I'm sad about her not being here to see my dream come true, I know she's looking down on me with a thumbs-up and a "You go, girl!"

In addition to Bobbi, years later when I finally had the courage to let a few others in on my secret, I was greeted with open arms by so many generous friends willing to read my (very!) unpolished drafts. I want to thank these early readers for their kindhearted encouragement and tempered constructive feedback: Cindy Carroll Nolan, Jeannette Colonna, Jennie Ruggles, Katie Stambaugh, and Aunt Linda Credit. And a special acknowledgment to my two "eagle-eye" beta readers, Julie Nichols and Mrs. Nancy Roselli. I couldn't have made *Maplewood* what it is today without your help, support, and dedication, and I appreciate it!

To my editor, Kira Freed, who continually challenges me and inspires me to be a better writer and to bring the best version of myself and my work to the reading world. And to her husband, Charlie Alolkoy, who makes my book covers shine.

To my readers—thank you for continuing to show up on this long, meandering journey of mine. You are the reason I get up in the morning (very early!) and the reason I keep pounding away like a deranged gerbil.

About the Author

Amy Q. Barker is a #1 Amazon best-selling author of women's fiction as well as a nature lover. She writes books about extraordinary women who inconveniently fall in love during a major life crisis. Amy was raised in a small town in Western New York and now lives miles from anywhere on a lake in Indiana with her husband.

Thank you for reading Amy Q. Barker's imaginings set to words. If you enjoyed this book, please consider leaving an honest review on Amazon or Goodreads.

To connect with Amy, check out her Instagram @amyqbarker_author and sign up for her newsletter on her website: www.amyqbarker.com.

Made in the USA
Las Vegas, NV
18 November 2023

81080108R00167